Happy Reading

Darlin Bess.

A Life of Crime

Darlien Breeze

Mystic Publishers
Henderson, Nevada
~ 2010 ~

Mystic Publishers
Henderson, NV 89015
www.mysticpublishers.com

Interior Design: Jo A. Wilkins with Mystic Publishers
Cover Art: Todd Aune with Books in Motion
Cover Construction: Brian Stalians

Thank you to all my family and friends who support me no matter what dopey thing I write.

Thank you to my editor Sherri Orrison who keeps it from being too dopey.

And thanks to Jo Wilkins who puts it all together.

A life of Crime

"Old man Cummings knows where all the bones are buried."

"What makes you think he'll talk to us?"

"George, if there's anything I know, it's that for the price of a bottle and some good cigars, Cummings will talk all night."

Steve Simon drove his black Honda Prelude down Maple Avenue. "Look for number 1980, there, that's his place."

The two young reporters made their way to the house at the end of Maple. "There he is on the porch." George pointed. A slim man about eighty years old with longish gray hair sat in a rocker with his stocking feet resting on the porch rails. His long frame moved gently back and forth with the movement of the chair as he drained the last of his beer.

"Hi, Mr. Cummings, it's me, Steve Simon, this is my friend George Smitts. We brought you a little something." He pulled out a bottle of Jack Daniels, and two very expensive cigars. George held a large, hot pizza. "We were hoping you'd tell us about some of your old cases."

"Why are you so interested? All that's a long time ago." He waved his hand dismissively. "I'm retired now. Don't like to talk about the past." The old man eyed the bottle.

"I understand. We don't want to stir up bad memories, maybe just have a drink with you."

"Let me get a couple of glasses. Do you boys want some soda or water in yours?"

"I'll take some soda water," George said.

"Me too," echoed Steve. "We'd like to do a story about your law career, but if you don't want to talk about it, then don't. Jess Haywood lives a few miles from here and I hear he had quite a colorful career as a police detective. Maybe he'll want to tell his story." He handed the old detective a cigar and poured a drink into the empty beer glass.

"George and I want to write a book about past crimes. We figured you'd know more about some of the really juicy ones than anyone else."

The detective took a sip. "Haywood, that blowhard, he wouldn't know a crime if it bit him in the ass!" He ran the cigar under his nose and inhaled deeply. "La Aurora Preferido," he said appreciatively. He went into the house and returned with a cigar clipper. "You boys know your cigars." Steve leaned over and held a lighter to the end. Cummings puffed the cigar to life.

The reporters waited. After a few more puffs and a couple of sips Cummings said, "I do remember this one case, we called it Diplomatic Immunity. It was a doozy; had us running all over the place. The FBI got involved because it was a kidnapping. I had just made detective at the time, local law was called in to help in the search for this woman. As I remember it. . ." The old man leaned back in his rocker.

Chapter 1

Diplomatic Immunity

So cold, I'm so cold. She wrapped her arms around herself, trying to draw warmth from her own body. "Let me out! Why are you doing this?" she shouted, shaking the bars of her cage. *Don't show fear, that's what he wants.* She heard the lock on the door turn. Tears rolled down her face. Kendra brushed them away and stood as straight as the wounds on her back would allow.

"I see you're awake, good. I brought you some food." He opened the cage door and placed a metal pie tin with a slice of bread and half an apple on the floor. "Here's some fresh water too." He slid a half gallon jug of water beside the food. She cringed, pressing as far away from him as she could get. He put the food inside. "Don't fret. I don't have time for you today. I have important things to take care of. Big important meetings must look like the dutiful son. You know how it is." He laughed, "Don't go away, I'll be back." He turned to leave.

"Why? Why are you doing this to me? What have I ever done to you?"

He turned ice blue eyes on her, his complexion becoming mottled with red. "So American, so many questions. A woman from my country would never dare to question me. I'll have to bring something special to teach you some manners. You should learn your place." He became calmer. "But, I'm a fair

man, to answer your questions you've never done anything to me, how could you? Kendra Maguire, you're nobody, you're nothing. Nothing, do you understand? I do it because I want to, because I like to. . . because I can."

He pulled the cage door closed with a bang and locked the chain. She got a quick look outside when he opened the cabin door. She could see nothing but sand and stunted trees. *Looks like the desert.* Where am I? The cabin door closed behind him. She listened as the deadbolt slid into place. She could hear a car drive away. Kendra tried to get comfortable sitting naked on the rough concrete floor. Her whole body was in pain. He poured salt water on the wounds after the beatings to stop infection. An old trick from the days of slavery, he'd said. The pain was nearly unbearable. *I have to keep my strength up as much as I can.* She reached for the bread and ate it slowly. *The water has to last, no telling when he'll return. I'll save the apple for later.*

In spite of the cold and her constant pain Kendra drifted into a dream-like state, reliving the events of the past week or two. She wasn't sure how long she'd been here. She remembered being dressed up, wearing a black beaded dress that showed off her honey-blond hair and green eyes. She remembered sliding into a limo. She had a flash of Hugo Dekker, not really handsome but attractive in a rugged way. Hugo said he wanted to get away from the embassy crowd and go somewhere more private. He'd opened champagne and poured a glass for her. That was the last she could recall until waking up, caged like an animal.

It had taken all kinds of persuasion from her kids to get her to accept this date. Widowed for only three years she didn't feel ready to go out and about. Her kids, twenty-year-old Sheila and eighteen-year-old Kenny thought it was high time she started to enjoy life. When they found out the son of the Ambassador from Olembe, a small principality off the coast of South Africa had asked her to dinner, they immediately started a campaign for her to go.

As personal assistant to Malcolm Fairchild, the head of the Department of Foreign Affairs in Los Angeles, her job included scheduling events to welcome foreign dignitaries. She arranged the events and saw to any special needs, such as extra lodging for the twenty wives of a Saudi prince. She met Hugo Dekker and his father the Ambassador from Olembe when she arranged a welcoming party in their honor. She understood that negotiations were taking place between their country and the United States that would have profound effects on the future of oil exportation. Kendra worked hard, loved her job and was careful to have time for her family.

Kendra lifted her head trying to see beyond the cage where she was confined. *The cabin appears to be of wood, one room, no windows, a rough cement floor and one door. The only light is coming through cracks between the boards that make up the walls. If I could get out of this cage I might be able to break through a wall. The building doesn't look too sturdy.* Kendra shook the cage. Putting all her weight, some one hundred and twenty-five pounds against the door, nothing budged. "Help! Help! Can anyone hear me? Is anyone out there?" She vainly shouted until her throat was too sore and dry to continue. She sat back down, trying to ignore the sharp edges of concrete digging into her backside and sobbed. "What is going on? My kids must be worried sick."

"Have you heard from Mom?" Sheila asked Kenney. "This isn't like her. She always calls even if she's going to be late." Sheila put her books on the table and headed for the kitchen. "I've got to get to the office. Professor Dunn kept us after the bell and now I'm going to be late for work. Kenny! Are you listening? I'm worried about Mom."

"I hear you, chill out. She's probably just enjoying her first real date in over three years."

"Kenny, wake up, she went out last night. It's now two in the afternoon. Something's not right I'm worried." The phone

rang. "Maybe it's Mom. Hello, this is Sheila. No, I don't. We haven't heard from her. I don't know, I'm worried sick. Yes, I'll let you know."

"Who was that?" Kenny came from the kitchen eating an apple.

"Malcolm Fairchild, Mom's boss. He's worried too. Mom was supposed to come into work this morning. He said she hadn't called."

"I thought this was her day off."

"It usually is but they have some big deal going and she agreed to work. Kenny, I'm calling the police, this doesn't feel right."

"Oh, come on. She's probably having the time of her life. She'll call when she's ready. Stop being such a worrywart."

Sheila called the police, "Hello, I want to report a missing person." The officer told her that the police would not get involved until the person had been missing for forty-eight hours unless there was reason to suspect foul play. After telling her brother what the police said, she grabbed her purse and left for work. As she wove her red Volkswagen through traffic a mantra, played over and over in her head, *Let her be okay, let her be okay, let her be okay.*

The week passed with no word. At the Department of Foreign Affairs, Malcolm Fairchild was worried too. He turned to his secretary, "Martha, get Hendrix on the line. I need him to look into something for me."

"Hendrix here."

"Boss needs a word with you," Martha said.

"I'll be right up." Minutes later Bob Hendrix sat in Malcolm Fairchild's office. "What's up? Martha sounded serious."

"Sit down Bob. I'm not sure but I've got a really bad feeling. Kendra Maguire hasn't been to work in a week and her kids haven't seen her since last Friday. Seems they were both out of the house when she went on a date with Hugo Dekker, the son of Ambassador Bram Dekker. See what you can find out will

you? Something's wrong. I know it."

"Of course. Give me a few hours. I'll get back to you."

At the sound of the lock clicking open, Kendra cringed. "Ah, waiting for me are you? That's a good girl. You're learning." Hugo opened the cage and yanked her out. "I've brought you something special. Now let's see you do a little dance." He flicked her with the whip he carried, raising a welt on her leg, causing her to jump. "That's a start. I know you can do better." The whip snaked out and hit the other leg. Kendra let out a cry. "Stop, you bastard, stop!"

"Good, good! That's what I like, a little fight." Hugo snapped the whip again and again covering her with small, bleeding cuts. At last when he tired of his cruel game, he handcuffed her to the outside of the cage bars. "This will keep you healthy until I'm through with you." A smile played on his face.

Kendra screamed from the pain and fainted as Hugo doused her with salt water from a bucket he kept in the corner of the room. When she woke up, she was once again in the cage, alone and freezing cold.

"Boss, this is what I found out. Hugo Dekker has a rep for getting into hot water. So far his dad has always been able to bail him out. The list of suspected infractions is from almost every country they visit. So far, the injured parties, usually lovely women I might add, have not testified against him. With the weight of his father behind him he seems to skate right though trouble."

"What about his connection to Kendra?"

Hendrix thought he noted more than a professional interest in Malcolm's voice. "Evidently Dekker asked her out. She's been a widow for over three years and according to office scuttlebutt, she was reluctant to go. Seems her kids encouraged her or she never would have gone. I guess this is her first date since her husband died. I think it's time to get the police involved."

"She's been gone since last Friday." Malcolm answered Detective Cummings. "No, this isn't like her at all. She's probably the most dependable person I know. She would never leave her kids to worry like this."

"What do you know about her personal life? I've been in touch with her kids. I understand she's a widow. Any office romances?"

"Her husband died a little over three years ago from a heart attack. She started to work here shortly after. It's just her and her children as far as I know. At least she's never mentioned anyone else to me. Look Detective, I know you get this all the time but believe me, Kendra would never just leave. She's too dedicated to her family." *Why didn't I get closer to her? My fear of getting involved has left me knowing almost nothing about her. Rats! I'm such a fool.*

"Mr. Fairchild, we're already looking into what happened to Mrs. Maguire. Her daughter Sheila called as soon as her mother didn't come home after her date. Meanwhile, if you hear from her give me a call." Josh Cummings called his partner. "John, I'm going to interview Hugo Dekker. Meet me at the Olembe Embassy at two. I understand he's in a meeting until then."

At the embassy they were ushered into the office of Bram Dekker. "Gentlemen, please sit down. This is my son, Hugo." The ambassador and his son stood side by side in the opulent room.

"Sir, I'm Detective Josh Cummings and this is my partner Detective John White. We're here about Kendra Maguire. She's missing." He turned to Hugo, "I understand that you were one of the last people to see her. You two had a date last Friday, isn't that true Mr. Dekker?"

Hugo smiled, "Yes, we did have plans; however, I had to cancel at the last minute."

Detective Cummings asked, "What happened? Why did you cancel?"

"There were some important business matters my father had asked me to take care of. I explained this to Ms. Maguire, she was very understanding." Hugo's smile did not reach his eyes. It was a *much* practiced political smile.

Bram Dekker broke in, "Missing, you say? Isn't she the girl who arranged our welcome party? Hugo, what do you know about all this?"

"Nothing, I assure you Father. I had no idea she was missing. This is the first I've heard of it. How awful. Do you suspect foul play, Detective?" Hugo managed to look sad. "I do hope she's found soon."

"Detectives, we wish to offer any help we can give. I know you must ask questions, please feel free," the ambassador offered.

"At this time we have no reason to suspect anything. We're just gathering all the information we can. Thank you both for your time and your cooperation." The detectives dropped their cards on the mahogany desk and left.

Once they were in the car, John said, "Don't tell me, I can guess. You don't believe Junior. You think he's a lying piece of trash. Well, for what it's worth, I agree."

After the detectives left, Bram Dekker confronted his son. "Hugo, if I find out you're lying, that will be it for you. I told you last time I'm not going to bail you out of trouble again. I mean it Hugo, this is it."

"Put your mind at rest, Father. I told you I don't know anything about the Maguire woman and I don't." Hugo turned and strode from the room. He opened his cell phone and called for his driver, Mikhail.

Bram Dekker called for his most trusted servant, "Polo, follow him. He's up to something. Find out what it is."

By the end of the week, Sheila and Kenny were frantic. They were once again in the office of Detective Cummings. "This is entirely our fault," Sheila wailed. "If we hadn't almost forced

her to go, none of this would have happened."

"Please, Miss Maguire," Detective Cummings held up his hand, "stop blaming yourself. This is in no way your fault. We'll find your mother. Try to stay strong. You need to do that for your brother and yourself. Can you do that?" *I just hope to heaven she's still alive when we find her*, Cummings thought. I don't know how I'll face these kids if she isn't. Then, thinking more practically, he asked, "Sheila, how are you and your brother getting along, financially I mean? Do you need help?"

Sheila wiped her eyes and tried not to cry. "We're okay. Mr. Fairchild, mom's boss, is seeing to it that the household bills are paid and he sent enough for food too. Kenny and I both have part-time jobs so we're fine. Thanks for asking."

Kenny put his arm around Sheila, "Come on Sis, let me take you home."

Before they could leave Cummings spoke up, "The best thing you two can do is keep your lives as normal as possible. Don't miss school. Don't miss work. I'll call you the minute we have any information, I promise."

Cummings mused. *"Only eighteen and already he's taking his place as the man in the family. He looks just like the picture I saw of his father on their mantel, tall thin, dark brown hair. I'll just bet the girls are crazy for him. That kid is a winner."*

"John." Cummings called his partner.

John stuck his head in the door. "Yo, what's up?"

"What say we go have a little talk with some of the personnel over at the embassy? I have the feeling that someone knows something. Let's find out what it is."

"Good idea. I'll bet Hugo has a personal driver. Big shot like him would want a special person in his corner, someone loyal to him and him alone."

At the embassy they asked around and found Mikhail. Detective Cummings identified himself and Detective White. "We're here about the disappearance of Kendra Maguire. I understand you drove the two of them a week ago Friday, is

that true?"

Mikhail continued to polish the already gleaming Rolls Royce Silver Cloud. "No, I never took the Maguire woman no place. I only drive the boss."

"You do know she's missing?"

"I heard. Has nothing to do with me."

"Where did you take your boss that Friday?"

Mikhail scrunched his face as if deep in thought, "We drive to the desert I think. Boss had meeting-it last a long time. After, he said he wanted to get out of city, too much noise and confusion."

"Where did you go?"

"Just drive. Out to desert, it's like home he said."

"Did you stop anywhere?"

"No, just drive." He smiled.

"Thank you for your time, Mikhail. You've been very helpful."

"What a crock!" John exclaimed. "That guy's into this with his slick boss, I'd bet anything. And did you notice his watch? How many chauffeurs wear a Rolex? He must make really good money."

Kendra thought she would go mad. The bitter cold crept into her bones. Weak from hunger, once again she felt all the bars of her cage hoping for a loose joint, some place she could shake loose. *Nothing. Nothing! I don't know how much longer I can hold on.* She heard the car drive up. Fear gripped her. This meant another beating. Against her will she also thought, *food.* This time, too weak to stand, she just sat against the bars.

Hugo brought a folding chair in from the car. He relaxed outside of her cage, legs stretched out in front, ankles crossed. He seemed to want to talk. "So do you enjoy your job with the Department of Foreign Affairs? How is your boss to work for?"

"What do you want? What do you care about my job?" *He's acting like we're old friends. What's going on?*

"This is just a friendly chat." Hugo leaned forward and put his elbows on his knees. "You probably are waiting for me to rape you. You Americans are all alike, you think about sex all the time. You want me to kiss you, fondle you take you here on the bare floor! I wouldn't soil myself with a dirty pig like you. What kind of woman leaves her home and her children to do the bidding of a man she's not married to? What kind I ask you!" His voice became louder and louder as he spoke.

Thinking to calm him Kendra responded, "I'm a widow, I had no choice. I have to work to support my family. My children are nearly grown, it's not like I'm leaving babies. My daughter is twenty and my son is eighteen. Both of them are finishing school. I know my family is worried. I'm sure they've called the police by now."

"No. No one has called the police. They know you for the whore you are."

"That's not true!" Kendra flared. "My boss has called the police and so have my children. I know they are looking for me." It was all she could do to keep from breaking down but she refused to let him see her cry.

He seemed to calm down and collect himself. "Don't worry. I will not touch you. However," he smiled, "my driver, Mikhail isn't nearly so choosy. I may let him have you before you die. Yes, that's a good idea. Maybe I'll watch." He laughed at the fear in her eyes. "I understand those Russkis like it rough. No sad weeping women for them. Ha!"

"You'll never get away with this."

"Of course I will," he laughed, "I can do anything I want."

"My country will declare you persona non grata, you'll be expelled."

Hugo looked at her as if she were a slow witted-child. "So what? I'm a prince in my country."

"Your country will punish you."

"Ha, not likely! Do you think my father would allow anyone in your country or mine to harm me? It would look very bad for us. No, that will not happen. The United States will tread

lightly. They do not want strained relations with us. You are not important to either side. They will make a few inquiries and then drop the case. Believe me, no one will waste time looking." He shoved two apples and a new jug of water into the cage. "Make this last. I may be gone for a few days." With that he left, closing and locking the cabin. Kendra was weak from hunger and relief that he had not beaten her, this time.

At the embassy Bram Dekker sat behind his desk. "Tell me what you found out, Polo. Were my suspicions correct?" The ambassador's face reflected his worry.

"Yes sir, I'm sorry to report your son is probably holding the woman somewhere in the desert. I followed him as far as Apple Valley, that's a community about ninety miles from Los Angeles. He then turned into the desert and I could no longer follow without being seen. What would you have me do now?"

"Nothing, it's time my son learned a lesson." After he dismissed Polo he called Detective Cummings. "Detective, this is Bram Dekker. I believe I have information that could help you in the disappearance of that young woman, Mrs. Maguire. Can you come to the embassy or no, better yet, can we meet somewhere neutral, a restaurant perhaps?"

Cummings said, "Of course. Meet me at the China Peacock, it's between Roja and Bazer near Ventura. I can be there in an hour."

Fortunately, the restaurant was not crowded. Cummings asked for a booth and ordered a diet coke with a slice of lemon while he waited for the ambassador. Bram Dekker arrived, looking far older than Cummings remembered from just a few days ago. *What ever this is, it's killing him*, thought Cummings.

"Detective, thank you for meeting me away from the embassy. As you will come to realize the information I have for you could be dangerous if it fell into the wrong hands and I'm proven to be wrong."

Cummings started to speak. The ambassador held up his

hand. "Wait please. This is hard for me but it must be said. Let me tell you a little about my son. Several years ago he fell under the influence of an extremist religion that wants to keep our country in the dark ages. Hugo was young and impressionable. He had just lost his mother who was abusive. Unfortunately, a touch of madness runs through her family. She committed suicide." Ambassador Dekker looked down and took a moment to regain his self control. "This group regards women as possessions no better than the family dog. This suited Hugo's frame of mind. I blame myself for not noticing his obsession with them. I should have seen the attraction. For years I've worked for our country's enlightenment and today I'm proud to say our women are educated and independent. When I found out Hugo had joined this disreputable band of fanatics, I sent him abroad to get him away from their influence. He has sworn to me that all of that is behind him, just a youthful mistake he tells me. Unfortunately, I believe he's lying. My servant followed him to a place called Apple Valley last night. He couldn't get too close but I'm fearful that he may be holding Mrs. Maguire somewhere in that area."

"Ambassador, I can't imagine how painful this must be for you. I give you my word I'll check it out. If your son is not involved no one ever need know of this conversation." He paused, taking a sip of his coke. "If he is . . ."

"Please," he held up his hand, "let's deal with that when the time comes."

In the embassy garage Detective Cummings once again spoke to Mikhail, "Hi, remember me? We spoke the other day."

"Yes, yes, I remember you."

"Good. I just had a few more quick questions. You said you drove your boss out to the desert. Can you be more specific? I mean the desert is a pretty big place."

Mikhail smiled, "I'm not sure, I don't know this place, we just drive for about an hour and come back here. That's all I know."

"I see, well, thanks again. By the way that's a beautiful watch. I noticed it the other day."

"Yes, present from Boss. You like huh?"

"Very nice." Cummings saw his partner emerge from the other side of the garage. He gave Mikhail a wave and quickly walked away.

As soon as the detective was out of sight, Mikhail began searching the Rolls. He went over every inch until he found what he was looking for. With a sleight of hand born of experience, he quickly removed the tracking device and attached it to the undercarriage of a limo parked next to him.

Kendra heard the car. She listened for the sound of the deadbolt snapping open. She didn't bother to try and rise. Curled in a fetal position she was too weak to care. Huddled against the bars of her cage, the rough concrete biting into her flesh, she thought, *I hope he kills me this time and gets it over with. I'm so tired, there are so many things left undone and unsaid. Why didn't I push Malcolm a little. I could see he was interested in me but he's so shy. I should have made the first move. Maybe we could have had something together. Now I'll never know. Thank God my kids are nearly grown, they'll be all right. I know they will.*

Hugo loomed at the door of her cage. "Well, looks like it's over for you. Let me check just to be sure." He unlocked the cage door.

"Boss!" screamed Mikhail. "Get out now. I just heard over the scanner the police are sending a helicopter. They'll see the car. Hurry! Get out!"

Hugo turned and quickly poured gas around the cabin from a metal can sitting by the door. As he ran out he flicked on his lighter and torched the pool of liquid. He jumped in the car as the cabin was engulfed in flames. "Drive! Get as far away as possible."

"What about the woman?" Mikhail asked.

"Dead. Never mind her—just get us out of here."

The sound of Hugo and Mikhail shouting and the smell

of smoke roused Kendra. The cabin was burning but the cage door was unlocked. With a strength she didn't know was in her, Kendra crawled through the cage door. *I have to get out. I have to find a way.* A section of a side wall collapsed leaving a space large enough for her to slide through. Her hair was singed, her feet were blistered but she was free. *Get away, get away, get away,* she thought, find help. She half-stumbled, half-crawled away with no idea where she was.

A family of rockhounds, returning from a day of exploring petroglyphs and searching for rose quartz and other rocks they could turn into jewelry, bounced along the desert. The father expertly dodged rocks and cactus while his two young sons argued about whether to have pizza or spaghetti for dinner. "Dad, look! A naked lady!" the youngest boy yelled, pointing out the window.

The truck screeched to a halt. The father shouted, "Stay here," to the boys. They watched out the window as their father grabbed a blanket from their camping gear and ran toward the stick-thin woman. A call to 911 directed them to the nearest hospital.

Overhead a helicopter searched the desert. "I see smoke, go that way." The co-pilot pointed. As they approached they could see the cabin, now in cinders. "Call it in. There's no way anyone could have lived through that."

At the hospital, the emergency room personnel took over. Kendra was soon hooked to an IV. Covered with cuts both old and recent, blistered and emaciated, she was barely conscious; the doctors were amazed that she was still alive. "Can you speak? What is your name?" the ER doctor asked.

He leaned close to her as Kendra tried to say her name through parched lips, "Ken, Ken," was all she could manage.

"Call the police," the doctor in charge ordered. "God only knows in the shape she's in, she'll be hard to identify. See if they have a missing person matching the description of this woman." Within the hour the hospital had a FAX with Kendra's

picture. "Call the number on the flier, tell them I think we have their missing woman."

After receiving the call, Detective Cummings requested a police helicopter. "John, I'm going to the Apple Valley General Hospital. Wait for my call. If this is the Maguire woman, notify her kids and Malcolm Fairchild. Ask him to bring them to the hospital. I have a hunch that he's more than a little interested."

At the hospital Cummings was able to identify Kendra because of her striking resemblance to Sheila.

Sheila and Kenny Maguire ran down the steps from the hospital's rooftop helipad. Malcolm Fairchild followed close behind. Doctor Linton ushered them into his office. "Where's Mom? I want to see her," Sheila cried.

"She's here and she's going to be fine. Understand that the ordeal she's been through has left her dehydrated and weak. We're administering fluids and treating her wounds. I'm going to allow you to see her for five minutes, one at a time."

Sheila tried not to cry at the sight of her mother. She sat on the side of the bed, "Mom, It's me, Sheila."

Kendra opened her eyes, "Sheila honey," her voice came out raspy and thin. "So glad to see you." She closed her eyes and appeared to go back to sleep.

"You go in," Sheila said to her brother. "I'm not sure she's awake so just let her know you're there. Talk to her, tell her you love her."

After Kenny returned to the waiting room, Malcolm went in. "Kendra, it's Malcolm. I'm not sure if you can hear me but I want you to know that I've been a fool. I should have spoken up months ago. I didn't realize how much you meant to me until I thought I'd lost you. When this is over I hope you'll give me a chance to show you how much I care." Kendra opened her eyes and he could see tears pooling. She smiled and squeezed his hand before dropping back to sleep.

Detectives Cummings and White arrived at the embassy and demanded to see Hugo Dekker. They were ushered into the same room where they had originally met. Ambassador Dekker and Hugo were waiting for them. "Mr. Dekker I'm charging you with the kidnapping and torture and attempted murder of Kendra Maguire. You had motive through your twisted association with those religious fanatics, you had ample opportunity and sufficient means to carry out your sick plan."

Hugo looked bemused, "Yes, yes, I also have one other thing that you didn't mention . . . diplomatic immunity."

Cummings glared at him, "What about your driver? He doesn't share your immunity. He'll be charged with the same crimes. He'll go to prison for years, maybe life."

Ambassador Dekker seemed to have aged in the space of a few minutes, "Hugo, you can't let this happen. Where's you sense of decency?"

"Come now, Father. Mikhail's only a servant, hardly someone with whom you should be concerned."

Unnoticed by the men talking, Mikhail had slipped into the room and stood listening behind a statue. When Hugo swaggered from the room Mikhail stepped in beside him. "Ah, Mikhail, I was just coming to find you. Take me for a drive. I need to clear my head. All this police nonsense has giving me a headache."

Hugo noticed the desert landscape outside the car window. "Where are you going? Turn around, go the other direction. Drive along the ocean." Mikhail did not respond. He made no move to follow Hugo's order. "Turn around! Did you hear? What's the matter with you?" The Rolls left the highway and headed into the vast open desert following dirt trails. Hugo screamed, "I command you! Turn this car around!"

"No, you no longer command me. You are no longer the master." Mikhail's demeanor had shifted from obedient servant to the one in charge. He pulled the car behind giant boulders, opened the door and drug Hugo out. Hugo could see a post

driven into the ground with a chain attached. "You would throw me to the wolves! I who have loved you and obeyed you for years. You said you loved me. You said we would always be together." As he spoke he forced Hugo to kneel while he attached a dog collar around his neck.

"I do love you! I meant it. I just said that to my father and the police so that we would have time to escape. We'll fly away tonight. We'll be together. I swear!" Hugo's eyes grew large as he watched Mikhail uncoil a long black whip- the one he'd used on Kendra Maguire.

"LIAR!" The whip snaked out and ripped Hugo's sleeve. Again and again Mikhail sent the whip on its vicious mission. Soon Hugo was on all fours, the few tatters of his clothing held on by threads, his body a mass of small bleeding cuts. "Don't go away," Mikhail taunted. "I have important business to attend to, I'll be back."

The desert turned freezing cold. Hugo could hear night creatures scuttling in the dark. He screamed, "Mikhail, Mikhail, come back! I'll make you a rich man, don't leave me, I do love you!"

The next morning Hugo heard the powerful engine of the Rolls as it came up the hill. He was relieved to see Mikhail get out of the car. "I knew you'd come back for me. I knew you wouldn't leave me," he sobbed.

His relief turned to fear when he saw the whip in Mikhail's hand. He also saw something else, a bucket. The whip began its deadly dance. Mikhail worked until sweat covered his face. Hugo curled on his side, trying in vain to escape the next blow, his naked body a mass of small bleeding cuts. Mikhail lifted the bucket, "Here, salt water for your wounds. It prevents infection you know." He watched without emotion as Hugo writhed in agony.

"Why are you doing this? What have I done to you?"

"I do it because I want to, because I like to, I do it because I can."

Josh leaned back in his chair took his time with a long sip of Jack and a few puffs.

"Hugo's remains were discovered about three months later. Animals had scattered the bones. All that was left was the stake with a chain and dog collar attached. If it hadn't been for DNA we might never have been sure. The Rolls was later discovered at a used car lot in Apple Valley. Last I heard, the police are still looking for Mikhail."

"Incredible! This is awesome stuff Mr. Cummings. We can't thank you enough." Steve checked the recorder.

Cummings held out his glass, "Please none of that 'mister' business. Makes me feel old. Call me Josh. Now here's one that you may find interesting. We called it Countdown. The young men settled back to listen.

Chapter 2
Countdown

Dr. Fred Jansen called police headquarters. "Yes, sir, how can I help you?" Detective Josh Cummings answered.

"I've just received a call demanding ten million dollars for the return of my wife. The voice gave me seventy-two hours from the time he contacts me again. I was warned not to get you involved, but I didn't know what else to do." Jansen's voice went up a notch.

"Believe me, sir you did the right thing. Give me your name and address. We'll be right over."

"Wait! You don't understand. My wife's right here. She's not missing."

There was a moment of silence. *"That means someone else is.* We'll need pictures of your wife, Dr. Jansen. It must be a case of mistaken identity." Josh turned to his partner, Dennis Kahill. "Someone has kidnapped a woman he believes is Ruth Jansen. They're demanding ten million in ransom."

"Fred Jansen, the inventor?"

"That's the one."

Dennis frowned. "You know, ten million doesn't seem like much for a person in his income bracket. I wonder why so little?"

"Good question. I haven't got a clue. Let's head over there

and see what we can find out."

Ruth and Fred Jansen's apartment was tastefully decorated with none of the excesses often found in the homes of people of enormous wealth. "This is not what I expected," Dennis said, glancing around at the simple furnishings.

"Ruth and I came from humble beginnings. We know what it is like to be poor. Neither of us feels the need to display our wealth. We prefer a simple life style. That's why this ransom demand comes as such a shock. My wife and I are often in the newspapers connected with this or that charitable organization. Whoever took this other poor woman must have seen our pictures."

"Yes. The problem is, as you're aware, if the kidnappers think they have your wife they may keep her alive until they get the money. Once they realize they have the wrong woman, there's not much chance they'll let her live. And so far we have no idea who this woman is."

"This is horrible," said Ruth, sinking to the couch. "Is there any way you can find out who's missing?"

Detective Cummings shook his head. "We'll do all we can but unless the husband or family contacts us, we're in the dark. Meanwhile, her family may not know she's been kidnapped. They may not have filed a missing persons report. We'll check. Please keep quiet about this for now. We need to find out all we can. It may already be too late."

Back at headquarters, Cummings and Kahill called a meeting with the other investigators. They outlined what had happened on a white board behind him. "Any ideas?"

One voice piped up, "Whoever was taken must resemble the wife. Maybe travels in the same social circles."

"I don't think she belongs to their same group," said Dennis. "The Jansen's would recognize someone in the group who looked like Ruth Jansen and they'd know right off if she was missing. We'll just have to play along until they make contact again. Meanwhile we'll check for all missing person reports on women with Ruth Jansen's approximate appearance. We'll have a phone tap on the Jansen place within the hour. Then we wait."

Cummings spoke to his investigative team. "I've asked Dr. Jansen to come here and educate us on his company and its latest research project."

The inventor nodded his head. "To start with, Jansen Development maintains state of the art security. The R&D optometric division can only be accessed by thumbprint and eye scan. Fewer than a dozen employees are ever allowed in the lab at any given time. The lab operates around the clock. Our scientists work in teams of twos and threes to insure that vital information cannot be lost if any of them should die or become incapacitated. Our collaborative method also insures that sensitive documents can be modified quickly should it become necessary. Among the various projects currently in progress is the Laser Eye. This is our current 'star.' Once implanted, the Laser Eye will permit a blind person to see with twenty-twenty vision. Currently, the cost of this device is about two million dollars per eye." He paused and looked thoughtful for a moment. "We are close to perfecting a way to make it possible for the average person to achieve sight with a cost of two to three thousand dollars per eye. Our dream is to make the device attainable by every blind person. 'Doable and affordable.' That's our motto."

"Do you have any idea what the Laser Eye would be worth to a rival firm?" asked Kahill. "Millions?"

"Make that billions, Detective. Think of all the blind people in the U.S. alone, not to mention around the world. Remember too, that almost as soon as the Laser Eye is perfected, new technology will render our present knowledge obsolete. Soon we'll be able to manufacture implants at a few hundred dollars each. Our project can be compared to the development of the computer, which went from being a huge box that weighed tons down to a hand held instrument in a few dozen years."

"Dr. Jansen, is your wife involved with the research?" asked

Cummings.

"Oh, yes, very much. My wife is a well-known scientist. Her specialty is sight restoration. In fact, she actually developed the process."

"I see. For now we'll have to ask that she stay away from the lab. If these people believe they have her then that's the best chance we have of rescuing this other woman."

"Of course. I understand."

Josh stepped up, "Thank you, Dr. Jansen. Now, back to the problem of who's been kidnapped. People, we haven't had any reason to suspect that the kidnapping is related to Jansen's work, but it would not be a stretch to assume that it is. The kidnappers may be holding this woman hoping to extract secrets from the lab. They may or may not know the value of the Laser Eye."

Dr. Jansen rang a small bell from his desk. "Everyone, may I have your attention, please? Ruth will be attending a convention in Delhi for the next week. She'll possibly stay longer to lecture on current advancements in eye care. Will this cause any problems?" He looked over at Rod and Julia, the other members of Ruth's immediate team.

"No. We're good," said Rod. "Isn't this rather sudden?"

"Yes, in fact it is. It seems the doctor scheduled to do the honors at the conference had an unfortunate accident. The director of the program called Ruth in a panic and begged her to fill in." He paused, trying to sound convincing. "You know Ruth; she can't say no. If you have any problems, just let me know. Ruth will be calling me every night so I can relay your concerns to her and hopefully she can resolve any issues."

Two days went by without any word from the kidnappers. Finally, on the third day, the phone rang. Immediately, the listening device kicked in. A muffled voice began to speak, "Deposit ten million in the following bank account." He gave the numbers to an offshore account. "As soon as the money is in place I'll release your wife. You have seventy-two hours. I'll call in one hour for your answer. *Tick, tick, tick.*" The line went dead. Jansen and his wife were perched above the phone, listening.

"Detective, I can put the money into the account…"

"Wait, Doctor. Don't be too hasty. We have no idea who this woman is and not a clue as to who's asking for the money. First, let's find out if she's still alive. When he calls back, ask for proof that 'your wife' is okay. Tell him you can get him the money *but not without proof.*"

The hour crawled by. When the phone rang Jansen picked it up. Before the kidnapper could speak he barked, "Let me speak to Ruth."

The altered voice said. "You're in no position to make demands. If you want your wife back, deposit the money. Now you have seventy-one hours. *Tick, tick, tick.*"

"I want to speak to my wife, right now! Prove to me she's alive or you'll get no money from me."

There was a slight pause. Then an angry sounding voice growled, "I'll call you back tomorrow. But you'd better be prepared to send the money or she goes up in smoke. Tick, tick, tick, Dr. Jansen, tick, tick, tick."

Ruth had tears in her eyes. "I hope this is the right thing to do, Detective. I feel so bad for that poor woman and her family."

The next day when the phone rang, Cummings and Kahill listened intently. The voice on the line was Ruth's. "Help me. They're hurting me. Need money. Don't wait."

The angry voice cut in, "You heard her. You have forty-seven hours left to send the money, Doctor, or your wife dies. *Tick, tick, tick.*" Again the line went dead.

Cummings looked at the Jansen's. "Ruth, that sounded like you, was that your voice?"

"Yes. I don't understand. How could they get my voice?"

"There are ways," said Kahill. "You make speeches at fundraisers. The words could have been spliced from talks you've given in the past. Another possibility is someone who can mimic your voice. We'll have to have the tape analyzed to know for sure."

At headquarters they discussed the message. "There's something not right here, Josh," Dennis said.

"I know. For one thing it didn't sound strained. Whoever was talking was too calm."

"Yeah, plus, what a strange message. If the kidnapper had let her talk she would have been crying and begging her husband to save her. If he had written a message for her to read, it would have had more sentence structure, don't you think? Also, what do you make of his comment earlier about her going up in smoke?"

"It's hard to say if that was just talk or a reference to her actually being burned up. Dennis, have the records searched for any buildings in the area that are scheduled for demolition."

"You got it."

"Let's take a look at the other members of the lab. I know we discounted them in the beginning because they know Ruth and would not have mistaken someone else for her. But now.... I don't know what to think."

"Whoever did this would have to have access to the tapes of Ruth's fundraising speeches," said Kahill. "And, he would have to have to know how to cut and splice to get the words he wanted."

"We're talking scientists here, pretty sharp individuals. I'd think they could figure it out."

"Not necessarily. Often people have tunnel vision when it comes to their work. Especially, I think, people working on such sensitive stuff like what goes on at Jansen Development."

"You may be right. Hey, look at this." Josh held a folder open for Dennis to see. "It says here that Rod Gibson's hobby is electronics."

"That doesn't mean he's involved,"

"No, but it's a start."

Kahill and Cummings went to Rod Gibson's home. The door was answered by a beefy man in a stained tee shirt and equally stained khaki pants. They identified themselves. "Rod ain't here," the man barked.

"Do you know where he is, Mr. Gibson?"

"My name's Johnson. Rod's my stepson. So what do you want?"

"Sorry, Mr. Johnson, do you know where he is? We want to talk to him. He may have some information about a case we're working on." The two investigators had already suspected that Rod Gibson would not be home. "Maybe you could help. Does Rod have a workshop? Something apart from the house?"

"Yeah. He rents part of an old warehouse on River Street by the Oak Avenue bridge. He plays around making recordings and selling them to friends."

"What kind of recordings?"

"I don't know. He records stuff off the Web and the radio and puts it together into some kind of music mish mash. I'm not into that stuff so I don't pay attention."

"You've been very helpful. Would you mind telling us where this warehouse is?"

"Down by the river, like I told you. Jeez man, I'm busy. Now, if you two don't mind." He shut the door a little too hard.

The agents ran back to their car. "This is the guy! I can feel it!" exclaimed Cummings. "Call headquarters! Get a team over there! Let's be careful; we don't want him to harm the woman."

A SWAT team poured out of the van, taking position around the warehouse. Josh and Dennis ran to the front of the building. The overhead door was down was and locked. They knocked on the walk-in door and waited. They could hear the sounds of running feet and furniture being overturned. Cummings went to the side door just in time to catch Rod trying to flee. "Search for the woman!" he shouted. The SWAT team swarmed into the building.

"All clear." The team leader reported. "No sign of her."

"I want a lawyer!" yelled Rod. He squirmed in vain, trying to release himself from Cumming's grasp.

"Of course you do. Let me tell you if that woman is dead or harmed, all the lawyers in town won't help you. The only way to help yourself is to tell us where she is."

Gibson just smirked at them from across the table at police headquarters.

The public defender arrived, she and Rod held a private conference.

"My client is prepared to tell you what you want know if you agree to no time served for the other offenses."

"Counselor, we already have Dr. Gibson on pirating CDs, and selling pornography…"

"Yes, yes, we know," she said impatiently. "What my client wants is to walk out of here in trade for the information you want."

"Help me out here, Gibson. Why the ruse about abducting Ruth Jansen? It's not like her husband wouldn't notice that his wife wasn't missing."

"No, but the old fool has tons of money. He gives to every sad sack organization that comes along. I knew he wouldn't let someone die for a measly ten million. Besides, I figure he owes me the money."

"How so?"

"If it weren't for me, Ruth would never have perfected her design on the Laser Eye."

"That's odd. When we spoke to the Jansen's, they indicated they were about to let you go. They said your work had become shoddy. Second rate at best."

"That's a load of bull! I'm smarter than everyone else in that lab put together. Stop blowing smoke! If you want your lady back, you'd better drop the charges. And," he looked at his watch, "*tick, tick, tick*. You'd better do it soon or it won't matter."

With that he sat back in his chair and glared at them.

Josh and Dennis stepped from the room. "Josh, if we let him go, we can get him later. By my calculations we have about twelve hours left. I have the feeling that without a job, he'll be back at his porno and pirating in no time at all."

Josh smiled. "Okay, but we have to clear it with the brass first. I'll go upstairs and see what magic I can work while you go back in there and get that guy to start talking. He has us over a barrel for now, but you're right, we'll get him."

Kahill stared with disgust at the man seated before him. "Okay, Gibson. You win, for now. But I warn you if that woman isn't in good health when we get her, we'll be back with a vengeance you can't even imagine. Now where is she?"

"It's Doctor Gibson and I won't say one word until I see the paperwork. I want it signed by the district attorney and notarized. Then and only then do you get the information." He looked at his watch and mouthed, "Tick, tick, tick."

They waited impatiently until Josh opened the door holding a sheaf of papers in his hand. "Got it!"

Gibson handed the papers to his attorney. "Look these over. If you say they're in order, then I'll tell them what they want to know."

It took a few minutes for the attorney to read the documents; finally, she nodded.

Gibson laughed out loud at the two men. "You don't get it do you? I can't believe you're so stupid. There is no woman. There never was."

Josh laughed, "Well, he thought he'd put one over on us and I guess he did for a while. In the end Dennis was right. We caught him less than a year later knee-deep in selling porn and pot to underage kids. "

He leaned back in his rocker, took another sip. A wreath of cigar smoke circled his gray head. *Imaging being able to pay ten million to ransom someone you don't even know. All I got was my piddly pay and the promise of a gold watch.*

Well, there was that little something . . .

George reached over to make sure the Josh had a full glass. The old man smiled. "Then there was the time up in Aspen Grove. This couple inherited an old house from an uncle who'd been murdered. The sheriff, a good friend of mine, told me this story." The detective puffed and sipped, George and Steve waited. "Seems the couple moved into the house and the wife found an old diary and started asking questions. . . Sheriff called it The Perfect Crime.

Chapter 3
The Perfect Crime

"What is it, Jen?" Mark asked, as he watched his wife dust off an old book.

"Looks like a diary or a journal. Funny, from what you've told me, your

Uncle John didn't seem like a journal kind of guy. Look at this; some of these entries date back to the sixties and continue off and on until 1983."

"That doesn't seem like a very big book for twenty years."

"They don't go day by day. Some of them are months apart. In fact, it looks like one whole year is missing."

"Well, never mind now. Let's clear out the rest of this stuff for Goodwill. We can read the journal later." Mark turned once again to old trunks and boxes of clothes, drapes, knick-knacks, and pictures—the accumulation of a lifetime. One entire box was filled with newspaper clippings. Mark could see at a glance they were about the auto accident that killed his Aunt Doris, Uncle John's wife.

Mark always thought of his uncle in terms of before and after. Before Aunt Doris was killed, Uncle John was an easy going, fun-to-be-with guy who took his nephew fishing, taught him to shoot and to ski. Mark was thirteen when his aunt was killed. After the accident his uncle was bitter and reclusive. He claimed someone from Tyson Electronics, his business rival, killed his wife. There was a large contract up for bid and John's company, Sparks Electronics, and Tyson were in competition. John hounded the police, said he had proof the brake lines on the car had been cut. He believed the "accident" was meant for him. Doris was driving his car that day. The police said they didn't have enough evidence; the brake lines could have been severed when the car went over the embankment. The case was kept open as long as possible, but without conclusive proof they could do nothing. To make matters worse, Junior Tyson spread the rumor that John himself had caused the accident to collect the life insurance. John became a caustic spokesman for police incompetence. He spent his time writing articles to the newspaper documenting cases of sloppy police work. He filled columns with names of people who had been unjustly incarcerated due to trumped-up police charges. He cited case after case of investigations that ended in the "Cold Case" files. He became a one-man crusade against poorly trained, incompetent police. He wrote of documented cases of "testa-lying," the training young police cadets received on how to make sure their notes back up their "evidence" in a crime. The newspaper articles came to an abrupt stop when John was murdered.

Mark and Jen finished for the day then left for their motel intent on hot showers and dinner. "What do you think?" Jen asked, they sat in the cozy booth enjoying an after dinner drink. "It's been nearly twenty years since your uncle was shot, and the police still haven't got a clue."

"Actually, the real problem was they had a lot of clues but none of them made sense. Uncle John was always calling the authorities and making complaints against people who were on his property watching him and shooting at the house from the woods. The police investigated, but there was never enough proof to hold anyone. Once or twice they questioned people, usually someone from Tyson Electric."

"When was he killed? 1983? The last entry in the journal is July fourth, 1983."

"The cleaning woman found him shot through the head on July sixth. Police figured he'd been dead two days. They also guessed that someone shot him from the woods. The bullet was too mangled to be of much use."

The house was in probate for years and, until recently, totally neglected. It stood on a hill overlooking a stand of trees and a stream that widened and narrowed with the annual rainfall. From the upper deck you could see Lake Tahoe just beyond where the stream fed into it. After work each Friday, the two of them drove to Aspen Grove and spent the weekend refurbishing the old Victorian house. Luckily, Mark was good at fixing things and was able to do a lot of the work. They hired out the big projects, the roof, new wiring and some plumbing, but he could handle broken porch planking and replacing windows. Jen was an able helper; the two of them enjoyed the prospect of making this home. It was going to mean a bit of a commute for both of them, but owning this beautiful home nestled among giant pines with a view of the lake made it worthwhile. In the fall, when the golden aspen were at their peak, the scene would be spectacular. Jen couldn't wait.

Mark's position as senior architect in the firm of Maynard and Shaw was both satisfying and demanding. He told Jen it looked like he would be made a full partner by the end of the year. The workload wouldn't be any less, but the raise would allow them to maintain Uncle John's gift in a style it deserved. The house was on the list to be considered for historical preservation. Mark felt privileged to be able to live there. It had been in his uncle's family for more than a century and Mark felt sure the murder wasn't the only secret the old girl was keeping to herself.

They worked every weekend through April and May. By the time school let out in mid-June, the house was ready. It now had a new heating and air-conditioning system, plus up-dated bathrooms and an indoor laundry. They moved in, both claiming the house would never be finished. Restoration was their new hobby.

"Honey, you take the basement and I'll take the attic. Okay?" Jen said.

"Suits me fine. That way we'll both have our own retreat."

Mark's space had walls outfitted with cupboards made especially to hold blueprints. Lighting focused on the work area, which included his CAD, computer assisted drawing, and a special printer designed to handle blueprints. He also had his regular computer, several file cabinets and a tilted drawing board. *Even with the CAD, I still enjoy hands-on drawing*, he thought.

Meanwhile, Jen transformed the attic. She put down colorful rugs, brought in a desk for her computer and a workbench for her projects. New lighting and a coat of yellow paint made the once gloomy area cheerful and inviting. "Come and look, what do you think?" Jen asked.

"I think it's almost perfect but how about enlarging the window? That would give you the wide-screen look."

"Great! I'd love that. I'll be able to see more of the lake and the woods."

On any given day Jen could watch deer quietly making their way through Indian paintbrush and aster lupine. Ground squirrels frolicked and gathered seeds. Once she saw a black bear ambling through the undergrowth. She stacked John's boxes in one corner. "I want to go through them at my own pace," she said.

"Listen to this, honey." Jen sat curled up in the big overstuffed chair by the window with Uncle John's journal on her lap. She read, "'Started going to Wiley's Pub today. After a while they won't notice.' That was dated April 2, 1980. Then it skips to June. 'Got some cigar butts from Junior's ash tray.'" Jen put the journal down. "What do you make of that?"

"Beats me. But I do think Uncle John lost it toward the end. It may be just the nonsense ramblings of a confused and bitter mind. Or, maybe it's something profound, but we'll never know. I did find something strange today. When I was putting the last touches on that built-in blueprint cabinet, I noticed the wood at the back sounded hollow. The boards didn't seem to be aligned just right, and when I applied pressure they moved to one side. There was a hidden compartment behind. It was empty but something had made small indentations in the wood. I'd say it had been used to store something fairly heavy. From the shape of the marks, probably a gun, rifle most likely."

Jen read through the journal, then began putting the newspaper clippings in order. Most of them dealt with the accident. Some were letters John wrote to the editor of the local newspaper, a few had been published. Next, she tackled the bills and miscellaneous papers. There was a paid invoice for a .30 caliber rifle from a gun show dated 1/4 and a bill from Peterson Medical Supplies for dissolvable sutures dated 1/18. Another mystery bill listed several bales of hay, yet another, helium balloons. After dinner Jen showed Matt the bills. "What would your uncle want with sutures? Or with hay, or helium balloons for that matter?"

"Beats me. I can't even imagine."

"Do you think the police would let us look at the case notes from John's murder? I'd like to see them."

"Jen, what good would that do? Even if they let you see them, the notes probably wouldn't make sense to someone outside of law enforcement."

"I don't know, honey, I just have this funny feeling that if I could see them maybe they'd make sense to me. This whole murder thing is so unsettling."

"Babe, it's been so many years ago. If the police couldn't solve it, what makes you think you can? Let it go." Mark glanced up in time to see the expression on his wife's face. He knew that look. It spelled determination. "Okay, okay. I'll ask Chief Watkins if you can have a look." He knew when he was beaten.

Jen sat with a copy of the old newspaper clippings that

she had copied from the archives at the local library. "Look at this—the article says there were a few pieces of hay on the upper deck where the maid found John."

"So?"

"I'm not sure. It's just funny that your uncle had a bill for hay and they found some pieces of hay near his body."

"Did they also find sutures?"

"You're being a smart-ass but I'm sure there's something here." Jen put the notes away and went back to reading the journal. Little by little Jen matched entries in the journal to paid bills or newspaper articles. One entry read, 'need to check wind patterns.' The next one read, "2/3 got the sutures today. practice time.' Another comment right after a paid bill for hay, 'how do U get hay on deck without questions?' A few days later, 'paint a bulls-eye—claim target practice. Buy bow and arrows.' The next invoice was from Thompson's Sporting Goods. "Did your uncle practice archery?" Jen wondered.

"Not that I ever knew about, but remember by the time of that entry I was living in the city and didn't have much contact with him."

"Where were the bales of hay? The police report mentioned pieces of hay, not bales."

"Funny. You're right, I never thought about it. You know who might know something, Alice Simms. She cleaned house for Uncle John, in fact she found the body."

A spry lady in her eighties, Mrs. Simms answered the door at first knock and welcomed them into a cozy living room dominated by a big-screen television and two huge cats. "That's Chocolate and Rum Puddin'." She waved at the dark brown and lighter brown cats. "Don't mind them, they own the place, just let me live here, and feed them, of course. Mark, I haven't seen you since, well, since your uncle…"

"I know, Mrs. Simms, I know. That was a terrible time for all of us."

"Please, let me get you some tea." Mrs. Simms appeared to

be trying to get past the awkward moment.

"That would be lovely. May I help?" Jen asked.

Once they were all seated in the living room, Mark began by asking, "Mrs. Simms, did my uncle practice archery? Did he have bales of hay on his upper deck?"

"Why, yes he did. I always thought it was a strange place to practice, what with all that open ground behind the house. But one day he had this big bale of hay with a bulls-eye pinned on it facing the woods. I never actually saw him practice but I did see a bow and some arrows on the table. They were there for several months and then one day I came to clean and they were gone. I just figured he'd lost interest."

"I'm sure the police asked you these same kinds of questions, did you notice anything strange about Uncle John before he died? Was he acting different or, I don't know… anything? "

"Well, this may or may not have been strange, but one day I was getting some of his clothes ready for the cleaners and I found tobacco in the pockets of two of his jacket. I never knew John to smoke, so it struck me as odd."

"Did you take care of his bills?" Jen asked.

"No, he did all that, but I did pick up packages from the post office now and then. And there *was* one package that stood out. It was from some medical lab. I have no idea what it was and, of course I'd never ask, but most of his packages came from seed catalog companies."

Mark put his arm around the old woman. "Thank you, Mrs. Simms, I know that was a hard time for you."

"It was. But that was a long time ago. Please come back. I enjoyed your visit."

"Let's go see if the Chief has the copy of the notes from the case ready for us."

Matt smiled at his wife, "A bulldog has nothing on you when you get something in your head."

Chief Watkins greeted them warmly. "Happy to see you

refurbishing that old house of your uncle's. House has a great history, you know."

"Hi, Chief. Yeah, I know some of the history but not all of it. Thanks for letting us see those notes. Jen is convinced there's something in them that will lead to the killer."

"Help yourselves. None of it ever made sense to any of us, so maybe a fresh pair of eyes will see something we didn't see."

"The hay," Jen said. "Where did the hay go?"

"All we found were a few pieces scattered on the deck. They didn't seem to mean much. I did ask Mrs. Simms, she said your uncle had been doing some target practice, but he'd lost interest and took the bales away. Seemed odd at the time, but other than that, odd was all it was. Another thing, we found bullet holes in the wood around the deck. Your uncle had reported being shot at a few times, but there seemed to be a lot of bullets embedded in the wood, way more than the few shots he'd reported. Look, you're welcome to read over these old notes and frankly, I hope you do see something new, just don't get your hopes up."

"You didn't tell me the house had a 'history' Come on confess. What's the story?" Jen was curled up in her favorite chair, sipping a glass of chardonnay. Mark stretched out on the sofa with his whisky and soda.

He laughed. "Well, like all history, this story is a mix of fact and fiction. Who knows which is which. Plus, I have the feeling that every generation adds its own spin. But the story goes, my great, great Aunt Imogene was an old maid, only in those days she was referred to as a spinster lady. Seems she was the very essence of decorum. Church on Sunday, Ladies' League volunteer, do-gooder, etcetera. She did her own housework and had a handyman come to take care of the grounds. Now, Lester Leake was by all accounts a good-looking guy about fifteen years younger than Aunt Imogene. He was slim and tall with jet-black hair and piercing blue eyes. He took care of her yard and the horses. . . remember this was back in the 1800's. Anyway, one day Lester up and disappears. No one knew it until my aunt started asking around for a new handyman. It seems Lester's sister came looking for him, only he's nowhere to be found. Then the sheriff starts to nose around. Seems the sheriff found out that Lester had a criminal record in another state. He waits until Auntie is at church one Sunday and searches the house. Lo and behold, he finds Lester's clothes hanging in her bedroom closet and short black hair on her pillow. Well, times being what they were, the sheriff didn't feel right about asking indelicate questions of a lady, especially one of Aunt Imogene's social stature, so Lester's disappearance remained just that, a disappearance. Seems old Les was never found, so the sheriff probably thought, 'good riddance.' Story has it that Auntie ordered several new aspen trees planted on the backside of the property about that time. You can still see the stand today. I guess no one ever asked why she needed more trees. It's not like this place is bereft of them. Now you have to decide for yourself what part is fact and what part is fiction. No one in the family knows for sure."

"Why on earth would a woman alone live clear out here? In those days this must have been really isolated."

"Seems she grew up here. Her father built the place, and by all accounts he was both wealthy and eccentric. Her mother died when she was a little girl, she never married. She just took care of her dad; when he died she continued to live here."

"Wow, whatever the truth, it makes for a good story. Maybe we'll hear Lester stomping around in the attic some dark and stormy night."

"Lord, I hope not. Between Lester and Uncle John, I've got about all the mystery I can handle."

"Maybe next spring we can dig around that stand of aspens."

"Jen, don't even think about it." Mark's voice took on a strident quality.

"Okay, okay, just kidding."

On Tuesday the rain came down so hard Jen didn't venture out of the house but spent her time with the journal and bills. When Mark got home they had beef stew, corn bread and salad for dinner. Jen had also baked a chocolate pie. "Boy, that hits the spot, honey; perfect rainy-day meal. I about froze my tail at work today. The heating system was on the fritz."

"Here, this should warm you up." She handed him a cup of coffee. "Let's have dessert in the living room. I have something to show you." Spread out on the coffee table was the journal with pages tabbed. The entries read, 'got some more butts today. About ready' and 'a few more practice runs should do it.'

"Look at this drawing, honey. What does it look like to you?" Jen asked.

He looked at the drawing for a while before finally saying, "It looks like a line drawn from the upper deck into the woods and back again. It makes a skinny triangle."

"Yes, but look at the point of the triangle. That looks like that outcrop of rocks just inside the tree line."

"You're right, but what does it mean?"

"To use your phrase, beats me. But I think John was planning something. I just can't figure out what." The chief was right. The case notes didn't say much beyond what they already knew. Jen put one thing together: the link between the cigarettes in the woods and the notes in the journal about pilfering butts at the local bar. "Uncle John was setting people up. He planted the butts in the woods, shot at his own house and then called the police."

"You can't know that for sure. Besides, where's the gun? None of Uncle John's guns matched the slugs the police found. Mark bolted upright. "The cabinet! John stashed the rifle in the hidden cabinet I found. I'll be! I think you're right. But what happened to it, where is it now?"

Jen went online the next morning and learned all she could about ricocheting bullets. Next, she looked into dissolving sutures, then called her friend, Thelma Norton.

"Thel, it's me, Jen. I have a strange question to ask but maybe you can help."

"Strange? What happened to 'Hi, Thel, how ya doing? I'm fine, thanks.'"

Jen laughed. "Sorry. You're right. I'm just so caught up in the murder of Matt's uncle, I get carried away."

"Murder? Wow. When did this happen?"

"Oh, it was years ago. It's just that they never solved the crime and now I have a bunch of notes and journal entries that seem to add up to something. I'm just not sure what. Since you're a nurse, I thought maybe you could answer a question."

"Shoot; I will if I can."

"Will dissolvable sutures dissolve in water or do they have to have body fluids?"

"You did say the question was strange, but the answer is they would dissolve in water. It might not be at the same rate as they would in the body, but water would definitely make them disappear."

"Thel, you're a doll. Thanks."

"Hey, don't leave me hanging. When do I get to hear the end of this story?"

"As soon as I know it, we'll have lunch. I promise."

Jen was so excited she could hardly wait for Mark to get home. "Honey, I've got it figured out."

"Hey, whoa, slow down, let me get my coat off. So what have you figured out?"

"Mark, your uncle wasn't murdered. He committed suicide!"

"Babe, what are you saying? The police ruled it a murder. What makes you think suicide?"

"Okay, I know it sounds a little far out, but just listen."

"Let me get a drink and then I'll hear your story. I have a feeling I'm going to need one."

Once they settled in the den in front of a warm fire, she began. "First listen to all the facts. One, John believed his competitor, Junior Tyson, killed your aunt. Two, he lost the big contract to Tyson after his wife's death. Three, he blamed the police for not catching the killer even after he provided what he felt was proof that someone tampered with his car. Four, he tried for years to get some kind of public outrage going against the police and Tyson.

Now, those are facts. What I've pieced together is a likely scenario. First, Uncle John gathers up cigarette butts from the local bar and plants them in the woods. Then, he shoots at his own house and calls the police. He hides the gun in that hidden cabinet you found in your workroom. Next, when no arrests are made, he buys hay and practices shooting into that outcrop of rocks until the ricocheting bullets hit the bale of hay."

"Honey, this is just too wild..."

"Hear me out, there's more. Once he feels confident that he can hit the rocks and have the bullets come back to the hay, he removes the hay. He then wraps the gun in dissolvable sutures, attaches a helium balloon or two and shoots until he's hit. Once he's hit, he automatically drops the gun. The air stream carries the gun out to the lake and dumps it as soon as the balloons start to deflate. It looks like murder, but John really killed himself. What do you think?"

"Well, I have to admit there's some sense to your theory. But there's no way to prove it."

"We could have the lake dredged for the gun."

Mark almost choked on his drink. "Forgetting the cost, you're talking about one deep lake. Did you know Lake Tahoe is the second deepest in the United States? I think it's about tenth in the world. No, sweetie, even if your theory is correct, that idea is out. You think the police would pay to dredge Tahoe for a twenty-year old gun? Besides, even if it were practical, which it isn't, the gun would most likely have rusted away or fallen apart by now."

Despite knowing he was right, Jen wanted to share her idea with the chief. "The theory is good," Chief Watkins told Jen. "I'm inclined to agree that's what happened. All the pieces seem to fit. I'd like to put this old case to rest. You know there's no statute of limitations on murder. Closing this case would mean no open cases for Aspen Grove, a pretty good way to end my watch. I'm retiring at the end of this year. I'd like to go out leaving the slate clean for the next chief. It would mean a lot to me."

Tony Milford, reporter for the *Aspen Grove T.V.*, had the piece about solving the John Blackburn murder ready for the six o'clock TV broadcast. The news was the most excitement Aspen Grove had experienced in a long while. Chief Watkins was gracious enough to give Jen the credit she deserved for helping to solve the decades-old crime. "While some of this still remains conjecture, I am now officially closing the file on the murder of John Blackburn."

Wiley's Pub was crowded with the usual Friday night after work bunch when the newscaster made the announcement. Older clients remembered the event. They remembered John as a good guy, one of them. Comments around the room were heard.

"Too bad. John was a good guy."

"Yeah, he went downhill after his wife was killed in that accident."

"Some didn't believe it was an accident."

"John sure didn't."

"Well, it's finally over…poor John."

Pete Raefield sat at the bar and said to no one in particular, "Can he do that? *Close the file,* I mean. Hey, I watch Cold Case Files on TV. They never close them unless the facts are solid."

"TV ain't real life. And this ain't exactly the big city." proclaimed the bartender. "TV's got an hour to get all the facts, solve the crime and put the bad guys away. This here's been goin' on for over twenty years. Time to put it to bed, I say."

"Besides," offered another patron, gesturing with his beer mug, "this is a small town. The chief of police can close a case if he wants."

The TV announcer finished by saying, "At last residents of Aspen Grove can rest easy. They can stop looking for John Blackburn's murderer. Next, the weather."

One lone man drinking at the end of the bar downed the rest of his drink and thought, *and I can stop looking over my shoulder.*

The old detective looked off in the distance, thinking of another time. "Chief Watkins was a friend of mine. He was happy to leave office with a clean slate." Josh sipped and looked into his drink. "Lucky thing too; he didn't live more than two months after he stepped down as sheriff. Cancer. No one knew. There were still some questions about the case but no one wanted to bring them up. Oh, well, long time ago. Lots of things happened back then. Lots to forget."

"What about that case where the woman, a niece, I think, inherited an old house out on the bay?" Steve prompted. "Seems there were a lot of twists and turns to it, at least from what I read in the newspapers."

"Ummm, you're talking about the one with the retarded daughter. You have been digging into some old files." He took a few puffs on the cigar and another sip of Jack. "Yeah, I remember that one." He rocked back in his chair. "Started out as a visit from a long lost niece:"

Chapter 4
CAITLIN

Long fingers of wispy fog draped the old mansion. Here and there the mist parted to allow a glimpse of turn-of-the-century elegance, a grand old lady long past her prime. High windows overlooked the bay. Lace curtains from another era protected the inside of the house from the casual or curious. Deep, red velvet drapes fell from the sides of each window.

Caitlin mounted the steps and rang the bell. The chimes barely sounded before a middle-aged woman wearing a navy blue wool dress with a lacy white collar opened the door.

"Mrs. Randolph?" asked Caitlin.

A look of surprise covered the woman's face, but she quickly regained her composure. "Goodness, no! I'm Eva, Mrs. Randolph's companion, but you must be Miss Caitlin. Please come in; the Missus is in the library. She's waiting for you."

Caitlin was shown into a large room with a cheerful fire casting out the chill of the fog-bound day. The lady seated in a comfortable chair having tea appeared much older and much closer to the image Caitlin had formed over the past several weeks of telephone conversations. Mrs. Randolph was a beautiful woman, well into her eighties.

Her snowy white hair, bound with pearls, swept into a bun at the nape of her neck. Her nails gleamed from a professional manicure topped with a light coat of clear polish.

"Caitlin, how wonderful to meet you at last. When my granddaughter called to tell me about you, it was hard to believe, but you're the spitting image of my mother. There's no doubt in my mind that you are my brother's daughter. Come, tell me how you came to start looking for your father's family. Please sit here, where are my manners? It's just so startling to see you. I know I'm prattling, but I'm so excited to meet you at last. I'll ring for Eva; you must be weary after your flight." She pulled a long bell cord and Eva of the blue dress materialized at once. Caitlin realized that she must have been standing just outside the door. "Eva, please bring fresh tea, sandwiches and some of that wonderful cake Mary made this morning." She turned to her guest. "Eva takes care of me. Not that I need taking care of, you understand, but she's a friend as well as a companion."

Eva brought a light lunch on a rolling cart, tiny sandwiches filled with chicken, ham and watercress, and pale wine served in crystal glasses. All of this was accompanied by monogrammed silverware that looked antique, well used, and expensive. Caitlin noticed the initials RR woven into a pattern of silver leaves were also embroidered on the linen napkins and tablecloth. She was having a hard time taking it all in. So far, she had hardly said a word. But her mind shouted, money, big money!

"Please, dear, tell me about yourself. I know from Twyla that you found us after you saw the name Wise on an advertisement for her art show. Other than that and the fact that Twyla was convinced that you're my brother's daughter, I really don't know a thing."

"What she says is true. I've never known anything about my father's side of the family and naturally, I've been curious. The only thing my mother ever said was that he had a sister named Martha. Well, she did say once that she didn't think Martha liked her very much. Mom died last year and left me still not knowing. When I saw the name Wise on the ad for the art show I took a chance that there might be a connection. We met, Twyla put me in touch with you, and here I am."

"As for my not liking your mother, please understand. I had been your father's nursemaid since he was a little boy. When he told me he had a sixteen-year-old wife and a baby on the way, I guess there was a certain amount of jealousy. I suddenly felt left out. Who knows, maybe I was feeling depressed because that was about the time realization of Missy's condition was beginning to sink in. Looking back, I can see that I did not act in a very warm and loving way toward your mother, and for that I'm deeply sorry." Martha suddenly looked very old and tired. "Well, I can see we have a lot of catching up to do. We have a room prepared and you're welcome to stay as long as you like."

"That's very generous of you. I hadn't planned on staying here. I mean, I just thought I'd get a room near the airport. I certainly don't want to put you out."

"Nonsense, there's plenty of room and I want, no, I need to get to know you better." The older woman leaned back, looking as if talking had taken her last bit of energy.

"Time for your medicine, Miss Martha, and time for your rest." Eva entered the room so quietly that Caitlin was a little startled to see her standing there holding a small silver tray with a glass of water and some pills in a silver cup.

"Oh bother! Don't be alarmed, dear; it's just this old heart of mine. A short rest and I'll be as good as new. Please make yourself at home. Eva will show you to your room and we'll meet again this evening."

Two women entered the room. "Missy, we have company," said Martha. The older of the two women looked at Caitlin and hid her face behind the younger woman. "This is my daughter, Missy. For all intents she remains a spoiled six-year-old. This is Carmen, Missy's nurse."

Carmen said, "How do you do," and turned to get Missy, who was playing on the floor.

Missy began jumping up and down chanting, "Missy wanta

go to the park, Missy wanta go to the park, Missy…" Missy's chanting changed to screams that were about to escalate into a full-blown tantrum when Carmen stepped in. "Why don't I take her outside for a little while?" She turned to Caitlin, "The park is just across the street. It has some swings she likes. Once she gets cold and hungry she'll want to come home. She'll sleep better for the exercise."

"Yes, yes, go on," Martha sighed. Missy smiled a sly smile at her mother, who didn't seem to notice.

Carmen led Missy away. Martha turned to Caitlin. "I should have put her in an institution long ago, but her father and I just couldn't. At first we held out hope that she would be right some day. We took her to every specialist we ever heard of, but in the end there were no answers. We hired people to care for her and did the best we could. Carmen is our latest in a long list of nurses. My son, Neil, found her. She's not only a trained nurse but she's very strong. Unfortunately, Missy sometimes gets out of hand and needs to be physically restrained, although not so much now that she's on this new medication. And Missy seems to like Carmen, so that's a plus. I don't know what I'll do when… I must take my nap now or Eva will be back to get me. We'll talk later, my dear. After you get settled in why don't you spend some time looking through some of these old family albums? I'm sure they will interest you. The first one shows your father and me when we were children. The others, you'll see, they're labeled. We can discuss who's who later."

The albums revealed a family she had never known. Here were pictures of a young Martha and her younger brother. Martha was holding young Joe by the hand. The boy, with his sandy blond hair blowing in the wind, was making a face for the camera. The pictures seemed to show Martha in charge of Joe and Joe rebelling against her authority. In one family portrait, Joe and Martha's parents sat stiffly in high-backed chairs while their children stood at either side. It was clear that Joe took after their mother with his light skin and clear blue eyes. Martha was her father's child, dark hair, dark eyes and pale olive skin. In another photo taken in someone's backyard, several people sat around a picnic table. The two adult men looked very much alike, probably Grandpa Wise and his younger brother. One woman held an infant while the other appeared to be cutting a cake. A smiling Joe and Martha held plates at the ready for their share.

The next album had pictures of Martha's wedding. There was a picture of a beautiful bride in flowing white and a smiling groom in formal tux, and Caitlin's father, Joe, standing on the steps of the church looking very dashing in his Navy uniform. Caitlin realized with a shock that her father must have been about twenty when this picture was taken. Farther in the album there was a letter, yellow with age, telling Martha that Joe had married and was about to be a father. The next page showed Joe, his tiny sixteen-year-old wife and their blanket wrapped infant in a park. They were standing under a tree looking out at the ocean. Caitlin had seen this photo before. It was one of only two pictures she had of her father. Tears sprang to her eyes as she read the next document from the Department of the Navy, which began, "We regret to inform you…"

After dinner Caitlin stood up. "How can you be so sure that I'm a Wise? All you really know is what I've told you, plus the similarity of coloring to your family."

"Come with me," said Martha, "I want you to see something." They went down the hall and entered a small, charming office; above the fireplace hung a portrait of a young woman about Caitlin's age. Caitlin's face showed her astonishment. The girl had her same bright blue eyes, tiny figure, blond hair and face. Caitlin might have posed for this picture playing dress-up in clothes found in an old attic trunk.

"Now you know why I am so sure. That picture was painted of my mother when she was twenty-four, just two years before Joe was born. I'm very tired now. Eva has your room prepared, so please go up whenever you're ready. There's a television in the library and many fine books to read. Please make yourself at home." Martha looked very pale and drawn.

"I won't be far behind you. It's been a long day." The upstairs hall was long and gloomy. Carpet absorbed the sound of her footsteps. Shadows played from old-fashioned lights filled with what appeared to be fifteen-watt bulbs. Funny, thought Caitlin, how cheap the very rich are. Maybe that's why they're rich. She knew it was foolish, but the hall felt creepy. Her room at the end of the hall seemed far away. She could hear muffled sounds from a room across the hall. As she approached, she could make out Missy's voice. "Missy doan wanna go to bed, Missy doan wanna go to bed."

"Be good, Missy. Tomorrow Neil is coming to see you and I want to tell him you've been a good girl," came the voice of Missy's nurse.

"Will Neil bring my pony?" asked the little girl in the aging body.

"We'll see," said Carmen. "I know he'll bring it soon."

Caitlin stopped eavesdropping and entered her room for a much-needed rest and some time to think. The day had put her on emotional overload. So much to learn about her father's family, and here were all the answers. It was hard to believe that Martha had lived so close, only an hour's plane ride away, for all these years, and now at last she had found her. *And she's so rotten rich*, thought Caitlin.

Since their first meeting nearly a year ago, Caitlin had become a regular, returning for weekend visits every other month or so.

She felt very comfortable now. The room had become her room. Everyone except Neil accepted her. Caitlin had even managed to form a certain rapport with Missy, occasionally reading to her in her room to spell Carmen for short periods of time. She and Aunt Martha were now very close, spending hours in front of the fire sipping tea and exchanging thoughts on every subject. "It's amazing," Martha commented, "how very much alike we think."

Yes, amazing, thought Caitlin and smiled.

Morning dawned bright and cloudless on this Saturday in June, a beautiful day. Mornings like this were especially welcome in foggy San Francisco. Caitlin made her way down the long curved staircase letting her sense of smell guide her to the kitchen and fresh-brewed coffee. The room was large. Clearly, at one time this kitchen had been designed for cooking on a grand scale. There were two restaurant-sized ovens, a floor to ceiling walk-in fridge, a bank of stainless steel sinks and enough pantry space to store half a supermarket. Caitlin assumed that at one time Martha and her husband had entertained on a luxurious scale.

"Ah, good morning to you, Miss Caitlin," said Mary. "If you'd like to go into the breakfast room, I'll bring coffee and whatever you'd like." All this came from a large, cheerful woman whom Caitlin judged to be not too much younger than Aunt Martha.

"Well, to tell the truth, Mary, I'd like to have coffee down here if you don't mind. Sitting alone in the breakfast room always seems like such a waste of space somehow." Caitlin smiled.

"You're welcome to have coffee anywhere you please," said Mary. "Why don't you join me, since we seem to be the only early birds? Carmen had me give Missy some of those sleeping pills in her evening milk or she'd be down here pestering me." A small frown passed over Mary's broad face as she made this last comment. Caitlin wasn't sure if it had to do with Carmen, the pills or Missy.

"I'd like that," said Caitlin. She followed Mary to a small cozy room off the big kitchen.

"This room," Mary explained, "used to be the eating room for the servants."

"To tell the truth, I like this, it seems friendlier somehow. How long have you worked here? I get the feeling that you and Martha are fairly close."

"Oh yes, I've been with Martha and her husband, Mr.

Randolph, since the first days of their marriage. In fact, John came to work here as their gardener and he and I were married here. We shared in the raising of Neil and the heartbreak of Missy's retardation. Miss Martha and Mr. Randolph took that child to all kinds of experts but no one could help. Poor little Missy will always be a child. At first it didn't seem so bad, but after a while people started trying to talk them into placing her in an institution, but Mr. Randolph would not hear of it. For a long time Neil was the only one Missy would listen to, but he was a mean one and would get his little sister to do bad things. Of course they were just children, but even so..."

"What kinds of things?"

"Oh, you know the kind of stuff a big brother would do to a younger sister, especially one who wasn't quite right in the head. Once he got her to take off all her clothes in front of a house full of important guests. Another time he told her if she held her new puppy under water, he would turn into a fish and swim around. Missy cried for a week after the puppy died. Of course, she was never allowed to have another pet, and Neil was punished but it didn't slow him down. After that trick, he told her she could fly, and she jumped from the second story balcony. As luck would have it she landed in a bush or she might have been killed. Young Master Neil got himself a good whooping for that one, but I'll tell you Missy loves him to this day in a way that's almost unnatural. Missy will do anything Neil tells her, anything."

Or anything she thinks Neil wants her to do, thought Caitlin.

Before Mary could go on, a bell sounded. "That'll be Miss Martha wanting her coffee and paper."

Carmen appeared in the doorway. She poured herself a cup of coffee as Mary prepared a tray to take upstairs. "I'll be taking Missy to the park, Mary. Would you fix a snack to take please?"

"All right," Mary answered tersely. "By the way, Mr. Neil is coming to dinner this evening," Mary said. "I'll fix dinner for Missy early. She'll be too excited to eat if I wait until he gets here." Caitlin listened to this exchange, sensing a tension between the two women. Carmen nodded at Caitlin and left the room. Mary cast a strange look at the retreating back of the nurse that was hard to miss.

"Many of the pictures had to be restored, they were so old and yellow. I'll tell you, I was amazed at the technical aspects of the restoration. They put the pictures on a screen and the first thing you know the image gets clearer until you'd think they were taken yesterday. In some cases I even had color added so you'd get a better idea of what they really looked like."

"I did wonder about that," said Caitlin. "I didn't think they had color photography as far back as some of these pictures must go."

As Caitlin and Martha worked their way through the albums again, a history she had long wondered about emerged. Here on these pages was her father's family all the way back to Great, Great Grandpa and Grandma looking like they did in the eighteen hundreds.

"Everyone looks very prosperous," mused Caitlin.

"Yes, there was money to spare, although not nearly as much as on the Randolph side."

I would have enjoyed getting in on some of that, thought Caitlin.

At the sound of the doorbell Missy flew down the stairs screaming, "Neil, Neil," in the high-pitched voice of a six-year-old.

"Okay, Missy, okay," said Neil as he tried to extract himself from Missy's arms.

"Did you bring my pony? Where's my pony?" shouted an excited Missy.

"Not today, Missy, soon, real soon," Neil said as he joined Caitlin and his mother in the library.

"Well, well, here's the long, lost cousin again." Neil's face twisted into a smirk that he was careful to hide from his mother. Somehow it came out like the slap of a wet towel on bare skin.

Neil's manner grated on Caitlin; it had been instant, mutual dislike from the moment they met.

"Carmen, please take Missy upstairs now," said Martha. "Missy, be good and Neil will come up later and see you." The lewd look between Neil and Carmen embarrassed Caitlin.

Over dinner and yet another discussion about money, Neil said, "It's just that you don't understand business, Mother. You have to lose a few before things really begin to pay off." The look he gave his mother was one of pure hatred.

"Maybe, but I'm through paying for your mistakes. Go to work, Neil. I'm not giving you one more cent. And on another subject, I won't have you filling Missy's head with this pony business. There isn't going to be any pony. It isn't right to get her hopes up the way you do."

"The devil with Missy, it's always Missy! Missy! Missy!" he shouted. "I'm sick of it! Sooo nice seeing you again, cuz. Do come again soon and hear more of the family dirt!" Neil threw his napkin down and stomped out of the room.

"Don't look so stricken, my dear. Neil has always been very foolish. His outbursts don't mean a thing. He'll call later and apologize; he always does. He has no money sense and that wife of his is too greedy by far. He may be right about one thing, though; I guess I've always paid a lot of attention to Missy. I feel guilty, but not guilty enough to keep throwing money down the rat holes he finds."

Neil called later in the evening and made up with his mother. He then asked to speak to Caitlin. "How long will you honor us with your presence this time?"

"Just until the end of the week; I've taken a few vacation days. Now that I've gotten to know Aunt Martha, I enjoy our time together. It's been wonderful getting to know my father's sister and finding out about his side of the family."

Neil chuckled in his unpleasant way, "I notice I wasn't included it that syrupy little speech. I suppose the old bat is sitting right there where she can lap up every word. How sweet!"

Caitlin replaced the receiver and turned to see Martha looking, what? smug? *Would that be it?* Caitlin wondered.

"Bedtime for this old girl," Martha said when Eva appeared with her evening medication. "Please stay up as long as you like." Martha kissed Caitlin on the cheek and disappeared up the stairs.

It wasn't much later when Caitlin met Mary carrying a tray laden with warm milk and a pot of tea. "Is that for Carmen and Missy?" she asked.

"Yes, I take it to them every night. The warm milk seems to help Missy sleep."

"Here, let me take it; I'm going up anyway," Caitlin offered.

Mary handed her the tray with a grateful look. "Those stairs are looking longer and longer as time goes by. These old legs are starting to rebel. Don't see how Miss Martha does it." As Caitlin took the tray it slipped, spilling milk and tea.

"Oh darn, now look what I've done."

"Don't worry; I'll fix some more quick as a wink."

"Nonsense, you go on. I'll heat some milk and fix the tea. After all, it was due to my clumsiness."

"Thank you, dear; I *am* tired. Oh, Missy's sleeping tablets are in the cupboard. Just drop two into the milk. And thank you one more time."

Screams tore through the gauzy curtain of Caitlin's sleep. Lights popped on throughout out the house, like bubbles rising to the surface of a boiling pot. With gut-wrenching effort she pulled on her robe and looked down the hall. The light at the end was assurance that the ungodly sound was coming from Missy's room. The screams kept on and on, but it was Carmen's voice, not Missy's. Caitlin forced herself down the dark hall. Missy stood just inside the door; even in the semi-lit room, Caitlin could see the dark front of Missy's gown and smell blood. Carmen abruptly stopped screaming when she saw Caitlin. Carmen seemed confused; she kept shaking her head as if to clear it. "Missy, what have you done?" Carmen began shaking the old child, demanding, "What have you done? What have you done?" Her voice was slightly slurred, as if she had been drinking. It was then that the light glinted off the knife in Missy's hand.

Eva, Mary and John were pounding breathlessly up the stairs. "What's going on? What's happening here?" demanded John. All of them seemed to notice the knife at the same time.

"Oh, my God!" The stunned moment of silence was followed by Mary's voice, "Miss Martha, has anyone checked on Miss Martha?" Fear made her voice tremble.

"You stay here, I'll go," said John.

"No, I have to know," Mary whispered.

The horror of what they were all thinking settled around the room. Carmen told Missy to go wash up. Missy made no move to obey.

The long keening sound from Martha's room confirmed their worst fears.

Detective Josh Cummings had seen many murders over the twenty-some years he had worked homicide. Retarded daughter stabs ailing mother was a first, although certainly not in a league with some of the criminals he had apprehended. In fact, everything about this case was so open-and-shut it caused him a moment of worry. *Josh, my boy, stop looking for deeper and darker, he told himself. For once you don't have to bust your balls wondering who done it and still you're not happy. Maybe nothing makes you happy, ever think of that?*

The coroner was still upstairs with Martha when the detective began his questioning. Not sure how to go about getting answers from this middle-aged, over-weight woman with the mind of a child, he jumped right in, "Missy, did you kill your mother?"

"Free widdle monkeys jumpin' ona bed, one felled off and bump his head," came Missy's singsong answer.

"Stop that, Missy, stop talking baby talk," snapped Carmen, "Can't you see she doesn't have any idea what you're talking about?" she said to the detective.

Josh was clearly out of his element with this one. "Perhaps you're right," he said. "Please tell me what happened."

"Well, I put Missy down about 9:30, as usual. She has trouble sleeping, so I give her some sleeping medicine that Dr. Wells prescribes. Mary brings it up in warm milk with cookies and some tea for me. We had our treat, then she went to bed. I read for a short while, before I fell asleep. I really don't know what time."

"Excuse me," Josh said. "Where is your room?"

"My room connects to Missy's. The door between us is always open in case she needs me."

"You didn't hear her get up?"

"No, I was sound asleep. Usually I hear her but for some reason I was really out of it. Generally, she sleeps through the night after she takes her medication. I didn't wake up until I heard her singing."

The detective ran his finger through his thinning hair. *I don't like it. It's too simple*, he thought. The sound of the doorbell brought him back to the task at hand.

The smell of whisky preceded a disheveled Neil as he stumbled into the room. "What's happened? The cop told my wife something happened to Mother. Tell me what's going on!" *Hey, that looked pretty good*, thought Neil. *Lucky Carmen called, or I'd still be in bed with that cute little waitress. Wonder how she knew where I was?* Caitlin caught the look that Carmen shot Neil, a look that fairly shouted, oh shut up and stop talking, you fool!

Missy broke free from Carmen's grasp and ran to Neil, nearly bowling him over in the process. Neil's demeanor changed abruptly from worried to irritated. "Carmen, take Missy. Get her off me, will you?" Neil shoved Missy hard. "Get away," he shouted.

Missy began to pout. "Where's my pony? Did you bring my pony? You said, you said…"

Carmen quickly took charge and pulled Missy away soothing her. "Not now Missy, not now. Neil's busy right now. Let's go up to your room. I have some candy for you." She looked at the detective for his approval.

"Yes, take her." He didn't see any advantage to having a disruptive Missy in the room. The coroner was finished; Martha's body was being removed from the house. Preliminary statements taken, they were all asked to make themselves available for further questioning. There was no doubt that Missy killed her mother, but why? What triggered her behavior? These questions had to be answered. He told Caitlin to extend her stay until further notice. He assured her that it would only be a matter of a few days, as the facts seemed pretty clear. Privately, he thought there was something else here, something that bothered him. He wasn't ready to put a name to the worry as yet, but past experience as a homicide detective made his bones ache on this one. He made arrangements for Missy to be taken to Child Haven for the night. He didn't know what else to do with her.

Caitlin was sure that no one could sleep any better than she could that night, but the house was quiet. If the others were awake they were not making any noise. She got up with the idea that some hot tea might help. The hall was dark and silent. Darkness always gave her the creeps. *Time to spend some money on 100-watt bulbs, brighten this place up.* The thought made her smile.

There was a dim light coming from under the door to the pantry at the bottom of the stairs. She could make out the muffled sounds of voices. Caitlin's instincts told her to run back upstairs and forget the voices, but curiosity won out. She mentally took herself by the collar and dragged herself closer to the door.

"Just a little while longer, be patient. It'll be over very soon."

"You said there'd be no inquiry. You said they'd just take her away and we'd get the money, you said…"

"Will you shut up? There's nothing to worry about. This is just routine stuff. Besides, how'd I know this detective would make such a big deal out of it? Just keep cool and everything will be okay. How did you get her to do it, anyway?"

"Me? Oh no, you don't! How did *you* get her to do it? That's the real question. Don't go trying to lay this off on me, you bastard. I had to track you down at that slut's house and..."

"Okay, okay, let's not fight about this now. Go back upstairs and we'll talk about it later."

"Fine! But I don't intend to wait much longer. I want out of here and I want the money you promised, understand?"

Caitlin stepped back into the recess under the stairwell just as the pantry door opened. The silhouettes of Neil and Carmen were still on Caitlin's eyes long after the door closed. She could hear their soft tiptoe sounds as they made their way to the kitchen door. A gust of cold, night air caused her to shiver. Carmen crept on bare feet back up the stairs only inches from where Caitlin stood holding her breath.

The office of Detective Josh Cummings was sparse: metal desk, metal chairs, not much in the way of personal belongings, other than one framed certificate of his master's degree in criminal justice from the California State University at Long Beach.

All those involved had been asked to arrive at the police station about an hour apart. "Please sit down," he said to Mary and her husband John. "This won't take long. I just have to ask some routine questions. You say you worked for Mrs. Randolph for the past thirty years?"

"Yes," Mary replied, her eyes red rimmed, swollen from crying. "I came to work for the Randolph's soon after they were married. My husband was hired shortly after me. John and I were married on the estate."

"Tell me about Missy," said the detective. "Was she violent?"

"Well no, not really. Sometimes she would throw a tantrum if she couldn't have her own way. She acted like the spoiled six-year-old she really is, you know, kick her feet, pout, make ugly faces, but most of the time she was sweet and easy to get along with. Even when she was being naughty she usually could be distracted with a cookie or a promise of a trip to the park."

"Usually?" asked the detective. "Were there times when she had to be restrained?"

"Only since Carmen came to take care of her. I never did like the way she wanted to give her shots and sleeping stuff all the time, but that wasn't for me to say."

"What about last night? Who was in the house?"

"Me and John, of course," continued Mary, "Mrs. Randolph, Carmen, Missy and Eva. Also there was Ms. Caitlin, Mrs. Randolph's niece."

"Was Mr. Neil Randolph there at any time yesterday?"

"He came earlier but he left after dinner." Mary made a face.

"What do you think of Mr. Randolph?"

A look passed between Mary and her husband that told the detective what he wanted to know.

"He was always a hard one to like," volunteered John. "Even as a little tyke he had a mean streak. Not just little boy mischief, but really mean stuff."

"Mean, like what?"

"Hateful stuff. Like the time he got Missy to run naked through the garden full of guests when the Randolph's was havin' a party for some bigwigs. Or the time he got her drunk and she puked up all over the Persian rug in the library. One time she ran away when Neil told her a witch was going to eat her. Took most of a day to find her. Poor thing was scared to death. Oh, he's a mean devil, he is."

"I understand that Missy does what Neil tells her. Why would she mind him any more than, say, her nurse or her mother?"

"Missy adores Neil; she worships the ground he walks on," said Mary, "always did."

"Shoulda put her in an institution. Shoulda done it right away, not wait till something like this happens!" John broke in.

Mary started to cry again. John patted her on the shoulder saying, "There, there, old girl."

"Where is Missy? What will become of her?" Mary asked, drying her eyes.

"Right now she's at Child Haven, but soon she'll be transferred to Angel of Mercy Catholic Home for Retarded Children. Her doctor is seeing to the arrangements. Evidently, Mrs. Randolph gave him the power to provide for Missy's health care in the event she wasn't around to take care of matters. Under the circumstances I'd say she was a lady of much wisdom."

The detective abruptly asked, "Do you know if Neil is the sole beneficiary of Mrs. Randolph's will?"

"I guess," said Mary. "Who else could there be?"

"She probably left some provision for Missy," said John. "She wasn't fooled by Neil's big act around her. No sir, the Missus wasn't nobody's dummy. She quit giving him money to finance his schemes after the first few failed big-time. I think they had another argument about that the other night over dinner."

The detective pondered some of the things Mary and John had said. "Check out the will and get a look at Neil Randolph's bank account," he told his assistant. "I still don't feel good about this one."

Eva was very uncomfortable sitting in the cold police office. Josh tried to put her at ease. "Please don't be nervous. This won't take long. It's purely routine. How long did you work for Mrs. Randolph?"

"About fifteen years."

"What were your duties?"

"Mainly I took care of Mrs. Randolph, brought her medication, reminded her to rest, sat with her in the evening and read, that sort of thing."

"Did you help with Missy?"

A shiver of revulsion crossed Eva's face. "No, I didn't have anything to do with her. That's Carmen's job. I just looked after Mrs. Randolph." Eva broke down and sobbed. "Why would she do it? Why would she kill her mother?"

"That's what I'm trying to find out," said the detective. "Is there anything you can tell me about that night? Anything that stands out?"

Eva dabbed at her eyes with a tissue, then shook her head. "No, nothing. Neil, Mr. Randolph, came to dinner. He and Miss Martha had an argument about some money he wanted and she wouldn't give it to him, but that was nothing new. They always argued about money. He left in a huff but he called later to apologize. That wasn't new either. He was always doing that."

"Anything else about that evening?" he prompted.

"Oh, Neil promised Missy a pony a while back and Missy wanted the pony right now. Mr. Randolph and his mother had words about that, too. Miss Martha had asked him so many times to stop making false promises, but he kept on. He seemed to enjoy getting Missy's hopes up. He told his mother Missy didn't know the difference anyway. But she did."

The detective recalled Missy's words: "Where's my pony? You promised." He also recalled how quickly Carmen had taken charge at Neil's insistence and removed Missy from the room.

Eva left. Carmen was called in. "Ms. Ruiz, you're Missy's nurse/companion. Is that right?"

"That's right," said Carmen.

"How long have you been employed by the Randolph's?"

"A little over a year, I came in April of last year."

"How did you come to work for Mrs. Randolph?"

"I worked out at the Family Fitness Center where Neil Randolph belongs. He told me his mother needed someone to take care of his retarded sister, so I applied for the job."

"Was this your usual line of work?"

"Not really, but I have a degree in physical therapy, and Neil said the job would only be for a few months. The pay was good and I got free room and board."

"Why only a few months?"

"Neil said he was going to talk his mother into putting Missy in an institution, so the job would be temporary."

"Please tell me about last night."

"After dinner, Caitlin brought Missy's warm milk with a sedative so she'd sleep through. It must have worn off. Sometimes she sleepwalks, so when she first woke me I thought that's what she'd been up to. Then I saw the blood, so much blood all over her. Her gown was soaked! I asked what she was doing but all I could get was mumbo-jumbo. I couldn't understand her. I went to get Mrs. Randolph, but then I saw what had happened. That's when I screamed and someone, probably John, came and called the police."

Interesting, Carmen knew the old lady was dead when the others came up the stairs, but she didn't say anything. He let Carmen go and called his assistant. "Anything?"

"Somethin.' The will was changed last Friday in favor of Caitlin Wise, with provisions for the staff and Missy. A trust was set aside for Missy to provide for her care until she dies. Neil Randolph is broke. His wife spends more than he makes, and he spends more than he makes. That boy is in real deep. Not only that but he has a taste for the ladies, Carmen among others."

"Hey, good work! I knew there was more to this than appeared on the surface."

"Yeah, but that doesn't take away the fact that it was Missy who killed her mother."

"No, but it points to who's behind it."

"Okay, but can you prove anything?"

"Good question. I'll think on it. Please call Ms. Wise in.

"Ms. Wise, I understand you were staying with your aunt for a few days. Is it true that you didn't know your aunt or any of the family before the past year or so?"

"Yes, that's true. I didn't know any of my father's family until a chance meeting with Twyla Wise, an artist who had a showing in Las Vegas, where I live. We met and she immediately saw the family resemblance. She called her aunt and put the two of us in touch. That was a little over a year ago. Since then I've been to see Aunt Martha several times. We've become very close. I often call her just to talk."

"What do you do in Las Vegas, Ms. Wise?"

"I'm an entertainer, at least I hope to be. Right now I'm a cocktail waitress at the Plush Bunny."

Isn't that a topless bar? Josh thought. *Low pay for being groped and taking your clothes off and no telling what else.*

"She was very kind, and we spent every evening going over old family albums so that I could get to know my family," continued Caitlin. "This is all so horrible." She looked ready to cry.

"Murder is always horrible," said the detective. "Would you know anything about your aunt's finances? Such as who benefits from her will?"

The question caught her by surprise, but Caitlin looked thoughtful. "No, I know nothing of her finances. The only thing I know is that Friday she went to meet with her accountant. Mary said that it was strange, because she had never known my aunt to go out to see her accountant. He always comes to the house. I don't know if that's important or not but it's the only thing I know. Oh . . . well…"

"Yes, was there something else?"

"Well, just that Neil and his mother had an argument at dinner over some money that he wanted to borrow for a business venture. Aunt Martha said no, and Neil stormed out. He called later to make up. Aunt Martha said this was his usual behavior and not to take notice of it. I don't know if any of that's important."

It did tell Josh a few things more about Neil's character than finances.

"Do you like Neil Randolph?" he asked.

"I really don't know him very well. I mean, I've only met him on a few occasions. I mean, I really don't know."

Caitlin's obvious discomfort told him all he needed to know about how Caitlin felt toward Neil Randolph.

"Is there anything else you can tell me? Anything at all?"

"Oh, I hate saying things about people I hardly know. It seems so dishonest, somehow, but, well, last night after everyone left, I couldn't sleep. I went downstairs to get some tea and I heard Neil and Carmen talking. They were in the small pantry at the bottom of the stairs."

"What did you hear? What did they say?"

"Nothing important sounding. Just talk about how this would soon be over and how Carmen was angry about something, but I couldn't hear exactly what. I got the impression she was mad about being mixed up in the investigation, but I can't be sure."

"Was that it?"

"Yes, that was it. I just thought it strange they were meeting in the middle of the night in the pantry, and right after Aunt Martha's murder."

Strange indeed, he thought. Evidently no one knows about the change in the will. Or possibly someone knows but isn't telling...yet. It's going to hit the fan when this comes out. Neil was called next to be interviewed.

"Mr. Randolph, where were you when your mother was killed?"

"You know exactly where I was because your man called me; I was at home."

"Why did you take so long to respond when my officer called?"

"Mmm, I'd had a little too much to drink so my wife couldn't wake me up right away."

"Isn't it true that you weren't home but were at the home of Mrs. Nancy Brewster? Isn't it true that your wife called you there and told you to come home because the police had called?"

True, thought Neil, *but it wasn't wifey who called. It was Carmen.*

"Yes, it's true," said Neil. "I didn't think it sounded too good to be over at Nancy's when something happened to Mother, so I lied. You can understand that, can't you?"

"I'm really not interested in you and your girlfriend. I'll leave that to you and your wife. What I want to know is what about you and Ms. Ruiz."

"Carmen? Why, she's Missy's nurse. I hardly know the woman."

"It's my understanding that it was at your insistence that your mother hired Ms. Ruiz."

"Not insistence! I only suggested that she interview Carmen. I met Carmen at the gym, and I knew Mother was looking for a new nurse for Missy. No big deal. We'd had a string of nurses and the last one just left. Other than tell her about the job, I had nothing more to do with it."

"Then tell me about the late-night meeting in the pantry."

Detective Cummings let Neil stew over this last remark. He excused him with a few more questions and called Carmen back for further questioning the next day. He hoped Neil and Carmen would try to meet, since he had them under surveillance.

Next he called Dr. Wells, Missy's physician, who agreed to come to the station.

"Dr. Wells, is Missy capable of telling us why she killed her mother? Can she tell us anything of value as to what prompted her to do such a thing? I'm having a real hard time dealing with this. I'm used to motive and reasons for acts of this kind."

"It's hard to say. Missy lives in a shadow world, with the mind of a six-year-old and the aging body of a postmenopausal woman. She has a lot to contend with. Furthermore the recent trauma of being removed from the only home she has ever known is making her difficult to deal with."

"What would happen if Neil went to see her?"

"There's no way to judge the reaction, but for her sake I believe it's better if she learns to adjust to the new environment with as few distractions as possible."

"Doctor, I need to get to the bottom of this. There's some reason Missy stabbed her mother. Something triggered the attack. I don't believe she just took it into her head to kill her mother."

"Yes, I agree with you. Missy always seemed to have a great deal of affection for her mother. I can't think why she would want to kill her. Of course she may not have realized she was killing her. To Missy it might have been a game, like in cartoons, where the Road Runner gets flattened by a steamroller and then gets up and runs away. I doubt Missy has a real concept of death."

"Doctor, thank you for coming, I appreciate your time. If I have further questions, may I call you?"

"Yes, of course, here's my card. I'll tell my nurse to put you through immediately if you call."

The two men shook hands. The detective was left with his thoughts. *A game. Yes, Missy, let's play a game. You kill Mommy and then you get a pony. Only one person had that kind of power. Now to nail him and maybe Carmen too.*

Mary watched for a moment from the doorway. Caitlin was walking…no, not walking, more like waltzing around the room, humming, as she let her hand trail across each piece of beautiful old furniture. "Miss?" Mary asked. "Aren't you flying home today?"

"Yes, of course, but I thought I'd visit this room once more. Aunt Martha and I had such wonderful talks in here that I…"

"You slut! You filthy piece of trash!" Neil's voice could be heard from out on the walk. He burst into the room, veins standing in cords on his beefy neck. "How did you do it? How? Tell me, or I'll smash your silly looking face to a pulp!"

Caitlin backed up as far as she could, her eyes growing large and round. "Mary, quick get John! Call the police! *Help!*"

Mary ran for the kitchen. "John! John! Call the police! Mr. Neil's gone crazy!"

John came out of the kitchen still holding a donut in one hand. "What's goin' on?"

"Quick, call 911! Mr. Neil's trying to kill Miss Caitlin!"

John ran to the library in time to see Neil choking Caitlin. Her face turning blue, she was clawing at his hands. "Let go you crazy bastard," he shouted. Neil was too intent on his task to pay attention. John lifted a poker from the fireplace and swung it, hitting Neil across the shoulders. The blow temporarily loosened his grip on Caitlin's neck. She crumpled to the floor gasping for breath.

"I've called them; the police are on the way!" Mary shouted. She ran to Caitlin, who was trying to sit up.

Neil started forward again in an attempt to kick Caitlin, but John held the poker high over his head. "Make one more move and I'll let you have it. This time I won't be so easy on you!"

Neil backed away, his face still red, the veins in his neck looking ready to burst. "I'll get you for this, you little tramp! I don't know how you got my mother to change her will, but I'll tell you one thing, you'll never see one red cent of that money. That money belongs to me!"

He turned to leave just as the police arrived.

"Take your hands off me, you morons!" he shouted, as the police twisted his arms behind and cuffed him. "She's the one you should arrest! That little whore stole my money! I'll make you pay for this you, you filthy tramp!" Neil glared in Caitlin's direction as the officers ducked his head and put him in the squad car.

At the station Josh was going over the report. "I knew there'd be the devil to pay when Randolph found out his mother had cut out him in favor of the new cousin," he said to his assistant. "Frankly, I didn't quite expect this. Was she badly hurt?"

"Naw, just some bruises and a good scare. Good thing

the old guy was there, or it might have gone the other way, though."

"I know that bastard did it. I know he got Missy to kill the old lady; I just can't prove it," he groused.

"At least he didn't get the money," said his assistant. "Missy Randolph is snug in her new home with enough money in trust to keep mosta the entire city in silk sheets for the rest of her life. Mary and John got a cottage in Carmel, plus an income equal to what they get now. Eva got her monthly salary and fifty grand as a going-away present. Even Carmen got enough to tide her over until she lands another job. Caitlin's the big winner and Neil's the big loser. That's the way it goes. By the way, Caitlin says she won't press charges against Neil."

"Why not? Without her charges he walks out of here. We can only hold him for a few hours." Josh was puzzled.

"Can't tell you. All she said was the family had suffered enough."

"Okay, then cut the jerk loose, but put the fear of God in him. I don't want a repeat of today."

Mary and John were packed, ready to leave. Eva had departed earlier for a three-month cruise, and Carmen moved back with an old boyfriend until she could get another job.

"Are you sure there isn't anything I can get you, Miss? John and I are going now."

"No, you go on. Cleaners will be in Monday to clean and I don't need much else, at least for now." Caitlin waved good-by, as John and Mary walked toward a waiting taxi.

The nun paused, watching Missy drip blood-red paint onto her paper and begin to spread it with arthritic fingers. Missy softly chanted to herself, "Free widdle monkeys jumpin'ona bed, one tooked a knife and killed the mommy dead. Now you get a pony, the doctor said, Free widdle monkeys…" Over and over and over.

"Poor thing, poor, poor thing," the nun murmured as she

went about her rounds.

The trees in the small park across from the mansion were wrapped in wisps of fog. From behind one gnarled trunk, Neil's red-rimmed eyes stared across the street at movement behind the velvet-draped windows. If hatred had been liquid, the street would have been filled with poison. The lawn would have been awash with a roaring wave that took the house and its occupant lifting them high and smashing them beyond recognition upon rocks placed there just for this purpose. "Soon, Miss Bitch, some day very soon," crooned Neil.

Caitlin continued the waltz interrupted days earlier by Neil's attack. One hand lightly touched the yellowing bruises on her neck, the other trailed over the beautiful old furniture, her beautiful old furniture. She softly hummed to herself, "Three little monkeys jumping on a bed. One took a knife and killed the mommy dead. Now you get a pony, the doctor said, three little monkeys…" Over and over and over.

The old detective took another puff and ruefully knocked the ash from the dwindling cigar. "Did you know these come from the oldest factory in the Dominican Republic?" George and Steve waited for him to continue.

"We all thought that was the end of the story. Seemed like it at the time." He sipped and puffed. "Strange how things change. One minute you're sure of your facts, the next minute they get blown sky high. This one was a real mind blower. Neil just couldn't leave well enough alone.

Chapter 5
WHAT GOES AROUND

Neil left the park, blind with a hatred that consumed him so completely it made him stagger when he walked. "Hey, buddy. You okay?" Neil, vaguely aware of a voice behind him, didn't slow down or look back. His only thought, *get home and start planning my revenge.*

Caitlin couldn't see Neil, but she sensed him. She knew he was in the park, hiding, like the coward he was, behind a tree. She knew he came nearly every day to watch the house. She'd alerted the police, but they said they couldn't do anything unless he made a move to harm her. Caitlin knew how frustrated Neil was and it made her laugh. *No wonder Aunt Martha left the money to me, I deserve it. He's such a loser!*

She walked through the grand old rooms admiring the antique furnishings and the beautiful marble fireplaces. *Mine, all mine,* she thought and hugged herself. *Hard to believe a hard-luck gal like me could've gotten so lucky. Talk about rags to riches.*

"That bitch! That worthless bitch! I'll see to it she pays me every penny of the money she stole," Neil ranted to his wife.

"What can you do, honey? Your mother left everything to her, everything except the money to keep Missy in that expensive nursing home." Terri Randolph was sick and tired of her husband's whining. When they first met, he came on strong, telling her that he was the son of a very wealthy family. He led her to believe that he was in line for millions of dollars as soon as his elderly mother passed away. They lived on the money his mother gave him for investing in his endless business ventures. She soon figured out that her husband's business sense was on a par with Bobo the Clown's. Neil's ventures never got off the ground. According to him, it was always someone else's fault, never his. Not too long before his mother was murdered, she'd cut Neil off. Mrs. Randolph was nobody's fool. She'd grown tired of Neil's failures and his weak excuses. And now, they were living on maxed-out credit cards and promises. If he didn't figure a way to take control of the family fortune soon, she'd be long gone.

"Terri, there has to be a way. I'll see my attorney tomorrow. I could claim my mother was mentally incompetent. That worthless bitch wormed her way into Mom's life claiming to be her long, lost niece. I'll fix her. That money belongs to me."

"Neil, honey," Terri said in a quiet voice, trying to soothe her husband before he worked himself into another rage. "We'll go to the attorney tomorrow, but I have to tell you, I know your mother had Caitlin checked out. She really is your cousin."

Neil and Terri sat in the office of their attorney, Sam Levine. Sam's father, Andrew, had been the Randolph's attorney before he retired. "Neil, Terri, what can I do for you?" Sam had a pretty good idea of what they wanted. He was just a few years older than Neil and had known him since he was a boy. He knew that basically Neil was no good. His mother had changed her will to prevent Neil from squandering the Randolph fortune. Sam had helped his father draw up the will when it became clear that Missy Randolph would forever be a child and Neil couldn't be trusted. "We're here to see what can be done about the will. My mother wasn't mentally capable of changing the will, and I can prove it," said Neil.

"Neil, I know how upsetting this has been for you, but I assure you your mother was of sound mind when she made the changes. What could possibly prove otherwise?"

"Simple," responded Neil. "She left Missy's trust to the nursing home and her doctor. Everyone knows how Missy loved me and I doted on her. Mother would never have left her care to someone else. Even if she left the bulk of the fortune to that bitch, she would've left Missy's care to me, if she'd been in her right mind." He sat back with a satisfied look on his face. It was clear that he'd given this a great deal of thought.

Levine sat back in his chair and shook his head. It was amazing how history had just been reinvented. True, Missy had always had an unnatural attachment to her brother. When they were children, he'd talked her into doing things that were dangerous or shameful. His parents punished him severely on many occasions, but he delighted in putting her in harm's way. Now, here he sat claiming a great love for his sister. He had a great love all right—for the fortune left in trust to care for Missy. Levine and Gold, Attorneys-at-Law, were the executers of the trust. The money went to the nursing home and the doctor who cared for her. The bad thing for Neil was that even if he had control of the money, his sister was younger by several years. What could he hope to gain? "Neil, this won't fly. Your mother was one of the most competent people I've ever met. Breaking her will or any part of it would be impossible. I know. I helped write the entire thing." Patience was not one of Sam Levine's qualities, and Neil's constant whining was getting on his last nerve. "Ever since your mother died, you've been trying different schemes to get the family money into your own hands. Remember all the failed business ventures you talked your mother into bankrolling? Remember how often she advised you, even begged you, to get a job? Now's the time to take that advice and leave the will alone." Sam stood and ushered Terri and Neil to the door. "Leave it alone, Neil. Go to work… make something of yourself."

Driving home Neil could still picture that night after Missy killed their mother. For weeks the police looked at him as the primary suspect. They said he was the only one with the control over Missy to make her do such a thing, he certainly had motive. In the end they couldn't prove their case, though it definitely wasn't for lack of trying. As it turned out, he didn't inherit the Randolph money. The will had been changed only weeks before to favor Caitlin.

"Until a year or so ago I never even heard of her. Suddenly out of the blue she appears. She claimed to have traced Mom through a distant relative with her same last name. Bull! That conniving bitch knew exactly where Mom lived and I'll bet a plugged nickel she knew to the penny how much she was worth. Caitlin came on all mealy-mouthed and syrupy sweet. She pretended to want to know more about her *long-lost relatives*. Poor Mom. She was a victim of that piece of trash. Imagine that tramp, living in Las Vegas and working at the Plush Bunny! I wonder how much acting like a bunny pays? Then she was always at the house, pretending she belonged there. She's been a constant pain in my neck, a thorn in my side. I don't know how she did it, but somehow I'll make that bitch pay. She got Mom to change her will and then finagled Missy into killing her." Neil fumed as he rehashed the details out loud, even though Terri had heard it all before. She did note that with each telling, Neil became more and more of the loving son and brother and less and less of the jerk he really was.

Neil drove in silence for some time, obviously plotting some new scheme. "What happens if Sam's no longer the family attorney?" he asked, not expecting an answer.

"Then the law firm appoints a new attorney. Nothing changes."

"But what if the new attorney's younger, less experienced, someone who didn't know my family. He'd be more likely to see things my way. He'd see how I've been screwed. Then we could break the will, toss that bitch out on her ass and put things to rights." Neil suddenly felt better, as a germ of a plan formed in his mind.

At The Alibi, Neil's bar away from home, he had a few drinks with an old acquaintance, Jason Wilkes. Neil and Jason met in jail—Neil, jailed for driving under the influence, and Jason on a connection to an insurance scam. Neil was released with a fine and community service. The case against Jason couldn't be proved. The police had to let him go. The two men formed a loose bond around the attitude that society was the cause of all their problems. "What you're asking costs money, and the last I heard, you're broke."

"Only temporarily. As soon as the will's changed I inherit millions. So what's the going price?"

"Depends. If you want a lot of pain and suffering it could go pretty high. If all you want is a simple slip-and-fall or car accident, I can probably get it done for around a hundred grand."

"Okay, a car accident will be fine, but it must be soon and, you understand, you won't get paid until my money comes in."

"Waiting isn't my best talent. How long do I have to wait?"

"It shouldn't take more than six months, max."

"Okay, six it is, but remember you owe me even if you don't get the will changed. I still get my money."

The tone of voice made Neil shudder, but the deal was done. Three weeks later he read in the paper that Sam Levine had been in a fatal car accident. The following week he received a letter from the law firm of Levine and Gold telling him of Sam's demise and announcing that a new attorney had been placed in charge of the Randolph estate. Neil shouted with joy. At last things were going his way. With Levine gone he could finally get his hands on what was rightfully his.

At the nursing facility where Missy Randolph was being

treated, Dr. Wells asked his patient, "How are you today Missy?" You seem much better."

"I'm fine. I feel good, thank you."

Dr. Wells spoke to the nurse in charge of Missy's care. "She seems to be responding to this new medication. What do you think?"

"Oh yes, Doctor, Missy is much improved. In fact it's hard for me to believe she's the same person."

"It will be a while before we can be certain, but it looks like her retardation was really the result of a chemical imbalance. I only regret we didn't have the benefit of these drugs years ago. The entire family could have been spared a lot of grief."

"Do you want me to notify her brother? They're very close, you know."

"Thank you, Nurse, I'd be grateful. Tell him not to get his hopes up, but we are making progress."

Missy Randolph looked from the doctor to the nurse. Things that had been tumbling about in the fog inside her head for a long time were starting to slow down and come into focus. Her big brother, Neil, was one of them. Missy had grown accustomed to people talking as though she were not there. "Hey! Remember me?" She waved her hand for attention.

"Sorry, Missy," laughed Dr. Wells. "I'll have to change the way I think about you; we all will. Also, I have some good news. I believe we can switch from injections to tablets. The research on this medication seems to indicate that after the initial series of treatment, switching to the tablets is just as effective."

"A lot easier on the backside, too," Missy said happily.

The letter from the nursing home came with the usual supply of bills. Neil threw all of them into the trash. "Don't you think you should at least look at those?" Terri asked.

"What on earth for? I don't have money for the bills and the nursing home just wants me to visit my sister. Why would I do that? Who needs that retard? Mother always saw to it that she was in my face every minute. Missy this, Missy that, do I care? I'm glad to be rid of her. She's just another pain in the ass."

"You know, Neil, that girl really loves you. The least you could do would be to visit her now and then. It wouldn't hurt."

Monday, Neil went once again to Levine and Gold. This time he met with Peter Levine, Sam's son. Peter was a much younger version of his dad. "No way, Mr. Randolph. The will and trust my dad wrote for your mother are as solid as the day they were written. You can't break the will; there's no way to do it and my advice is to stop trying."

Neil stormed out of the office. He ran down the steps and slammed into his car. He careened out of the parking garage and fishtailed into the street. "Caitlin, that bitch! It's her fault. She'll pay for this. I'll break her neck. I'll burn the house with her in it! I'll kill her! She can't do this to me!" he screamed. The cords on his neck stood out. His face turned bright red. On the way to the park for his daily spy session he began to plan how he would kill his cousin. "Just remember, what goes around comes around," he shouted to no one.

Back at The Alibi, Neil drank with Jason Wilkes once more. "I know, I know, Wilkes, I promised, but if you do this one I'll double the money. Don't you see, with her out of the way, the money reverts to me and my sister, and Missy's in a home for the mentally challenged."

"Mentally challenged? You mean retarded?"

"Yeah, she's a retard, can't take care of herself."

"I don't know. I'm not used to waiting for my money. I've got expenses too, you know. Besides, what makes you so sure? How do you know the old lady didn't set it up so it goes to some funky charity if this cousin cashes in her chips?"

"No, no, I've seen the will. It all comes to me. No worries there," Neil said, trying to sound confident. The fact was the very thought gave him a sick feeling in the pit of his stomach. He'd never even given a thought to the possibility that he might not be in line for the family fortune. This was something he would check out with his attorney as soon as he could.

"Okay, but this one is going to cost big-time. When do you want it to go down?"

"As soon as possible. Make it look like an accident. The furnace in that place has to be as old as I am, so it could catch fire."

Neil had not been to the park for several days and didn't know about Caitlin's new friend, Fang, a pit bull. Fang was generally sweet-natured, but he did not like strangers. Each night he made the rounds of the house and inspected his territory.

Saturday was the cook/housekeeper's day off. Caitlin had had a wonderful day. In the morning she went for her workout at the gym where she spent an hour with her personal trainer. Next, she had brunch with a man she recently met. The rest of the afternoon was spent shopping. She usually bought two or three of the same items, just because she could. She was making up for years of scraping along, just getting by. Her drawers and closets were stuffed with garments never taken from their original wrappers. Caitlin thought about Neil and laughed. *That worthless coward, hiding behind trees, spying on me. What does he think? I'm going to faint when I see him?* She went to bed after the eleven o'clock news.

At one, when the house was quiet, Wilkes slipped the lock and went to the basement. Neil was right; the furnace was as old as the hills. It didn't take long to plug up the ducts. This would cause the furnace to back up and explode. This old place would go up like tinder. Neil's cousin would be toast. Just to make sure, he planned to creep upstairs and kill her. A pillow over the face should do the trick. The fire would cover the evidence, and no one would be the wiser. He prided himself on being professional.

Fang heard the faint creak of the stairs. He let out a bark and hurled down the stairs, throwing his stout body at the intruder. His strong jaws closed around Wilkes's neck. The man was so surprised that he fell backwards, hitting his head

~ 78~

on the marble landing. Caitlin woke with a start. She raced into the hall and saw Fang at the bottom of the stairwell holding on to a man. A 911 call brought the police in a matter of minutes. The first policeman smelled smoke. He saw tendrils of smoke coming from the basement and called the fire department. The firemen quickly saw the problem and were able to extinguish the fire before much damage had been done.

Caitlin told the police that she had never seen the man before. Detective Cummings asked if she thought this had any connection to her cousin Neil. "I honestly don't know. I do know Neil watches the house from behind a tree at the park across the street. I've reported him to the police, but unless he tries to hurt me, they say there's nothing they can do."

"I've been keeping tabs on your cousin. I've never been completely satisfied with the way the case was closed when your aunt was killed. Something about it just never set right with me."

The next day Josh had a hunch. He turned to his assistant. "Call Neil Randolph and tell him it's important that he come to the station."

"Will do. What do you want me to say?"

"As little as possible. Just allude to evidence connecting him to the fire and attempted assault of his cousin."

The following day Neil came as requested. "What fire, what are you talking about? I was across town Saturday night and I can prove it."

Bingo! "Who said anything about Saturday? It's just that we have an old friend of yours from The Alibi in one of our guest rooms. He's been telling us some pretty interesting stuff."

Neil's heart sank. *The rat! The filthy rat! He gave me up to save his own skin.* "It was his idea. I never wanted to hurt my cousin. He told me if I didn't go along with his scheme, he'd hurt me and my wife. You hafta understand." The detective listened while Neil dug a deep pit for himself, one he wouldn't be able to crawl out of soon.

In her room at The Home, Dr. Wells spoke quietly to Missy. "You understand this medication has been nothing short of a miracle. The advances we've made in this area are phenomenal. You'll be able to live in a home of your own, in time possibly without assistance."

Missy had been busy catching up on life, her reading skills were already at fifth grade level and comprehension scored far above that. It would be some time before she was fully functional in the outside world, but Dr. Wells felt confident that she would be capable of living a fairly normal life. Each day she worked with a tutor, increasing her skills in reading, writing and math. One of the volunteers took her shopping. She could manage the bus system and even a movie.

"Missy, how would you feel about talking to the police? I know they would like to clear up the mystery of your mother's death. I think you would feel better about getting the facts out in the open."

"Yes, I want to talk to them. I'm ready now. I need to do this." Even though she uttered the words bravely, the thought of talking about *that night* made her mouth go dry. She'd been holding the information inside for a long time now. It had taken months of medication before her mind cleared enough to separate fact from a dream-like haze.

Dr. Wells determined that she was stable enough to handle the meeting with the police. "Detective, it's Dr. Wells here. I thought you'd like to know that Missy Randolph is almost fully recovered and is capable of telling you what happened the night her mother was murdered."

"Dr. Wells, I guess I have to say that I'm astonished. How on earth did this come about? I thought Missy Randolph was hopelessly retarded."

"We all did, but through the latest high-level research it was found to be a chemical imbalance. She's responding better than anyone could have hoped."

"Doctor, I'm grateful. It's always bothered me that I

couldn't get the truth of what happened that night. I'll come there; I don't want to upset her."

"Thank you. She's anxious to tell her story but this will make it easier. She isn't completely comfortable talking to strangers."

The detective, Dr. Wells and Missy sat in the pleasant living room of the nursing home. Dr. Wells began by asking Missy if she remembered the detective. "I remember, you came to my house the night my mother was killed."

"That's right. I was there. I want to thank you for taking the time to see me. Now, please, just take your time and tell me what happened. And please know that I'm not here to blame you in any way."

She started her story in a hesitant voice but gained confidence as she went along. "It was Caitlin. Every chance she got, she took me to the park and taught me that song. *Three little monkeys jumpin' ona bed. One took a knife and killed the mommy dead. Now you get a pony, the doctor said.* I remember that Neil was always promising me a pony but he never brought it. In my childlike mind I thought it was my mother who was keeping the pony from me. Caitlin said it was a game. I would stab my mother, then she would let Neil bring the pony. After that, Mom would get up like they do in cartoons. You can't know how sorry I am."

"No, don't be. This wasn't you. It was another person, someone not in control," said the doctor.

"He's right. You're not the one to blame. Now that I know the truth, your cousin has a lot to answer for."

In the months that followed this conversation, Caitlin was indicted for the murder of her aunt, Martha Randolph. Neil was held for hiring Jason Wilkes to burn the Randolph mansion and attempting to kill Caitlin. "Proving I had anything to do with this won't be that easy," Neil bragged to the detective. "All you have is the word of a convicted felon against mine. Now that Caitlin is out of the picture, the money reverts to me. I can hire the best attorney in the business."

"Guess again, Flash. I have enough against you to put you away for a long time. Your buddy Wilkes made a deal. And it looks like the best you can afford will be a public defender. I'll try to see if the judge can't appoint some first-year P.D. to give him some practice." This was a bluff, but Josh didn't care. He just wanted to see Neil twist in the wind.

"You're crazy! I'm rich. I'll call my attorney." Neil asked for and received a phone. "Peter, this is Neil Randolph. What about my money? Now that the bitch is out of the way, the money's mine, right?"

"Actually, Neil, the money is mine." An astonished Neil looked up from the phone. What he saw nearly took his breath away. A stylishly dressed woman stood in front of him. At first he thought it was his mother. It was moments before his brain caught up with the image before him. It was Missy! A Missy he had never seen, or even imagined. "Mom knew who you are, or better yet *what* you are, a conniving con man. You're a loser, Neil, a born loser. As it happens, the money and everything else belongs to me. You and dear cousin Caitlin will both get exactly what you deserve: *Nothing!*"

The old detective seemed to have drifted off, actually he was thinking, *all that money and me with my detective's paltry salary*, then he lifted his head, took another sip and continued. "It does my heart good when a case ends with the bad guys getting what they deserve and the good guys coming out on top." He looked at the end of his cigar, "Did you know that a cigar like this tastes different at different stages of smoking it? See how it's fat in the middle and tapered at the ends . . . gives off different smokes." He leaned back. "There was another case. Wealthy businessman, his wife, then, his daughter. We couldn't really prove what happened but everyone had suspicions . . ."

Chapter 6
WORTH THE WAIT

Jo ducked behind the filing cabinet in the supply room pulling her friend, Nora with her. In an excited whisper she said, "Lori's getting married."

"*No way!* Who'd marry her? What am I saying? With her father's money she could buy just about any man she wants."

"Don't be unkind. Lori's kinda sweet... I mean, in her own way. Admittedly she's not too bright and her fashion sense could use a major adjustment but hey, no one's perfect."

"Not too bright!" Jo hooted. "She was so excited when we asked her to join the office pool she showed up the next day in her bathing suit."

"Cut it out, Jo, that's not true and you know it." Nora laughed at her friend's exaggeration.

"I can see the wedding now," Jo went on. "Overstuffed bride in wedding gown by L.L. Bean with matching Birkenstocks. Handmade veil by Fisherman's Friend. Flowers by Burpee Seed Company. The wine, of course, will be imported from France. Her father will see to that."

Nora doubled up in laughter at the image Jo painted.

"Any idea who the victim, I mean, bridegroom is?" Nora asked.

"Hold on to your pantyhose girl, you're not going to believe this. It's Tom Markham."

"Oh Jo, say it isn't so." Nora put her hands over her heart. "Tom? Gorgeous Tom? The Tom of my most outrageous sexual fantasies? Tom with the smile that melts half the typing pool every time he walks through the office?"

"That's the one." Jo went on in a conspiratorial tone. "Sara, Mr. Allen's personal secretary, overheard Tom ask Mr. Allen when they could set a date. Not that she was eavesdropping, you understand," Jo lowered her glasses and winked at Nora, "but she told me that old man Allen actually shook Tom's hand and offered him a drink. They're going to lunch Wednesday to talk about the details."

"Wow! I can hardly believe it. Details? I wonder what details. Usually the mother of the bride takes care of the wedding stuff."

"I don't know for sure, but Sara said she wouldn't be a bit surprised if Tom suddenly became Vice President in charge of whatever."

"Sounds like a match made in heaven. Fabulous Tom and the Allen money with poor plump Lori thrown into the mix." Nora let out a long theatrical sigh. "Trust me I'm just green with envy. Except for the wedding outfit, I'd give anything to be in her shoes. Anyway, now she can stop pretending to 'work' here. She can retire to her mansion and play housewife."

Mrs. Allen could easily have passed for a general in the German army. She shouted orders, checked and double-checked for every last detail. This was to be a wedding the likes of which this city had never seen. It hadn't escaped her notice that all of her friend's daughters were well-married and producing grand-kids at a respectable rate. Her daughter might be the last to marry but she would have the biggest and finest wedding of them all. "He who laughs last…" she was fond of saying. Lori had fitting after fitting until she was exhausted. She actually lost ten pounds, which made her only fifty pounds overweight.

The wedding took place in the church the Allen's attended. The congregation was the richest; the members were among the city's most elite. When Mr. Allen complained about the cost his wife assured him that it was their obligation to their only daughter to give her a proper send off. They were after all, *"Allen's."*

Tom and Lori honeymooned in a villa in the south of France. When they returned it was to the small ten-acre estate presented to them as a wedding present by Lori's parents.

To everyone's astonishment Tom seemed to enjoy married life. He stopped going to the club after work and soon fell into the routine of social life to which the Allen's were accustomed. He worked hard at the office and earned the respect of the other attorneys. He never abused his position as son-in-law of the owner and in time people forgot that he probably offered himself as husband to Lori in exchange for his title and considerable salary.

Lori, ever mindful of her weight, tried every diet plan she could find, to no avail.

"Lori, honey. Stop trying. I like you just the way you are, honest. Weight isn't everything, you know." With that Tom would bring her a box of Godiva chocolates. The following week it would be Nirvana and then a box of Bugge from Belgium would arrive. Even though these took a little longer to be delivered Tom assured Lori that they were worth the wait. At first he brought them every week, but after about six months he started bringing them two or three times a week, and then he brought them as soon as he could see the last box was empty. Lori ate until she could barely waddle around the room. She had to use a dressmaker to cover her increasing girth. There was no way she could buy anything ready made.

Lori was so grateful that Tom didn't nag her about the extra pounds that she never questioned him about why sex just wasn't part of their marriage. Lori's knowledge of sex was limited to the first night of their honeymoon; after that it was never mentioned again.

The household help, ever ready to gossip, reported that handsome Tom was very attentive to his roly-poly wife. He kissed her goodbye each morning and greeted her each evening with another long and passionate kiss. The maids tittered behind closed doors and some speculated as to how long it would take their handsome employer to stray. They were somewhat disappointed that he never showed the least sign that all was not well.

As time went on everyone began to accept that Tom truly loved his wife. "Martha," he said one morning to the housekeeper. "Please watch what my wife eats. She's highly allergic to peanuts so anything with peanut or peanut oil could send her into anaphylactic shock."

"Of course, Sir. I'm glad you told me, I had no idea."

"Actually, I didn't either until her mother called me at work yesterday and happened to mention it. I'm surprised that Lori didn't tell me herself. Her mother says she periodically will sneak a little peanut butter or a few peanuts in the shell, like a child who will do a naughty thing just to gain attention. I'll speak to her myself but if you'd help, I'd be grateful."

That evening after dinner Tom asked his wife to join him in the library. "Lori honey, your mom told me about your allergy to peanuts. Why didn't you tell me? I'd have been more careful about the candy I buy."

Lori looked downcast. "I'm sorry. I didn't think it was a big deal. When I was a kid I got so tired of everyone watching my diet. I guess I used a taste of peanut as a small revenge. Trust me, it won't happen again. Besides, I read that some people outgrow the allergy. Maybe I'm one of them."

"Maybe, but why even take a chance? Please say you'll be careful."

In May of the third year that Tom and Lori were married, Mr. and Mrs. Allen, at Tom's urging, prepared to take their first vacation in over ten years. Mrs. Allen was so excited she insisted that Lori go with her to pick out new clothes, at least three outfits for every possible activity. They were taking a cruise to the Caribbean. They would fly to Florida in their private Learjet and begin the cruise from there. Mr. Allen asked Tom to take care of the details, letting him know that he wouldn't be the least bit unhappy if he were called home on urgent business. Mrs. Allen could carry on by herself in the capable hands of the ship's staff.

Tom called the airport and spoke to Tim Riggs, the Allen's pilot. "Captain Riggs, this is Tom Markham, Mr. Allen's son-in-law. He asked me to check with you to make sure all was ready for their trip. In fact, he asked me to come and personally take a look. I don't want to step on any toes and frankly, I wouldn't know a propeller from a wing span, but if you don't mind I'll come and pretend I know what I'm doing."

Riggs laughed. "Sure, come take a look. And just so you know, Learjets don't have propellers."

Tom laughed easily, "I knew that. Just testing." Tom dutifully went to the airport and "inspected" the plane. He made sure to look at everything in case anyone questioned him later. Most important, he figured, was the well-stocked bar. He made sure there was plenty of the scotch his father-in-law preferred. His mother-in-law liked white wine, a Chablis or sometimes a rose.

The Allen's were into the fifth day of their cruise when sure enough there was an emergency that made it necessary for Mr. Allen to come home early. Mrs. Allen bravely carried on.

This set the pattern for the Allen's annual "vacation" for the next three years.

In the fourth year, they took off to meet with their cruise ship but something went wrong. The plane exploded at the end of the runway, killing the pilot and Lori's parents. The funeral was well attended. Lori had to be sedated. Tom took charge. After the funeral Lori holed up in the house, barely eating except for the candy Tom continued to supply. Six months after the funeral Lori got up from her bed washed her face and stepped into Tom's adjoining room. "Sweetheart!" he cried, "I'm so happy to see you up. Come here and let me look at you." Lori crossed the room and threw her arms around her husband.

"Tom. You've been so good to me. I don't know how I would have managed without you."

"I have to go to the office now, but why don't we have a late dinner and celebrate when I get home?"

Lori followed Tom to the front door. The housekeeper observed them holding hands and hugging each other. Tom stepped out of the house and then stepped back in and gave Lori a long kiss that would rival any Hollywood smooch from the big screen.

The housekeeper called Tom at his office at ten that morning crying so hard she could hardly get the words out. "Mr. Markham, please come home, its Mrs. Markham. I think-I-I, think," she faltered. "Oh, please come!" she wailed.

Tom raced across town. The doctor was there. "Mr. Markham, I'm so sorry. It was sudden. The housekeeper said your wife went back upstairs after you left. She went to bring her some tea about nine-thirty and found her passed out. She called me and I came right away but your wife was already gone. It looks like she died from anaphylactic shock. Is she allergic to anything?"

"Peanuts, but we're extremely careful not to have any around."

"I'm sorry but it looks like she may have ingested something with peanuts. There'll have to be an autopsy but I'm sure that's what caused her death."

The Allen's left their considerable estate to their only daughter. Tom, of course, inherited from his wife.

After the second funeral in six months, Tom announced to his office and friends that he would take some time off. Everyone agreed that he deserved some space to grieve. On the plane to Aruba he opened his briefcase and took out a bag of peanut butter cups. He slowly unwrapped one and savored the rich chocolaty taste. *Definitely worth the wait*, he thought.

"It appeared that the plane had been tampered with but the evidence wasn't conclusive. The peanut candy to the wife? Who knew? If he did it, he got away with it, along with the family fortune. Well, I guess you can't solve them all." Josh looked at the ash on his cigar. "You boys must really be keen to hear about these old crimes. This cigar runs about fifteen, sixteen bucks." *Sure couldn't have afforded one of these babies in the old days.*

"You're worth it, Josh," Steve said. "We can get the bare bones of a story from the newspaper but it takes someone like you to give us the inside scoop. We really appreciate your time."

Josh, chuckled, "You came to the right place for inside scoop. Anymore of that?" He tilted his head toward the bottle. George poured some of the amber fluid into the old man's glass and waited until he'd taken another sip. "You boys like ghost stories? I know a couple. Never met a ghost myself, but both of these make you sit up and think . . . ummm maybe. The first one takes place outside of Reno. I'll loan you the book later and you can judge for yourselves."

Chapter 7
DANA'S HOUSE

"Now here's a little beauty; two bedrooms, one bath, nice size kitchen and sun porch. Just right, for a single lady like yourself." Fred Montclair glanced at his image in the rear view mirror and smoothed the few hairs on his otherwise bald head before aiming for the curb and preparing to step out.

"No! I've tried to make myself clear. I need at least three bedrooms, two baths and a room for an office. I'm a freelance writer. I have to have an office." Exasperation punctuated each word. "I am *not* interested in some tiny cracker box of a house. If I wanted that, I'd stay in an apartment! I want some yard and some space!" The Sunday drive through the residential section of the city wore on Dana's nerves. Clearly, Montclair had not listened to a word she said. "If you don't have anything in the category that I requested, then please take me back to your office. This is a waste of time!"

"Ms. Hollister, I pride myself on fitting people to their property. In your case, a single woman needs to be near her neighbors for support and companionship. Two bedrooms should be sufficient. You can put your computer on a desk in the second bedroom so you can do your little writing stuff. As for the small yard, you certainly don't want the extra work of lawns, gardens and such. Besides, the homes I have in mind are ready to move in. You won't even have to paint."

Gritting her teeth, Dana struggled to speak in a slow, controlled voice. "Take me back to your office *now!*" *How dare this insensitive oaf try to dictate what's right for me.* Dana could barely contain herself during the ride back.

Montclair, oblivious to her mood said, "As long as we're going back, I'll take the scenic route and show you some of our countryside manors. These aren't for you; however, they *are* lovely to look at." He steered the car through lush, gently rolling hills dotted with homes. Beautifully manicured lawns and fountains flashed between trees. Children dashed here and there, playing. *This is more like it. This is what I want.*

Dana saw a rundown house with a fading "FOR SALE" sign posted near the driveway. "Stop! I want to see this one."

"Oh, you don't want to see this one. It's been vacant for years. Totally rundown. Cost a fortune to restore. No. This is not for you."

"Mr. Montclair, stop this car! I'm sick and tired of you trying to tell me what I want and don't want! Now either show me this house or I'll find someone who will!" Dana glared at him. She had never met such a blatant sexist in her life and she didn't intend to put up with him another minute.

Montclair set his jaw in a grim line as he steered the car up the drive. Dana could see the place suffered from years of neglect. Under peeling paint and overgrown trees was a beautiful jewel of a house. Her heart took a leap. *This is my house.* "I want to see the inside." Without waiting for him, Dana got out of the car and started for the front door.

"Now see here, little lady—" His voice trailed off when he saw her determined look. Reluctantly, he opened the lock box and took out the key. "No one's been in here in ages. No telling what we'll find," he said gruffly. Dana thought she detected a quiver in his voice. She put it down to his fear of another outburst from her.

"How much?"

"How much? You aren't serious. Do you have any idea of

the cost to restore this place? Besides, you haven't even looked at it. The upstairs is probably rotted out. Let's go." Now she was sure he sounded afraid.

Dana ignored him and went upstairs. There were five bedrooms, one medium size and four very small ones. One bath. No closets in the small bedrooms only pegs on the walls for clothes and a wardrobe still holding dusty, child size clothes. Her mind was already remodeling. One large bedroom and bath. One office. Two medium bedrooms with a connecting bath or maybe . . . . She joined Montclair in the foyer. "I'll need a complete workup of costs. Give me the names of at least three home inspectors. I want to know the condition of the roof, plumbing, electrical and so on. Why has this property been on the market so long?"

Montclair turned to leave. "I'll get you the names. I have another appointment back at the office." He practically ran to his car.

"You didn't say why this property hasn't sold."

"It's been in court battles for years. It's just now been released for sale."

This isn't the entire story. I'd bet on it. Montclair retreated into silence. He went from talkative to moody, then silent. Once they reached his office he lightened up a little and said he'd get the information she wanted and send it to her hotel.

Weeks later, keys in hand, Dana walked up the drive of her new home. What a struggle, Montclair fought me every step of the way. *You'd think the old windbag didn't want a sale.* Her thoughts ran over the purely frustrating ordeal of what should have been a simple purchase while she waited for Brett Nielsen. He was going to give her some ideas on refurbishing and the costs of bringing the old place up to code. A dusty truck with a Nielsen Architects logo pulled into the driveway. "Brett Nielsen," said a tall, sandy haired man with green eyes and a boyish grin held out his hand. "I love the look of this house. My idea, with your approval of course, is to preserve the look as much as possible and still bring the old girl into modern times."

Dana was already impressed with what he had to say. Two other architects had wanted to all but destroy the house to modernize it. That wasn't what she was after. "Let's go in," she said. "I'm anxious to hear your thoughts." As they entered the dusty foyer Dana thought she heard the sound of children laughing. "Did you hear that? Someone's in the house."

Brett stopped and listened. "Stay here. I'll check." He ran lightly up the staircase. She could hear him going from room to room. "Nothing. Maybe just the wind through a broken window."

During the next two hours the two of them checked for necessary repairs, discussed possibilities, rejected ideas. "I'm starved. Besides, I think my brain is on overload from all these notes." He waved a book of lined pages filled with comments and scribbles. "Let me take you to lunch, ply you with wine and we'll dream of the finished product."

Dana laughed. "Look at us; we're both covered with dust, hardly fit for fine dining."

"Not to worry. I know just the place. The tablecloths are paper and you can get wine in a plastic cup." He noted that even covered with dust Dana was an attractive woman. Her light brown hair contrasted with her almost black eyes and pale skin. She barely reached his shoulder and he was over six feet tall. *She must be five five or six*, he thought.

"Lead on. I could eat dry macaroni I'm so hungry."

"Even I can offer better than that!" he said, looking at her in mock horror. Once they were seated in the restaurant Brett said, "I figure this project will take at least three months if all goes well. I'd like to start on the roof in case we get some rain, that way the work can go on inside."

"How much damage is there to the roof? Are we talking totally new or patch job?"

"Luckily there isn't that much damage. I figure we can get the damaged places repaired with foam and the places that show from the ground can be fixed without too much trouble.

Honestly, it's in much better shape than I would have expected given the length of time it's been sitting there."

"Speaking of which, don't you find it strange that a property of this quality would be on the market so long? The real estate agent said it had been tied up in court; somehow I don't think that's the whole of it."

"No, it isn't."

Dana looked at him, surprised. "You know the story, don't you?" She leaned across the table and rested her hand on his arm. "Please tell me. I've felt from the very first day that something was off-kilter. I just didn't know what."

Brett sighed. "I hope this doesn't spoil it for you. The family that owned the house was murdered. The mother and two children were stabbed to death. The father was held responsible and went to prison proclaiming his innocence. He died in prison. The property was put on the market to pay his legal fees. It never sold. That's why it's been vacant for so long. The real estate agent should have told you."

"Yes, he should have. It doesn't change how I feel about the house. I don't feel uncomfortable being there. It does explain why the neighbors have not been around to introduce themselves." *It also may explain the sounds I hear from time to time when the house is quiet*, she thought.

"Give them time. People say they're not superstitious; the reality is we all harbor some old fear of spooks, as unrealistic as it is."

Over the next three months, Dana went to the library and looked up stories from the newspaper archives about the murders. The headlines were lurid, the stories pretty much the same. According to the father, Robert Helms, he returned home from work to find his family dead or dying. His wife was still breathing. He called the police. The paramedics arrived and took April Helms to the hospital. She never fully regained consciousness before she died, but kept calling her husband's name. The police took that to mean she was identifying him as the killer. The first officer on the scene described Robert Helms as being covered in blood. Helms said he ran to his wife, took her in his arms and tried to revive her. The murder weapon was missing; police surmised that he had disposed of it before calling them. No motive for the killing was ever found and Robert Helms maintained his innocence to the end.

Another article on the same page caught Dana's eye. It noted that a cousin of Mr. Helms, George Gross, was negotiating a business deal to build a factory on some land held by the two of them. The deal was being blocked by Mr. Helms' refusal to sell the land to his cousin. The incarceration of Robert Helms might have prompted him to sell to his cousin; unfortunately, George Gross was killed in an auto accident on the same day the family was murdered. Dana copied the articles and headed home. She was building a file of information on the Helms' murders.

She drove up the long driveway and stopped. Yellow banners fluttered from the roof and a bright red ribbon stretched across the front of the porch. Brett stood at one side. As soon as she got out of the car, he handed her an oversized pair of scissors. "You may christen the house, my lady," he said, bowing deeply from the waist.

Dana laughed. "I don't know what to call her. I've never named a house before."

"Your choice. How about Dana's Diggs or Mansion Dana."

"Wow," she laughed. "Such pretensions. How about something a little more down to earth? I know." She took the giant scissors and cut the ribbon. " I christen thee, Dana's House."

Brett and the workers cheered and clapped. A worker with a bottle of champagne and glasses appeared from behind Brett's truck.

"With your architect's eye maybe you could give me some advice on colors. I want to create a mood of tranquility and cheerfulness." *And give you a reason to come back*, she thought.

"I know a lot of really great places to buy furniture, and we could go through some books I have to look at finished rooms. That way you could get an idea of color schemes that appeal to you. I could bring the books by this evening if you like." *Also I would have a good reason for seeing you again, he thought.*

That evening as they poured over Brett's scrapbooks, Dana was sure she heard someone upstairs. "There. Did you hear that? I know it's not a broken window. I hear children playing."

Brett listened. "Yes. I do hear it. Hold on. I'll check." He went up the stairs quietly, stopped on the landing and listened. "The sound is coming from the master bedroom." He stepped into the room, seeing only empty space. He joined Dana in the kitchen. They sat across from each other at the table. "I don't know what to think. There is definitely the sound of children playing coming from that room, when I look—nothing."

That night Dana slept on the hide-a-bed she was using until she picked out bedroom furniture. She fell asleep listening for the sounds of children playing; all she got was silence.

Over the next few weeks, Dana and Brett shopped for furniture, chose colors and grew increasingly fond of each other. "The rooms will be finished tomorrow. The first of the furniture can be delivered, and as soon as you decide on your bedroom furniture you can stop sleeping on that lumpy hide-a-bed."

"I can't wait. My back is beginning to get a permanent ache. I'm still trying to choose between the set we saw at the antique mall and the one from Hill Brother's Furniture." *My real problem is the mattress size. If I'm by myself, a queen will be fine if Brett's going to be part of this, I'll need a king. Brett hasn't really said what his intentions are.*

"Both are nice." He took her face in both hands and kissed her, long and hard. Abruptly he said, "I have some work to do. I'll be back around six. How do you feel about Chinese take out? I know this terrific place."

"Chinese is good." Dana was a little stunned at the intensity of the kiss. *Well, I guess that answers the intention question.*

Just before six, Brett's truck pulled up in front of the house. He struggled to lift a king size mattress and frame from the back. "Hold the door for me, please." He called. Dana held the door wide while he carried them upstairs. "Now you can choose what ever bed style you want, as long as it fits a king-size mattress."

"Hey, did it ever occur to you that I might say no?"

"No." Then he looked panicked. "You weren't going to say no. Were you?"

Dana flew into his arms, "No, you big fool. I wasn't. But a girl likes to be sure."

"Will this make you sure?" He took a small velvet box from his pocket and opened it. Inside was a beautiful square cut diamond ring. "I was going to wait until the right moment. . . you know, maybe over Chinese."

Dana laughed. "This moment seems right to me with or without won ton and spicy duck."

Late that night Dana woke to the sound of weeping. A young woman, dressed in the style of the thirties, was standing at the foot of the bed. "Help us, please help us," she cried. Dana tried to speak but the woman was gone

The next morning, over coffee, Dana described what she had seen. Brett listened intently. "I can't be sure if it was real or a dream, but the woman was the one from the newspaper articles, the one who was murdered."

"This house has a lot of secrets. I think she's trying to tell you something."

Dana was relieved that Brett didn't think she was imagining things. "What should I do? What can I do?"

"Just wait. She'll come again. She must know what she wants from you."

The next time the young woman came she was not alone.

Dana could see the back of a man dressed in a dark brown suit. The woman had a terrified look on her face. Her clothes were torn and there was a bruise on her face. She held out her hand and pleaded, "Please, no!" Then she cried out for her husband. "Robert! Robert! Help!"

At breakfast the next morning, Dana said, "Brett, she was calling for her husband to help her. She wasn't calling the man I saw with her Robert. Someone else killed her and the children. She's trying to tell me who."

The nights were quiet until August Sunday the 25th. Dana woke to the sounds of April Helms calling for help. "April, what can I do?" Papers appeared in her hands. Dana could see only the heading: County Recorder.

"Why now? Was there anything special about the date?" Brett handed her a cup of coffee.

"I'm not sure, but I'll go to the County Recorders office and see what I can find out about August 25, 1932, the date of the murder."

"Do you need me to go with you? I have some free time this morning. My ten o'clock appointment was postponed until tomorrow."

"I'd appreciate it. You know the 'two heads are better than one' thing."

At the county recorder's office, they were directed to the microfiche department in the basement. Dana worked backward from the date of the murder and Brett worked forward. After an hour Dana said, "Look." There on the screen was a copy of the transfer of land from Robert Helms to his cousin George Gross. It was unsigned, with "pending signature" stamped on the area above the signature line. It looks like cousin Gross had everything in order, just waiting until he could get Robert to sign.

Brett stopped his machine and pointed to the screen, "This is significant. It appears that Gross was deep in debt and after he was killed, several companies including the one he had lined up to build a factory on, filed to recover money from his estate."

That would certainly be a motive for killing Robert Helms."

"It would. But why his family?"

"Yes. Why?"

The mystery continued to occupy Dana's thoughts and the only possible source of information left was a dead woman's ghost. The next time April Helms appeared her clothes were torn, her hair disarrayed and her wrists were bruised. The man in the scene was adjusting his pants. Two children were peeking into the room.

"Brett! Wake up! Now I know why he killed them. He raped April and the children saw it happen."

Brett sat up and pulled Dana close. "I have a friend on the police force. Let's call him and see what we can do."

"You present a good case, Ms. Hollister; however, I'm afraid citing evidence provided by a ghost is going to be a hard sell to my superiors. Besides, a case this old...what seventy some years, is really a cold case. Unlike TV where they solve these old crimes, we have so many more pressing issues on our hands. I'm sorry. The best I can offer is a suggestion that you look up the report on George Gross's auto accident. I can get you access to the police files. See if anything shows up. Frankly, I don't know that it will do any good. We have the murder listed under 'solved.'"

"So really you're saying there isn't anything we can do." Brett said to his friend.

"I'm afraid that's right. Sorry to disappoint you."

They left the police station, both lost in thought. "What now? What can I do?" Dana said. "I feel so defeated."

"First, let's follow his suggestion and see what we can find out about the old accident report. It couldn't hurt and maybe it will help."

"The archives in the police library barely go back that far on microfiche. Let's see what we can find." The librarian, a short, stocky man with gray, bushy hair and had been the police historian for twenty years. He pulled a canister from the shelf and placed the film in a machine. He quickly went to reports dated August 1932. "Here you go. We weren't nearly as detailed or as careful about documenting things as we are now. Anyway, you're welcome to take a look."

Brett and Dana scanned through the documents until they came to the auto accident of George Gross. "The librarian was right. Look at how these are written. 'Car going too fast. Lost control- maybe brakes failed. Slammed into tree on curve. Hit head on wheel. Vic covered in blood. DOA.'" Dana searched through the rest of the report; it shed little light on anything until a sentence at the end. "Brett, look, right here; almost an afterthought." He could see scribbled at the end of the report one sentence. "Too much blood for small head cut."

"That was April and the children's blood. He was trying to get as far from the murder as he could get. Probably panicked, lost control and crashed. The question is what can we do now?"

"I've been thinking about that."

That night April and the children appeared. For the first time, Brett could also see them. They were all dressed in their Sunday best, as if on the way to church. No one spoke, they just smiled. Dana could feel their happiness. As they turned to walk away, April waved. Before they faded, Brett and Dana could see Robert Helm arms out stretched waiting at the end of a long bright corridor.

"The end. I just wish the world could know."

"They can. That's what I've been thinking about. You're a writer. You have all the material for a novel. It's perfect. You've done the research. You even know the main characters personally...Okay, in a way."

"A novel. But I write articles. I'm not a novel writer. But I guess...." Brett could see the idea beginning to take hold. "It would have to be presented as fiction. No one would buy the ghost factor."

"So? As long as you get the story out, does it matter? And, I'll bet there will be locals ready to believe the ghost parts. People around here have long memories and they still believe in haunted houses."

Dana kissed Brett, "You know for an architect you're a pretty savvy guy. What should I call it?"

"How about *Dana's House?*"

"It's getting late. I'll share this next one, then let's call it a night." George noticed that the bottle was down about half. Both cigars were gone. He could tell the old man's voice was getting tired.

"This one stretches from Las Vegas to Scotland. My buddy, Denny Griffin who wrote *Policing Las Vegas*, *Cullotta* and crime in Las Vegas, used to be a cop. He told me this one . . ."

Chapter 8
CASTLE McCLOUD

At first it sounded like babble, but then the sounds began to sort themselves out into many languages, filling the great hall, English, with an attractive Scottish burr, the predominant one. The atmosphere at the Royal Highland and Agricultural Society of Scotland in Ingliston was super-charged. Chantel Petit was here as a free-lance photographer to cover the opening of the annual wool merchants' convention. Deals would be brokered between grower and distributor, old friends would meet for a "wee drop," and rivals would try, once again, to outbid each other.

Chantel loved the energy of the place and took copious notes and many pictures. She particularly enjoyed the booths set up to show off wool and cashmere garments woven from fine Scottish yarn. When she stopped for a break and a bite to eat, she put her backpack, with its precious camera equipment and notes, on the chair next to her. She noticed a briefcase on the floor, partially hidden under the table.

She bought grilled chicken, a fruit plate and a cup of tea." Pointing to the burgundy leather case on the floor, she told the waitress, "I think someone left this. I'm sure the owner needs it back."

"Yes, I'm sure. You can take it to the admissions desk.

Someone will check it."

Chantel finished her lunch, half-expecting the owner to arrive searching for his lost goods. No one came. She finished, took the case and made her way to the admissions desk across the hall. The desk was unoccupied; she was reluctant just to drop the case off. It seemed too valuable to leave in the open.

Inside she found a name: Ian McCloud. She went in search of someone who could give her a roster of attendees. When she finally found a person in charge, she was told, "Sorry, Miss, we can't give out that information." It seemed the closed mind of the professional worker bee was the same the world around: Follow the rules, no matter how stupid. She tried to leave the case with him and let him deal with it; of course, he could not be responsible. Frustrated, Chantel figured McCloud must be staying in one of the nearby hotels. She would spend a few minutes trying to locate him, and after that, she would drop the case off at convention security.

She returned to her hotel and made some calls. The third call produced results. She told the clerk at the front desk, "Please tell Mr. McCloud that I believe I have his briefcase. If he can identify it, I'll be happy to give it to him." She gave the man her name and number.

"How could I have been so stupid, so careless!" Bruce was berating himself. "I just walked away and left the blasted thing!" Ian and Bruce McCloud retraced their steps in the convention hall, trying to locate the lost briefcase.

"We'll find it. Stop beating yourself up. After all you're not used to carrying my case around. It's here somewhere." They went back to the food court and found the waitress who had served Chantel.

"I told the lady to take it to admissions. She seemed a responsible sort, wanted to do the right thing." They headed for the admissions desk, but no one there could help. Back at their room they got Chantel's message. "Probably holding on to it for a reward," Bruce said sourly as he called the number. He left a message at Chantel's hotel describing the case and suggesting there was a reward.

Chantel took the briefcase to the front desk of their hotel and left it, telling the clerk to please return it to Mr. McCloud. Bruce was standing nearby and stepped forward. "Miss, I'm Bruce McCloud. My brother Ian is the owner of the case. We appreciate you bringing it back." He reached into his wallet and began counting money.

"You're welcome. Please don't feel a reward is necessary." She turned and walked away, happy to be rid of it.

Bruce returned to Ian's room. "Here 'tis. A very attractive lassie returned it but refused a reward. She left before I could say anything to her. But now I feel guilty for assuming she was after money."

Ian looked at his brother, a slightly younger version of himself. Both had raven black hair and eyes the color of the sky on a cold rainy day. "You must be in the mood for guilt, wee Bruce." Ian placed a hand on his brother's shoulder and gave him a mock frown. "First guilty over losing the case, now guilty for getting it back. I've never known you to have so much guilt."

"Guess you're right." Bruce gave a short laugh. "I'll have to think of a new hobby. This guilt thing just isn't working for me. By the way, how's your talk going with McIver? I've spoken to the American, Dan Hal, and he's willing to take a shipment of cashmere to try it out."

"Everything's good. McIver says we can finalize the contracts tomorrow."

The mass of people in the great hall thinned. Most buyers and sellers finished with their negotiations were headed back home. Chantel packed the last of her camera equipment and turned to leave. As she did, she bumped into a man, causing a moment of confusion. "Sorry, sorry, hope I didn't hurt you."

"No, no, I'm fine," Ian said. "Besides, I believe this was my fault. I'm the one to say sorry."

Bruce came from across the hall. "Ian, this is the lass who found your case. Ms. Petit, this is my brother Ian. I'm Bruce McCloud. We met briefly, yesterday."

"Thank you for returning my briefcase. I really needed the papers inside for today. I appreciate getting it back. Bruce said you refused a reward, I'd be honored if you'd join us for dinner. We just finalized two major contracts and it would please us both if you'd find it in your heart to help us celebrate." He gave Chantel his most winning smile as he took in her slim build, honey blond hair and brown, brown eyes.

She hesitated for a moment. The thought of spending a lonely night in her hotel room prompted her to say, "That's very kind of you. I'd like that. Tonight's my last night here, so it would be a lovely way to finish my trip."

The Vermillion Room at the Scotsman boasted more than one hundred wines. The cream leather sofas in the bar area beckoned weary travelers to relax and shed their cares. The bronze-fronted cabinets sparkled with reflected candlelight. Chantel, Bruce and Ian chatted while waiting to be called to dinner. "So, you two seem very happy. I take it your negotiations went well."

"More than well. Ian and I have been trying for several years now to build our cashmere trade, and this is our first major American contract."

"Bruce is right. We're very gratified to finally get our foot in the door, as it were."

"But you also sell regular wool too, don't you?"

"Aye, but careful lass, we McClouds tend to think our wool is anything but regular." Bruce flashed a smile. "Each wool merchant thinks his sheep and goats are special. The others, of course; are wrong, McCloud wool is special. Our sheep trace their lineage back to the first McCloud lamb over two hundred years ago. We raise Shetland and Scottish Blackface. The goats came later, they're pure Kashmir."

Ian put his hand up, "Whoa, Bruce. Ms. Petit isn't interested in our family history." He turned to Chantel. "As you can see, we tend to be very passionate about our animals and wool."

"Yes, I can see that." She smiled. "And please call me Chantel. It's refreshing to find people who are passionate about their work."

"If you could bring yourself to stay an extra few days, I'd love to show you around," said Ian. "Not just sheep and woolen mills, but some of the highlights of Edinburgh and surrounding areas."

During dinner the brothers kept Chantel amused with tales of their boyhood escapades. Chantel told them of her life as a freelance photographer and her home in Las Vegas, Nevada.

"Chantel Petit, French for little song?" Ian asked.

"Yes. My parents had a poetic streak. My mother was a singer and my father wrote her music. I think they both had hopes that I would follow in their footsteps."

"And now? How do they feel about your journalism career?"

"Unfortunately, they're both gone now. Dad died of lung cancer and Mom followed him two years later. I believe she died of a broken heart."

"I'm so sorry." Ian covered her small hand with his.

After the meal they all declined dessert and Ian suggested they go back into the bar area and sit by the fire. Bruce excused himself. "Thank you for joining us. It's been a pleasure meeting you." He shook Chantel's hand. "I have some paperwork I want to finish."

Bruce left and Ian said, "Methinks wee Bruce's 'paperwork' has big blue eyes, a soft red mouth, and willing ways."

Chantel laughed. "I can see you are very fond of your brother."

He looked down at his wine. "Yes, sometimes he's the only one I feel I can trust." His gray eyes became dark and a worried look passed over his face. When he looked up though, he smiled. "You didn't answer when I asked if you could stay an extra few days. Please say yes. There are so many wonderful places to see and I make an excellent tour guide. You could stay with Bruce and me. We have an extra room in our cottage and it's not far from here."

"That's a very attractive sales pitch," adding to herself that Ian McCloud was a *very* attractive man. "I'll tell you what. I would like to stay and see some of the sights. I understand that whale watching is spectacular, and I've never seen heather in bloom. I wouldn't feel comfortable staying with you. So I'll stay for the rest of the week, at the hotel. The rates should go down now that the convention is over." She thought for a moment. "Maybe I can take pictures, turn it into a sightseeing story and call it a working vacation."

"It's settled then. I'll pick you up in the morning. Dress warmly. It can be pretty chilly near the water." Ian walked Chantel back to her hotel and saw her to her room. To her relief, he didn't offer or suggest that he come in, he did kiss her softly on the cheek. "Good night, Chantel Petit, little song. The name fits you."

The week flew by. Ian took Chantel on a whirlwind excursion of the Scottish Isles. She was treated to whale watching off the Isle of Mull, and Ian identified many of the seabirds. He took her to see heather in bloom. They had lunch overlooking a valley of heather so beautiful it took Chantel's breath away. Ian sang, "I will build my love a tower by yon clear crystal fountain, and on it I will pile all the flowers of the mountain. Will you go, lassie, go?"

"Ian, that's beautiful. Did you . . ."

" No, no. I canna take credit. It's from an old Scottish ballad called 'Wild Mountain Thyme.' There are many more verses, but we'll have to wait for Bruce to sing them. He knows them all."

By the time she had to leave, she and Ian knew they had something special between them. "I'll be in Las Vegas at the end of next month for the trade show. Maybe you can show me a bit of your world." This time when he kissed her it was softly on the lips. The kiss was filled with need.

"I'll be happy to show you, however, consider yourself warned. Las Vegas will be a stark contrast to your soft heather-covered hills and windswept seacoast. If we're lucky, you'll be getting there just before the really hot temperatures set in."

She returned to Vegas. Ian called nightly, running up an obscene phone bill. Six weeks later, Chantel asked, "How soon will you be coming to Vegas? I can't wait to see you."

"Well, lassie, just look out your window." She looked out to see a long white limo pulling into her driveway.

"Ian! I can't believe this!" She threw her arms around him. "I'm so happy to see you, but what's with the limo?"

He handed her a bouquet of white heather. "I didn't think it was proper to propose from the back of a Chevy. I would have rented a horse, but I couldn't find one." His smile went through her like a shot of warm brandy on an empty stomach, leaving her lightheaded and bringing a flush to her cheeks.

Chantel laughed. Her eyes sparkled. "Did I hear you say 'propose'?"

"Aye, lass." He opened a small velvet case and showed her a marquis diamond in an antique setting. "I'm asking you to be Mrs. Ian McCloud, if you'll have me."

Chantel answered by kissing him and holding out her hand. He placed the ring on her finger. "Now I can stop holding my breath! Little Song, I love you so much. You've made me the happiest man in Scotland or Las Vegas or wherever we are." They looked around at the sound of clapping. The neighbors had gathered.

Chantel waved at them and laughed. "I think we should take this show inside."

The ride from the Edinburgh airport brought Ian and the new Mrs. McCloud out of the city and into the countryside. "Ian, I'm a little nervous."

"Nervous? Don't tell me you're having second thoughts about us. A bit late, don't you think?" He gave her his special smile that melted her heart. At the same time he squeezed her hand.

"Not us, love, but this will come as something of a shock to your family. Won't it? Tell me about them. I just realized that except for Bruce, I really don't know much." And deep within, Chantel was nervous about the living arrangements. Ian always spoke of his 'cottage' and she knew Bruce lived there too.

"Where to start? I guess with my first wife. We were married when she was sixteen and I was eighteen. We were so young, and so in love. She died two years later. We didn't know she had a weak heart. She would get short of breath and have to sit down for a while, kid-like we didn't pay too much attention. Then one day when I came in from tending the sheep, she was in the hospital. My mother found her unconscious at the foot of the stairs. Poor little thing, she never came home. It was ten years before I got over it. About that time I met Lorelei." His expression changed to one of dismay. "That was a whirlwind affair. I was lonely and ready and she was determined. She came with two little girls, Fia and Odara, aged five and seven, and a mother, Moira. She left me a year and a half later. We heard she married a prince or a count or some such. She promised never to return to Scotland and she has never contacted her children." He looked grim for a moment. "We've made do, but I'm afraid Moira has made sure the girls blame me for their mother leaving. Nothing I say or do changes that."

As they crested the hill, a beautiful hotel at the end of a long curved road came into view. "Oh, Ian, look. How lovely. It could be on a picture postcard."

Ian turned into the long drive toward the building. "I'm starving. Let's stop here for lunch. Okay with you?"

"Yes, of course. I'm hungry too."

They walked into a large room with a great fireplace at one end. Much to Chantel's surprise it was furnished in glass and chrome. The floors were polished oak; the overall effect was cold and inhospitable. A shiver went through her, a chill put goose bumps on her arms. "Let's eat in here." Ian led her into a small, cozy room next to the kitchen. The aroma of fresh bread made her mouth water.

"Ian! You're back. Why didn't you call?" A short woman about Ian's age with iron-gray hair gave him a hug. "And you must be the new little missus." She turned to Chantel with a welcoming smile. "I'll call Kirk. He'll be wanting to say hel-lo."

A stout pug of a man a full head shorter than his wife came into the room. Ian turned to them. "This is Kirk and Cora, two very dear friends." He hugged them both. "I'll tell you all about the trip as soon as we've had lunch. We're starving."

Chantel and Ian sat with Kirk at the table while Cora fed them homemade chicken soup and fresh bread with strawberry jam. Ian filled Cora and Kirk in on the details of his trip to the trade show and ended with his wedding to Chantel. All the while Chantel was a little bewildered. Finally, she had to ask, "So do you two own this hotel? I don't see any other guests. Is it off season?"

"Aye, lass, you could say that." Kirk frowned at Ian. "I suppose he didn't mention that this hotel is his *cottage*, his family home."

"Cottage? Why this place is huge. It's more castle than cottage. Ian, why didn't you tell me? I feel like a fool."

Ian looked down but she could see the smile tugging at the corners of his mouth. "Well, it used to be twice as big until it was nearly destroyed by fire in 1898. My grandfather had it rebuilt on a smaller scale. Since then we've always referred to it as the cottage."

Cora spoke from the kitchen counter with her back to them. "Will you be wanting a family dinner tonight?"

Chantel thought she detected a note of displeasure in the woman's voice.

Ian, too, sounded less than thrilled. "Yes, let's have everyone here."

The table in the dining room was set with silver and china dating back to the time of the first McClouds. Chantel was nervous about meeting Ian's family. He chided her. "You're a McCloud now, too. And I'm very proud of you." He kissed her. "You're my wife. Nothing is more important to me than having you here. Go in there, head high and smiling. You are Lady McCloud."

Ian made the introductions. "These are my stepdaughters, Fia and Odara. Their husbands, Blair Shaw and Dario Luna, and this is the girls' grandmother, Moira Bane."

Chantel guessed that Fia looked like her mother from what Ian had told her; tall, thin, dark red hair and brown eyes. Odara resembled her grandmother Moira, younger and older versions of Cruella De Vil.

Dinner was a strained affair with Fia and Odara ignoring Chantel, and Moira asking rather pointed questions about how long she and Ian had known each other, how they met, who was her family. After dinner they went into the great room for drinks. Although the fire was blazing, once again Chantel felt a chill.

"Do they all live here?" Chantel asked Ian once the evening finally ended and they were in their own part of the mansion.

"Aye, they do. Except for Moira. She lives in the guest house."

"What about Bruce?"

"He lives here too, in this wing, but he's seldom here. He spends most of his time at the ranches. Kirk and Cora have a separate house on the grounds as well. I know this is a bit overwhelming. I was afraid if I told you, you'd never agree to come here and live. Can you forgive me? I'll try to make it up to you." With that he turned off the light and slid his hand over Chantel's silk-clad back.

"Maybe. We'll see." She turned to him and held him close. "This is going to take a lot of making up."

"Well. What do you think?" Fia stood with one hand on her hip, a glass of Burgundy in the other.

Her husband, Blair, got up from an overstuffed leather chair and asked, "Fresh drinks anyone?" Odara and Dario both held out brandy snifters.

Moira stared at her sherry. "Mine's fine."

"Well?" Fia demanded. "We have to get rid of her. You can see he's besotted. She'll have him changing the will before sunrise, wait and see."

"Calm down, Fia, we have no idea that he'll change anything. He hasn't changed it in almost fifteen years. What makes you think he'll do it now?"

"One careful look at the books and we'll be out on our collective asses."

Blair looked at his wife, but he could see she wasn't going to give up so easily. "What do you say, Dario? You work in the office. How often has Ian come in and looked at the books?"

"Never, to my knowledge. And I've been especially careful to cover each expense. The books look good. But Fia's right. We need to be very cautious."

"So does that mean I can't go to Paris for a new gown? The annual Christmas ball is next month," Odara pouted. Dario put his arm around his wife.

"Of course not, darling. It would look out of place if you showed up in last year's gown." He pulled a mock frown and did a theatrical shiver. "Heaven forbid." Odara punched him lightly on the shoulder.

"One thing we must all do," Blair put in. "Act like you accept her. Otherwise anything that happens throws suspicion on us."

"Like what?" said Fia.

"Like who knows. Accidents happen all the time."

Chantel stood looking at the room that gave her the shivers. Cora came up behind her. "You don't like this room, do you?"

She didn't want to hurt Cora's feelings, yet it was hard to hide the fact that all of them avoided the room and almost never sat in it. "It just doesn't seem to fit with the rest of the house," she began cautiously. "I picture it with warm rugs and overstuffed couches and chairs. I don't know, it just seems so cold. I actually get goose bumps when I come in here."

Cora pursed her lips. "That's Lady McCloud. She's letting you know she's not happy."

"Cora, what are you talking about?"

"It's true. The ghost of the first Lady McCloud is here. When she's happy, the house has a warm and friendly feeling, when she's not, a chill comes over the place. According to the tale, robbers trapped the young wife when her husband was away. The servants were slain and the wife left for dead. She lived long enough to tell her husband who the attackers were, but they escaped and were never caught. Since then her ghost walks these halls."

"What about this ghost?" Chantel asked her husband. "Why didn't you tell me?"

Ian put his arms around her. "Chantel, my love. Not everyone accepts living with a ghost." He smiled. "In fact, not everyone believes in her. If I hadn't grown up with her in this great old house, I might have had my doubts too."

"Have you ever seen her? What does she look like? Please tell me Ian, because I think she's been with me. I haven't seen her, it's more like . . . oh, I don't know—it's like I sense her."

"Aye, that's it. All my life, and Bruce will tell you the same, she's been a presence chilling us to the bone when she's displeased and making things warm and cozy when she's happy. She hates the great room. I know you've felt the chill when you go in there. Legend has it that's where she died. Go ahead and make your changes. I for one will be happy to see the end of all that cold, hard glass."

"Cora, please help me, this room is just too out of place in this old castle. I need to soften it, warm it up."

"Come with me. I want to show you something." Cora led Chantel down to the basement. There, stacked against the walls, was furniture from years gone by.

"Oh my, this is beautiful!" Chantel ran her fingers across a carved wooden side table. "Why is it all hidden away down here? This is exactly the look I envisioned for that room."

Cora explained, "Ian's second wife, Lorelei, wanted to change everything, 'modernize it,' she said. Ian let her have her way. Fortunately, she ran off before she could wreak more havoc."

"Well then, let's set about 'unmodernizing' it." It took Chantel less than a month to turn the room back into a warm and inviting sanctuary. She redid the walls in antique yellow, added couches in rich butternut leather and had the side chairs brought up from the basement and recovered in tapestry that blended the colors. The rugs were deep wool in soft browns and off-white.

One evening, while waiting for Ian to come home, Chantel sat curled up in a soft chair, sipping hot cocoa and reading a novel. The feeling that someone else was in the room came over her. "Who's there?" she asked. There was no answer and she didn't expect one. A warm feeling came over her. She felt strangely secure. *She's here and she's happy.*

"Ian dear, look at me." Chantel turned her husband to face her. "What's wrong? Something is on your mind. Can't we talk about it? Please don't shut me out. I'm concerned."

Ian held Chantel close. "It's probably nothing. Just a business problem." He ran his fingers through her hair and kissed her. "It's nothing to worry you."

"Ian, stop right now. I am worried, and the more you tell me not to worry, the more I worry, so spit it out!"

He sighed. "Come, sit with me. I need a drink." He poured a scotch for himself and a glass of Chardonnay for his wife. They sat in the small alcove off their bedroom. "It's the profits from the ranches. Something is off-kilter, I don't know what. The books are in order but we don't seem to be making the profit we should. I spoke to Dario. He takes care of the books, and he says it's due to higher costs of production. I'm sure he's right; it's just that I still get a strange feeling about it, like there's something I'm overlooking. I'm not an accountant, so I may be just imagining a problem. It's driving me crazy."

"What does Bruce say? Has he looked at the books?"

"Aye, but he's like me. We hired Dario because we're ranchers, not bookkeepers." Ian turned to Chantel. "Would you take a look? Maybe a fresh pair of eyes could spot the problem, if there is a problem."

"Honey," Chantel rubbed Ian's neck. "You know I'd do anything for you, only remember, I'm not an accountant either."

"Actually, maybe that's best. You wouldn't be prejudiced by any accounting rules. Just take a look and tell me what you think."

"Does Dario do your taxes or just the day-to-day bookkeeping? I'm thinking he might regard it as snooping if I went in and asked to see the books."

"You're right. Besides, if there is a problem I don't want him to know I know. I'll call Laird and James. They're the CPAs we use. They're in London. They do the actual taxes. Dario provides them with the information. Milton Laird is an old friend. He'll understand that I want to be discrete."

Odara came into the great room. Chantel was making an arrangement of holly and pinecones for the center of the table. "I guess Ian told you about the ball next month? It's the social event of the year. This year it will be held at Culloden House. It's a castle turned hotel."

"He said something about it. I'll have to get a dress. I'm not sure what's appropriate."

"I figured as much. Men are so dense about these things. Let me help you. I know you don't want to show up in something that's not suitable."

"Thank you. I'd really appreciate your input. Your dad just said it's formal."

"Yes, formal. But for a person in your position, wife of one of the richest merchants in Scotland, custom would call for dark gray. Something loose. Low, sensible shoes and a hat that matches. I'll call Edina. She's been our dressmaker for years. She'll fix you right up."

"It's kind of you to help. I certainly never would have chosen gray. It's not my best color."

"Next year you can be a bit more colorful, but the first time out you don't want to make the other wives envious." Chantel was surprised at Odara's offer of help. Maybe this was the beginning of a thaw between them. She hoped so.

"Odara, you didn't! She'll look like a hag. Ian will kill us," Fia scolded but couldn't hide the laughter bubbling up inside.

Odara fluttered her eyelashes. "Oh, Daddy dear, it was all for fun. I never thought she would take me seriously. I'm so, so sorry." She laughed at her own cruel joke.

Chantel drove to Edinburgh to see Edina. Her heart was heavy as she thought of the dress Odara had said would be appropriate. *Yuk! Gray! My worst color, she thought. And a hat! How grim can it get?* After the fitting she headed for lunch, more to lighten her spirits than out of hunger.

In London Ian picked up copies of the bookkeeping ledgers at the office of Laird and James. Then he met his wife for tea. "You have to be ready for a barrage of questions," Chantel said. "I'm sure there will be a lot I just don't understand."

"Ask away," Ian replied. "As soon as you've had time to look things over, we'll discuss any items in doubt. As long as we're here, wouldn't you like to do some shopping at Harrods? I need a few things, so we might as well kill two birds, as they say."

"I told you! See? Didn't I tell you?" Fia fairly screamed at her husband. Blair had mentioned seeing Chantel in downtown

Edinburgh. "She's spying! I knew it! We have to do something and do it now before this whole thing gets out of control."

The following week Chantel was driving back from Edinburgh. She had picked up her new dress. *Ugly thing*, Chantel shuddered at the thought, *if that's what Ian's wife is expected to wear, then that's what I will wear. The last thing I want is to embarrass him in front of his friends and colleagues.* She was lost in thought as she came over the hill and realized the road was slippery from morning rain. She applied the brakes. Nothing happened. The car picked up speed, going much too fast to make the curve. The brakes were useless, the power steering would not respond. Chantel screamed as the car went out of control, careening off the road and into a tree.

Kirk Brodie looked up at the sickening sound of crumpling metal followed by an ominous silence. He spurred his horse into full gallop. Cresting the hill, he saw the front of Chantel's car nearly wrapped around a huge tree. She slumped over the wheel, honey blond hair spilling over her face. "Chantel! Chantel!" he called. "Speak to me, girl!" Chantel groaned. "Thank God, you're alive." Kirk quickly grabbed his cell phone. "Cora, call Doc Campbell and get Ian. There's been an accident."

The room would not stand still. The people's images blurred like they were underwater. Slowly, slowly, things began to settle down. She could make out Ian's worried face peering down at her. "What happened? What's going on?"

"You're going to be okay. The doctor says you have a concussion, but bed- rest for a few days will make things right again." She could see her husband had tears in his eyes. "Kirk found you. Luckily, he was riding nearby."

"How could this happen?" Ian asked, as Bruce and Kirk examined the car's brakes and power steering. It appeared that the lines under the car had worn away. Ian looked like thunder. "Could this really have been an accident?"

Kirk spoke up. "I check all the cars on a regular basis, as

you know. I would have replaced any hoses or power lines with this kind of wear. This looks deliberate to me."

"Put an extra watch on the garages. If someone is out to hurt us, let's find out who. Meanwhile, don't let on that we suspect anything." Kirk and Bruce nodded in agreement. Just as they started to close the overhead garage door a chill blast of air frosted the windows. They looked at one another. "She's here," Kirk said, "and she's not happy."

Chantel came out of the shower with one towel wrapped around her head, another around her body. "Darling, I didn't know you were back. I was just about to get ready for the party."

"We don't have to hurry. There's plenty of time. Are you sure you're up to this?"

"Absolutely. Besides, I'm going stir-crazy. A party is just what I need." She took the towel from her head and shook out her long, damp hair.

"Well, in that case, I think we should get the party started right away." With that he pulled the towel away from her body and she stepped into his arms.

Ribbons, each displaying a different tartan, decorated the ball-room.

Chandeliers ablaze with light, highlighted everyone laughing, having a good time as Ian and Chantel arrived. Fia, Odara and their husbands were waiting in a small cluster, ready to laugh at the gray-clad frump Odara had invented. What they saw was a sparkling Chantel descending the long staircase, dressed in a body-hugging gold sheath under a gossamer float studded with rhinestones. Gold high-heeled sandals completed the ensemble. Champagne-colored diamond earrings, presented by her loving husband just hours before, sparkled in her ears. Both of them still bore the flush of recent lovemaking. "Ian said he didn't like gray," she whispered as she passed them, giving Odara a wink.

Bruce came with his girlfriend. "Chantel, this is Mary. She

works at the Vermillion Room where we had dinner that first night after you found Ian's briefcase."

"Mary, it's nice to meet you. I'm happy to have a friendly face in the crowd," she said, glancing over her shoulder at her husband's stepchildren and ex-mother-in-law.

Moira stood with a disapproving look.

Bruce danced with Mary. Ian took Chantel for a fast spin about the floor. "Time to exchange," Bruce told them, waltzing Chantel away.

"This is all so lovely," Mary told Ian. "I see your son-in-law Blair at the hotel quite often and occasionally Dario. This is the first time I've met the rest of the McClouds."

Chantel held up a yellow legal pad. "Ian, I'd like to go over some of these figures with you. Just to make sure I know what I'm looking at."

"Tonight after dinner, love. I have to speak to Kirk for a bit, then we'll spend the rest of the evening going through everything. Are you sure you're okay? You look a little peaked."

"I'm fine, really I am."

He kissed her and held her. "I know I worry too much. It's just that since the accident . . ."

"Hush now. It's okay. We'll talk when you get back."

Ian returned looking angry. When Chantel tried to question him, he held his finger to his lips whispering, "Later."

Behind the closed doors of their own suite, Ian said, "Kirk talked to the police today. The brakes and power steering were definitely tampered with."

"Oh, Ian! Who would do such a thing and why?"

"I intend to find out. Bruce told me that Mary has seen Blair having drinks at the Vermillion with the same man on two or more occasions. She's sure Blair passed him some money. She said it wouldn't have made her think twice, except the man is the mechanic who repairs her father's car. She thought the Vermillion was a pretty expensive place for a mechanic to be having lunch."

"I don't know what to say about all this. I hope it's just a coincidence." She brought out her legal pads. "Let's go over these figures. At least that's something positive we can do."

"Aye."

"The figures in column A are the expenses I can identify—feed, medical care for the animals, etcetera. Now here," she pointed to a row of figures, "are the ones I question. I put the figures into American money so I could understand. Here it shows $10,000 a month going to Fia and another $10,000 to Odara."

"Yes that's right. When their mother left me, that's the amount we negotiated in exchange for her promise never to return. I also had to promise to take care of Moira. At the time it seemed a bargain to be rid of her."

"That explains that. I did wonder. Okay, what about these charges?"

She used her pencil to point to the next row of figures. "Here are monthly credit card charges ranging from $1,500 to $2,500. This comes to an average of $2,000 a month, about $24,000 a year. Now these were all labeled farm expenses, but when I looked further I found they were really for purchases of clothes and jewelry. And here, $1,200 a month for a second office in downtown Edinburgh, plus four car payments of . . ." She went on and on. "Ian, both Blair and Dario draw very substantial salaries working for you. It seems to me . . ." She looked up at Ian's stricken face.

"It seems to me that we have a nest of vipers living with us." He gathered his wife in his arms. "You know, my love, I'm in the mood for . . ." Chantel snuggled up to Ian. He dumped her unceremoniously on the bed, giving her a wicked smile. "That too, but the word I have in mind is revenge!"

She laughed. "Let's plot, oh husband mine! I love a challenge." Far into the night they schemed and revised, agreeing that just kicking them all out wasn't nearly enough.

"First, the credit cards have to go," she said. "I'll call and have them canceled. The girls can hardly complain. When they try to use them, the bells will go off telling them their credit is no longer good. The manager of the store will invite them to come to the office and explain. Imagine how humiliating that will be. With luck, they'll be shopping with friends."

Ian laughed. "Yes, and next month a notice will be posted announcing failure to pay rent on the 'office in town'."

"What shall we do about the cars? I mean a Porsche, two Fiats, a Mercedes, not to mention Moira's vintage Bentley. The monthly garage bill alone should pay off the national debt."

"Kirk can help us there. He and I talked. He'll do a little 'creative' mechanical work. Not enough to cause accidents, but enough to send the cars to the shop. One by one, the little vipers will be driving loaner cars. They'll figure out that something's going on, but again, what can they do?" He rubbed his hands together, clearly enjoying this game. "Once they're all in loaners, the more tattered the better, I'll cancel all the leases."

"A disclaimer of responsibility should be in the newspaper by no later than the end of the month." Chantel was busy making a list of the things they intended to do.

"Just what is a 'disclaimer of responsibility'?"

"Well, in America, when you no longer want to be held responsible for another's debts, usually in divorce cases, you post the notice so their creditors can't say they didn't know. I'm assuming you have something like that here."

"Call James Laird. He'll set us straight on that one."

"Now the biggie. What about the $10,000 a month to the girls. And what about the jobs you gave their husbands?"

"I told you!" Fia screeched. "I told you! Now that little bitch has stopped our credit. One by one the cars go to the shop. Next we'll be out on our asses, just like I said."

"What can we do?" whined Odara.

"You!" her sister screamed. "You and your bright idea about the dress."

"Well, it wasn't me who fixed her car," she retorted, staring at Blair. "Just too bad she didn't die."

~ 122~

"Shut up! Shut up both of you," Moira ordered her dueling granddaughters. "Now is the time for planning. We can play who's to blame later."

"What about poison? We can plan a dinner party and spike the wine. Later we'll just say we had no idea the wine was bad." Odara looked at the others. "What do you think?"

"I think you have your head up your ass, as usual!" Fia could hardly get the words out, she was so angry. "And what will we tell the police is the reason not one of us took even a sip of wine? Not even Blair, who's practically the town drunk!"

"Hey, watch your mouth!" Blair turned to Dario. "Take control of your wife before I do," he shouted.

Dario looked thoughtful. "Everyone calm down and listen. Ian, Bruce and Chantel live in the oldest part of the house. The wiring's got to be ancient. Fire wouldn't be out of the question."

"Yes, but what about Kirk and Cora?" Moira asked. "They have to be out of the way."

Blair spoke up. "Don't they go on holiday every year to see her parents or something? That would be the ideal time for 'an accident.' But who knows how to rig the wiring? We certainly aren't prepared for anything as sophisticated as all that."

"Don't be too sure." They all turned to look as Moira spoke.

"Moira, what are you saying. Do you know someone who knows about wiring? It has to be someone we can trust." Fia looked puzzled.

"You're all too young to remember, but during World War II, I worked wiring airplanes. They hired women because of the great shortage of men. And, much to everyone's surprise, we were darn good at it. Because of our size, we could get into places that were hard for the lads. I haven't forgotten the basics and with this old place, it shouldn't be difficult. We just need to pick the right time. I'll need one of you to do the actual work, but I can tell you which wires to fray and how and where to cause a spark."

"The time will be when Kirk and Cora leave and Bruce is home for a few days. We, of course, will be in town at various parties, and you, Moira, should plan to spend some time with your friend on the coast. I understand she hasn't been all that well." Blair looked at the others. "We've all got to be committed to this or it will fail."

Dario downed the last of his drink. "It's this or wait until they throw us out. Personally, I rather enjoy our life here. I don't have a wish to go job shopping. Besides, I have my eye on a new Bentley."

"Well, wee Bruce and Mary, let's hear it. The two of you have looked like cats with cream on their whiskers all through the meal." Ian smiled at his younger brother and waited for a response.

"Mary and I, well you see, Mary—"

"Oh, for heaven's sake, man, tell them!" Mary seemed about to burst with their news.

"We're getting married." Bruce let out a long sigh as if this were the hardest thing he had ever done.

"I'm so happy for you." Chantel reached across the table and kissed Bruce, then Mary.

"Congratulations! This is wonderful. We haven't had a wedding in years.

This will be a grand thing for the McClouds. We'll invite every relative and friend in the Scottish Isles. We'll . . ." Ian looked up at Bruce's stricken face. "What?"

"Actually we thought a small, simple ceremony with just you, Chantel and Mary's sister . . . Maybe next week?"

"Next week! Why so soon? It would be great to have a big lavish wedding and a grand party. What's the rush?"

Chantel came to their rescue. "How about we have the wedding very soon and a big party to celebrate after?" She laid her hand on her husband's arm. "Ian, darling, you are about to become an uncle."

"Well, I can be a bit dense," he said, laughing, "but you'd

have thought I'd have picked up on that one." He held his glass up. "To the bride and groom and the newest little McCloud." The chandelier tinkled, the room grew warmer. "She's here and she's happy," Ian said.

What in the dickens am I doing crawling around the attic of this ancient building freezing my back side off? Blair asked himself. His breath came out in puffs of white. Am I nuts or what? I must be daft to let the others talk me into this. Moira's as mean as a snake and none too stable if you ask me. Be just like the old biddy to get me up here and call the police on me. Blair kept up a running conversation with himself, trying to allay his fears, as he inched his way along rafters that had been in place when his own grandfather was a young man. *Here! This is what she was talking about. Spool and knob wiring tied into more modern wiring. Modern. If you call fifty years ago modern. Still, it's what Moira described as the perfect place to fray the wires. She said if I do it right, the fire will travel down the walls. Now, Dario just has to close the vents to the rest of the building so the smoke only goes to their wing.*

The phone startled Ian and Chantel out of a deep sleep. "Who is it? It's almost two in the morning," Chantel asked, as Ian cradled the phone to his ear.

"It's Bruce, they just called him from the South Ranch. The ewes are lambing. It's a bit early and they're short-handed. I have to go and help. Go back to sleep."

She bounded out of bed. "Not on your life. I'm coming to help too. What about the girls and Dario and Blair? Couldn't they help?"

"Not likely," he said with distaste. "Besides, they're all in town at parties." Ian shoved his feet into boots and grabbed a sweater. "Better dress for a long night. Lambing can be bitter cold work."

When they drove in, Ian and Bruce went immediately to the barn. Chantel set about making coffee and sandwiches. She took a tray to the barn and announced, "Hot coffee and food, everyone." The men looked at her gratefully. "Is there anything else I can do?"

"Aye, lass, come hold this lantern. The light's not too good in this part of the barn." Bruce handed her an old-fashioned kerosene lantern and directed her to hold it up high. The men worked through the night helping the new little lambs into the world. Chantel held lights and passed out coffee and sandwiches. At daybreak, Bruce yelled, "We've got trouble here!" Chantel could see the ewe struggling to expel her baby. The plaintive cries tore at her heart. "We need some small hands to go in and turn the lamb. It's caught sideways."

Chantel acted rather than thought. "I can do it." Startled, Bruce and Ian both looked at her for a few seconds, before Bruce explained what had to be done.

Later, over brandy, three exhausted people sat in the kitchen. Too tired to move, Ian looked at his wife covered with pieces of hay and drops of blood, her hair wild about her face. He thought she had never looked so beautiful. Bruce lightened the moment by saying, "So, okay, you know how to help with the lambing, but can you run a tractor?"

"Oh, Lord, do I have to do everything around here?" Their laughter was born of weariness and relief that the night was over. The lambs were safe.

Smoke curled down the walls, out the vents and into Ian and Chantel's bedroom. The room filled with noxious fumes meant to kill.

"Cora, tell me again why we're coming home early." Kirk seldom had cause to question his wife's notions. This time he was curious.

"I don't know why. I just know we have to get back." She patted her husband on the back. "Trust me. And hurry, please." They drove down the long driveway toward their house. "No, no, the big house. We have to get there now!"

Kirk turned toward the family home. Cora fairly jumped from the car before it came to a full stop. Kirk ran ahead of his wife. They burst into the entry. "Smoke! It's coming from Ian's wing. Call the fire department. I'll check to see. . ." Not finishing, he ran up the stairs, calling, "Ian! Chantel! Bruce!" Smoke furled so thick in the hall he couldn't see, the fumes made him cough. "Ian! Chantel!" A coughing fit seized him. Despite all the smoke, the house was freezing. Kirk was blue by the time Cora grabbed his arm and led him back down the stairs. "She's here and she's furious," he told his wife. They could hear the wail of the fire engine.

Ian and Chantel had followed the fire trucks. Frantic, Cora and Kirk were sitting in their car as firemen swarmed the house. "Thank God," Cora whispered when she saw the couple.

Kirk looked up and smiled. "I can't remember ever being so happy to see you." He hugged Ian and Chantel to him.

"What's happened here?" Ian asked. "And why are you two home so early?"

"It was Cora," Kirk explained, "she got one of her 'feelings' and insisted we come back 'ear."

"The wiring in this place is older than I am," the fire inspector told them. "It should have been upgraded twenty years ago. You have a lot of smoke damage, nothing irreparable, but here's something that worries me." He showed Ian and Kirk the vents. "All closed. Except for the ones to your wing. Where's the rest of your family tonight?"

The investigation was swift. Faced with criminal charges, Fia, Odara, their husbands and Moira chose permanent exile over prison. "Losing all their privileges will be worse for them." Ian looked sad for a moment. "I tried my best. It was just never going to be enough."

With Mary and Cora's help, Chantel brought the mansion back to its former splendor. The wiring was upgraded. The wing that had housed Ian's stepchildren was refurbished for Bruce, Mary and their new family.

After a marvelous dinner that Cora insisted on preparing,

Ian, Chantel, Bruce, Mary, Cora and Kirk sat back completely satisfied. Ian held his champagne flute high.

"To us."

"To us," they all echoed.

"It will be good to hear the laughter of children once again in Castle McCloud," Ian told his brother and sister-in-law.

"One little voice won't seem like much in this huge place," said Bruce.

"I'm counting on you to fill it with more than one," laughed Ian.

Bruce did his best to look serious. "We'll try. But this could take some time."

Chantel spoke up. "Possibly, could you use some help?" They all turned to her.

Ian looked at his wife, at first with surprise, and then with wonder in his eyes. "Little Song, are you sure?"

"Just like a man to ask such a question!"

The chandelier tinkled and the room grew warm. They all looked up. "She's here and she's happy."

"Okay, fellas, that's it for the night. Thanks for coming by. Enjoyed talking to you." Josh shook hands with George and Steve.

"Thanks, Mr., er, Josh. Can't tell you how much we appreciate hearing about all of these old crimes from you. Would it be okay if we came back on Saturday? That is, if you're not busy."

"Sure, Saturday's fine." He laughed, "Just happens I've had a cancellation in my social calendar."

"Saturday it is. We'll be here about five with hot pizza."

The two drove away filled with amazement at the wealth of information delivered to them. Steve commented, "We'll have to give him an acknowledgement in our book. He's saved us years of research. Not to mention the personal touch. Imagine knowing all those people."

Cold weather had George and Steve rushing up the stairs and into the house with pizza, whisky and fresh cigars. The old man waved them into the living room. "Put everything on the coffee table. I'll get some glasses and napkins. That pizza smells great." The three of them made short work of the food. George helped clear the table while Steve poured drinks for everyone. Neither Steve nor George smoked, so Josh had the cigars to himself. "Let's see, where to start?"

"How about one of your own cases, some of your favorites?" Steve asked as he put his digital recorder on the table.

"There's so many that I remember." The old detective made himself comfortable in his easy chair. "Ummm. You might find this one interesting. I did. It happened at the main library in Las Vegas. At least that's where it started. The newspaper called it . . ."

Chapter 9

MURDER IN THE STACKS

"The Experienced Book store motto: Why take chances with a new book? These books have experience!" store manager Amelia Pruitt, had told her with a small, tight laugh.

Kathy viewed the organized shelves. Each genre placed by author, each book waiting for the next avid reader to realize its worth. *I don't know why I'm so on edge tonight. I usually enjoy my time here. Maybe it's the full moon. Who knows? Probably it's because the rest of the library is so quiet.*

To get to the computer room, people passed the store in the basement of the library. Often they stopped to peruse the shelves or asked if a certain book by their favorite author had come in. But not tonight. *This is my first time to man the store by myself and it had to be on a holiday weekend.* A chill went down her spine. Stop it! she willed herself. To pass the time she turned to a box by her desk and began marking books that had been donated. She stacked each marked book on the floor. She would restock the shelves, as soon as there was space.

Kathy's friend Laura talked her into volunteering one day a week. Laura, with beautiful dark eyes and a ready laugh, said this would be fun. She forgot to mention it was also a lot of work. Laura also showed Kathy where Ms. Pruitt hid the key to the rare books room. She remembered her friend's grin as she told Kathy that Ms. Pruitt thought she was the only one who could get in. "I found the key by accident," she said. "Pruitt is so worried that someone else will touch her precious books. I thought they must be the rarest of the rare first editions, so I snuck in and took a peek. They're firsts, but nothing special. Pruitt says she saves them for antique book collectors, but the truth is I've never seen a book leave that room."

Kathy pictured Ms. Pruitt's tall, rail-thin figure and horsy face. *I guess we all have quirks.*

"Well, well who do we have here?" Kathy jumped back to the present with a jolt. She hoped never to hear that voice again, but the face didn't register.

"Don't tell me you don't recognize me." The voice oozed false friendliness. "It's me, the love of your life, come to take you away from all this." He waved his arm, taking in the small room. His smile reminded Kathy of a rabid dog about to pounce.

"Dentin? Is that you, Dentin? I don't get it. What are you doing here? Why do you look so different?"

"Always with the questions. I thought you'd be happy to see me. Prison just wasn't my cup of tea, love. Even after they put me in witness protection, all I could think about was getting home to my Kathy."

"You sick bastard! Stay away from me! How'd you find me?"

"For a smart man like me," he pointed to his chest, "finding a dumb bitch like you," he made a gun out of his fingers and pointed at Kathy, "was a piece of cake. And now get your coat. We're leaving."

"Never! I wouldn't go two steps with you!"

"Actually, you are." He grabbed her hair and twisted it until she screamed. The books on the shelves absorbed the sound. "Come quietly now, or this will get much worse."

Kathy did not plan to go willingly. When they were married, Dentin liked leaving scars. She twisted and grabbed the heavy library stapler from the desk with her left hand, bringing it down hard on Dentin's head. He howled and eased his grip enough for her to pull away. Kathy, blind with rage, pounded the stapler, letting it take on a life of its own. Chest heaving, Kathy stood for a moment to catch her breath. *He's dead! What now?* Laura's words flashed into her mind. "The stacks of boxes have grown until you can hardly get in there. She just hoards them. It's her own little quirk."

Before she could think about what she was doing, and before panic froze her in place, she found the key to the rare books room and dragged Dentin in. By moving a stack of boxes, she made a hollow place and covered the body with more cartons of books. The boxes should have been hard for her to move, but pumping adrenalin gave her the strength she needed.

Back in the bookstore, she was surprised to find that most of the blood had landed on the books she was marking. The small amount of splatter wiped up easily with Windex and paper towels. She shoved these and the stapler into her large handbag. She turned to lock the store and leave, but then had a thought. *When they do find the body, how will they think the killer, Killer! Oh GOD That's me! Shut up Kathy, shut up and think. How did the killer get into the rare books room? Who knows? Who cares? This has nothing to do with me. Just get out of here!*

Kathy drove home trying to control her breathing and turn her mind off. It wasn't working. *Dentin the Demented. Here! I thought he was gone for good. The only thing that had stood between him and lethal injection was his willingness to trade his inside information on a huge drug ring for a lesser sentence. If he got into witness protection, then the information must have been really worthwhile. Give Dentin a few bucks to get started, he could steal the rest and disappear like smoke on a windy day. A good plastic surgeon to make him look like a new man . . . . Now you have A-1 creepazoid back on the streets. Why would he risk coming here for me? I guess I'll never know now.*

Tuesday, Laura called. "Kathy! You won't believe this!"

Kathy stopped breathing. She tried to sound curious, but not over the top. "Tell me. What has you all in a lather?"

"Pruitt came back from her vacation today. When she went to check on her precious books she started screaming like a banshee. I wasn't there, but the other librarian called the police and then me."

"Police?" Kathy squeaked. "What for?"

"A body!" Laura exclaimed. "Pruitt found a body in the rare books room. I guess she went ballistic. Kept crying 'Ridley, Ridley' over and over. The cops had to have her sedated."

"Ridley? Who's Ridley? Oh, wait. Isn't that the guy you told me about? The one Pruitt was supposedly in love with years ago. He liked her, she liked him, and then one day he didn't show up for work and no one's seen him since."

"That's the guy. After he disappeared, Amelia Pruitt had a complete meltdown. It was months before she came back to the bookstore and, according to gossip, she was never the same."

"Why on earth was she calling Ridley?" Kathy said, more to herself than to Laura.

"That's what the police want to know."

"Do you think this man could be Ridley?"

"I have no idea. I never saw him. He was long gone and only a juicy rumor by the time I started volunteering."

"Is the store open?"

"No. The officer said it would be closed for a few days. The library will let us know when it reopens. The cop did say they would want to speak to all of us. Just a formality. I doubt if anyone knows the dead guy."

The TV news flash called it, "The Murder in the Stacks," but the police had little to go on. Ms. Pruitt withdrew into a world of her own. The only word she spoke was to call out "Ridley," from time to time.

"You seem nervous, Miss Benton," said the man at her door.

"Of course I'm nervous," Kathy snapped. "It isn't every day someone is killed where I work."

"I'm Detective Josh Cummings." He held out a business

card. "I understand, but try and relax. This won't take long."

Kathy led the way into her living room, pointing to a seat. Manners insisted that she offer him coffee, a soft drink, something. "No, nothing, but thank you."

"Do you know who the man is?"

"Yes. His name is Frank Thomas. We found his driver's license and credit cards in his wallet. Does the name mean anything to you?"

"No. Not a thing."

"I understand that you were not at work Tuesday. Is that correct?"

"Yes, that's right. I'm a volunteer. I only come in on Fridays."

"We believe Mr. Thomas was killed over the weekend. Because of the temperature of the rare books room, it's hard to pinpoint the exact time. Do you have a key to that room?"

"No. Ms. Pruitt carries the key with her. No one else is allowed to go in there."

After the detective left, Kathy poured herself a glass of wine, amazed at how steady her hands were. *I never had to lie, not once. He never asked anything to which I couldn't give a straight answer.* She sighed with relief.

Doctors continued to try to get through to Amelia Pruitt, but she refused to emerge from her safe cocoon. Periodically, she rocked back and forth crying, "Ridley, Ridley, you came back."

Josh Cummings had a problem with riddles. In his usual methodical fashion he wrote questions on his yellow legal pad:

1. Why was Thomas in the library?
2. Who's Ridley?
3. Did Pruitt kill him?
4. Does Pruitt think Thomas is Ridley?
5. IS Thomas—Ridley?
6. Why is that room kept under lock and key?

7. Where's the murder weapon?

8. Does Pruitt have the answers?

The answers to two and five came to him through questioning the library staff. He checked off the numbers on his pad and thought to himself, Ridley's the old love who disappeared, rare books were Pruitt's passion after Ridley took off, and she became obsessed with keeping them to herself. Amateur psych time—she transferred love of Ridley to love of rare books. *Okay, I guess I can buy that. Sorta,* he thought.

A check at the house listed on Thomas's driver's license showed a man who lived alone. His address book was sparse: a number for the local drugstore, one for the dry cleaners, his dentist, a tire-repair shop and a few other businesses. No personal numbers. No friends. No family. Josh took a picture to Dr. Ben Drisan. The dentist confirmed that it was Thomas. "Had he been a patient long?"

"No, not long, only a few months. He just came in for a routine cleaning and X-rays. Nothing out of the ordinary."

"Thank you, Doctor. You've been a great help." *Not really,* he thought. *He just confirmed Thomas's identity, but we already knew that.*

Josh went home. His wife took his coat and told him to sit. "Honey, you look beat. Let me get you a beer." He gave his dog Biscuit a scratch behind the ears. His wife brought the beer, frosty in the bottle, the way he liked it. "Dinner will be ready shortly." Linda, used to seeing him lost in thought, finally gave up on conversation attempts and drifted off.

The next morning he went through cold cases and found the file on the disappearance of Lamar Ridley, July 29, 1975 more than thirty years ago. Ridley was here one day and gone the next. Nothing had ever been found on him. Josh found an address and phone number for Ridley's sister and called. The number wasn't working, but through the magic of a police computer, he was able to track her new name and phone number. "Ms. Hastings? I'm Detective Josh Cummings. I'd like to talk to you about your brother. May I come over?"

"Ridley? You want to talk about Ridley after all these years? Have you found him?"

"If I may, I'd like to meet with you. It won't take long." He showed up at the address a half hour later. "Ms. Hastings? I'm Detective Cummings."

"Yes, please come in. What's this about Ridley?"

"Ma'am, would you mind looking at this picture and telling me if that's your brother?" He fished a photo out of his pocket and handed it to her. She looked at it for a long time before saying, "No. That's not Ridley. Although, it does bear a striking resemblance to him when he was young. Odd, we always called him Ridley even when he was a boy. I really don't know why. But, remember, my brother would be in his late sixties by now. This man looks no more than thirty-five or forty."

"Thirty-eight, actually. I knew it was a long shot—a very long shot. But I had to find out. Thanks for your time."

Josh visited and revisited the crime scene. He came away frustrated and no more the wiser. On Sunday after dinner he told his wife, "Honey, I'm taking Biscuit for a walk. I have to get my head around this case. It's driving me crazy. Come on, Biscuit, old boy, let's you and me get some air." The park surrounded the library. Biscuit let out a bark of pleasure at this unexpected outing.

After half an hour of throwing a stick, Josh said, "Come on, I can't stand it any longer." Holding his badge up and pointing to Biscuit, he told the security officer, "Police dog," then proceeded to the basement crime scene.

"Sit, stay," he ordered Biscuit. Once again he made the circuit of the bookstore, finally going into the rare books room. Nothing had changed. Come on! "Why am I so convinced I'm missing something?" he said to the totally uninterested dog. He moved things around, looking under books, hoping for some insight. Biscuit, bored with sitting, wandered in to smell and nose around the musty boxes. "What are you doing?" asked Josh as Biscuit was pawed the wall and made snuffing sounds. "Is there a mouse in there? Can you smell a mouse, old boy?" Biscuit started digging at the wall in earnest, stirring up a dust cloud of drywall plaster. "Hey, stop that! What's gotten into you?" Josh came around the stack of boxes to drag Biscuit away. The dog had already made a sizeable hole. Josh reached for his dog's collar when he saw a glint of metal. "What . . .?" A gold cufflink. The cufflink attached to a shirt. The shirt wrapped around a skeleton's arm.

In the morgue, the head medical examiner stood at one side of the sheet-covered body. "Ladies and gentlemen, may I introduce you to," he drew the sheet back, "Mr. Lamar Ridley. And before you ask, yes, I'm sure."

"Give me a thought, something, anything I can tell the press," Captain Burk pleaded. "The feeding frenzy is just heating up. I need something, Josh. Help me here."

"Okay, here's my theory. And remember, until Pruitt gets out of the nut hut that's all it is-theory."

"Lay it on me. I'm a desperate man."

"Think about this. Thirty years ago Pruitt and Ridley were a hot item. They get into it over something—who knows what. She kills him and plasters him up in the rare books room behind a new piece of drywall. After that she won't allow anyone else to go in there. Then, three weeks ago, she comes back from vacation and sees this guy Frank Thomas and thinks it's Ridley come back to haunt her. She kills him, drags him back into the room, and covers him with boxes until she can dispose of the body. But! She's gone over the edge, so she puts it out of her mind and goes berserk when she 'finds' him on Tuesday after her vacation. Now she's retreated into her own world, safe from harm and repercussions from the crime."

"Do you think that's what really happened?"

"No. But it's the best I can do. I have no idea what happened. Thomas doesn't seem to have existed before he came to our fair city. No bank records, old addresses, no nothin'. We may never know the real story, but until *and if* Amelia Pruitt comes back from fog town, that's the best I can come up with."

Kathy read the story in the paper. "Laura, I can't work there any more. It's too creepy for me."

"Are you kidding? The murder has given the bookstore celebrity status. Our sales are out of sight!"

"Good grief, Laura, that's ghoulish!" But she laughed, mostly from relief. Now all she had to do was pray Pruitt stayed safe and sound in her own cloudy world, behind padded walls.

"And!" Laura said in a rush. "Guess what?"

Kathy smiled at her friend's exuberance. "What? I can't wait to hear your latest, and I'm sure greatest, mind-blower."

"Think of this. A new combo reading room, mystery theater and restaurant. We'll have readings of new mysteries, the occasional short play, offer light refreshments and have a fully stocked mystery library. What do you think?" Before Kathy could respond, Laura rushed on, "I've got the perfect location picked out. My brother will help set it up, my cousin will cater the food. You can be in charge of scheduling readings and overseeing the pricing of incoming books. Well, what do you think?" Laura repeated.

Kathy was, as always, amused by her friend's enthusiasm, but this time she did think Laura's idea had merit. "It sounds good. But remember, I do have to work. I need an income."

"I know, I know, but don't worry. As soon as we turn a profit you'll be the first to get a salary. Come on, Kath, this could be fun!"

"Okay, I'm in. By the way, what's the name of this new place?"

"You're gonna love it! We'll have a grand opening! We'll have music and champagne and lots of shrimp and little meatballs! We'll have a big banner printed! We'll get TV coverage!" Laura was fairly bouncing up and down. "We'll call it Murder In The Stacks."

Two years later.

Josh's partner looked at the open file on the desk. "Why the big interest in this old case?"

"Alex, this case has always bugged me. Before you came to the department, about two years ago, we found a guy named Frank Thomas with his head bashed in, in the basement bookstore of the library. At the same time, we found Lamar Ridley, a former lover of Amelia Pruitt, the head of the bookstore, plastered up in the wall of the rare books room of the same bookstore. Mr. Ridley had been a resident of the wall for over thirty years. Frank Thomas seemingly came out of nowhere. No past, no present, and certainly no future. Another strange twist to the case was that Lamar and Thomas bore a striking resemblance to each other. *And* the only one with any knowledge of the crimes was locked up in a nut hut." To paraphrase someone, he couldn't remember who, he said, "Oh man!" and dug the heels of his hands into his temples to stop the merry-go-round of thoughts.

To keep from thinking about the crime-crimes-he started on the pile of paperwork before him. "What's this?" Josh held up a fax from the FBI.

"Came in yesterday, while you were out." said Alex. "The Fibbies want our help finding Dentin Kramer. Seems he's a bad guy with some really good info they needed so they stashed him in witness protection; only, he disappeared. The name doesn't ring a bell; I thought you might know him."

"Not offhand. Looks like he's from Denver originally, little out of my territory." Josh put the flyer in the "to keep" file on his desk. "Anything else exciting happen?"

"Oh, yeah. That hospital where they're keeping that old gal, what's her name? You know Prim or Prunes or . . ."

"Pruitt?"

"Yeah, yeah, that's the one. Some doc called, said you'd want to know she's showing some signs of coming back to the real world."

"You bet I want to know! Did he leave a call back number?"

"That yellow sticky. On top of your 'urgent to do list."

The detective quickly dialed the number and asked for Dr. Simmons. "Doctor, this is Detective Josh Cummings. You called about Amelia Pruitt."

"Yes, I did. She's beginning to regain her sense of reality. In a few days, she should be able answer some questions."

"Thanks, Doctor, I appreciate the call. Will next Tuesday be okay?"

"It should. If there are any problems, I'll let you know."

"Hey, how about we work on some of these other cases?" said Alex. "It's not like that old case is the only one needing our fine minds and astute police work."

"Right, right, I'm on it." *Until Tuesday*, Josh thought.

The drive to Quiet Haven, the sanitarium where Amelia Pruitt was recuperating, gave the detective time to think. *There are just too many loose ends. I need to find out what went on between Pruitt and her boyfriend Ridley nearly forty years ago. And how does this guy Frank Thomas fit into the scene. Or does he?*

Dr. Simmons ushered him into a private room. He rang for the nurse. "I'll introduce you to Ms. Pruitt, then leave so you can have some time alone. Please bear in mind that she's very fragile. Try not to upset her. Let her lead the conversation as much as possible."

"I understand. I'll take it slow and easy."

Amelia Pruitt arrived in a wheelchair, pushed by a nurse. The doctor made the introduction before leaving.

"Ms. Pruitt, I don't really know how to begin. I need . . ."

Josh was at a loss as to how he should approach this frail old woman, none of the questions he had rehearsed seemed to fit. Before he could go on, Amelia Pruitt saved him the trouble. "Detective, I'm sure this is difficult for you, as it is for me, but I've lived with this secret for many years. I think it's time to set the record straight. I've kept a diary." With that she pulled her sweater aside and took out a book with a tattered red binding. "Here. Take this. It will answer your questions. After you read it, if you need to know more, you may come back. Now I must rest. I'm not feeling well."

Josh took the book and thanked her. That night he sat up until midnight reading. The dates on the entries started over forty years ago. The first were obviously a continuation of the year before.

Jan 4

"Accidentally" ran into R at the restaurant. I know he eats there almost every night. He asked me to join him.

Jan. 6

Invited R to a concert. Told him I had an extra ticket.

Feb. 2

Told him I'd been given tickets to see The Rat Pack—he agreed to go.

Feb. 10

Talked R into escorting me to a play being put on by the theater group. After the play I invited him to my apartment. I guess we both had too much to drink. My greatest fear is the age difference. Nine years. Ridley says he doesn't care. I dare not tell anyone yet. They're sure to think he's after my money. They just don't know him. June! I want a June wedding.

Mar. 4

I have to talk to R. I think I might be pregnant. This will move my plans ahead by several months but I know he'll be happy.

Mar. 6

Ridley didn't take the news as well as I'd hoped. He just needs time to adjust. I know he loves me.

Mar. 10

He's avoiding me. I'm getting worried. Part of it is that I'm so sick. I have to talk to him. I can't go through this alone.

Mar. 20

He called, said we need to talk. We'll meet tonight. I know everything will be OK.

Mar. 21

Abortion! *Never! R wants me to end the pregnancy. I can't! I won't! He just has to marry me.*

April 1—April Fool's Day—

How fitting! Ridley came to the bookstore after hours. I was just finishing up. He said he could not marry me. It would ruin his plans. His plans! What about my plans! He said he never wanted children. Never wanted to marry. I don't know what happened. I just went crazy. I've been so sick for weeks and now this!!! It was an accident. The sharpened screwdriver was just in my hand. Then it was in his back. I don't know how it got there. The rare book room is being remodeled. I only remember how hard it was to stuff him into the space in the wall. Pushing the dry wall into place and taping it up took all my strength. I didn't mean it! I'm so sorry! God knows I'm so sorry!

Nov. 12

The past months have been a nightmare. All the lies. All the subterfuge. Finding a home out-of-state for unwed mothers. I feel like a dinosaur- all those teenagers and ME. I could be their mother.

Dec.15

Coming back home. Everyone thinks I ran off because Ridley dumped me. Better to let them think that than the truth. At least the baby is healthy- the agency said they have several qualified parents waiting to adopt-Thank God.

Josh put the book aside and rubbed his eyes. *How sad,* he thought, *different times. Today no one would raise an eyebrow about an unwanted pregnancy. Now, forty years later, this old lady is still suffering the fallout from her affair.*

Monday morning, Josh gave Alex the low down on Pruitt's diary. "Forty years ago, an unwanted pregnancy and a moment of madness ultimately unhinged her."

"Well, at least one crime is solved. Do you think there'll be any repercussions for Pruitt?"

"Unlikely. It's doubtful that she'll ever get out of the sanitarium. She's pretty sick. And if she does, she'll be so old, a trial would most likely kill her."

"You know Alex, I've been thinking. Her son would have been about the age of Frank Thomas and Ridley's sister said he looked a lot like Ridley. What if . . .?"

"Yeah. Sounds possible. Can we get the name of that home where she went? The one where she had the baby? That might lead us somewhere.

"We've been meaning to get all these on the computer. Getting the time and the money to pay someone just hasn't happened," said the gray-haired man who led them down the stairs. The smell of mold and dampness rose from the basement floor. "There you are." He waved his arm around and pointed to the walls lined with file boxes. "Help yourselves. I think the years you're looking for are on the back wall. Some of our records were damaged when we had a flood, so I can't guarantee anything."

"Alex, you start from that wall and I'll start from this

~ 144~

one. Hopefully, we'll find something before we meet in the middle."

Four hours later, covered with dust, Alex said, "Hey. I think I have something."

"Right!" Josh exclaimed. "This is it. Baby boy born to Amelia Pruitt adopted by Frank and Emma Kramer. 1976. Here's their address."

The Kramers had moved several times. Frank had passed away. They tracked Emma down in Huntsville, living with her sister. After introductions were made, Detective Cummings asked, "Do you know the whereabouts of your son?"

"Dentin? No. I haven't heard from Dentin in years."

"Lucky about that! Good riddance to bad rubbage I say!" Emma's sister blurted out. "That boy was trouble from the start. I warned her not to adopt that boy. No telling what kinda trash his mother was. I warned them. Said he'd be trouble, and he was!"

"Now, now Sadie. That's all in the past." She put her hand on her sister's arm. "It's true, though. Dentin just couldn't stay out of trouble. Little lies when he was a small boy, then bigger and bigger lies. Then, setting fire to the school. He spent time in a reform school for that. From then on, he was always in some scheme, always into fights. I don't know what was wrong with him. Frank beat him every time he got into trouble, but he just wouldn't stop. He had a cruel streak. Hurting small animals—sick stuff. Once he actually hit me in the mouth when I wouldn't give him money. After that, we told him to leave. He joined the Army but got kicked out for assaulting an officer. That's the last we heard of him. He was about twenty at the time."

"Do you have a picture of Dentin?" Josh asked.

"Only baby pictures and they're packed away."

"Dentin Kramer. Not our boy, unless . . . Let me see." He rummaged through the stack of papers and found the FBI bulletin. "Here it is. Alex, look at this. The age and build are the same. The general appearance is the same. Straighten that nose, lighten the hair, add some contacts and you could have Frank Thomas."

"You know, you're right. Now what was he doing in that bookstore? And why is he dead? Do you think Amelia killed him thinking he was Ridley?"

"Possible. Or maybe someone who knew his real identify followed him there and killed him." Josh rubbed his temples. "Too many unanswered questions. I'm getting a headache. "

"Maybe it's time to speak to Pruitt again."

"Good thinking!"

Josh turned to the phone and dialed the sanitarium. "What? Oh, I'm sorry to hear that." He turned to Alex, "Pruitt just died. She was our last link. Now what?"

Kathy was busy shelving new books at the Murder in the Stacks Bookstore. "Kath, did you see this?" Laura burst into the room waving a newspaper. "Pruitt is dead."

"Dead?" Kathy repeated stupidly. "Dead? How?"

"She died in that sanitarium where she's been since the murder."

"Here, let me see." Kathy took the paper with shaking hands. The paper did a complete rehash of the crime, including the unsolved murder of Frank Thomas and the finding of Lamar Ridley, Pruitt's old lover stuffed in the wall. "Looks like Pruitt came out of her meltdown before she died and talked to that detective, Josh Cummings." She broke out in a cold sweat.

"Hey, are you okay? You look like you're about to faint." Laura led her friend to a chair. "Sit here while I get you some water."

"Yeah, I feel a little shaky." Kathy said. "Maybe a touch of the flu. I think I'll go home and lie down."

"Good, go, go, I'll handle things here."

At home, with a glass of wine for fortification she began to think. *What am I going to do? What did Pruitt tell them? Actually, what can I tell them? Kathy's breathing began to slow down. I'm over reacting. The police still don't know that Frank Thomas is Dentin Kramer. Blast it! Just when I thought all this was buried forever this new worry comes along to bite me. If I'm not careful I'll end up like Pruitt.* She drained her glass and reached for the bottle.

Bill Bundy, Dentin Kramer's old cellmate, rubbed his whiskery chin as he lit another cigarette. "If I can track Dentin down and find out he's remade himself, then so can the cops . . . eventually. As soon as they realize Dentin and this Frank Thomas are the same guy, they'll start putting two and two together. They're slow and dumb, but dogged."

Junior, Bill's son, said "What difference does it make. The guy's dead."

"Yeah. That's the point. As soon as they connect the dots they'll start looking for me. Kramer and I shared a cell before he made a deal with the Feds. He had info they wanted, so they put him into witness protection. They'll think I killed him for that information. I couldn't care less about all that crap. All I want is the money he stashed. The Feds don't even know about that."

"How much?" Junior asked.

"Over six mil . . . more than enough to kill for."

"Holy Sh— Where'd he get that kinda money?"

"Robbed the First National Bank in Tulsa. Wore a dog mask. Never caught. In fact, no one ever even came close. No one was hurt so it wasn't top priority for long. He got swept up when he worked for the mob in East Harlem. That's where he got the goods on several crime bosses that he traded for the witness program. All he had to do was testify and he would have been home free. Stupid jerk. When we were together, all he ever talked about was getting out and hooking up with his ex, Kathy. She must know where he hid the cash. I think it's time I paid her a visit."

Alex leaned over his desk and handed Josh a yellow sticky with a phone number. "That's Agent Morris, FBI. He says he has some more info on Dentin Kramer to share."

"Agent Morris? Josh Cummings here. You called about Dentin Kramer?"

"Yes, Detective, I did. We just found evidence that ties Dentin to an old bank robbery. One of the men with him was in prison on an unrelated crime. He got sick and said he wanted to clear his conscience before he died. More like he wanted revenge. Seems Dentin made off with over six million and no one else got their share."

"Pretty interesting, but how does that concern us?"

"Dentin had a wife, Kathy something, wait, here it is Benton. Kathy Benton. She may or may not know about the money; they were divorced about ten years ago. But according to my sources, he talked about her all the time. Always saying how he was going to find her and get her back. He conveniently forgot that he nearly beat her to death. But the point is, if I know this, you can bet others do too. She may be in danger. My information is that she's in your area."

"Benton, Benton, Benton." Josh snapped his fingers. "She worked at the used book store where Dentin Kramer/Frank Thomas was killed." *Well as the White Rabbit would say, things get curiouser and curiouser. Or was it Alice who said that?*

It didn't take long to find Kathy Benton at her new place of employment. "Ms. Benton, remember me? Detective Josh Cummings, we spoke after the murder at the bookstore."

"Yes, of course, how may I help you?" she answered. Josh couldn't help but note how pale she looked. "I read about Ms. Pruitt's death, too bad. I was sorry about it."

"We have come to believe that Frank Thomas and Dentin Kramer are one and the same. Ms. Benton we know that you were married to Kramer."

"It's true. Dentin and I *were* married. We've been divorced for about ten years. I haven't heard anything about him since the divorce. I never wanted to know anything about him. Why do you think he's this Frank Thomas? You never mentioned that before."

"We didn't know before, this is new information. Did you know Kramer was out of jail?"

"As I said, I didn't keep track of him. I didn't even know he was in jail. It certainly doesn't surprise me." She put her hand up to her head. "Detective, you'll have to excuse me, I've had the flu and I'm still not too strong."

"Ms. Benton, we're assigning a man to watch over you."

Before he could go on Kathy blurted, "Watch me? What on earth for?"

"Please don't be alarmed. Kramer's old cellmate may be looking for you. He may believe you know where a large amount of money is hidden. Did your ex-husband ever mention any cash that he had stashed away?"

Kathy gave the detective an angry look, "I just told you, I don't know anything about Dentin. I didn't know or care that he was in jail. What are you suggesting?"

"Nothing. It's just a question I have to ask. If you see anyone who looks suspicious or if you feel like you're being watched or followed, please call me." He handed her his business card.

"Of course, I'll feel watched and followed! You just told me you're assigning a man to watch and follow! How am I supposed to know your man from this old cellmate?"

"Please calm down. I'll have my man identify himself. He'll show you his badge."

"Well, that went well." Josh ran a hand over his face. *Next time Alex can do the honors. I seem to raise her hackles every time I open my mouth.*

"May I help you find something? Are you interested in anything special?" Kathy asked.

"No, thanks. I'm just looking." He noted her name on her tag.

"Let me know if you need any help. And here are some brochures about our next mystery production that might interest you."

Back in the car, Junior said, "It's her." Her nametag says

Kathy Benton. But she fits the description. Guess she didn't want to be known as Kramer's ex. Don't blame her."

"We'll be paying Miss Kathy a visit soon. But first let's check out where she lives and keep track of her work hours. I don't want any nasty surprises like a mad-dog boyfriend or a real mad dog for that matter."

Over the next few days Bundy and his son watched Kathy. They soon realized that she was being followed by one or more plainclothes cops everywhere she went. Now the problem was how to get to her. While Kathy and her shadow were at work, Bill and Junior let themselves into her apartment and "fixed" the plumbing so that her sinks would overflow when she tried to use them. They also made sure the water in the shower came out in tiny drips. Next, they left a business flyer with the apartment manager that promised service within the hour or no extra charge. When Kathy's call came in, the manager immediately called the number on the flyer.

"Plumbing service, ma'am." The Bundys stood on the porch dressed in overalls with Speedy Plumbing embroidered on the front and back. Their panel truck, loaded with plumbing supplies and painted with the same logo, stood at the curb.

Officer Forester stepped up, flashed his badge, "May I see your identification, please?"

"Of course, Officer. We're just here to fix the plumbing." Bill and Junior both took out I.D. cards with the plumbing company logo.

Kathy opened the door. "Officer Forester, my apartment is flooding! Please let these men in before everything here is ruined!" She stepped aside while the two "plumbers" came in. They immediately set to work turning valves, clanking and banging under the sink and in the shower.

"We were able to stop the flow of water but we'll have to return with a new sink. This one is old. It cracked when I tried to fix it." He saw the look on Kathy's face. "Don't you worry, ma'am. The manager said all costs would be covered." Bill Bundy gave Kathy his most reassuring smile.

"Oh no! What will I do for water! When will you return?"

"Not to worry, little lady. We'll be back within the hour." The two men left, giving a nod to Officer Forester as they got into their van. "We'll buy a sink at the Home Depot down the street. We'll get the biggest model they have."

The officer stood on the front porch of Kathy's unit. "This is Forester checking in. Everything's quiet here. The lady had a plumbing problem, the plumbers are on it."

"Did you check them out?" The hair on Josh Cumming neck rose. "Never mind. Give me the name of the plumbing company."

"Here it is. I even wrote down the phone number."

Bill and Junior returned with a large box. Once inside, they quickly removed the contents. Bill called, "Ms. Benton please look at this sink and tell me if it's okay with you." When Kathy entered the kitchen, Junior hit her, knocking her out. "Quick, help me get her into the box," said Bundy. "Close the flaps and tape it shut. We'll say we're just taking the old sink away if anyone asks."

Josh and Alex screeched to the curb outside the apartment. Josh was out of the car and running before it came to a complete stop. Guns drawn, they entered the apartment, surprising Bundy as he finished taping the box. "What's the problem, Officer?" Bill Bundy said in his most ingratiating voice.

"Hold it right there. Where's Ms. Benton?"

"I have no idea. We were just called to fix a leak in the plumbing. Maybe she's at the store." A groan from the box caused Junior to step from the kitchen and shoot. His shot went wild but Alex returned fire and caught him in the leg causing him to scream as he fell to the floor. Bundy pulled his gun from his overalls. Josh killed him before he could get off a shot.

At the hospital a bandaged Junior remained silent. "What were you and your father doing in Kathy Benton's apartment?" Josh asked.

Junior, no stranger to police strategies said, "I want a lawyer."

"Sure, sure you can have a lawyer. We'll send over a first year Public Defender to help you out. Let's see . . . attempted kidnapping. Assault with a deadly weapon. Attack on police officers, accessory to the death of your father . . ." Josh turned to Alex, "What else can you think of? Oh, I know, violation of parole. Looks like at least twenty . . . thirty years. Before the P.D. gets here, you might want to help yourself."

Junior looked expectantly at the two detectives. "In what way? What're you offering?"

"Look Junior, we know your old man was the brains behind all this, we'd like the details. What can you tell us about the death of Dentin Kramer/Frank Thomas? You help us and we'll put in a good word for you."

Junior really wasn't quite as stupid as he looked. So he wove a tale for the detectives using information from his father, ending with, "My old man followed Dentin to that bookstore and killed him when he wouldn't tell where the money was hidden. He figured the wife would know and she'd be easier to convince. He waited for about a year until the dust had settled, then we went for her. How'd you get on to us anyway?"

"Simple. A few phone calls to the non-existent plumbing repair shop." Josh shook his head at the stupidity of the whole thing.

"Wow! Kathy, look at this." Laura waved the morning paper. "Here's the whole story about those goons who attacked you. It says here that the father, Bill Bundy, killed Dentin Kramer because he thought Kramer had about six million dollars stashed away. When Kramer wouldn't tell they came after you figuring you knew. Junior Bundy traded the story about his dad in exchange for a lighter sentence. You know, Kathy, this would make a good play for our next Murder In The Stacks production."

Kathy touched her sore head. "Laura, please! I never want to hear or talk about this again in my life." She sent up a silent prayer. *Please God, let this be the end of it.*

The old detective rubbed the back of his neck. "This cold weather makes my bones ache." He reached for his glass, held it up and peered at the amber liquid. "This helps." He sipped then took a long puff of his cigar. "You boys don't know what you're missing. A good cigar is a fine thing." He watched the smoke float toward the ceiling. "Well, that should have been the end of the story but there was more . . ."

Chapter 10

Murder in the Stacks continued

"Mrs. Kramer? These are for you. Please sign here." The man handed her a standard UPS form to sign for proof of delivery. Beside him on the porch were several boxes. Kathy looked confused. "I haven't been Mrs. Kramer for years. What is all this stuff?"

Kathy looked confused. "I haven't been Mrs. Kramer for years. What is all this stuff?"

"No idea, ma'am. Please sign here," he repeated.

Reluctantly, she signed the form. The return address indicated the boxes came from the police department. *A call to the department of the police listed on the form should clear this up*, she thought.

"Hello, this is Kathy Benson. I just received several boxes of my former husband's belongings. Can someone explain why?"

It took the usual maddening trek through the bureaucratic jungle until finally Mrs. Truax in the community liaison department explained, "You are named as Mr. Kramer's beneficiary."

It shocked Kathy to think that Dentin even had a will. "What about his parents. I'm sure they would appreciate these things far more than I do."

"He specifically named you as beneficiary when he went to prison. Feel free to donate what ever you don't want to charity. They're yours."

Good idea. I'll call the Salvation Army and have them pick the stuff up. I won't even bother to open it. I'll call Laura and tell her about this. See what she thinks. "Hi, it's me. You'll never believe what just happened." Kathy explained.

"Wow. What a way to start the day. What's in the boxes?" Laura asked.

"No idea. I was just going to send them over to charity. Anything to get rid of them. I sure don't want anything of Dentin's."

"Whoa. Hold on," said Laura. "First, if its papers or books, it's likely the charity won't even take them. Second, it might be interesting to see what's in there."

"I swear, Laura, you do have a ghoulish streak." Kathy had to admit to herself that she was just a tiny bit curious. "Come on over for lunch and we'll have a 'search for treasure' party. Just the two of us. You bring the wine."

"Aren't pirates supposed to drink rum?"

"Yeah, but a good pinot grigio beats rum every time. You can bring a parrot, if it will make you feel any better. Just don't let him poop on my carpet."

"Smart mouth."

The girls spent the afternoon going through boxes of clothes, books and papers. They found nothing of interest until Kathy took out a suit jacket she recognized. "Laura, look at this. I can't believe it. Dentin was wearing this when I first met him. Good grief, that would have been almost twenty years ago. Why on earth would he still have this old thing?" She ran her hand into a pocket and felt something under the cloth. The small inside pocket revealed a key. "Isn't this a safety deposit key?" She held it out for Laura to look at.

Laura turned it over. "I think so, but it doesn't tell us what bank. The numbers must have some meaning. Like the first number might be the bank and the second number could be the city and so on. You know like your social security card."

"Who do we know in banking? We need an interpreter. Someone who speaks fluent bankeze."

"I know. My cousin Carl. He works for Fidelity Federal. He can help."

"Laura, is it your family's ambition to have one member in every single industry? You always have an uncle or cousin or, or someone who has a finger in every pie."

"Don't fuss. Just let me call Carl." Laura made a few calls and reached her cousin. After she explained the numbers on the key to him, he said, "Sorry. Those aren't bank numbers. They sound like some kind of private system."

"Well, what else is there? Lockers at the airport. Lockers at a club. There must be thousands of lockers in the world." Kathy looked discouraged.

"Don't give up so easy. Let's think this through. Where would Dentin most likely hang out? What were his hobbies? Did he have a special place he liked to spend time?"

"You're right, Laura. Dentin was a health nut. Health food, daily workouts, the whole nine yards."

"Okay, that's good. Where did he live? I mean, where did he live just before he went to prison?"

"Hmmm, let me think. I really don't know. I do know how to find out." She called Josh at the precinct. After reintroducing herself, Kathy asked, "Detective, where did they arrest Dentin? I mean what city? I want to find out how close he was to me all those years before the arrest. I'm just curious."

I guess this is a female thing, the detective thought. "He was captured in Boise Idaho. Pretty far from you. Why?"

"I'm not sure, his clothes and belongings were just delivered and some of the things brought back a flood of memories. I guess I always believed that I'd somehow sense him, if he got too close. Thanks. I appreciate your help."

"What was *that* all about?" Laura asked. Why did you give him that stupid excuse?"

~157~

"I'm not sure. At first I was going to tell him about the key, at the last moment something held me back. Anyway, it looks like Boise is the best bet for clues to the key."

With the help of the computer, Kathy made a list of what appeared to be top-notch health clubs in Boise. She reasoned that Dentin would go first class. Next, she sent emails to all of them with the information that Dentin Kramer had passed away and she, as his next of kin, was searching for a gym locker that matched a key she held.

"You know Kathy, he may not have used his real name. Then what?"

"You're right. Then what?"

Nothing came of the emails. "So what's the next step? Laura, where else could he have a locker?"

"What about private clubs? You know, more the spa variety."

"Good thinking." Kathy made a search for private spas and retreats. She sent the same email. Two days, later her computer sang out, "You've got mail." The email read:

Dear Mrs. Kramer. We're sorry for you loss. Mr. Kramer keeps a locker here. He's been paying three years in advance so he gets our discount, which is why there have been no late notices sent. If you'll bring the proper identification, we'll be happy to release the contents of the locker to you.

"Laura, I have to go to Boise. Please say you'll come with me. I can't bear to do this alone. It may be nothing but I just have a funny feeling that Dentin didn't keep a locker just for old gym clothes."

"Okay, let's go Friday. We could be there by noon and back here by Saturday with good plane connections."

"Ever the optimist." Kathy made the reservations. As luck would have it they were able to get tickets to Boise for Friday at seven a.m. and return Saturday at two p.m.

The large locker held boxes stacked all the way to the top. They were wedged into the space so tight, it took both Laura and Kathy to pull one out. "Let's not open it here," Kathy whispered. "Too public."

"Open it? Never mind opening. How in heck are we going to get them out of here? It's not like we can carry them."

"Leave them here. Let's take one box back to the hotel and see what's in it. We can come back for the rest later."

They made their way to their hotel and threw the box on one of the double beds. "This is making me nervous." Laura ran her hands down the sides of her jeans. "My palms are all sweaty. Go ahead, Kathy, let's take a look."

"Oh, oh, oh!" Kathy exclaimed, as bundles of one hundred dollar bills tumbled out of the box. "I came close to being killed over this money! I can't believe it. Dentin had it all the time."

"The question is, now what?" Laura looked at her friend. "This is a problem, Kath. Do you want to call and tell the detective you found the six mil? Do you want to keep it? How would you explain it?"

"I don't know what to do. Let me think. The first question is, how do we get it out of the locker? How do you suppose Dentin got it in there?"

"You know, Kathy, I have a cousin who's an accountant." Laura looked thoughtful. "If there's a way to keep it and not break any laws, he'll know about it."

Kathy stared at her friend, "Laura, tell me again what part of the mafia your family is from."

Laura laughed, "Not exactly mafia. It's just that growing up in Las Vegas you learn about a lot of stuff. You know, my family worked in the casinos from the beginning, so hiding a little money isn't such a big deal to them." She made a call to her cousin. A few calls later her brothers, Pete and Charlie agreed to meet them at the airport before they flew home Saturday. "The boys will take care of getting the money. They'll bring it to you."

"But how will they get the boxes out of the . . ."

Laura held up her hand, "Don't ask. . . Leave it to them. Trust me, they know what to do. Next, we go see my cousin."

Back home in Vegas, Kathy and Laura left the accounting office of cousin Nick. "Okay, I have the instructions written down. This is doable. It will take time. Laura, let's get one thing straight right now. We're in this together fifty-fifty. No argument."

"Girlfriend, that's way beyond generous. I mean three million dollars! You must be crazy to even think like that! Just give me a little something to keep Murder in the Stacks afloat until it can stand on its own. That would be more than fair."

"No. We're a team. I'll need you to help put your cousin's plan together. Besides, with two of us, it will go much faster."

The next week, each of them went to different banks and opened non-interest bearing accounts with an initial deposit of two thousand dollars. At first they chose six banks in Las Vegas and six in nearby Henderson. The way they calculated things, it would take about four years to deposit all the cash. That was way too slow, so they refigured and chose twelve more banks. Over the next two years, depositing money became their part-time job. They traveled to several cities in Nevada, California and Utah, depositing $8500 into each account every week. They went at different times of the day and week to avoid seeing the same tellers as much as possible. They also deposited in the outside teller window to keep conversation to a minimum.

According to Cousin Nick, you could put that much cash into an account and still fly beneath the banking radar. It seems the bank keeps internal records, they don't share with the IRS.

"After the money is safe," Kathy said. "We can quit thinking about keeping afloat, and make plans for expansion. Think, Laura, what we can do with this kind of money. We can offer scholarships for young people. We can sponsor worthy efforts like the Henderson Writers' Group. There's no end of the good we can do. Frankly, it would make me feel better about, well," she swallowed and bit her lip, "a lot of things."

"Gosh, you're right." Laura looked pensive for a moment then said, "Or, we could call the authorities and give the money back. I'm sure they would do the right thing and make sure it gets back to the rightful owners." Both women thought for a moment and then, said in unison, "*Noo way!*"

Old Josh leaned back, took a sip and puffed for a few minutes, "You know, I always had the idea that there was more to the story than any of us ever found out, but sometimes it pays not to keep digging. This next case is a story right out of the pages of a horror novel. If I hadn't been involved, I might have questioned it. I called it. . ."

Chapter 11
Evil—A Family Affair

The cool, dark interior of the bar made Ellie relax. She sighed as plopped her oversized bag, filled with papers to be graded, on the floor by the barstool. She stretched her neck and rotated her shoulders before looking up to see Hank, the bartender, smiling at her. "Double anything. Right?"

This was their ongoing joke; Hank knew Ellie's usual consisted of one, at most two glasses of white wine on Friday night. She would say, "This is my reward for surviving another exhausting week."

"Tonight though, make it a triple, Hank," Ellie replied. "My head's killing me."

"Coming up, pretty lady. Just relax. The week's over. Why don't you stay awhile, dance a little, have some fun?" He knew her routine. She came in after school on Fridays, had a glass of wine and left, always alone. He also knew she had been a widow for some time. *Such a nice person deserves to have someone special in her life.* "Here you go." He placed the wine on a napkin in front of her. At the far end of the bar, a man sat nursing his beer. Hank moved away from Ellie to ask the man if he needed anything.

"One more beer, then it's time to go."

"Stick around. The food's not bad and the band will be here

in about an hour."

"Thanks, maybe next time." He placed several bills from his wallet on the bar, drank his beer and left.

Ellie could see the man's reflection in the mirror behind Hank. He appeared good-looking in a rugged, out-of-doors kind of way. Dark brown, sun-streaked hair worn a little too long, hung just below his ears. His slim body fit nicely in jeans and work shirt. *Maybe a construction worker or landscaper*, she thought. *Now, now Ellie, don't go complicating your life. The last thing you need is a man.* She smiled at her own thought process. *We're doing fine, just Billy, Emily and me. We've mourned Tom, now we're okay again.*

Over the next few Fridays, Ellie came in for her weekly "reward." Twice she noticed the same man sitting alone. On the Friday before a much-awaited four-day holiday, she decided to stay for dinner. Her kids were away for the weekend. Billy went camping with friends and Emily was at the farm with her grandparents. It wasn't often she had this much time to herself. She planned to savor every minute.

"Well, look who's here," Nan handed her a menu. "It's nice to see you. We have a really good roast pork tonight and the salmon is especially nice. I'll give you a few minutes to decide."

"Thanks, Nan. Everything sounds great. Just give me a few." Ellie chose the salmon with a garden salad. She also splurged and ordered strawberry pie for dessert.

After dinner, she was gathering her things to leave when the band started their first song. She lingered a few minutes longer to enjoy the music.

"Care to dance?" Ellie looked up at the man she had noticed a few times in the bar. "I'm not very good, but if you can put up with my mistakes, I'd really appreciate it. By the way, my name's Ken. . . Ken Holland."

"Hi, I'm Ellie Bovac. And yes, I'd like to dance," she was surprised to hear herself respond. Ken led her to the dance floor, and despite his earlier comments, he proved to be an excellent dancer. "Do you work around here? I've seen you in here a few times."

"I'm an engineer. My home base is in Colorado Springs. I'm here to do some work on the dam. I'll be here for the next few months, no way to tell how long. There's a problem with the controls to the main turbine so I'll be staying until it's ironed out. How about you? I see you in here with a big bag of papers, so my guess is you're a teacher." He held her close for the next slow waltz. Then, at the end of the set, he led her back to her table. "Thank you. May I buy you a drink?"

"A glass of white wine would be nice. Please sit down." Again, Ellie wondered at her response. Ken joined her. They spent the rest of the evening getting to know one another. Ellie couldn't remember when she'd enjoyed herself more.

They met at the bar each Friday for the next few weeks. Slowly, after Ellie became comfortable, she invited him home for dinner. Billy took to Ken immediately, pleased to have a man around. Emily was polite, but cool.

"What's wrong, honey?" Ellie asked her daughter one evening as they washed up after dinner. "You look like you just ate a lemon."

"It's Ken, Mom. I don't like the way he looks at me."

"What do you mean? Has he said anything . . .um um . . .you know, anything bad?"

"No. He says I'm pretty." She shrugged her shoulders. "It's the way he says it. He's always touching my hair or rubbing my arm. He says I look just like you, then, he'll say, 'My mother had red hair.' He gives me the creeps."

"Maybe he's trying to be nice and just doesn't know how. I don't think he's been around teenagers very much. Don't worry about it. Do you have homework?" Ellie wanted to change the subject. She wanted her kids to like Ken. In spite of her resolve not to get involved, he was becoming an important part of her life.

Ken's suggestion that the four of them go camping over Easter vacation met with mixed reviews. They would be staying in his friend's cabin. Billy was keen to go. Ken promised to teach him to hunt. Emily wasn't interested. She said she'd rather stay with friends or her grandparents. Ellie was anxious for her family to like Ken and viewed this as an opportunity for them to get to know him better.

Catching Emily alone, Ken cooed, "Come on, Em, Let's all go. It'll be fun." He ran his hand down her arm. When he got to her hand he picked it up, turned it over and kissed the palm, giving it a wet lick. Emily jumped as if she'd been burned. "Leave me alone! And leave my mother alone!" she yelled as she ran from the room.

No, that's not what I had in mind, not at all. He laughed to himself.

Safe in her room Emily called her girlfriend. "Hi, Beth Ann, it's me. No, nothing's wrong, not really. It's just Mom's boyfriend. I hate the way he looks at me and when he touches me, my skin starts to crawl. He wants us to go away with him for the Easter break. No way am I going anywhere with him! I can't understand why my mom likes him; he gives me the creeps."

On the last day before vacation a speaker from the State Bureau of Water spoke to the graduating seniors. He explained some of the fascinating things he had learned as an engineer. "Recently, I've been assigned to the dam, making sure there are no hairline cracks that could cause trouble down the line." Students interested in careers as engineers asked questions about the job possibilities.

At the break, Ellie asked if he knew Ken Holland. "No, can't say as I've heard of him, but you know, a lot of people work for the Bureau."

A silent alarm sounded in Ellie's head. "I heard there was some trouble with one of the turbines. I heard they were trying to fix it."

"No, there's no problem. Believe me, if there's a problem, I'm the first guy they call. The last thing the Bureau wants is to have to shut down a turbine. We support a high-level maintenance program just to ensure a problem like that won't sneak up and bite us." The bell sounded. Teachers and students moved toward their classes.

Ellie had some questions for Ken. There was probably a simple explanation. She drove to the supermarket to pick up supplies for their stay at the cabin.

Emily threw her books on the bed and went to the kitchen for a Coke. When she returned to her room, Ken was there. "Well, well, Miss High and Mighty. You've been swishing your little butt in my face for a month now. Let's see if you can put out for ol' Ken. I know you're makin' it with that pimply-faced boyfriend of yours." His speech slurred; he smelled of whisky. "Come on, give Uncle Ken a little kiss." He grabbed Emily by the front of her sweater and pulled her to him. The sweater ripped, leaving Emily standing in her bra and skirt. She screamed and ran for the door. Ken was drunk but still fast enough to grab her by the arm.

"Leave me alone! Don't touch me!" She swung the Coke bottle hitting Ken on the side of the head. The blow didn't knock him out, it just made him mad. Emily fought like a tiger, still, she was no match for Ken. He tied her to the bed and gagged her with duct tape. He cut off the rest of her clothes with his hunting knife. Smiling, he undid his belt buckle and let his Levi's drop to the floor.

"Now, little spitfire, we'll see what you're made of."

Emily tried to scream through the tape. She shook her head from side to side. He could make out a muffled, "Don't, don't."

"Don't? Don't? Don't what? Don't do this?" He sat on top of her and slowly drew the blade down one cheek. Blood beaded along the line left by the knife. "Maybe, don't do this." Ken made another shallow cut on her other cheek. "Now for the fun part." He placed the point of the knife at the base of her neck and pushed until blood ran down both sides and on to the bed. Emily twisted her head; it made her blood run faster.

"How 'bout this, sweetheart?" He angled the blade between her breasts and pushed slowly, entering her at the same time. His climax and final knife thrust came at the same moment. "Sorry it's over sweetie, but your mom'll be home soon. I have to save a little somethin' for her." Ken rolled off Em's body, pulled on his clothes and moved to the back of the door just as he heard the sound of a car coming up the drive.

"Hi, I'm home. Can someone help me with the groceries?" Ellie called from the kitchen.

"Hey, sweetheart, we're in here," Ken called from the bedroom.

"What's going on?" Ellie asked as she came down the hall. "My God! My God!" She stood looking at the blood-soaked figure on Emily's bed. "Em!" she screamed, "No God, no, not Em!"

Ken hit her from behind. Ellie never knew what happened. "Sorry babe, wish I had time to make things more fun."

Billy ran home, eager to pack for the trip to the cabin. "I'm home," he called. "Where is everybody?" He raced down the hall to his room. As he passed his sister's room, he saw her lying on the bed, covered in blood. "Em! Em! Mom! Where are you? Somebody help!" He ran out of the house. A police cruiser making a routine patrol of the neighborhood saw Billy and stopped. "Help! Help! My sister's hurt bad. There's blood everywhere!"

Officer Perez followed the boy into the house. "You wait here," he cautioned Billy. "I'll check and be right back." Perez drew his gun and started down the hall, calling out, "Hello, anyone home? Police." Everything in the kitchen and living room seemed to be in order. He glanced into Emily's bedroom, and immediately called for backup. He quickly checked Emily for signs of life; finding none, he went back for Billy. "Come with me, son." Billy followed him, crying.

Within minutes, police cars converged on the peaceful neighborhood, sirens howling. Billy was placed in the care of a female officer who called his grandparents. The officers began a room by room search. Wallace, Perez's partner, yelled, "Found another body." Ellie's bound and gagged body was stuffed into the closet in her bedroom. According to the M.E, she had been dead less than two hours.

With a healthy lead, Ken headed for his mother's house in Colorado Springs. He ranted to himself as he drove. "Redheads, they always think they're better than everyone else. Just like dear old Mom. Too good to take care of me, too busy with her 'work.' Work, yeah, that's what she called what she did with every man she could con into dropping his pants and paying a few bills. Work, while I stayed locked in a closet, too scared to cry or ask for water. Anyone doesn't think she got what she deserved should take a look at my back. Scars like these don't come easy. It took years of beatings to get these babies." Ken continued his monologue while pushing his white Cadillac past the speed limit toward Colorado Springs. "Ellie and Emily . . . two redheads just waitin' for a chance to do me in. I know their type. Been around them too long; they can't fool me. I love that look in their eyes when they know they're about to take their last breath. Love it when their eyes go big, just as the knife goes in. It's more fun if I can shove it in a little at a time. Gives 'em time to think. Yeah . . . lots of time. Too bad I couldn't take more time with Ellie. It would have been fun to watch her die slowly. Ya gotta get 'em before they get you! That's my motto. The kid, Billy, he's just like them. Give him a little time to grow up and he'll be gunnin' for me. Gotta think on that one." With miles behind him Ken began to relax. "Gotta think. Mom's place isn't too smart, first place they'll look. Ellie's old man had a trailer. We went to look at it after he died. She was going to fix it up and sell it, maybe after school lets out." Ken took the next off-ramp, circled back and headed for the mobile home park. A flood nearly wiped out the park two years ago and parts of it were still in ruins. *Last place they'll think to look*, he thought. He parked behind the trailer and broke the lock to get in. The place looked dusty and unused, the air smelled stale; there was no electricity. Fortunately, the water was still hooked up and the toilet worked. He covered the windows with aluminum foil and went to sleep.

When the police questioned her, Beth Ann could barely talk for crying. "Em and I have been best friends since kindergarten. We were going to visit our boyfriends the night she was killed. I had to call it off when my mom made me clean my room. If we'd gone like we planned maybe she'd still be alive. She was supposed to go camping with her family the next morning. Em said she didn't like her mother's boyfriend. She told me he gave her the creeps."

The hunt was on. Newspapers and TV reported this to be the most intensive manhunt in the history of this small community. One officer stated that he'd never seen so many men and women searching for one individual. Mounted police searched culverts behind the Bovac's house looking for any sign of Ken Holland. Neighbors, only too happy to help, gave any information they could think of and many of them went out looking as well.

A search of police records turned up the fact that Ken Holland had a lengthy record using different aliases. He'd been convicted of breaking and entering in three different states. He received a suspended sentence for the rape of a seventeen–year–old girl, his girlfriend's daughter. Testimony indicated that he had not been entirely to blame; the girl had earned quite a reputation for herself.

When contacted by police, George Holland, Ken's older brother stated, "Ken was always in trouble. He isn't welcome in my home or around my children. Neither of us is close to our mother. She abused us as kids. Ken got the worst of it, being younger. I could escape, but poor Ken was too little. Unfortunately, now he's turned into a monster."

Billy stayed with Mr. Jordan, a teacher from his school, until the end of the year when he would live with his grandparents.

He immediately began working with a psychiatrist to help him through the trauma. A month from the time of the slayings, the coroner released the bodies.

The funeral was scheduled for the following week. Mr. Jordan took Billy home to get his dress clothes. As they approached the front door, Billy hung back. Seeing his reluctance, Mr. Jordan tried to put him at ease. He put his arm around the frightened boy. "It's okay. We'll get through this. Don't forget your dress shoes." Billy wanted some of his toys and his lucky ball cap. They brought along a small suitcase to carry the items. "Got everything? Let's go then." Mr. Jordan wasn't any more comfortable than Billy at being there. They turned to leave. The hall closet door silently opened behind them. A tall figure wearing a ski mask and gloves jumped out, swinging a baseball bat. He hit Jordan on the side of the head, knocking him to his knees. "Run, Billy, run!" the teacher yelled. Billy didn't stop to think; he took off, hitting the front door at a dead run, screaming at the top of his lungs. Dazed, Jordan rolled to one side; using a judo move, he caught the intruder around the waist and squeezed. He couldn't hold on. He did manage to fell the man, take the bat, and hit him once. The intruder broke away and fled through the back door.

The news quoted a source within the police department saying the recent attack prompted a dramatic increase in the number of officers assigned to the case. "Our intention," said the source, "is to make sure nothing else happens. We want the community to feel safe. We're planning ahead for further unforeseen problems." The source went on to state that previously they'd been confident, due to lack of sightings, that Ken Holland had left the city. However, evidence at the scene proved that Ken Holland was the intruder.

One columnist wrote, "Obviously the police were dead wrong about the perpetrator leaving the area. Now they are not expecting or predicting anything. One officer, who chose to remain anonymous, told this reporter that she couldn't recall a situation where an offender was identified and publicly known yet stayed in the vicinity to stalk the victim's family."

The search raged across the city. People began reporting sightings; police followed up on every report. "More sightings than Elvis," commented one officer. Once again they contacted Ken's family. His brother George said he hadn't seen or heard from Ken in years. He said their mother left a message on his answering machine several weeks ago, announcing that she would be on an extended vacation in Europe. She didn't say when she'd return. "I was surprised to get the message. We're not close." Police were stumped as to how Ken could stay hidden without help from family or friends.

Finally, a break in the case came from a surprising source, Ken's own computer. A search showed pictures of Ken posing in several disguises: with and without glasses, several types of beards, light and dark hair of varying lengths and some with a mustache. The child pornography found on his computer would be handled in a separate charge. Police distributed flyers showing his different looks. They were taking it as a personal affront that he had slipped past them, returned to cause more damage and once again escaped.

Ken began to relax. The neighbors hadn't noticed him. He stayed in during the day, going out only at night for food and beer. *Soon it'll be safe to move, maybe go to Mom's place in Colorado Springs. George thinks she's on vacation, probably figures she's with some old geezer. Lucky we're not friendly, he won't even ask questions.*

Dawn Clark looked over the fence at Ellie's dad's trailer. She couldn't be sure but she thought she saw some movement. *And aluminum foil on the windows. . . was that always there? Strange, I look over here every day and I don't remember seeing it.* Dawn liked Emily and her family; she worried about Billy. *This is awful for the poor kid.* She was taking out the trash, a job her son usually took care of, when she saw the parked Cadillac.

"Metro. How may I direct your call?"

"I think I have information about Ken Holland, the guy

who killed Ellie Bovac and her daughter."

"Stay on the line, please. I'll connect you to the detective in charge."

"Cummings here. What have you got?"

"I'm not sure," said Dawn in a hesitant voice. "But I think Ken Holland's car is parked out back."

"Hold on." He shuffled through papers to find the number on the license plate. "Okay, describe it to me."

"A white Cadillac." She gave him the license number.

"I'll be right there. Don't go near the trailer. If you see him, don't go near him."

Josh and his partner Alex Romero arrived at the mobile home park. They stationed their car well away from the Bovac's trailer, taking care not to be seen. As soon as they were sure the Cadillac belonged to Ken, Josh called for backup. The neighbors were quietly evacuated. Armed police and K-9 dogs surrounded the area. A helicopter hovered overhead. Josh pounded on the door. "Come out, Holland. We have you, you can't get away!"

The door opened. Everyone braced for whatever might happen next. Officers stood, hoping he would try to run. They were disappointed when Ken, dressed in jeans and tee shirt with his hair tousled from sleep, offered no resistance. He stepped onto the ground; an officer handcuffed him, read him his rights, and put him in the patrol car.

Newspapers reported the peaceful capture of Ken Holland. "Thus ends the most intense manhunt in local history. His capture brings relief to the community and to the friends and family he terrorized." Some of the younger officers may have wanted a little more fireworks; everyone else was ecstatic. Cars filled with teenagers, drove by the mobile home park, blowing horns and yelling. Billy Bovac cried. He was too overcome to talk about the capture. When asked, he couldn't bring himself to respond. Even with around-the-clock protection, he had felt uneasy, always looking over his shoulder and jumping at each new sound. Maybe in time he would feel safe again.

When interviewed, the neighbor, Dawn, said, "I had a bad feeling. I saw that foil on the windows and knew things weren't okay." She dabbed at her eyes, "To think he was right next door all this time."

Ken, of course, pled not guilty to the charge of murder. He told his attorney, "Ellie and me were taking Billy and Emily to a friend's cabin in the mountains over Easter vacation. We had an argument the night before we were supposed to go and I took off. I was at my mom's place in Colorado Springs when they were killed and I have proof. I didn't even know about the murder until I was coming back to make up with Ellie and heard it on the car radio. I knew the cops would try to pin it on me because of my past record. Then, I remembered her old man's trailer and figured it would be a good place to lay low until they found the killer. Those schmucks! Of course they found my fingerprints; we were together at her place every day. Ellie and I were thinking about getting married."

"Does Holland seem a little too smug? I'd like to wipe the smirk off that SOB's face," Josh whispered to Alex. "Says he was at his mother's and can prove it. Well, that creep better have something ironclad, I'm telling ya. The DA's going to push for the death penalty, and I'm going to volunteer to pull the handle."

After months of preliminary procedures, including jury selection, court was finally in session, Judge Alden Anderson presiding. Twice, the bailiff had to admonish people in the packed room to quiet down. The mood was mixed—excitement, relief and revenge. Ken Holland kept a smirk on his face. His attorney, a public defender, warned him to give up the attitude. Ken looked bored. "They can't prove a thing. All they have is wishful thinking. Bunch of morons; if they had brain one, they'd be dangerous." He laughed at his own dark wit. "This is too funny. All these high-priced attorneys, all these 'good citizens' lusting for my blood, and they don't have squat." *I'm too smart for these hicks. If they're waiting for tears of remorse from me, they've got a long wait. There's another redhead in the jury. When this is over maybe she'll be next. Redheads! Vultures waiting to kill your spirit and pick out your eyes. I'll show 'em who's boss.*

Police testimony revealed little more than what the public already knew. No one saw Ken Holland the day of the murders and further, no one saw him on the day Mr. Jordan was attacked. By now, any bruises Ken had from the fight with Jordan had healed. He maintained his story about being in Colorado Springs with his mother. "I have no idea who could have committed this horrible crime," he said. "And, I certainly have no idea who attacked Billy's teacher." Ken's prior record was ruled inadmissible.

Cummings was going ballistic. "This jerk is as guilty as anyone I've ever seen. If he walks, I'm throwing in the towel!" He called Holland's mother again and left yet another message on her answering machine; so far, no response.

The facts were not in dispute. Ken's fingerprints were all over Ellie's house. Neighbors claimed that Emily didn't like Ken, some said Billy seemed to like him. People who saw them together stated that he treated her well and there was no doubt that she was more than fond of him. There were no witnesses to the crime. Even with Ken's dark past, the defense attorneys claimed that nothing on his computer or in his records supported a charge of murder. The trial continued for three weeks. The evidence was circumstantial, still the detectives and the prosecuting attorney felt they had a good case. People had been convicted on circumstantial evidence before. Ken's demeanor worked against him. No one, including the jury and his own attorney, liked him.

On the last day of the trial, Ken took the stand. The prosecuting attorney stepped up. "You told the police that you were at your mother's house in Colorado Springs the day Emily and Ellie Bovac were murdered. To date, we've not been able to verify this statement. All attempts to reach your mother have failed. What proof can you offer that you were there on that date?"

"My mother can vouch for me and if that's not enough she'll show you ticket stubs from the movie we went to see. I believe she even called my brother and told him she was home and that I was there with her."

"The truth is, Mr. Holland, we can't verify that your mother's anywhere around. Frankly, we're not sure she exists."

Ken looked at the attorney as if he thought the man was totally stupid. "Oh, she's around, that's for sure. In fact, if you turn around, you'll see her."

The court turned to watch a woman of about sixty, dressed in a pale blue suit, dark-blue pumps and carrying an expensive handbag, walk into the room. Her marked resemblance to Ken was noted by some.

Josh hissed to his partner, Alex, "Quick, get a picture of Holland's mother from his file. I remember seeing her in a newspaper clipping from one of his earlier cases."

Alex hurried from the room, called the station and asked to have the picture faxed to the court immediately. He then raced upstairs to retrieve the picture as soon as it came through.

"Rats! I was so sure she was a phony." Josh gazed at the picture of a younger Mrs. Holland. "This is going to throw a brick right in the middle of this case." Jury deliberations took three days. Everyone was on edge. In his heart, he knew Holland killed Ellie and her daughter. He also knew, "a shadow of a doubt" is the rule to which juries must adhere. Mom showing up cast a big shadow.

"Not guilty!" the foreman announced the verdict. A thunderstorm broke lose in the courtroom. Judge Anderson pounded his gavel in vain.

As Ken and his mother exited the courthouse, he gave the gathered reporters the finger and had a special wink and a laugh for Detective Cummings. He and his mother departed in their car.

Josh stomped down the courthouse stairs. "He's guilty, Alex. You know it, I know it, he sure as shootin' knows it. Son-of. . ." He threw his jacket on the steps.

Josh and Alex stood on the sidewalk watching helplessly as the dark-blue sedan drove down the street. "Come on, Josh, let's find ourselves a drink. There's nothing we can do. You win some, you lose some, you know how it goes. He'll get his. Trust me, he'll be back in the crosshairs of the law soon enough. We'll get him next time."

The dark-blue sedan sped away with Ken and his *mother*. Ken couldn't stop laughing. "Did you see their faces? They even had a picture of *you*. Lucky you and Mom looked so much alike. What did folks call you . . .identical twin cousins?"

"Yes, sometimes first cousins look more alike than sisters; we sure did. What now? What shall we do first?"

"First, let's get the out of here. Head for Colorado Springs. We'll sell Mom's house and car. You can go the bank, cash in her stocks and clean out her account. We'll split everything down the middle."

"You know, I never asked, what ever did happen to dear old Mom?" Ken gave her a look and raised his eyebrows. "Yeah, that's what I thought." Both of them doubled over in laughter. Ken gleefully stepped down on the accelerator.

As the detectives watched the car speed toward the corner, a Shell tanker backed out of the gas station after filling the underground tanks. Ken hit it square on. The driver leaped from the cab just as tanker and sedan exploded in a ball of flame.

"Well, maybe justice was a little faster this time," Josh said. "Let's have that drink Alex. Suddenly, I feel like a celebration is in order."

The old detective thought for a moment, "Now, here's one for you. In a way, it's a love story. I was working with the organized crime unit down in San Diego. This must have been twenty, twenty-five years ago. I labeled the file My Lara; you'll see why."

Chapter 12
MY LARA

Ann paid for her coffee and sat outside. She leaned back in her chair enjoying the soft breeze and ocean view. Thoughts of what to do after lunch were just entering her mind when a deep male voice intruded.

"You're perfect."

"What?" Ann was startled.

"I'm sorry. I can't help staring; you are so perfect."

Ann laughed, "Of course, you're right; however, it usually takes people a bit longer to realize it."

"You must think this is some corny pick-up line."

"Well, now that you mention it."

He stuck out his hand. "Hi. I'm Josh Cummings. I'm with the organized crime unit of the San Diego Police." He produced his badge and identification card. "May I sit down?"

Puzzled, Ann motioned for him to sit. She was a little apprehensive but since she was in full view of the waitress in the coffee shop, she thought she was safe enough. "I think you'd better explain. What's this all about?"

The waitress came to take his order. She turned to Ann, "Your food will be right out."

"Just coffee for me, thanks," he told the girl, then turned to Ann. "This is rather a long story, but please bear with me. I know who you are. We've been following you for weeks now."

"Following me? Why on earth…?" Her hand flew to her chest.

Josh held up his hand. "Please, it's okay. Let me explain. We know your husband was a police officer killed while fighting organized crime." He reached into his pocket and withdrew the picture of a woman several years older than Ann's thirty-six years. The resemblance was striking. It could have been Ann's mother. "This is Belle Giacomo. She died about five years ago. Her husband is the head of a large, powerful, organized crime syndicate. Actually, he's been turning his interests into legitimate businesses for some time now. The problem is his nephew Phillip; he seems determined to keep the old enterprises alive and well."

"This is all very interesting, Mr. Cummings. I'm curious. Why are you telling me?"

"Because we need your help. We're hoping that what happened to your husband will help persuade you. Here. . ." He waved his hand to indicate the restaurant. ". . .is not the place for this discussion. May we come to your house? Say about seven?"

"We?"

"Yes, my partner, Nicole Evans and I. Please, listen to our proposal. If you're not interested, no problem."

Intrigued, Ann said, "And if I am?"

"Naturally, I hope you will be. We'll discuss it tonight. And, sorry, I must ask you not to mention this conversation to anyone."

Ann picked at her lunch, finished her shopping and hurried home. She couldn't help wonder what this Nicole Evans and Josh Cummings wanted from her. Every idea that came to mind seemed completely ridiculous. By seven, when the agents were due to arrive, curiosity consumed her. She could hear her late husband's voice, "Curiosity killed the cat." She had always had an insatiable need to know, often to her detriment.

When Ann opened the door, Agent Cummings and a

woman were standing on the porch. "Ms. Davidson, this is my partner, Nicole Evans."

Ann held out her hand. A small, dark haired woman about Ann's own age shook it. "Please come in." She led them to the living room and offered coffee or soft drinks.

"I'll have a diet coke, if you have it," said Nicole.

"Coffee for me," said Josh. "Nice place you have. I love all this polished wood."

"I love it too, until I have to polish it," said Ann. "Please, the suspense is eating me up. What is it you want with me?"

Cummings put his cup down. "You saw the picture. You could be Belle Giocomo at age thirty. She died in a car accident about five years ago. Her husband is Jules Giocomo. We want to put you inside the Giocomo estate to help gather information. We suspect that a major delivery is about to be made."

"Delivery? You mean drugs?"

"No. Teenage girls from Thailand. They're brought here and forced into prostitution."

Ann gave a shudder. "How horrible! What can I do? How could I help? Besides how would I get on the estate? I really *don't* understand."

"Our plan is to let Phillip Giocomo see you. He eats at Philippi's Pizza Grotto on India Street every Friday night. We want to put you where he can get a good look at you. His uncle, Jules, has been in mourning since his wife's death. Hopefully, Phillip will see an opportunity to get on his uncle's good side and also keep the old guy out of the way; you'll go with Agent Evans, your new best friend. If we're right, Phillip will do anything he can to keep his Uncle Jules occupied. We believe he'll think of some way to get you to come to the estate. If the old man knew what his nephew was up to, he'd kill him. Phil pretty much runs things now, but the old man still has a lot of clout and Phillip doesn't want him to interfere."

"You don't have to worry," Nicole gave her a friendly look. "We just want you to keep your ears open and try to remember faces you see. I'll meet with you every week to get any information you have. Remember, I'm your new best friend. Of course, all of this is moot if Phillip doesn't take the bait. Another thing. There is someone on the inside who calls us from time to time and feeds us information."

"If you already have someone, why do you need me?"

"We don't know who it is," Nicole broke in. "We can't rely on him or her to call. We have no way to call back. Given all this, are you willing to help us?"

Ann thought of her husband, David, dying in the pursuit of men such as these, and his years on the police force, trying to make the world a better place, "Yes, of course. I'll do what I can."

The restaurant was crowded. Fortunately, Nicole had made reservations. The waiter led them to a table in the center of the room. Ann would have preferred a dark quiet booth; however, this was better suited to their purpose. At first, Ann was afraid their conversation would be stilted. She feared everyone would know this wasn't a normal dinner with a friend. Nicole soon put her at ease with small talk. The two women discovered they had many interests in common. Both liked art films and had seen *Like Water for Chocolate* recently. Nicole modeled in college to help pay her tuition. Ann did some freelance fashion design. By the end of the evening they really were friends. Nicole raised her eyebrows when Phillip Giocomo and his group walked in. Once they were seated, Ann went to the restroom, making sure to pass in front of their table. Soon after, Nicole and Ann got up to leave. Nicole held her ticket out to the parking attendant. "We don't want to seem in any way eager to stay around. If this is going to work, he has to come to you."

The following two Fridays they ate at Philippi's, had a glass of wine each and left the restaurant after making sure Phillip had seen them. On the third Saturday of the month promptly at nine a.m., Ann's doorbell rang. Her heart gave a leap when she looked through the peephole and realized she was staring at Phillip Giocomo. She could see two men seated in a black car at the curb.

"Good morning, Ms. Davidson. My name is Phillip Giocomo. May I come in? I have a business proposal for you."

"I'm sorry, I was just leaving." Ann had been coached not to seem too eager or to recognize the nephew. "Besides, what ever you're selling, I'm in no position to buy right now. Sorry." Ann started to close the door.

"Please! I'm not selling anything." He held up a picture of his aunt, Belle Giocomo. Although not the same picture Agent Cummings had shown her, the resemblance was still evident. "Please, let me explain. My uncle, a widower, is very old and lonely, and not too well. He needs assistance cataloging his library. I think you could help. I've seen you in Philippi's on several occasions and I took the liberty of having you checked out. Once I realized how much you looked like my deceased aunt, I knew you would be perfect for the job. I know you're a teacher on summer vacation. I also know you're a widow. I'm offering you employment as an assistant for my uncle. I love my uncle very much and it hurts me to see the old gentleman trying to do the work himself. I'm prepared to offer a substantial salary. You would live at the estate. Of course, you would be free to come and go as you please."

The estate sprawled just north of San Diego, hidden behind working ranches with acres of green lawns surrounded by white fences and dotted with Black Angus cattle. The gates swung open to reveal old brick and ivy covered walls, high windows overlooking the courtyard, plus an elegant fountain creating a rainbow of multicolored sprays in the noonday sun.

Dual staircases led upstairs leaving a reception area the size of a small ballroom between them downstairs. The aroma of candles and furniture polish competed with an open fire and leather chairs. Small tables nestled beside each chair as though waiting for a snifter of old brandy and a good book.

Cross-paned windows on either side of the fireplace looked out at a beautifully manicured lawn. She could see well-tended flowerbeds filled with pink and white roses. The sprawling estate was enormous. It reminded her of an English castle.

"The maid will take you to your room." He saw Ann's look and hastily added, "The one you will be staying in if, hopefully, you accept the job after you meet Uncle Jules."

The maid led upstairs and down a carpeted hall. Ann raised her eyebrows and smiled. Her *room* was a small suite complete with bedroom, dressing room, sitting room and kitchenette. Rose-patterned wallpaper with matching spread gave the bedroom a warm, welcoming feel. The sitting room was well-appointed with a writing desk in one corner. A soft, inviting couch covered with light green fabric graced the opposite wall. The chairs were green print, complimenting the couch. Lampshades diffused the light to a soft, ivory glow. Deep carpet beneath her feet completed the feel of elegance. The maid, a pleasant round-faced girl with olive shaped black eyes and a halo of shining black hair, said her name was Mercedes. "Like the car," she smiled. "Mr. Jules say my real name is Porsche. He say I just like to pretend I'm Mercedes." Ann laughed, immediately liking the girl. "Mr. Phillip say to get some rest or have a swim; he will come for you at six. I will be your maid. Anything you need please just ask me."

Ann decided to stroll through the garden. When she returned, her things were put away in drawers and closets. Mercedes had left a tray with sandwiches and a soft drink. *Phillip seems pretty sure I'll stay*, she thought.

Promptly at six, Phillip escorted Ann to his uncle's apartment. She noticed the beautiful dark woods and gleaming wood floors. The walls were covered with ancient masterpieces; even at a glance Ann could tell they were originals. Ann's room was upstairs at one end of the hall. She was surprised to find that Jules Giocomo's apartment was on the same floor, at the opposite end of the hallway.

Jules greeted them at the door. "Phillip. To what do I owe

this pleasure?" At that moment, Jules looked at Ann. A sharp intake of breath let Phillip know he'd guessed right. "Come in, come in."

"Uncle, this is Ann Davidson. She's agreed to stay with us for a while and help you catalog your books. She's a teacher and works in the school library. I think you'll find her skills helpful."

Phillip looked at his watch, "Uncle, I have a meeting. I'll leave you to get acquainted."

"A meeting? This late? Who are you meeting?" Jules frowned at his nephew. "What's going on, Phillip?"

He glanced briefly at Ann. "Don't worry. I'll explain everything later."

Jules turned to Ann; he *could not* take his eyes off of her. "You must think me rude. It's just that you remind me so much of my late wife. Your honey blond hair, the shape of your face, even your eyes are the same hazel color. Please, come in. Sit down. May I offer you something? The cook made this wonderful chocolate cake for desert tonight and I haven't eaten it yet. Come, share with me. She always makes way too much. Oh, and let me introduce Samantha." He petted a beautiful coal black cat with huge green eyes. "Sam is pure alley, but don't tell her, she thinks she descended from royalty." Ann stroked Samantha and was rewarded with one of the loudest purrs she had ever heard. "My dear, tell me about yourself. How did Phillip find you? I had mentioned needing an assistant, actually; I'm surprised that he even listened."

The Jules Giocomo seated before her was definitely not the man she had envisioned. This man was bursting with vitality. Though was well into his eighties there was nothing frail about him. His eyes burned with intelligence. Ann could feel herself being drawn to him. "I'm a widow. My husband was a police officer killed in the line of duty. I was staying home, trying to keep the baby I was carrying. I had trouble conceiving and we wanted this child so very much. When David was killed, the shock made me miscarry." Agent Cummings told her to stick to the truth; it was easier than trying to remember a lie. "I went back to teaching after my husband was killed. Now I'm looking for summer employment. David's insurance didn't go very far. I responded to an ad your nephew placed in the paper." This was far from the truth. Phillip had asked her to go along with this harmless deception. Ann told him of growing up in southern California, going to college and ultimately marrying. "My family members were blue-collar workers. My father was in the navy and my grandfather was a jack-of-all-trades. Both my mother and my grandmother worked in a cannery, packing tomatoes, fish, whatever was in season. "

Jules placed his hand over Ann's. "How brave you are. It must be very hard for you, a young woman alone." He paused, "We'll start on the library first thing in the morning."

Ann realized that by comparison she must seem *young* to Jules Giocomo. Later, in her room she couldn't get him off her mind. He was so old world courtly, so warm, so genuine, so interesting. He seemed like a European aristocrat. It was even harder to remember the things Josh Cummings and Nicole Evans had told her about him.

They soon fell into a routine. Mornings were spent working on the collection of fine and rare books Jules accumulated over the years. At noon, they had a light lunch and Jules retired for a brief rest. Ann went for a swim or walked in the garden. Evenings, they met again for dinner. She enjoyed these times. Jules was a wonderful conversationalist: humorous, witty and filled with stories of his early life. He was open about his early career, as he built a name for himself in organized crime.

"Now, that's all past me. I've been turning all our businesses into legitimate enterprises for years now. In my declining years, I came to realize there's as much money to be made on this side of the law as there is on the other. And," he added, "you don't always have to walk backwards so you can see who's chasing you. Now, if I can just convince my nephew. He still has the young bull's need to prove his worth." He would place his hand over his heart and lament, with a twinkle in his eye. "Oh, to be young again." At other times, he would tell her of his beautiful wife, Belle, and his son Jules Jr. "Belle was my love and my life. I can't remember a time when I didn't love that woman. She was my, everything, until Jules Jr. was born; then I felt I owned the world. Belle and I took little Jules with us everywhere. Many of our friends hired nannies. Belle wouldn't hear of it. She was an old fashioned girl. She would raise our son the way our mothers raised us. When Jules was older I began to groom him to take over the business. That's when Belle insisted I sell off the illegal parts and build up the legitimate portions. She wanted Jules Jr. to get his law degree and then take over a business that was clean and free from problems with the law."

"Where is he now?"

Jules paused before speaking, sadness flooding his features, "Jules is gone. He and his mother were killed in an auto accident five years ago."

"I'm so sorry. I didn't know." Without thinking, Ann reached for his hand. His skin was warm; she felt the warmth travel up her arm.

"Of course not, my dear, how could you? Forgive an old man's reminiscing."

At midnight, Ann heard voices. She crept from her room and looked over the railing. There were four men going into the wing where Phillip kept his office. She had been warned not to try anything clever; she was there simply to observe and report. A quick look couldn't hurt. She crept down the long hall to get a better look. She was about to descend the stairs when a hand touched her shoulder. Ann jumped and stifled a scream.

"It is only me," Mercedes stood there in her nightgown and robe.

"I . . . I got turned around. I wanted to go to the garden. I can't seem to get to sleep. I thought a quiet walk might help."

"Of course, it is easy to turn around in this house. The

garden is cold. I'll get you some warm milk or would you like hot chocolate?" Mercedes led her back to her room.

Lately, when she returned from her swim there would be a beautiful evening gown with matching shoes waiting for her. "Mercedes, where are these gowns coming from?"

"Ah, Mr. Jules has me put them there for you. Are they not beautiful?"

"Very beautiful, where do they come from? Every night there's a new one."

"Mercedes put her finger to her lips. "Come, I show you." The two crept softly down the stairs. Under the stairwell a door opened into a room outfitted like the biggest closet Ann had ever imagined. There she saw row after row of beautiful ball gowns, furs of every length and shoes to match each outfit. "Sometimes Mr. Jules lets me choice," Mercedes beamed.

"Choose?"

"Choose, my English isn't so good."

"You're doing fine. I admire you for trying." Voices came from behind the wall. Mercedes quickly turned off the light and led Ann from the room.

"That is the office of Mr. Phillip on the other side of the closet. He would be angry to find us there." She put the key to the closet in her apron pocket.

After dinner Jules would put a record on his old-fashioned phonograph. They danced to the old tunes, everything from swing to waltz; his favorite by far was "Lara's Theme" from *Doctor Zhivago*. He often called her, "My Lara," as he held her close. Jules was an accomplished ballroom dancer. Ann had never felt so beautiful or so desired.

Once a week she called Nicole, aware that her conversation was being recorded. They would agree to meet in town for shopping. Ann was always accompanied by a driver; she was never far from his sight. Ann had little to report. The few men she had seen coming into the estate quickly disappeared down the polished halls to the other wing. Nicole assured her that all such information was useful. She felt torn. Her commitment to Agent Cummings and Nicole was mitigated by a growing affection for Jules Giocomo.

On Valentine's Day she returned to her room to find a sequined, red ball gown spread across her bed. That evening she and Jules shared a romantic candlelit dinner accompanied by wine and coffee. Jules presented her with a ruby necklace. Ann knew she should protest. He just made it seem so natural. He took such pleasure in her happiness.

It was after midnight when Ann got into bed. The satin nightgown she wore was smooth against her skin. Her mind was a jumble of conflicting feelings. A light tap on her door preceded Jules, as he stepped to the side of her bed. Ann's throat constricted. *Oh no, not this.* Jules smiled. He placed a red rose on the nightstand and bent to kiss her forehead. "I had to thank you for such a special evening. I hope you don't mind." He left as quietly as he had come.

At about three that morning, Ann awoke to the sound of angry voices. She opened her door, tiptoed out and looked over the railing. She could see several men gathered at the entryway. Something was happening. She tried to get closer to hear what they were saying. All she could make out were gruff voices. She couldn't make out their words. She stepped back into the shadow of the hall just as Phillip turned to look up. She prayed he hadn't seen her.

Ann called Dr. Berry, her dentist the next morning. It was the prearranged signal that something was happening. Dr. Berry's office made an appointment for her at one o'clock. She told Mercedes that she had a toothache and asked her not to mention it to Jules. She said she would be back in time for their evening session and she didn't want to worry him needlessly. "What happened?" Nicole asked once she was safely inside the office. "We had a call from our mystery informant last night. He says Phillip is about to accept a shipment of girls. He wants us to track Phillip and put a stop to it. *Who* did you see?"

"I didn't hear their names. There were four of them plus

Phillip. They were arguing. I couldn't make out the actual words."

"We'll get some pictures to you when it's safe. Meanwhile, go back home and listen for anything else you might hear."

Ann didn't mention that Phillip might have seen her last night. Dr. Berry gave her a shot and looked at her teeth. She now had a slightly swollen jaw and a good excuse for being here.

Jules was waiting for her when she arrived home. "I was worried. Mercedes told me you had a toothache and went to the dentist. Oh, I see your jaw. Let me get some ice for it. Mercedes," he called, "get an ice pack for Ann, hurry."

When the girl arrived with an icepack she hung her head. "I'm sorry, Miss, Mr. Jules, he ask where you are. I didn't like to lie."

"It's okay. Don't worry about it."

Ann felt like such a fraud. While she felt guilty for deceiving Jules, she did enjoy his attention. He insisted she come to his apartment and lie down. He tucked a blanket around her legs and put on some soothing music. "When the swelling goes down, I'll order some soup. Mrs. Fiorella makes the best soup you ever tasted." Ann noticed Jules looking out the window several times during the afternoon. He made light of it when she asked; she knew he was troubled.

That evening when Mercedes came to help her dress for dinner, Ann was able to slip the key out of her apron pocket. Later, when she heard the sound of Phillip's friends, she quickly ran on bare feet down the stairs and hid in the closet. She could hear them talking in the office. The voices were arguing about where the shipment was to be housed until it was time for the buyer to pick them up. Phillip's voice was clear, "What is this? We always put them in the warehouse by the naval shipyard."

"Can't do it this time," came a second voice. "There's Navy inspectors crawling all over the place. Some big military exercise comin' down. Can't take the chance."

Ann could hear the frustration and worry in Phillip's voice.

"Okay, bring them here. Put them in the old barn, the one that isn't used. How long will they be here?"

"Just overnight. The buyer will pick them up Thursday. It'll be over before you know it."

A crash sounded as Ann backed into a manikin, sending it tumbling to the floor. "What the . . .?" Phillip ran from the room and opened the closet door. He turned the knob on the old fashion light switch, flooding the room with florescent light. Ann made herself as small as possible, holding her breath, hiding behind the last row of ball gowns. She could hear Phillip as he began a search of the room. Her heart pounded as she tried to think of a plausible reason for being there. "Hey, Sam old girl. What are you doing in here? Get trapped and couldn't get out?" Ann could hear Samantha purring as Phillip picked her up, crossed the room and left, closing the door behind him.

Phillip joined the men in his office, "Just Sam." He showed the men the cat and then released her to run back upstairs. "Not to worry, she just got trapped in the room where my uncle keeps a lot of things that belonged to my aunt. "I think the old goat's making a play for his new library *assistant*." The men laughed at the implication. "Back to business. How many are we talking about?"

"Fifteen… and all virgins between ten and twelve. They arrive on the *Nightingale*, a freighter from Thailand. The customer will go crazy when he sees them. We have to get them off the dock as quickly as possible and loaded onto the truck we'll have waiting. They'll be asleep in boxes marked as clothing from Thailand bound for the wholesale market. All the documents are in order, only we can't keep the girls out too long. The doctor will give them a sedative to keep them quiet. We have to move quickly. We can't take any chances. The sedative only lasts a short time."

Ann couldn't stop shaking. She waited for hours after the men left before she dared return to her room. She had to find a way to warn Nicole and Agent Cummings. She couldn't use the dentist ploy again so soon and her lunch with Nicole wasn't scheduled until next week. She hated to chance it but maybe she could use Mercedes.

The next morning Ann waited for the girl to bring her coffee. "Mercedes, please sit down, I have a favor to ask."

Bewildered, the young woman took a seat on the green print chair next to the desk. "What do you need? I am happy to do what you want."

"Listen, this is going to be hard to understand, there are some really bad things going on. The men who come to see Phillip are buying young girls in Thailand and selling them over here. They make the girls become prostitutes. Do you understand that word?" Ann thought back to high school Spanish but couldn't remember the word for prostitute.

"Prostituta?" Mercedes looked aghast. "Niñas, little girls?"

"Yes, yes, that's it. I need you to call this number." She handed Mercedes a piece of paper with Josh Cummings number written on it. "Make an excuse to leave the estate so you can call from a pay phone. Don't let anyone see you. Tell whoever answers the phone that Ann Davidson said to be at the estate Thursday night. Tell them they're bringing the children here. Remember, Thursday, that's when they're bringing the girls. Tell them to bring a doctor. The girls are drugged and asleep in boxes."

Mercedes crossed herself, put the slip of paper in her pocket and turned to take Ann's tray. "I'll call for you."

Ann was miserable for the next two days. She hated what had to be done. She knew her betrayal was going to hurt Jules. There was no way out. She would testify that he knew nothing about Phillip's business. She would tell the court how Jules tried to make Phillip give up the illegal business. She could say that Phillip acted entirely alone; that his uncle was completely in the dark. What was the use? No matter what she did, he would end up hating her.

Ann pretended not to feel well in answer to Jules'

concerned questions. He said she looked pale. She wasn't eating; she couldn't concentrate. By Thursday, she was no longer pretending. The weight of her deception was eating her alive. She prayed to have it over with. Thursday dawned bleak and dreary with dark clouds heavy with rain threatening to pour misery upon the earth. At nine that night, she heard cars in the courtyard. She could see lights from her window headed toward the out buildings. Minutes later Phillip shouted something from downstairs; Mercedes rushed into her room. "Get up! Come with me!" Mercedes grabbed her arm and threw a robe at her.

"What's happening?" Ann asked.

"Shut up! Just come." Mercedes pulled her down the hall and down the stairs. Phillip was standing there with a gun pointing directly at her.

"Bring her with you. We're leaving. Get her to the car. She's our insurance. They won't shoot as long as we have her." Phillip waved the gun in the direction of the door. "Hurry up! The cops are at the barn; they'll be here any second!"

Ann was confused. She turned to Mercedes. "If you're with Phillip, why did you call?"

"Don't be stupid. I didn't call anybody. My job is just to spy on you and report to Phillip." She grabbed Ann's arm and began dragging her to the door. Ann noticed that the girl's English had improved markedly in the past few hours.

Jules stepped from the shadow of the stairway. "I made the call. I warned you, Phillip, I'll have none of this trafficking of young girls in my house. You're nothing but scum. If my son had lived, you'd never have gotten away with any of this. Belle warned me about you. She knew you were no good from the start. I should have listened."

Phillip's laugh was ugly. "Yes, dear Aunt Belle. I knew what she thought of me. I also knew that as long as Jules Jr. was in the picture, I'd never have a place in the business. I'm so much smarter than your lame-brained son; I could have made you wealthy beyond your wildest dreams. Too bad you got old and satisfied. That's why they had to have that *accident.*"

Without warning, Jules struck Phillip across the face with a poker from the fireplace, opening a gash from ear to chin. Phillip shot twice, hitting Jules in the chest. At that moment, Agent Cummings appeared at the door and shot Phillip in the arm, forcing him to drop the gun.

Ann dropped to the floor beside Jules. She took off her robe to make a pillow for his head and bent over him crying. "Jules, Jules, I'm so sorry. I never meant to hurt you."

"It's better this way." His voice was weak. "Don't blame yourself. I've known all along why you were here. Please, forgive this old man. You gave me so much happiness. I've had two great loves in my life, my darling Belle and you, Ann, my Lara. No man could wish for more." Jules closed his eyes and passed quietly from all cares.

In the weeks that followed, indictments were made and investigations continued into the business affairs of Phillip Giocomo. Mercedes was released on her own recognizance and promptly fled to Tijuana in an attempt to cross into Mexico. She was stopped at the border and quickly returned to San Diego for trial.

Ann was applauded for her role until finally, other news items began to take over the front page. Ann asked Agent Cummings about the money Phillip had deposited in her account for helping Jules. "That was fairly earned. You keep the money. And," he paused, thinking of the lovely ruby necklace Jules had given her on Valentine's Day. "anything else that Jules Giocomo may have given you."

A year later, Ann, with the Giocomo incident behind her, was teaching and trying her hand at some freelance fashion design, an interest she dropped when she married David. She wanted very much to devote full time to her design work. But bills beckoned, mortgage and car payments clamored for attention, even her newly adopted cat, Samantha, had vet bills and food to be purchased.

The post brought a letter from an attorney she had never heard of. The letter requested her presence at the reading of Jules Giocomo's will. Flabbergasted, she had never given a thought to Jules estate. Phillip was in prison for life and as far as she knew, Jules had no other kin.

Benson Lee of Benson, Benson and Benson welcomed Ann into his office. She was the only person there, other than Mr. Lee. "Ms. Davidson, I will read the contents of the will to you in a moment, just as a formality; the gist of it is, that Mr. Giocomo left his entire estate to you."

For a moment, Ann was too stunned to respond. She just looked at Mr. Lee with wonder on her face. "That can't be! I'm not related to Jules Giocomo."

"True, but his only living relative, Phillip is never going to get out of prison. The Feds had the house bugged; Phillip's confession to killing Belle and Jules Jr. was recorded. Other than a few bequests to old servants and a large donation to the Society of Fine Arts and Literature, everything else belongs to you. You inherit the house, land, the cars, furniture and jewelry. The farm alone brings in several million each year. The investment portfolio brings in several million more. Jules Giocomo knew he didn't have much longer to live and the thought that Phillip might get control of all he had worked for was more than he could stand. He had no other heir. He wanted you to have it all."

It took time and a giant mental adjustment for Ann to finally accept her new role as heiress. She moved into the Giocomo estate. Only Samantha seemed at home. The cat simply took her rightful place as queen of the manor and continued receiving food and attention, as was her due.

Valentine's Day brought back a flood of memories. She went to Jules' apartment. In the closet she found the beautiful red gown. On impulse she dressed in the gown and did her hair the way she had worn it that magical night. The ruby necklace sparkled at her throat. Ann opened the old-fashioned record player to play *Lara's Theme* one last time. Tears streamed down her face when she saw an envelope addressed to her in Jules' handwriting.

My Dearest Ann,

I instructed my attorney to wait until a year after my death to advise you of your inheritance. I wanted to be sure there would be no reprisals from Phillip. What he doesn't know can't hurt you.

Something must be done about Phillip. I have to find a way to stop him. I'm hoping that your friends in the police department will take my message seriously. Secretly, I guess I want them to do the job for me. If they don't do something soon, I'll have to take matters into my own hands. I'm too old to be playing these games. Phillip cannot be allowed to continue.

There is no way I can ever repay you for the hours of pleasure just being in your company gave me. Each evening I looked forward to picking out a gown that I thought would compliment your eyes and coloring. You can't know how I waited each evening to see you come through my door. It was like seeing you through the eyes of a lover. You made me young again; for this I thank you. I can think of no one better suited to enjoy the fruits of my labor. Rest assured that everything you receive came from legitimate business enterprises.

Please, for my sake, have a happy life. Follow your dreams and from time to time, if you think of me, remember the man who loved you beyond all age barriers and beyond reason. Try to think of me with affection for the wonderful hours we shared.

Good-bye Ann, My Lara,
For eternity,
Jules

"That story always made my wife a little weepy." Josh appeared to forget the two young reporters seated on his couch, then he looked at the glowing end of his cigar. "You know, these have been around since 1903. Did I already mention that? These are all aged in oak barrels for several years. It gives them a very unique flavor. They come in a variety of wrappers including the Platinum Cameroon, the Red Maduro and the Gold Corojo." He looked up at their confused faces. "Guess you're not cigar types. Oh well, I just find these things interesting." *All those millions! Helen and I struggling along on my pitiful public servant's salary. Never did seem right.* He sighed.

"Now, here's a good one for your book, good for a laugh too. This one came from an old hillbilly buddy of mine. It should have been called Dumb and Dumber. The file label reads . . ."

Chapter 13
TROUBLE TWINS

The old rattletrap car left a cloud of oil-choked debris as it bumped its way down Highway 95. Dexter and Delbert Pervis had received an invitation from the sheriff to leave Dog Leg Creek and never return. The only thing that saved them from incarceration was the small town's sympathy for their mother.

From day one the Pervis twins, most people called them the pervert twins, had been trouble. There wasn't a week went by but what poor Ms. Pervis was down at the school or over to the sheriff's getting those boys out of trouble. Each of them always blamed the other but there was no way to tell them apart. They often said they themselves weren't even sure which of them was which half the time.

Actually, there was a way, but only the boys and their mother knew about it. Tired of trying to tell her infant sons apart, she racked her brain for a foolproof way to do it. She was on her way to the outhouse one night, when it came to her. The next day she took the babies to the city and had a star tattooed on Del's butt and a moon tattooed on Dex's.

"We're outta here," said Del, the smarter of the two, having done well up to the third grade.

"Does this mean we can never go back, not never?" Dex had tears in his eyes.

"Shut up, Dex. What's the matter with you? The sheriff said git and that's what we're doin. We're gittin, big time. The money ma gave us won't last long. We gotta find a way to make a score, a big one, and soon."

"Ma said we was to git ourselves jobs and act right," whined Dex.

"Shut up, Dex. What kinda job do you think you could do, you moron? You ain't never goin' to be nothing. Now let me think, I gotta plan." They rode in silence for several minutes before Del said, "Shut up, Dex."

Dex, looking bewildered said, "But I didn't say nothin'."

"I know, but you was about to and it was gonna be stupid."

By the time they reached the Nevada State line, Del had the outline of a plan. Now all he had to do was fine-tune it. "Takin' you to Searchlight. Then I'm headed to Laughlin. From now on, we'll only talk on the phone."

"This'll be a blast. They'll never know there's two of us. Let's go! Why wait?"

"Dex, sometimes it's hard for me to believe you're as dumb as you are. We can't just go in there. We need to plan, like they do in the movies. We need to go over the plan so we get it right. We got to synchronize our watches."

"Sink-ro-nize? What the heck is that? Talk English. Sometimes I think you make words up just to mess with my head."

"Shut up, Dex. It means be sure our watches tell the same time so we're doin' the job at the same time—you doin' your stuff in Searchlight and me doin' my stuff in Laughlin. Now start lookin' for a place to stay. We'll circle the block and I'll let you off. You can walk the rest of the way."

"Aw, how come you always get the car? Why can't I have it this time?"

"Shut up, Dex. Did you ever hear of a bank robber runnin'

away from the bank carrying the money? How stupid can you get?"

Around the next corner they found a Motel 6 and not two blocks away was a Seven Eleven. Everything was working just right. Del dropped Dex off and headed for Laughlin. "I'll call as soon as I get settled. Don't be goin' nowhere," he yelled out the window.

At eight that night, Del called and got Dex's room number. "Okay, here's the plan. At exactly noon tomorrow, you go the Seven Eleven and buy a lot of candy and junk. Get some porno mags and be sure to get noticed. Make a lot of noise. Yell about the price. Knock over a newsstand, or better yet, bump into one of them stands with a bunch of bottles or cans, let 'em roll around on the floor. Be sure they remember you. Got it?"

"I got it, Del. I'll make such a dust up they'll be tryin' to kick my ass out. They'll 'member *me*, that's fer sure."

At exactly twelve o'clock the next day, Del went into the Bank of America in Laughlin, figuring, rightly, that most people would be at lunch. He stepped up to the teller holding a note carefully lettered with an orange crayon. "This here is a stic up give me the mony" The teller started to laugh believing it to be a joke. The security guard coming from lunch saw Del standing there with a gun.

"Stop right where you are!" the guard shouted.

At exactly the same time, Dex walked into the Seven Eleven in Searchlight. First, he rifled through the girly magazines, dropping several and dog-earing others. Next, he threw several in the general direction of the magazine stand. Then, he went to a large refrigerator at the rear of the store. "Where's the choc lit milk? What kind of a cheap joint is this? I want choc lit," he yelled. He picked up ten candy bars, four packs of gum, a bag of potato chips and threw them on the counter.

Mrs. Halpren, the owner, just looked at him. *This little weasel has a real need to be noticed. Too bad he doesn't put all this energy into something useful,* she thought.

"That'll be $11.95."

"Are you nuts!" Dex yelled. "This junk ain't worth no more un five dollar." George and Pearl Bronson entered the store in time to see Del shake his fist at Mrs. Halpren. "Get out of here before I pound your ugly face in!" George yelled. Pearl retreated to the back of the store ready to use the pay phone to call the police.

"That will be $11.95," repeated Mrs. Halpren. "Just pay up and get out or leave the stuff and get out. Either way, you leave or I call the cops."

Dex started to leave, when he got to the door he pulled his pants down and 'mooned' the camera on the wall. "Take that! You old bitch!"

Mrs. Halpren turned to George and Pearl, "That boy was working overtime to be sure we remember him."

"I'll remember him all right. I say we call the cops," George huffed.

"No. Let it go. Just forget him. Pretend you never saw him before if we see him again. It'll serve him right."

Del was so surprised at the sudden turn of events that he started backing up and tripped over his own foot. The gun went off as he fell, shooting the guard and killing him. Del scrambled to his feet and ran. He made it to the car and was gone before the police arrived. "Dex, get out now!" he screamed into the phone. "We got ourselves a little problem. Go to Vegas. Stay at the Motel 8 on Tropicana. Wait for me there."

"Did you get the money? Del, how much did you get?"

"Shut up, Dex! Forget the money! I killed the guard! We'll be okay but you gotta leave now. Walk to the bus station and for God's sake keep your stupid mouth shut. Don't talk to no one, you hear?"

Dex kicked the dirt as he reluctantly made his way to the bus station. *I'm tired of bein' told to shut up. Sick a Del always telling me what to do. Sick a him callin' me stupid.* Dex spotted a big sign over an office that said, "Be All You Can Be. Join

~202~

the Army." There was a picture of a smiling guy in a snappy uniform. "That's it!" he said out loud. "I'll join up and I won't never have to take orders, never again. That jerk Del thinks he's so smart. I'll show him." Pleased with himself, Dex walked into the recruiting station.

It didn't take the police any time at all to have Del in custody. The camera at the bank clearly showed him shooting the guard. Mrs. Halpern, George and Pearl read the news article about the bank robbery. They were surprised to see the face of the young man who had caused such a ruckus in the store just two days before. The article commented on Del's boyish looks and stated that the only distinguishing feature he had was a star tattooed on his left buttock.

"Star?" said Mrs. Halpren, "no way. That was a moon on that kid's butt." George and Pearl agreed. "There's two of 'em sure as I'm standing here. What say we all come down with a case of CRS (can't remember stuff) about now?

"It wasn't me," Del told his public defender, "and I can prove it. I was in Searchlight. Just ask that old woman who runs the place."

The judge questioned George and Pearl who both said they were at the store on the date of the robbery but neither of them remembered seeing the young man. Next, he called Mrs. Halpren to the stand. "Thank you for coming," he said. "Do you remember this man?" He pointed to Del.

The old woman adjusted her bifocals and peered at Del. "No, no, I can't say as I've ever seen him before," she said in a quivery voice.

"Take your time now and be sure," the judge said.

Again the she made a show of squinting and peering at Del. "Nope. Never laid eyes on him before today."

"Blind old fool!" Del hissed. "Make her show you the video from that day. You'll see." He sat back and glared at her.

The public defender asked, "Mrs. Halpren, do you have a

tape taken from the store camera on May fourth?"

She looked embarrassed. "I'm sorry. The camera isn't real. My nephew hooked it up for me to make it look like I had security. Never dreamed I'd really need it, being way out in Searchlight and all."

The trial was just a formality. Del got life with the possibility of parole after twenty years, only because he had not intended to shoot the guard.

As the guards led Del away they passed close to Mrs. Halpren. She smiled, "Nice tattoos. *Always did like outhouse art.*"

The three men shared a laugh over that one. "Wonder how long it took Dex to figure out he had gone from the frying pan straight to the fire." George laughed.

"Sounds like you must have done a stint in the service. Which branch?"

"Yeah, both of us. Army. In fact, that's where we met. We both realized that we were far more interested in writing about war than we were in being in one."

Steve broke in, "Then we turned our attention to local crime. That's when we got the idea for this book *and* with your help we think we have a bestseller on our hands. But don't worry, we'll give you full credit for your part."

The old detective looked at them and smiled, "Now, that would be nice. If you like local tales, here's one for you. It's right out of that TV program *Desperate Housewives.*

Chapter 14
EXTRA $$$

"Myrna, you may have to get a job." Seeing the look on his new wife's face, he quickly added, "Maybe just something part-time. You know, a little something extra to help make ends meet." Money was tight, as usual. Hal griped about every expense. The fact that everyday living was on a never-ending upward spiral didn't help.

"And just when am I supposed to do this 'part-time' work?" She looked at him in disbelief. "Between keeping your house immaculate, yes, I said your house, as you're quick to remind me, caring for the *kids*, need I remind you, *your kids*, *your dogs* and playing hostess to *your* endless poker parties, tell me just when do I have time for another job?"

"Calm down. Don't get your bloomers in a twist. I thought maybe something you could do from home. I see these ads asking for home workers to stuff envelopes, make doll furniture and . . ." He stopped when he felt the temperature in the room drop. "Well, there must be something. Come on, Myrna, we need extra money!"

"I see you've researched the job market, Mr. Thorough. Have you also looked into how legitimate these job prospects are? Have you done your homework, Mr. Know It All? Or are you, as usual, just going off half-cocked, shooting your mouth off without looking into things?"

"Look, Fred and his wife do okay. He makes about the same as I do, but he said Francie brings in a little extra doing alterations at home. Why don't you talk to her, see what she has to say?"

"Francie, it's Myrna. Do you have time to get together for coffee this morning? There's something I'd like to talk to you about. That's great. Come on over when you can. The kids'll be at school. We'll have the house to ourselves for a bit." She put the phone down and started for the laundry room. A mountain of sheets and unwashed school uniforms met her. Hal's kids didn't believe in wearing anything more than once and certainly wouldn't stoop to doing their own wash.

Later that morning, Francie rang the doorbell. "What's up? You sounded stressed."

"That's putting it mildly. Hal wants me to get a part-time job! Just when would I have time and what on earth could I do? He says you take in some sewing. Is that true?"

Francie laughed her raspy smoker's laugh. "Alterations. Yes, that's it. I alter men's anatomy, temporarily." Myrna looked blank. "The truth is I turn a few tricks on the side. It brings in extra cash, Fred never questions me about it and no one is the wiser. Plus no one gets hurt."

"Tricks! You don't mean . . ." Myrna looked horrified.

"Of course, I do. Oh, grow up, Myrna. This is not the dark ages. It's not like I'm hurting anyone."

"But how? I mean where do you get . . . them? How do you get away with it?"

"Easy. Once I caught on that several of the wives we know are doing it, then I just started offering my 'services', for a fee, of course. I spread a few bits of thread and some pins around for effect; Fred's just happy for the money." Francie winked. "Let me explain the ins and outs of doing a cash business." Over the rest of coffee and Danish, Myrna got a crash course on this particular home-based opportunity.

The company awards dinner was a lavish affair, everyone in evening finery. Hal made it clear that Myrna should look especially prosperous in an expensive new gown. At dinner Myrna caught the eye of Brad Turner, Hal's competition for sales, and made a special effort to talk to him. He seemed very interested, especially when Myrna rubbed his leg under the table with her stocking-clad foot.

"Meet me at my house Wednesday at ten. We'll have the house to ourselves," she whispered to him later, out on the balcony as they sipped champagne. "Bring five hundred dollars. I'll make it worth every penny."

On Wednesday, Myrna put fresh sheets on the bed and fresh towels in the bathroom. She had needles, pins, thread, a few shirt buttons along with scissors in a tray placed on a table in the den. First, she was too hot, then too cold. Her palms were sweaty. *I can't go through with it. I can't do this. What if Hal catches me? What if I can't . . . perform?'* she agonized.

Brad Turner was prompt. Afterward, he gladly gave Myrna five hundred dollars. "I'll be back for more of that."

Hal's tires squealed into their driveway. He barely waited for the car to come to a stop before he was out. He rushed into the house shouting, "Myrna, did Brad Turner come here this morning?"

Good grief! He knows! She was sick to her stomach. *How on earth . . .?* Afraid to lie, she stammered, "Yes, yes, he came by about ten."

She was ready with the alteration story when Hal blurted, "Did he give you five hundred dollars?"

Myrna felt faint. "Yes," she whispered. Her knees buckled. She sat down hard on the sofa.

"Good! I've been a nervous wreck. Brad asked to borrow five hundred dollars yesterday. I couldn't let him know how strapped we are for money, so I loaned it to him. He said he'd come by this morning and pay it back. What a relief!"

It took Myrna most of the evening to regain her equilibrium. Once back in control, anger replaced her sick feeling. Rage soon followed. *What a fool I've been! What a naïve, stupid fool!*

The next morning after Hal and the kids were gone, she called Brad Turner's house. When his wife answered Myrna said, in her most professional voice, "This is the Clark County Health Department, Division of Sexually Transmitted Disease. May I speak to Mr. Turner?"

"Mr. Turner's at work." Puzzled, she said, "This is Mrs. Turner, may I help you?"

"We need to inform Mr. Turner that it is imperative that he report to the Health Department immediately. Failure to do so could have dire results."

Hal was out of breath when he rushed into the house after work. He grabbed Myrna in a bear hug and twirled her around. "Get a sitter. We're going out for a special dinner to celebrate!"

"What on earth, Hal. What's going on?"

He fanned several hundred-dollar bills in her face. "This!" he said. "Look at this!"

"Honey, stop. Take a breath. Tell me what you're talking about? Where did you get that money?"

"Okay, okay, but you have to promise never to breathe a word of this to anyone. I mean, cross your heart and hope to die." He was grinning like a fool. "Brad, the jerk, came into my office this morning. He looked like something the cat dragged in. After he closed and locked the door, he told me about this call he got from the health department. Of course, he told his wife it was some big mistake. He begged me to go down and take some tests in his place. He even gave me a thousand dollars to go. Can you believe it?"

"Wow! No. I can't believe it. But what if . . .?"

"Oh, he'll sneak off to a private doctor later. Just to be sure. But, meanwhile let's celebrate! Remember, not a word of this to anyone, ever."

"Oh." She smiled, "you can trust me on that!"

Josh chuckled at the memory of the story. He savored the taste of his cigar and watched as blue smoke rings wafted toward the ceiling. "This next one takes place in Coeur d' Alene and Las Vegas. The Idaho police concentrated on the murder and we handled the phony cards. I call this one . . ."

Chapter 15
CLUB CARD

Pete's Hole In The Wall Casino was anything but. When they first opened the doors, visitors were met with large airy rooms filled with video poker machines and the cries of winners and losers. The sound of a country western band drifted through the casino and into the dining rooms. Felt lined tables for more serious gamblers were positioned in rooms off the main floor for privacy. The latest movies could be seen at the Cinema. There was something for everyone, fine dinning to fast food. Plush rooms were on the upper level and a first class bowling alley occupied the basement. This was a local's place, however; people came from all over the world to see the famous Hole In The Wall. The grounds boasted an RV park, swimming pool and both valet and self-parking. Around the clock transportation to the Strip and nightly shows were offered.

Morgan came there now and then to relax, enjoy a good meal and gamble a little. Although she would tell you playing was no gamble. It was a sure thing. "I put my money in the machine and sure enough, it takes it." Still, occasionally she would walk away with enough to pay for dinner or a new dress. She called her losses the price of entertainment.

"Do you come here a lot? Hi, I'm Rhea Jones."

Morgan looked over at a plump, slightly disheveled, little

lady with bouncing magenta curls pushing the "hold" buttons on a nickel poker machine. "I come now and then after work. Are you from around here?"

"No. My husband and I live in Coeur d' Alene but we come here once a month. My husband loves to gamble." She smiled. "And so do I."

"Morgan Whitefield. Welcome to Las Vegas." Morgan shook the woman's hand and turned back to her machine.

"Oh, there it goes again!" Lights flashed and music rang out, signaling a royal flush. Rhea sat back waiting for the attendant to arrive with her payoff. "Looks like twenty-five hundred. That's why I like the progressive machines."

"Hey, way to go! Good for you!" Morgan said. "Wish my luck would turn. The most I seem to be able to get is three of a kind or the occasional full house. Just not my night, I guess."

Rhea played beside Morgan for several more hands before saying, "Would you like to take a break and get some coffee or a soda? I can't drink, but we could get you whatever you want."

"That sounds good. Actually, I'd like some ice cream. They have a 31 Flavors in the food court. I'm ready for a break since I'm not winning anyway."

"My treat. I'm the big winner tonight. Next time it'll be your turn to get a jackpot."

Morgan laughed. "I wish it worked that way, but unfortunately, all the turns seem to be in Pete's favor."

They ordered their ice cream and found a table. "That's funny." Rhea said. "I never lose. Guess that's why I like to gamble. Every month I take home an extra five or six hundred dollars."

"Really? That's incredible. Do you have a system?"

"No, just blind luck. My husband says the machine knows I'm the boss. He's always saying cute stuff like that to me. In fact, there he is now." Rhea pointed across the room to a tall, beautifully dressed gentleman with styled gray hair talking to a man Morgan recognized as one of the casino managers.

Rhea and her husband seemed an unlikely pair. Morgan figured there was no accounting for what attracted people to one another. "Rhea, I'm tired. I think I'll be going now. Thanks for the ice cream."

"Maybe I'll see you next month. It's been fun talking to you."

The next month Morgan was in Pete's looking for a machine to play when she heard someone call. "Yoo-hoo. Morgan! It's me, Rhea Jones."

"Rhea, how nice to see you again. How are you doing? Any big wins?"

"Not yet, but I haven't really started to play. Let's sit together so we can chat."

"Sure, and you can show me your winning strategy."

"It's not much of a strategy. I just put my card in and start to play."

"With your luck, why don't you play the dollar machines?"

"I thought of that, but Russ said he thought I'd have better luck with nickels. He's so smart. I always do what he says. And look. I always win."

They sat side by side at video poker machines. Rhea started out with three of a kind, followed by a full house. After one or two losses, she hit a four of a kind and then a flush. Morgan had her usual luck, many losses and then a pitiful three of a kind. She held her own for a while with two face cards and two pair; still, she was losing, again. She glanced at Rhea's machine. The cards on the screen were two of diamonds, five of spades, seven of hearts, six of spades and a nine of clubs. A throw-away hand. Rhea held the seven and pushed 'deal'. Hearts jumped up across the screen. A six, eight, nine, ten and the seven she held. Straight flush.

"Rhea, I can't believe it! You won again! I would never have saved any of that hand. What made you save the seven?"

"Oh, I always save hearts. I like them best."

Over the next half hour, Morgan sat back, watching Rhea

win time after time by holding cards with little or no chance to win…but win they did. "Let's take a break. All this winning is making me thirsty." Rhea started down the aisle then turned back. "Mustn't forget my club card. Morgan, will you pull it out for me?"

"You left a hand on the screen. Don't you want to play it out?"

"Oh, okay. Just hold any card; it doesn't matter which one."

Morgan held a pair of threes and, sure enough, two more popped up. She pulled Rhea's card from the slot and waited for the receipt to slide out, giving the amount of money to be collected from the cashier.

Over the next few months, Rhea and Morgan met and enjoyed an evening of conversation, poker and ice cream. Rhea, Morgan learned, came from a well-to-do family and would inherit her father's money upon his death, since her mother had died years ago. Rhea confided that her eighty-year-old father had cancer and was not expected to live much longer. Russ Jones, her tall good-looking husband, was into investments. Rhea wasn't sure just what kind, although she assured Morgan that he was very successful.

When Rhea and Morgan met in November, Rhea looked sad.

"What is it, Rhea? Did something happen?"

"My dad. He's gone. It certainly wasn't unexpected, but still. I guess you're never quite ready are you?"

"I'm so sorry. Is there anything I can do?"

"No." Rhea patted Morgan on the shoulder. "Thanks for asking. Let's play awhile. It'll keep my mind busy. I didn't really want to come this time, only Russ said he had important business and didn't want me to be home alone. Wasn't that sweet?"

"Yes. Russ seems to take good care of you. Let's play over here." Morgan pointed to an area not too far from the escalators." I haven't played here in a while. Maybe my luck will change."

They played for about forty-five minutes before Rhea said, "I think I'll go back to the room. I'm not feeling well. I'm sorry, Morgan. Maybe we can meet tomorrow."

"You go on. I can tell you're not up to this. If I don't see you tomorrow, I'll see you next month." Morgan pulled her club card. "I'll walk you to the escalator. I think I'll call it a night too." Both women turned to get off their stools just as a waitress serving drinks came through the crowded aisle. Rhea's purse strap caught on her chair as she twisted to get out of the way. The contents spilled all over the floor. Morgan bent to help, her, dumping her own purse in the process.

Rhea sighed, "What a mess. Between the two of us, we've managed to completely cover this aisle with debris. Is there such a thing as purse debris?"

Morgan laughed. "There is now. I guess lipsticks, keys, combs and loose change would qualify as purse debris." They quickly gathered their things. "See you next time. Hope you feel better." She hugged her friend.

Morgan was concerned about Rhea and called the casino hotel the next day. Russ Jones picked up the phone. "Mr. Jones, this is Morgan Whitefield. Your wife and I have been playing together over the past few months. I just called to see if Rhea is feeling better."

"Yes. She's mentioned you. Nice of you to call. She is a little better thank you. She just had a little too much to drink. The doctor gave her something to help her sleep it off. I'll have her call you, if there's time before we leave. What's your number?"

She gave him the number. Something about Russ Jones didn't sit right. She didn't know what. He was polite. What was it? Rhea didn't call, so Morgan assumed her friend didn't have time to call before going back home.

Over the next few months, Morgan looked for Rhea. The next time she came to the Hole In The Wall, she spotted Russ Jones talking to the same casino manager she had seen him with some time earlier. She hurried across the casino and caught up with him. "Mr. Jones, I'm Morgan Whitefield, Rhea's friend. Is she here? I haven't seen her in several months."

"Oh yes, Ms. Whitefield, I remember you. No, I'm sorry. Rhea has been taking care of her mother since her father passed away. I'm afraid the old dear isn't doing too well."

"I see. Please tell Rhea I asked about her when you next speak to her."

"Certainly. It'll be my pleasure."

Taking care of Mom my foot. Rhea's mother is dead. Now I know there's something up with this guy. And then it hit her. *He told me she had too much to drink! Rhea didn't drink.* Morgan went home and got on the Internet. She looked up the phone book for Coeur d'Alene, Idaho. *Jones, Jones, Jones; good grief there must be a million of them. Here…R. Jones.* She called the number, only it turned out to be Ruth Jones who didn't know Russ or Rhea. The next call she placed was to the police in Coeur d'Alene. "Hello, this is Morgan Whitefield. I'd like to request, a well-body check on Mrs. Rhea Jones. Her husband is Russ Jones."

There was a moment of silence before a voice said, "Ms. Whitefield, this is Detective Barnes. What is your relationship to Rhea Jones?"

"I'm just a friend. I haven't heard from Rhea for several months and I'm concerned."

"Do you know her husband?"

"Not really. I introduced myself to him the other night at Pete's Hole In The Wall Casino here in Vegas. He told me his wife was taking care of her mother, only Rhea told me her mother passed away years ago. I know her father just died . . . and . . . I'm worried."

"We're worried, too, Ms. Whitefield. If you see Russ Jones again, stay away. Until we find Rhea, we're investigating. Frankly, we're not sure what to think at this point."

Over the next few months, Morgan monitored the Coeur d' Alene newspaper over the Internet for any news of Russ or

Rhea Jones. Finally, in October, an article appeared detailing the arrest of prominent investment counselor Russ Jones for the suspicious disappearance of his wife. Jones had given conflicting accounts as to the whereabouts of his wife, first saying she was at her mother's, later he said she was visiting her sister. Then he switched his story completely, saying that he and Rhea were having problems and Rhea had left for an undisclosed destination to think things through.

The voice on the phone said, "Ms. Whitefield, this is Detective Barnes. We spoke several weeks ago when you called about Rhea Jones."

"Yes. Of course, I remember you. I read the article in the newspaper. Do you believe something has happened to Rhea?"

"In fact, we do. That's why I called. As far as we can tell, you seem to be the last person to have spoken to Mrs. Jones. Would you mind going over everything you can remember about that night."

"I'm happy to, there isn't much to tell."

Morgan related what she could remember of the evening with Rhea. She told the detective about calling her the next day. "I didn't think too much of it at the time; later, I remembered her husband telling me she wasn't feeling well because she'd had too much to drink. Rhea told me she couldn't drink. It wasn't an issue since we usually had ice cream and tea."

"Was there anything else that you remember? Anything at all?"

"No. Not unless you count Rhea's incredible luck. She told me she always went home with an extra five or six hundred dollars every month."

"That *is* lucky. Thanks for your time."

Before he could hang up Morgan said, "Detective I have the feeling there's more."

He was quiet for a moment, then he answered. "There is, however, I can't discuss it right now. Thanks again for your help."

It was late November when Morgan saw an article in the *Las Vegas Review Journal* reporting the murder of Rhea Jones from Coeur d'Alene. She went to the Web and got the full story.

"Fishermen found Rhea Jones, wife of prominent investor Russ Jones, yesterday. She had been murdered. Donald Levin, real estate developer and father of Rhea Jones, recently died, leaving Ms. Jones an estate of several million dollars. Jones is suspected of killing his wife to gain control of her fortune.

"Russ Jones has been under investigation for some time for his connection to Las Vegas underworld crime. Jones is suspected of being a participant in a card-manipulating scheme. The club cards held by many steady gamblers have allegedly been programmed, magnetically, to change the numbers and suits of the cards on video poker machines, producing wins. The gamblers then shared winnings with Russ and his partners. Jones would invest the winnings to launder the money. Police are still trying to trace all the players. There is no way of knowing exactly how many altered cards are out there."

That explains all the luck Rhea had. Poor thing, she didn't even suspect. By keeping her on the nickel machines she was low profile and wouldn't cause much of a stir. Russ just gave her a card to keep her occupied while he conducted business with his buddies. He was making plenty of money, he didn't have to kill her. What a slime.

Eventually, Russ Jones was convicted of murdering his wife. He was sentenced to life without the possibility of parole. The fortune he killed for went to several charities.

It was after Christmas before Morgan ventured back to Pete's Hole In The Wall. She wore her black silk pantsuit and took the purse she carried the last time she saw Rhea. She chose a machine near the aisle believing that aisle machines were more apt to win. According to casino lore, casinos programmed them to win to attract other players passing by. She slipped her club card into place and began to play. Flags played across the front of her machine; she had a four of a kind. Two more plays; then a full house, followed by a straight flush, two losses, then a royal. Lights flashed and a merry tune played. Attendants arrived to make the pay off. Morgan passed them each a twenty-dollar tip. The change girl smiled as she cleared the machine. "Thank you, Ms. Jones. Good luck."

Old Josh looked at the bottom of his glass. "There was more than one of us wished we could find one of those special cards," he said as Steve gave him a refill. "Yeah. That would have made my day," he sighed wistfully. He stopped for a sip, puffed his cigar a few times and tried for a smoke ring before saying, "Did you read about the boat race on the lake? This one was hard to investigate because a lot of the evidence was under water . . ."

Chapter 16
PLAN B

"Ready?" Brock asked. He stuffed the bag of coins into Colby's life jacket. They put the jacket back under the seat to be sure no one tampered with it.

"Yeah, all set," Colby said "That should do it."

"Let's go then." Brock turned to Kojo. "I'm freezing my butt off in here."

Colby had one last comment. "Stay out of trouble. What would we do if you got caught breaking parole?"

"Well, then we'd go to Plan B. I always have a Plan B," Brock smirked.

The night before, Kojo used the master key to let himself into the area where the ancient coins were on display. As night watchman at the museum, he was responsible for checking each display once an hour to make sure all was well. He carefully picked up a coin and replaced it with one that looked just like it. He had been doing this for over a month now. With fake coins supplied by Vern Brock, Kojo hoped to get enough money to fulfill his dream.

The huge warehouse Colby Burns used to build his boat, Road Runner, had no windows. This was to insure secrecy during the building phase. Rival boat racers would be keen to learn of his design. The building was freezing cold. Another one of the sponsors' shortcuts, Colby thought bitterly.

Colby patterned his boat after the *Discovery II*, built by Lee Taylor in 1980. Until a tragic accident in 1978, Taylor held the over-water speed championship. After two years in the hospital he was making a come-back. On its maiden run, *Discovery II* broke apart halfway across Lake Tahoe, sinking to the bottom of the second deepest lake in the United States, taking Lee Taylor with it.

Kojo and Brock left Colby, they didn't want anyone to see them together. The party for the vendors was due to start in a little over an hour. "Why would Colby give up his chance at a world record to help steal the coins?" Kojo asked.

"Money. His share is about five million after the dealer takes his cut. Five mil will go a long way in some Third World country. Beside, there's no guarantee he'll win. And even if he does, he'll have to compete year after year to hold the title. Hard work. Every year, someone is out to take the title away. That means newer and better boats, lots of money, lots of work. Colby's getting up there. He wants to retire in style. I think he also wants to stick it to the press for calling him a copycat who couldn't come up with a design of his own, a loser had to steal from Lee Taylor."

Colby ran a hand through his thinning hair, popped another antacid tablet, and opened wide the doors as the first of his guests arrived. "Come in, come in, welcome. Take a look at what your money paid for." He greeted each sponsor by name, hugging many of the wives and girlfriends. "Help yourselves to food; there's an open bar, plenty to drink." As the evening progressed, over forty sponsors, their spouses and friends came to inspect *Road Runner*. It was painted jet black and looked more like a bullet than a boat. The driver had to lie down, then the canopy was pulled over him. The effect was of a long black bug with one huge bubble eye. *Road Runner's* logo was painted in silver on both sides of the hull.

"She's beautiful, Colby. Looks like a winner," said a portly man, coming up to him, holding a glass of champagne.

"You bet she's a winner. Wait till you see this baby skim over the water. I think we'll only get our feet wet when we land," he laughed. "Be ready to collect the prize money for me. I'll be too busy kissing babes to bother with that."

"Yeah, right. And pigs fly." He left as a new group of well-wishers approached.

"Ready to take the title?" asked the wife of his biggest sponsor.

"Angie, you have no idea how ready I am. This is just a practice run, but it'll show all of you what you paid for." He leered at her

"Never mind that." She brushed past him. "I think my husband's calling me." She sounded offended, then turned to wink at him.

The party lasted until well after midnight. Colby was tired, still, he was too wired to sleep. *Three days from now, I'll be on a sunny beach somewhere in the Greek Isles, with more money than I ever dreamed of. No more beating my brains out trying to squeeze cash from sponsors. The cheap bastards! They want their names on the program, they want the glory, then they go cheap when it comes to materials. Well, this will show them. I can't wait until the investigation shows inferior material used for the hull.*

When they drag it up for examination, they'll find the seam where I switched low-grade bolts for the ones the specs called for. They'd all be shocked if they knew how easy it was to make the switch. They'll say, "No wonder the thing blew apart under pressure." The press will have a field day. Couldn't happen to a more deserving bunch. But five million: that's my Plan B.

He put his hand to his chest as pain made his eyes water. Just stress, he thought. I*t'll go away as soon as the trial run is over. The doc's wrong. It isn't serious. Stress, plain stress. And no wonder, with all the years I've been working to beat the record. I'm* *so tired.*

"Did you give notice?" Brock asked Kojo. "Or are you just going to disappear?"

"I gave notice two weeks ago. I told them it was necessary for me to go home for a short visit. I didn't want anyone at the museum thinking this was a last-minute decision."

"What do you care? The coins will bring enough money so you can go wherever you want. Think you'll go back home?" Kojo didn't answer. He didn't trust Brock and preferred to keep his personal plans to himself. "Ah, keeping secrets are we?" Brock commented. "Well go ahead. I don't mind telling you, when I get my share, I'm off to Mexico. I've got a sweet little chickadee down there and . . ."

"I'm going to check the equipment." Kojo could only stand Brock's babbling for so long.

"Yeah, yeah. Go check. Be sure those oxygen tanks are full. I don't want anyone running out of air down there." He chuckled in that nasty way he had.

The day of the trial run dawned clear and crisp, flags snapping smartly in the brisk wind. Reporters vied for position as they threw questions at Colby.

"How does it feel to be the challenger?"

"How fast do you think *Road Runner* will go?"

"Do you think patterning your boat after Lee Taylor's jinxed *Discovery II* was a good idea?"

"*Road Runner* is an improvement on Taylor's design. We've built in a lot of new safeguards. Plus, remember this is Lake Superior, not Tahoe." Colby turned to look toward the Canadian shore. He knew another group of reporters and supporters were waiting on that side of the lake. *Too bad*, he thought.

Colby answered questions until it was time to start the clock. An assistant helped him into his lifejacket. He slid into position. He held his breath, counting five, four, three, two, one! The flag came down. Road Runner roared away, causing a rooster tail of water to drench those standing on the dock. His fans waved wildly as he neared the middle of the lake. People with stopwatches were yelling, "He's doing it! He's doing it! He's breaking the record!" Cameras followed his streak across the lake. Reporters followed him in the news helicopter, feeding live footage to the newsroom, where it was transmitted to televisions across the world. If this run bested the time from his last trial run, he would have a good shot at the world over-water championship title.

The crack sounded like thunder. The silence that followed was as deep as death itself. People stood in stunned silence as *Road Runner* like its predecessor, *Discovery II*, sank out of sight.

Under freezing cold water, Brock waited in a submersible. As soon as the boat went under, Colby freed himself and swam toward the sub. As planned, an oxygen mask and tank were strapped to the outside of the little vessel. Colby quickly slipped the breathing tube into his mouth and gave the thumbs-up sign. Brock steered the submersible away from the wreckage, resurfacing miles away, in a covered boathouse on the Canadian side of the lake.

"We did it! I can't believe we really pulled it off!" Colby was blue from the cold, elated and having a hard time standing still.

"Turn around. I'll help you off with the vest." Colby dutifully turned his back to Brock, who untied the vest with twenty million in gold coins stuffed inside. "Sorry, pal." Brock quietly slipped a wire around Colby's neck. When he was sure Colby was dead, he weighted the body and took it back to the middle of the lake. He knew it would be days, perhaps weeks, before the body was found. Then, presumably it would be presumed that Colby had succumbed in the accident. Brock counted on water and fish to help cover the crime.

Kojo was waiting with the airline tickets. "We should go now. The plane leaves for Amsterdam in three hours." He looked around. "Where's Colby?"

"He didn't make it. He was killed in the crash." He held the bag of coins up for Kojo to see.

"How'd you get the coins then?"

"He lived long enough to tie them to the submersible."

Kojo just stared at him. "Bull."

"Hey, look at it this way, now the split is two ways. More for us."

"Brock, you're a piece of work."

Brock laughed. "Let's just say, this is Plan B."

Hotel Condor in Amsterdam overlooked a beautiful park. Two men, one with a nondescript leather briefcase made their way to an address in a less than upscale part of town.

Antiquities dealer, Marvin Gold examined the coins. "Beautiful, beautiful. But unfortunately, not authentic. Whoever did this work was a master craftsman. These coins are a work of art."

"What! You're lying! You old fool, do you think you can cheat us?" Brock had his hands around the old man's throat.

"Don't be stupid!" Kojo pulled him away. "Let him go! The last thing we need is a murder. Don't you know the authorities would be on us in a heartbeat?" He turned to the dealer, who was massaging his neck. "You're saying these coins are worthless?"

"No, no. That's not what I'm saying. They're excellent replicas. Ancient coins are easier to fake because they were all struck by hand, so they have variations. These, these . . ." he lined the coins up in a row, "are all identical. See here." He began to point out the sameness of the coins. "They're definitely worth something. Just not the twenty million you expected."

"How much, then?" growled Brock.

"If I sell them to collectors one at a time, you can expect

about one million. Give or take."

Brock paced the hotel room. "One lousy million! This blows all my plans."

"Maybe not. Let's think this through for a minute."

"What? You have something in mind?"

Kojo sat on the edge of the table and poured Brock a drink. He lifted his own orange soda and took a sip. "Yeah. Think about this. What if we go back? I'm sure the museum will be happy to see me again. I'll take more coins. Your man can get us more fakes. I'll exchange them for the 'real' thing, the same as last time. I'm sure he'll do it for a cut of the action. We'll have to devise a new plan for getting them out of the country."

"Sounds doable. But this time, be sure the ones you steal are real. I'd hate to go to prison for stealing fakes." Kojo knew that Brock couldn't afford to be arrested. The three strikes law would put him away, probably for life.

"The ones I steal are already fake, just quality fakes. We'll be careful. You won't be going to prison," Kojo assured him.

"Easy for you to say. Your record's clean. You'd just go back to that mud hole you're from with a 'do not return' sticker on your butt." Brock was looking a little green. "I don't feel good. Must be something I ate. Airline food never did agree with me. I'm gonna crash for a while." With that he keeled over on his back, eyes wide open.

Kojo leaned over him. "This was my Plan B. The dealer will give me half a million cash. The rest is his profit. Half a million dollars is a fortune in my country." *In my country,* he thought, *I will be like a king. My family will no longer live in poverty. My village will have a school and fresh clean water. I will build a clinic and hire a doctor. My mother will never scrub another floor. My sister will marry well and my brothers will be prosperous businessmen.* He smiled as he picked up his airline ticket and headed out the door.

Bart Manning, the museum director, looked over the coins, statues, goblets and various other objects on loan from Lincoln Bradshaw. "Fred," he said to his assistant, "Please get Mr. Bradshaw on the phone. I'm dreading telling him that his entire collection is fake. All of the pieces are replicas."

"Bart, your assistant sounded so grim." Bradshaw said on the phone. "What's wrong?"

"Mr. Bradshaw, you have no idea how I hate to tell you this, but there's just no easy way. Your collection has been examined by two of the museum's top people, and I'm afraid the entire collection has been replicated. Excellent replicas, mind you, but fake just the same. Naturally, you're free to call in your own experts. In fact, I'd welcome it."

He was stunned by Bradshaw's reaction. Expecting the worst, he was shocked to hear Bradshaw laughing. "Replicas! Well, I'll be! There's no fool like an old fool, is there? Serves me right for thinking I got such a good deal. Tell you the truth, I thought the stuff was stolen."

Trying to hide his astonishment at not being reamed out, Manning said, "What do you want to do?"

"Fake or not, the collection is still worth a lot. What do you suggest?" Bradshaw responded.

"Let the museum display it. We'll advertise it as the Bradshaw collection of fine replications. We can even show how each piece is the same or how it differs from the real thing. We'll act as though this was our intention all along. That way we all save face."

"Go for it." He could hear Bradshaw laughing as he hung up the phone.

"Wow!" said Fred. "That was some save. Does this sort of thing happen often?"

"Not often, fortunately," said Manning, whose color was becoming more normal. "But I always like to have a Plan B."

Cummings leaned back in his chair, puffing his cigar. "These come from the Dominican Republic, you know. Used to be if you wanted a good cigar you went for Cubans or Havanas; that's all been outlawed now. Rotten shame, too." He made himself comfortable before going on with his next story.

"You know, over the years you hear just about everything there is to hear about human behavior. Personally, I've tried to remember some of the lighter side of things, whenever possible. Here's one that gave everyone, including the captain, reason to do a little head scratching, and end up laughing at themselves. This story really isn't from too long ago; in fact, it's fairly recent. For obvious reasons, the police never revealed all the details . . ."

Chapter 17
PRESTO CHANGE-O

The areas around Green Valley Parkway and High View were generally not considered high crime sections. Lately, though, a series of robberies of the higher end homes had changed that perception. Several residents returned home to find valuable pictures and statues missing.

Police went from door to door, asking if anyone noticed strangers or something off-kilter in their quiet neighborhood. Detectives Ben York and Amanda Goode knocked on the door of Richard McIntyre. "Sir, sorry to disturb you. I'm sure you've heard about the robberies in the area."

"Yes, of course. It's been in all the papers. How may I help?"

"May we come in for a minute? We're just asking routine questions to see if anyone has any information. Sometimes people see or know things they don't think is important; later it adds a piece to the puzzle."

"Please, come in. I can't think of what I might know, but I'd like to help if I can. Why all the sudden police activity? These burglaries have been going on for some time now."

"True, but unfortunately, a man was killed last night during the course of a robbery over on Green Valley Parkway, just a few blocks from here. This changes the investigation from burglary to homicide."

"My God. How awful!" Richard led the detectives to the living room. They noted the lovely furniture all in muted tones of beige and dark brown. The drapes were drawn, a soft light from a floor lamp gave the room warmth. "Sorry about the drapes. I'm photosensitive and can't be in the sunlight. Even my lamps have special bulbs."

"What kind of work do you do?" Detective York opened his notebook.

"I'm a freelance journalist. I work from home. I mostly do pieces on exotic vacation spots." He noted the look of surprise on the detectives' faces. "No, no, I don't travel." He smiled, "Most of my information I get from local chambers of commerce, *National Geographic*, and occasionally I hire photographers to take special pictures. No, I really am a homebody."

"Have you, or your wife seen or heard anything unusual in the past few days?"

"I'm not married. My brother and I live here together. I haven't heard anything and if Robert has, he hasn't mentioned it."

"Where is your brother now? We'd like to ask him these same questions."

"He went into work early today. He's a night auditor at the Golden Eagle Casino over on Boulder Highway. I'll have him come to the station tomorrow, if you like."

"Thank you, that would help. We're just gathering all the statements we can. Never know when a lead will pop up."

The detectives finished their questions and went on their way. It was after eight and the sun was down. Richard took the trash out front for a morning pick-up. "Richard, I'm glad I caught you." Mrs. Tobin called across the fence. "The neighbors are pretty upset by all the goings on. We want to start a neighborhood watch program. Charlie has volunteered to coordinate and we need people to help out."

"That's a good idea, Mrs. Tobin. Tell your husband I can

take the ten to midnight slot or any after dark duty. You know, with my problem, that works out just right for me."

"What about Robert? Would he be willing to take a shift?"

"Well, you know Robert. He's not willing to do much of anything. But, I'll ask." Richard and Mrs. Tobin lingered to chat for a few more minutes before going in.

Robert came to the station the next day and spoke to the detectives. They could see the resemblance between the brothers. Where Richard was about 5'8" and slim with sandy brown hair and blue eyes, Robert was around 5'11" with dark brown hair and brown eyes. They had the same build and facial features. Their voices were very much the same. The big difference was their personalities. Richard was open, friendly and given to smiling. Robert was somber, gruff, acted like this was a great imposition on his time. *Thoroughly unlikable*, thought York. "Piece of work," pronounced Amanda Goode.

Three days later, another robbery took place, this one on Warm Springs Avenue. Fortunately or unfortunately, depending on your view, the homeowner's dog took exception to the thief, chasing him out a second story window where he jumped, leaving very clear footprints in the soft earth. It didn't take long for the prints to be identified as size ten Reebok running shoes. Amanda commented, "Seems he's still out there. I would have bet he'd back off, knowing we've intensified the search."

"Some guys get off, living close to the edge." Detective York remembered Robert

McIntyre wearing Reeboks when he came to the station. Not much of a lead. Everyone wears running shoes.

That Saturday evening Richard lowered the window of his car as he was pulling out of the driveway. "Hi, Mrs. Tobin. Nice evening, huh?"

"Sure is. Enjoy it while you can, they say we're in for a hot summer."

Richard laughed. "I didn't know we had any other kind. Well, take care. I'm off to pick up Reba. We're having dinner, then going out to visit Mom."

Mrs. Tobin smiled. *What a nice young man. He looks after his sister and his mother. It must be hard on the family with Mrs. McIntyre in the nursing home with Alzheimer's. Too bad Robert's such a butt. He lets Richard do all the work. I guess the mother is too far-gone to notice. Still, if it were my mother, I'd visit.*

Detectives York and Goode were discussing the case. A map of the area hung on the wall with flags showing the homes that had been robbed and the house where the man was killed. All of them were in a six-block circle surrounding the street where Richard and Robert McIntyre lived. Amanda said, "Interesting. Look at the pattern. Everywhere but on the street where the McIntyre boys live. Also note, we've never had a clue as to how this guy gets to the neighborhood. What? Walk? Ride? Carrier pigeon? How about we go have another talk with the neighbors?"

"Richard is a saint. He sees to his family. His mother is ill, you know. They're quiet and mind their own business." Mrs. Tobin said in a way that let detectives know she thought they should do the same.

Detective Goode asked, "What about the sister. Where does she live?"

"Somewhere over by the Flamingo Library. She reads the books the library is considering and recommends whether or not to buy. Richard usually takes her to dinner every week. He says she is very shy and doesn't go out much. He's such a nice boy."

"What about Robert?"

"Well...He's not so friendly. I know he works nights, that's about all."

"Let's pay *the boys* another visit."

The detectives walked next door and rang the bell. "Hi, Mr. McIntyre. We're just doing a routine follow up. May we come in?"

"Sure, can I get you a soft drink, lemonade, glass of water?"

"No, thanks. Is your brother home? We'd like to speak to him also."

"No, in fact, he's out of town. Left yesterday on vacation."

"That a fact. Where'd he go?"

"Truth is, I don't know. Robert's the quiet type. Seldom tells me anything. It's just the way he's always been."

"How about your sister? Would he tell her where he's going?"

"I doubt it, you can call and ask." Amanda wrote down the number.

"Her name is Reba. She works from eight to three; she's usually home after that."

On the way back to the station Amanda asked her partner, "Notice anything?"

"You mean like a shadow on the wall where a picture used to be?"

"Yeah. Exactly like that."

Reba's answering machine picked up when Detective Goode called. "This is Reba. I can't come to the phone right now, leave a message. I'll call back." Amanda left her message, just asking if Reba knew the whereabouts of Robert.

At four-thirty, Reba called the station and asked for Amanda Goode. "Detective Goode here."

"Detective, this is Reba McIntyre, Robert's sister. You called to ask if I knew where he is."

"Yes. Richard told us he went on vacation he doesn't have any idea where. Did Robert say anything to you about going away?"

"No, only that's just like Robert; he's always been very closed up. He seldom shares his thoughts or plans with the rest of the family."

"What about your mother. Would he tell her?"

Reba's voice held a slight tremor. Goode thought she was about to cry. "I'm sorry. Mom's pretty far-gone with Alzheimer's. She doesn't even recognize Richard and me when we visit. Robert won't go anymore, says it a waste of time. He always was a little cold."

"I'm sorry to bother you, Ms. McIntyre. If you do think of anything or if Robert calls, please let us know." Dead end. The detectives wondered aloud how they could get a search warrant for Robert's room. "All we really have is the imprint of a pair of sneakers, size ten. You know, Ben, Richard has been pretty friendly and open through all this. What would you think about just asking him if we could look in Robert's room?"

"Worth a try... why not?"

"Hi, Detectives. York and Goode. Right?"

The two stood on the front porch. They waited until the sun went down in deference to Richards's photosensitivity. "Hello, Mr. McIntyre. We're here asking a favor. We have one clue, a set of prints from a pair of size ten Reeboks. I noticed that your brother was wearing Reeboks when he came to the station the other day. Would you mind if we took a look at his room? We just want to eliminate him as a suspect."

"Well, I guess it would be okay. Robert's real fussy about his stuff though, so please be careful." He led the way upstairs to Robert's room.

Amanda hung back while her partner looked over Robert's room. "This is a beautiful home, Mr. McIntyre. You have so many lovely things."

"Thank you. Robert's the decorator. These," he waved his hand to take in the statues and painting, "are reproductions, with the exception of a few old pieces Mom had. Robert collects art like crazy. Every time I come home he has a new piece. Now and then he gets tired of something and sells it, but he usually replaces it in a matter of days." Amanda noticed the blank spot on the wall was now covered with a new picture.

"Thanks." Detective York said. "We really appreciate your cooperation."

"Happy to help. Find anything?"

"These." He held up a pair of running shoes. With your permission we'll take them back and have our lab tech match them to the prints we have, just to eliminate Robert." He said with what he hoped was a friendly tone of voice. "By the way you haven't heard from your brother have you?"

"Not a word. That is so like him. I'm sure the shoes won't match. Robert's a strange duck in many ways, but a thief? No way!"

On the way back to the station house Ben asked, "Well, what's your take?"

"I'm not sure and I'm no art expert, but I'd be willing to bet some of those paintings are the real thing. I think Robert is up to his neck in this and poor trusting Richard is clueless."

"Let's drive out to the nursing home and have a talk with Mrs. McIntyre. Maybe Robert told her where he was going."

"What good would that do? She doesn't know her own children or her own name. If he did tell her, she wouldn't remember. Alzheimer's victims have a hard time with the here and now. She might remember something from twenty years ago and nothing from yesterday. According to the sister; the poor old thing is completely gone."

"I know it's a long shot. But even Alzheimer patients have lucid moments now and then, good days and bad days. Don't they?"

"I think it has to do with what stage they're in. From what Reba said, it sounds like her mother is in the last stages."

York called the station to ask if they had a positive I.D. on the Reeboks. "Looks like we have a match. Now let's find him."

The reception area at Bedford Manor was quiet and spacious. The receptionist was tall and slim, she wore her dark hair in a French twist. Her beige dress and black pumps seemed to make her blend into the wallpaper. The nameplate on the black lacquered desk said Madeline Dupree. She looked up and smiled when Detective York handed her a card and showed her his badge.

"This is my partner, Amanda Goode. We'd like to see Mrs. McIntyre."

"Let me ring for the director. She can take you to her." Ms. Dupree spoke into the intercom and turned to the detectives. "Mrs. Blackstone will be right out. Please have a seat."

Mrs. Blackstone bustled in, a grandmotherly figure, all smiles and welcome. "How may I help you?"

"We'd like to speak to Mrs. McIntyre, if we may. It concerns one of her sons, Robert. He's missing and we're trying every approach we know to find him. So far we haven't been able to get a clue as to where he might have gone. I understand that she has Alzheimer's and may not be able to tell us much. If she could remember anything at all, it might help."

Mrs. Blackstone looked blank, then frowned. "I don't know what gave you *that* idea. Beth McIntyre is frail but she's as sharp as they come." They had arrived at the door to a private suite. "Let me go ahead and prepare her for your visit. Please don't stay long; it's too tiring for her."

Ben York and Amanda Goode were speechless. They stood in silence, each with their own thoughts until Mrs. Blackstone opened the door and waved them in. "Beth, this is Detective York and Detective Goode. They'd like to ask you some questions."

Beth McIntyre, a woman in her late seventies, sat in a comfortable chair with her walker at one side. White hair formed a cap of ringlets around her head, setting off bright blue eyes. She was dressed in dress of pale blue silk. She wore navy blue short-heeled pumps and her nails were buffed and shining from a coat of clear polish. "Please, come in. Sit down. I can have some tea brought in. What is this all about? I must admit we don't get much excitement around here, so having the police show up will give us something to talk about for days to come," she chuckled.

It would be hard not to like this gracious, charming lady. Amanda could easily see the resemblance to Richard. "Mrs. McIntyre, we're here to ask about your son Robert. We need to ask him some questions concerning an on-going investigation. According to Richard and your daughter, Reba, he's gone on vacation and no one seems to know where he is. Do you have any idea?"

The look of surprise rivaled that of Mrs. Blackstone's few minutes earlier. "Detectives, you are mistaken. You must have the wrong person. I have only one child. His name is Richard."

"Son-of-a-b. . . !" Ben hit his head with his hand. "That son of a gun. He took us in like a couple a rookies." Ben smacked his hand on the steering wheel The ride back into town was much faster than the ride out to the rest home. When they explained it to the Captain he asked, "How did he pull it off?"

"Simple, now that we know the truth. No one ever saw them together. A dark wig, heel lifts, contacts and presto change-o, Richard became Robert. We never saw Reba, only talked to her on the phone. A call to the library told us there was no one by the name of Reba working there. The deal about being sun-sensitive covered him staying in during the day and the Robert disguise went to work at night. Jeeze, I feel like such a schmuck!"

The Captain laughed, "Pick him up. In fact, pick all three of him up."

The old detective was obviously enjoying the recap of these old cases. He took his time with a few puffs and drained his glass. "No matter what you read about crime statistics, the truth is that the police are fooled as often as they catch someone. Here's one that had us fooled for a while. Shouldn't have. We just weren't looking in the right places . . ."

Chapter 18
THE FIRE BRIGADE

The shrill sound made Gale groan and roll over. Tim sat up and grabbed the phone. "What's up?"

"The old Coley barn out on Route Twelve between…"

"Yeah, I know the place. Everyone on the way?"

"You bet. Be right there."

Tim hung up and jumped into his clothes. As he opened the doors to the big barn that doubled as a fire station, the first of the volunteers drove into the yard. Within minutes, ten men dressed in fire-fighting gear were racing through the night toward the latest fire.

"Lucky it's empty," said John Vogel, "hasn't been used in years."

"Surprised it didn't go up before now. Must be dry as a bone," responded Jeff Thompson. The men stood around looking, as the last of the building collapsed into a smoldering heap. They made sure there were no embers left to rekindle and possibly blow over to neighboring farms before they packed up and left.

"I swear, I think you love that old engine more than you do me," Gale said, when she brought Tim's lunch out to him. Tim industriously polished every bit of chrome on Engine

Ninety-nine.

"Not more," Tim said with a thoughtful look, "but maybe just as much."

Gale gave him a playful swat on the arm. "Isn't it strange how many fires we've had lately? We went for ages without one and now suddenly, we've had… what? Three or four this month."

"Not so strange. It's been very dry. Those old places are like tinder, just waiting for a lightning strike or a bum to forget his cigarette." Tim said, taking a last bite of his sandwich.

"I suppose. But all the buildings have been abandoned. Not one used for years. Just seems odd, that's all," she mused.

Another person who thought it strange was Ralph Wilson of the *Gardendale Clarion*. Ralph had been a crack investigative reporter before he retired, got bored and then started the newspaper.

Ralph called Tim, "How about if the two of us get together and discuss these fires."

"Sure, come on over. I'm just finishing my clean up."

"I just need some details for my article," said Ralph. "What do you suppose is causing all the fires lately?"

"Unusually dry for this time of year. Gale asked me the same thing this morning. Those old buildings were an eyesore anyway, so it's no great loss, I guess."

"Seems strange, that's all. Just when the city council's about to vote to do away with the volunteer fire department, we have more fires than ever."

"The council's a bunch of old fools," Tim said. "How can we rely on fire departments from cities more than fifteen miles away? No way could they get here in time if we ever had a real problem." It had taken Tim and several of his neighbors months of arguing with the council before they had agreed to buy old Engine Ninety-nine, in the first place. The engine was being retired from a big city fire department and was just right for the needs of a small community. The next hurdle, to get a stipend approved for upkeep. Tim promised to keep the engine in his barn and take care of it; all he asked were some funds for minor repairs. Tim shook his head at the memory. He smiled, *small town politics.*

A week went by before the next fire. "Why are fires always in the middle of the night?" groaned Gale.

"Fires are like babies, they come when they darn well please."

This time the fire started closer to town. The men pulled up in old Ninety-nine and immediately began hosing down Tony's Garage and Fix-It Shop. The shop burned brightly. Containing it was difficult. As soon as one area came under control, another place started to burn. The fire had a mind of its own. The men worked through the night. The shop was a total loss but they were able to save the house next to it, where Tony and Emma lived. *I hope they have plenty of insurance,* thought Ralph. He had started trailing the firemen whenever he heard the warning bells.

The *Clarion* carried pictures of the fire the next morning. Tim and his band of volunteers were shown, soot covered and working to save the structure. Tony and Emma were off to one side dressed in their nightclothes, holding on to each other. "Something's not right. This doesn't add up." Ralph muttered to himself. He began researching articles about the other fires, looking for anything that would explain the rash of recent outbreaks. He found information he already knew. Tim was chief and the only paid member of the fire-team. He had talked the council into the purchase of the old engine several years ago when he moved to Gardendale.

The next fire broke out in an abandoned warehouse by the river on Water Street. The fire brigade worked as fast as the flames allowed and had it under control in record time. They were checking for pockets of embers that could rekindle when John Potter screamed, "Hey, there's a body here! Help me! He's under this fallen beam. I can't lift it! Oh, God, it's Matt Brody, the night watchman."

Ralph began an investigation along with the police. Mrs.

Brody, holding back tears, told him, "Matt's usual night off is Monday. He was putting in overtime to earn extra money to put a new motor on the boat. Matt and young Matt have been planning this trip since last summer. The old motor kept breaking down. They had to row home from the middle of the lake more than once. It was to be a surprise." She broke down and cried.

Tim sat on the porch with his head in his hands. Ralph drove into the yard, got out and walked over to where he was sitting. Tim looked up. "It's over, Tim. It's a miracle no one was hurt before now."

"How'd you know? No one should have gotten hurt."

"I got suspicious. The fires were just too convenient. You're the only one who knows how to set fires so they would ignite at a certain time. You're the only one with that kind of background and training. And frankly, you're the only one with a motive."

"The council, that bunch of old fools, planned to do away with the job of Fire Chief. They had to be stopped. This was the only way. Besides, I couldn't bear not being chief any more. Call it job security."

Just then the police drove into the yard. "May I have a quiet word with my wife before we go?"

Jeff Thompson, the deputy and one of the fire brigade volunteers nodded. "Don't be too long."

Tim went into the house. Gale stepped into his arms. "Why'd you do it? We didn't need the money."

"I know. I just couldn't bear having them take away your toy. You loved being Chief. And I loved being the Chief's wife."

"Okay one more, then this old man is off to bed. This is a south of the border story. Happened while I was still working in San Diego." He took a sip and ran his tongue over his lips. "Good stuff." George and Steve settled back to listen.

Chapter 19
VIVA MEXICO

"Clay, it's me, Allison Scott. Please, you've got to help us!" She burst into wracking sobs.

"Allie, what's the matter? Calm down; I can't understand a word you're saying." Clay Claymore had been the Scott family attorney for more than twenty years. Family crises were not new, however, for Allison to call at night, he knew the matter was serious. "Allie, what's wrong. I can't help unless I know."

"Oh God, Clay, it's Megan. She's been arrested!"

"Arrested?" He sagged down on the side of the bed and ran his fingers through thinning gray hair. "Where is she? I'll go to the jail and post bail." He knew that for her not to take her medication could be life threatening. An overnight stay in the San Diego jail would be very hard on her, both physically and emotionally. Of the three Scott girls Megan was the least likely to do something that would land her behind bars. He couldn't imagine what she had done. Unpaid traffic ticket? Seemed the most likely.

"Mexico! Clay, she's in Mexico!" Allison once again broke down.

"I'm dumbfounded, Allie, where's Sara?" He considered Sara the most level-headed of the three sisters.

"Sara's gone to tell Mom. Clay, what are we going to do?"

"First, I need facts. There's not much we can do until morning. You, Sara and Lilli be in my office tomorrow morning, eight o'clock sharp. Meanwhile, try to get some rest and calm down. I know an attorney across the border. I'll call Jorge and see what I can find out."

The next morning Allie, Sara and their mother Lilli arrived at Clay's office. The Scott women looked so much alike that at first glance one could hardly to tell them apart. Even Lilli had blond hair, blue eyes and a slim figure. Today, none of them looked as if they'd had much sleep. Allie seemed ready to collapse, Sara and her mother appeared stronger, more determined. "Okay, start at the beginning, tell me what happened."

Allie gave Sara a quick nod. "We have nine days off from teaching, you know; it's spring break. We decided to go to Tijuana for a day of shopping. I wanted a new leather purse and some sandals for summer. We would have taken the bus down, then walked across the border, only Allie and Megan wanted some large pots for plants. We didn't want to lug them around." Sara took a deep breath. "On our way back we were in line at the border, waiting like everyone else to get across. Boys were pestering us to wash the car for a few pesos. When we got up to the border station, the Federales were there, checking the cars, pulling one out of line every once in a while. When it was our turn, they asked to see inside our purses. We thought they wanted to see receipts for the stuff we purchased; then, when they looked in Megan's purse they found the prescriptions she always carries." Tears welled in Sara's eyes. Lilli put her arm around her daughter. Clay handed her a glass of water.

Allison picked up the story. "They literally yanked Megan out of the car and held her at gunpoint. When we protested, they turned on us telling us to get going or we would be arrested, too. We were terrified. Meggie was crying. Sara and I tried to tell them the drugs were prescriptions, they wouldn't listen. All of us speak Spanish, so it wasn't as if they didn't understand. We didn't have much choice. We crossed the border and called you. Your secretary let us have your home number when she heard how serious it was. Clay, what can we do? We're out of our minds! Poor Megan must be scared to death! Please, you've got to help."

Lilli spoke up for the first time. "Clay, if it's a matter of money…"

"Lilli, stop right there. Of course I'll help. Like I said on the phone last night I have a friend in Tijuana, Jorge Lopez. We went to law school together. I've already put in a call to him. I expect to hear from him any time now. Meanwhile, why don't the three of you go home and get some rest? Frankly, you all look like worn out." He gave the women each a hug. "I'll call as soon as Jorge contacts me, should be sometime this morning."

Lopez called soon after the women left. "Clay, it's been a while. If I know you, this is more than a social call. What's up?"

Claymore quickly outlined the problem. "What can we do, Jorge? Megan Scott is a good kid. No way would she be carrying illegal drugs. She has some health issues, which she controls with prescription meds."

"I don't know what's going on. I'll find out. Megan Scott isn't the first American to be jailed in the past few months on false drug dealing charges. All of them young women."

"Why, Megan? Why not all of the girls? The three of them are within a year or two of each other."

"Again, old friend, I don't know. Let me see what I can find out. First, I'll go to the jail and see Megan. I'll call as soon as I see her."

Megan pressed her face against the car window, screaming for her sisters. "Sara, Allie, help me!" A border guard jerked her roughly back to her seat.

"Senorita, sit back and shut up. I don't want to hurt you, but I will."

"*You are hurting me!*" Megan cried as the guard pulled

her away from the window by her handcuffs. "What do you want?"

"It's illegal to have drugs in Mexico. You have drugs in your purse. You are under arrest."

"Drugs? Are you crazy? I have two prescriptions. Look at the labels. A doctor prescribed those medicines. That medicine is for me!"

The guard shifted his eyes away from Megan. "No more talk!" He turned to the driver. "Hurry, Jesse, I don't want to miss dinner."

The late model Chevy raced through back streets. Jesse zigzagged around potholes; the swaying motion made Megan sick. They stopped at the corner of Calle Ocho and Ave. Constitutione, where the Tijuana jail, called La Ocho, is located. The Federale pulled Megan out of the car and handed her over to a guard at the reception area. The two men had a whispered conversation. Megan was led away and pushed into a cell with four other women about her own age. They were all dressed, like Megan, in casual clothes suited for a day of shopping and walking on uneven streets. Megan looked around at the other women. One sobbed, holding a hand over her bruised face. They all looked shell shocked.

The Mexican system of justice stems from the Napoleonic Code. A defendant is guilty until proven innocent. Megan knew that a mistake had been made. She would be released as soon as her family could prove her medications were prescriptions for her own use.

"Hola, Senorita Scott. I am Jorge Lopez. I am your attorney. Clay Claymore called and asked me to see you. First, please tell me what happened."

Megan went over the events of the past twenty-four hours in a halting voice. "Mr. Lopez, this is a big mistake. I don't do drugs and I certainly don't sell them."

"Yes, your story is the same as the one your sisters told Clay. I will talk to the judge today. You must understand that

Mexico works on a system of *mordida*, 'bribes.' We will find out how much your freedom will cost. Meanwhile, I will leave you with some money so that you can buy better food. Further, I will also bribe the guards so that you will not be bothered."

"Bothered? What do you mean, *bothered?*" Megan put her hand up to her mouth to stifle a moan.

"Miss Scott, this is a rough, ugly place. You are a young, lovely woman. The guards are poor and uneducated." He shrugged his shoulders. "I just want to make sure that you will be safe."

"Mr. Lopez, I must have my medication. I can't go very long without it before I get really sick."

"I'll see what I can do. Meanwhile, I'll call your family. They can visit on Sunday."

On Sunday, Sara, Allie and Lilli arrived at the jail. Nothing Clay or Lopez had told the women prepared them for the horrific conditions. Amid the squalor and filth, children were playing, running up and down, tossing balls and laughing. They were offspring of incarcerated parents. Some of them, born in jail, had never lived on the outside.

The women found a semi-private corner. All four were crying. After the first shock wore off, Lilli said, "Clay and Lopez are working on getting you home. We just need to find out how much it will cost. Lopez says the system is corrupt, bribes are the norm. He doesn't think it will take too long." Megan looked wan. Dark circles bruised her eyes. It broke Lilli's heart to see her daughter suffering.

"Mom, I've got to have my meds. Please see if Lopez can get them for me. I can't hold out much longer."

Lilli knew that going too long without medication could result in seizures and possibly death for Megan. "We've got to get her out. The legal crap is taking too long! Meggie needs her medication. She can't go without it." Lilli paced up and down in her living room. Allison and Sara sat with glum faces while their mother ranted.

Sara held the phone tight to her ear, listening to Clay. "Sara, I just spoke to Jorge Lopez in Tijuana. He's doing everything possible to get Megan out of jail. It doesn't look like it will happen as soon as we thought. As we speak, he's negotiating the price."

"But we already knew that. Why is it taking so long? How much? Find out how much, Clay. Please, Megan will die in that horrible place!"

"I'll find out. Jorge is working on this as fast as he can. Most likely the judge is checking on your finances and will demand every penny. Hang in there, Sara. Don't let your mom go to pieces. We'll get Megan. Try to be patient."

"Good news, my friend," Jorge told Clay the next day. The judge will take $50,000, and he wants another ten to pay off the guards. He will bring Megan to my office, and we'll do the exchange. Let me know as soon as the family has raised the money."

Clay called and spoke to Sara. He told her what he had learned from Jorge. "Please, I know how hard this is but tell your Lilli and your sisters to be patient."

Sara related their conversation to the others.

"Patient, my ass, I want my daughter home now! We're going visiting." Lilli outlined a plan. Allie and Sara were reluctant; Lilli would not be dissuaded. Clay obviously didn't know their mother's real strength . . .action under duress.

In less than two hours, Lilli, Sara and Allison were crossing the border. The girls dressed in summer slacks, light blouses and sandals. Lilli chose a long, dark, loose skirt and over-blouse. She tied a scarf over her hair and wore oversized sunglasses. On her feet were the worn, comfortable Birkenstocks that she and Megan favored.

Entering the jail, Lilli hung her head and shuffled along, with Sara on one side, Allie on the other, supporting her. The three made their way to the visitors' waiting area.

Once again they were appalled at their surroundings.

Megan's condition had worsened since the week before: skin clammy, eyes swollen, nose running. She needed her meds. They drifted to a corner of the yard where they had a small degree of privacy. There Lilli quickly pulled off her blouse and pulled it over Megan's head. The loose wrap-around skirt was easy to take off and rewrap around Megan. Underneath, Lilli was wearing slacks and a blouse much like the ones her daughters wore. Megan was already wearing sandals similar to her mother's. The last touch was the scarf and big sunglasses. The women hugged and cried as Allison and Sara led their ailing sister out and away from the jail. They held their breath; the guards never so much as looked up.

In the car, Sara gave her sister a bottle of water and her medication. They drove across the border to the San Diego airport and put Megan on a plane to friends in Montana.

"You what? Please, tell me you didn't do this. Do you have any idea what trouble you're in?" Clay pressed a hand to his eyes and tried to hold at bay the headache threatening to overwhelm him.

"Clay, calm down. We couldn't wait any longer. Megan *has* to have that medicine, you know that. Besides, as soon as they discover they have the wrong person, they'll let Mom go."

"Sara, I have to call you back. I'm going to call Jorge and see what we're up against. I still can't believe this."

Jorge took the news better than Clay expected. "Actually, this may be a good thing. Lilli is obviously stronger than her daughter and the judge only cares about his money."

"They'll have the money by next week. When can we make the exchange?"

"Be in my office Wednesday at eight p.m. The judge will bring Lilli to trade her for the money. Plan to spend the night at my villa. Crossing the border at that time of night is not a good idea."

Wednesday morning, two a.m., the same men who had taken Megan at the border crossing herded Lilli and her four cellmates into an unmarked van parked behind La Ocho. Rushing the women into the van, one guard looked directly at Lilli and hesitated. A deep, frown wrinkled his forehead. Lilli appeared much younger than her forty-three years, still, she didn't look twenty. The guard spoke to the driver in rapid Spanish. Lilli couldn't understand every word, it was something about this one being old. The driver looked at Lilli, then shrugged his shoulders. "Not our business." The women were told to lie down and be quiet. They were being released.

At eight Wednesday night, Clay, Allie and Sara were in the office of Jorge Lopez waiting for the judge. When the knock came they all stared at the door, waiting for Lilli to come through.

The judge entered alone. He stood just inside the room, leaving his armed guard standing outside the door. "There has been a slight change of plans. You pay me now and pick up the prisoner from the jail in the morning."

"This was not our arrangement. You get the money when we get the girl. Not one moment sooner. What is this? I thought you were an honorable man."

The judge argued for several minutes, then left when it became clear that he was not getting the money. In the morning, Jorge went to La Ocho to see Lilli; she was not there.

The van rumbled along for hours. When at last it came to a stop, Lilli and the other women were herded aboard a fishing boat. The men jostled them down into the cabin. Lilli lost track of time. The boat followed a rocky shoreline before they landed and were transferred to a windowless van. They finally stopped. The driver slid the door open; the women were inside a yard with high stone walls. At one end stood a centuries-old gray-brown building covered with ivy. A wooden cross, eight feet tall, rose in front of the back entry of what Lilli thought must be a convent. The night sounds of the jungle rubbed their frayed nerves raw.

The women huddled together tearfully in a wooden storage

shed. At first light a nun brought sweet bread and weak tea. She said her name was Sister Maria. She led the way to a water faucet and the privy, which were located behind their hut. Sister Maria provided them with worn army blankets and helped them set up cots for sleeping. Although they generally had the run of the walled enclosure, there was no place to go.

Lilli began to check the enclosure, looking for a way to escape. The only ways out were through the convent or through the locked and chained gate. The women tried to get information from the little nun; she would not or could not tell them anything. The men who transported them came and went at different times, but none of them would speak to the women.

The four gathered around Lilli for comfort and to see if anyone had an idea of why they were here. Monica came from Mexico City to Tijuana with her husband on business. She went shopping while her husband was in a meeting. Two men jumped from a van, pushing her into it and driving immediately to the Tijuana jail. She was charged with shoplifting. "My husband has money, he will pay the *mordida*. But why are we here and not in the jail?"

Carmen lived in Tijuana with her husband and a new baby. She was sick with worry about her child, her face swollen from crying. "My baby, my baby. They will think I left her. What's going to happen to us?"

Like Lilli, Olivia lived in San Diego. "This is all so unreal! My family won't know what to do or who to call. My boyfriend will go ballistic once he finds out I'm not at the jail."

Esmeralda was the only one who did not speak any English. She was withdrawn, speaking only when asked a direct question.

At first they were all terrified. As the days passed and nothing happened; they began to relax. Each morning and evening Sister Maria brought food. Lilli tried to ask her about their situation, she still would not respond.

Late one night, Pepe, one of the guards, staggered to the

door and demanded that Olivia come with him. He grabbed her arm. She began kicking and screaming. Jesse, the van driver, rushed up. "What are you doing? Let her go. You will get us all in trouble if the merchandise is bruised."

Pepe's breath reeked of beer. "I'm not gonna bruise her, amigo, I just want a little taste of what she's got."

"You fool! Do you want the Patron to kill you? That's what he will do if he finds out. Let her go. Now!" Sullenly, Pepe let go of Olivia. She stumbled back to the hut.

"Lilli, he called us 'merchandise.' They're going to sell us."

"That's it!" cried Carmen. "I've heard of this. They kidnap women and sell them to buyers from Japan, Arabia, Europe, all over. That's what they're up to. We're being sold as slaves. We'll go to the highest bidder for sex slaves. Oh my God! What are we going to do? Our families will never know what happened to us."

For the first time Esmeralda, spoke. In Spanish, she said, "We must kill them. It's the only way!" She spoke with such force the others were stunned. "My family is very poor. My parents had to sell my sister into prostitution so the rest of us could live. That's why I was in Tijuana. I heard she was being held there. I wanted to buy her freedom. Now she's lost and so am I." Tears rolled down her beautiful face.

When Sister Maria came with their evening meal Lilli took her aside. "Sister, do you know what's going on here? We're being sold like sheep to the highest bidder. Please, can't you help?"

The little nun looked around to be sure they were not overheard. "My child, I'll do what I can, but Mother Superior is very strict. She takes money from these men. If she catches me talking to you, she will lock me in my room. Tomorrow morning early, I walk to the village for supplies. I will pass a note to my cousin who lives there. His name is Felix. That's all I can do."

"Offer a reward, Sister. Tell Felix it's worth ten thousand dollars if he gets the note to my family. I'll write down some phone numbers. Just bring me a pencil and paper."

"No, no, ten thousand is way too much. This is a very poor boy. He will not believe that much money. I'll tell him two thousand and say he must give half to the church. He will still be rich and the church will benefit."

"Whatever you say, just please get me that paper. And bless you, Sister."

At first light, Sister Maria brought their food, then went around back by the privy. Lilli followed. "Sister, you don't look well." Her face was very white. "Are you all right, Sister? You look pale." Lilli noticed the little nun was shaking. Before Sister Maria could answer she put her hand up to her heart and collapsed. Lilli felt for a heartbeat, there was none. She ran back to get Olivia, the strongest of the women to help her. They pulled Sister Maria's habit off and quickly dragged her body behind the outhouse, where they buried it under a pile of firewood. Lilli retrieved the paper and pencil, donned the habit, and pulled the hood down low to cover her face as she had seen the nun do. The tricky part would be to enter the convent and pass undetected, out the front door. Lilli figured with any luck it would be at least a day before anyone noticed she was missing. She wasn't sure how long it would be before Sister Maria was missed.

Lilli walked straight through the convent as rapidly as she dared. The other nuns went about their daily chores, paying no attention. Once outside, she hurried down a well-worn path, passing a field of corn being worked by nuns. She walked for about five miles before smoke from cooking fires let her know the village was near. Once there, she asked for Sister Maria's cousin, Felix. *Thank God, they understand my Spanish.*

At first Felix was wary. When he heard his cousin was dead, he cried, "Such a good person. She did so much for all of us!"

"Felix, you have to help. Please listen. Five of us are being held at the convent. There are men, bad men. They plan to sell us."

"Sell you? Senora, what do you mean?"

"Slaves, Felix. They will send us to other countries. We'll never see our families again. Sister Maria was going to tell you, but she died before she could. Please, Felix, there is a reward, two thousand American dollars if you will go to a telephone and call this number. Tell them where we are. You must hurry, I don't know when the men are coming to take us away." She pressed the paper into his hand with the telephone numbers and Jorge Lopez's name.

Felix looked at the paper with trepidation. "Senora, I can't read. I've never used a telophono."

"Oh, Lord. I never thought of that. Can you take it to someone who can read? Do you know someone you can trust? Please, Felix, this is important. These women are depending on you."

"Si, Senora, I know a doctor, an American, he lives in the next village. I will go to him. I will run like the wind. You can stay in my casa and hide while I am gone." He led her to the edge of the village and escorted her into a small, clean adobe house. The house had one room and one window without a pane. The window overlooked the privy and the jungle growing at the back. The furnishings were sparse: a rough wood table, two chairs, and a neatly made-up bed with a colorful quilt. Left alone, there was nothing Lilli could do but pray, and pray she did.

The call came to Jorge Lopez in Tijuana first. He took the information and called Clay. "We've located Lilli, Clay. She's about a hundred miles inland at an old convent. I've already called the monsignor here in Tijuana. With his backing, the governor has no choice. He has to go after Lilli and the other women. I understand there are four others. The last thing President Fox needs is another major scandal. We will bring them home."

The jungle was too dense for helicopters to land, but armed troops arrived by truck and deployed in the area surrounding the convent and posted lookouts. The men waited. Soon after sunrise, a beat-up Chevy van rumbled up to the gate. Jesse climbed down and unlocked the chain, allowing the van to drive into the yard. Before he could relock the gate, soldiers stormed the opening, ordering Jesse, Pepe and two other men down on their knees at gunpoint.

Felix came running into the little house. "Senora, I have the doctor. He is here with me."

Lilli turned to see a tall, lean man with light brown hair and glasses enter. "David? David Evans? What on earth? How did you get here?"

"Lilli Scott! I couldn't believe it when Felix brought me the note." He held up his hand before she could ask the next question. "I've called Jorge Lopez. He's alerted the authorities. Help is on the way."

"Oh, thank God! I thought we were all lost. But, David, seeing you here. This is all too much."

"Believe me. I'm as surprised as you are. I'm with Doctors Without Borders. I've been assigned to this area for the last six months, working with the villagers. The last time I saw you was, when? Twelve years ago, at Mike's funeral?"

"Yes, that was it. When Mike was killed, I was such a basket case. You were his closest friend. I should have stayed in touch."

"No, losing your husband is hard enough without the burden of thinking of everyone else. All these years, you never remarried?" He paused for a moment. "Lord, your girls must be grown. We have a lot of catching up to do. Start by telling me how you came to be in this mess."

"When we're back home and safe, I'll tell you all of it. Trust me. It's been a nightmare."

The reunion at Lilli Scott's apartment was better than any Christmas the family had ever experienced. Jorge Lopez and David Evans were there, as well as Clay Claymore and Olivia, plus a host of friends and relatives. Megan had regained her health and looked happy and robust once again. The food was wonderful, the champagne cold. Everyone gave a silent prayer of thanks for the way things turned out.

Jorge brought letters from Carmen and Monica. Carmen was back with her baby daughter and thanked Lilli for risking her life to save them. Monica said she was going to help Esmeralda find her sister and buy her back if possible.

"Well now, hopefully, things can get back to normal," sighed Clay.

"Yes, some peace and quiet would be appreciated," said Sara.

Lilli tapped her glass, "I do have one small announcement." All eyes turned to her. "David and I are going back to the village." David came to stand beside her. "Yes, the people in that village helped us and they need David. And I, well, I think it's time David and I got reacquainted."

"Mom! After all that's happened? You'd go back?" Megan cried.

"Yes, it's *because* of what's happened. Maybe in some small way, David and I can make a difference. The people are not to blame for the actions of a few bad men. The church replaced the Mother Superior, and I'd like to feel useful and needed."

"Oh, you're needed. Yes, you are." David kissed her cheek. "You're very much needed."

"Well, there you go, another weepy one. Boys, I'm off to bed. See you next Saturday?"

"You bet." George picked up the pizza box and empty bottle and threw them in the trash. "We'll be here."

As they left the house, George said, "You drive. I want to look over some notes I took while he was talking."

Steve nodded. "Josh says his wife liked the *weepy* stories. I have a feeling the old guy likes them too. Maybe, as you get older, you just have a need to remember the times things worked out right."

"Could be. His wife's dead, isn't she? I think I read that somewhere."

"Yeah. I get the feeling he misses her. He seems lonely."

"Saturday may be the highlight of his week. Hope so anyway."

The following weekend Josh once again waited for them on the porch. The weather brisk, not too cold to be out. He raised a hand in recognition as they got out of the car. George had a large bag from the Lo Fat's. "Hope you like Chinese. Give us a change from pizza."

"Sure, Chinese is fine as long as I don't have to eat with chop sticks."

"No, forks all around." Steve and George arranged the food on the small table by the old man. A filled glass and two more cigars were placed on the floor by his chair.

"I've been thinking about some old cases, trying to remember some that you might like for your book. A story came to me that isn't a real story at all just a way for a lot of frustrated policemen to let off steam. This story sorta evolved over time with the episodes changing with the teller, but the version that sticks in my mind is . . ."

Chapter 20
THE DREAM JUDGE

It looked like an operating room. There were two male nurses in green scrubs and a doctor standing by a hospital bed. A large-screen TV monitor sat at the head of the bed, some kind of machine with many dials stood at one side. Wires with suction cups trailed from the machine to the floor.

The prisoner, Sam Sampson, entered Judge Benton's courtroom very frightened by the punishment awaiting him. He'd heard stories. When asked to plead, he whispered, "Guilty," in hopes that by confessing he would escape the punishment.

"Good, that's good! Now let's see just how guilty you are." The gavel came down.

The bailiff read, "The prisoner, having entered his plea, will now be subjected to the Dream Machine. Let the record reflect that the prisoner will enter a dream state where he will experience the exact same pain and fear that he induced in his victims. If, in fact, he is innocent of these crimes, he will incur no pain, nor will he experience any fear, or suffer any dire consequence, real or imagined."

The nurses rushed forward as the prisoner started to cry. He was strapped to the bed, kicking and screaming. The IV soon quieted him. "Find out what crimes our friend here has been involved in." The judge sat back to watch.

Images of a much younger man filled the screen. He could be seen entering a small neighborhood convenience store, pulling a gun and ordering the owner to empty the cash register. Sam morphed into the image of the owner, who moved slowly due to a bad leg. He was near collapse from fright. Sam could be seen hitting himself, knocking himself to the floor and stealing the cash. Since the owner had never regained consciousness, Sam had not been identified.

Next, a little older Sam. He waited outside a local nightclub for a couple driving a Lexus to leave. He followed them to their own driveway. Then he herded them at gunpoint into their home, where they were blindfolded and bound. At this point, Sam became the man. Terror filled his being. Sweat ran into his eyes. He felt helpless to beg for his wife's life and the life of their unborn child. Sam then raped the wife and robbed them. Laughter filled the air as their car became his means to get-a-way.

Sam was shown over the years committing increasingly violent crimes. Judge Benton said, "That's enough. Adjust the dials to inflict maximum fear and pain at even the thought of committing a crime." The machine hummed. Sam bucked and shrieked. He squealed and sweated until the machine turned off. His legs would barely carry him as he wobbled from the courtroom.

Virgil Moran was the next prisoner. He pled "not guilty" to the crime of molesting a seven-year-old girl at the park. The sight of the bed, the wires, the TV and the machine with all the dials was terrifying. The nurses attached him to the monitor while the doctor worked the dials. The screen showed a lovely day at the park, clear sky, bright sun, temperature in the low eighties. Virgil was enjoying the day when he heard a child cry out in pain. He rushed around a fence of low bushes in time to see a man dragging a little girl by the arm. At the sight of Virgil, the man dropped the child and ran. Her clothes were torn, her face red from being struck. She still had her panties wrapped around her neck. Virgil picked her up and carried her to the picnic area, calling for help. The police arrested him. The little girl was too traumatized to make an identification, Virgil was the only one around. Judge Benton banged her gavel. "Stop! I've seen enough. Doctor, make the necessary adjustments. Release the prisoner. Mr. Moran, it's clear to this court that you are not guilty and only tried to help. We have left you with happy, positive recollections of that day. Thank you. You are free to go."

Virgil left the courtroom feeling that he had just had one of life's most wonderful experiences. He just wasn't sure what it was.

"Who'd you get?"

"Joe Hardaker."

"Wow! Old hard-ass Joe. Tough break."

"You?"

"Marion Benton. Lucky me." He smirked. "The Dream Judge. Guess we know who'll be walkin' outta here." The other prisoners on the long bench stole furtive glances at the new guy. "I hear she's a piece a cake. Doesn't believe in long prison sentences. I heard guys leave after only a few hours or at the most a few days inside. Can't believe my luck." He laughed. "She must shake her finger at you and give you a 'don't ever do that again' speech. Or maybe she does the shame-shame-on-you sign. I'll be back on the street in time for my next job. Got it all set up. Hate to waste the time in here, but hey! Ya gotta do what ya gotta do. If they had any real evidence, they wouldn't be handing me over to a cream puff like her." Pleased at his good fortune, he hugged himself.

The tunnel from jail to courthouse was long and lined with benches for prisoners waiting to see their assigned judges. The only ones shackled were the potentially violent cons, usually the repeat offenders, unable to adjust either to prison life or life as free men. At one end of the tunnel were doors leading back to the jail; at the other end was the door leading into the courthouse. Guards stood watch at both ends, ready for any disruption. Even the guards smiled when Eddie Smalie made his comments about his luck in drawing Judge Benton. No one said a word.

The door leading to court opened and a guard appeared. Each prisoner waited with a mixture of resignation and trepidation. Finally the guard intoned, "Eddie Smalie, front and center." Eddie, almost gleefully followed the guard to room eight, Judge Benton's courtroom. The hospital operating room atmosphere shocked him.

"Are you ready to proceed?" Judge Benton asked.

"Yes, your Honor. Attorney Alvin Baker for the defendant." Eddie stared at the man claiming to be his attorney. He had never seen Alvin Baker before.

The judge looked down at Eddie from her high bench and asked, "How do you plead?"

Baker leaned over and whispered into Eddie's ear. Eddie, disoriented, managed to stammer, "Not guilty."

"We'll see." The gavel hit with a resounding blow.

The nurses led Eddie to the bed. They stripped off his prison-issue shirt, handcuffed him to the bed and attached the suction cups to his chest. A nurse started an IV in Eddie's left arm. Within moments he was asleep. The doctor began to adjust the dials. He read from a sheet of paper. "Remember the events of July Fourth of this year." Slowly, a picture formed on the screen. At first, it was fuzzy, as adjustments were made the image became sharp. The screen showed Eddie entering the apartment of Hazel and Fred Waters. He raised a baseball bat over the head of the elderly Mr. Waters and started to crush his skull. Before the bat struck, Mr. Waters' image was replaced with that of Eddie, giving the effect of Eddie striking himself. Eddie screamed from the bed, the pain unbearable until his on-screen visage blacked out. Next, the picture showed Eddie tying Hazel Waters to a chair. Again Eddie's image changed places with his victim's. "Please don't! Please!" he screamed as he held lighted cigarettes to his own bare feet. His TV self laughed and yelled, "Where's the safe?" He took great pleasure in inflicting small cuts with his pocketknife.

Eddie moaned in pain. He finally sobbed, "In the bedroom, closet floor." With more torture, he gasped out the combination. The safe yielded only a few documents, yellow with age, and one small locket. "You bitch!" he yelled in frustration. The knife he held came down into his own chest. Eddie's bowels released on its impact.

"Is that enough, your Honor?" the doctor asked.

"No. Let's find out what else he's done."

Once again the doctor adjusted the dials while the nurses cleaned their patient, not for his benefit, for theirs.

The machine hummed. Eddie was instructed to recount his first violent crime. The screen displayed a date ten years prior to today. This would have made Eddie twenty-two. He moved into his mother's kitchen, lifted the lid from the pot where spaghetti sauce simmered. From a vial he carried in his pocket, he poured in poison and stirred the sauce. At dinner that evening he said, "Pass the salad. I'll wait for my spaghetti." As his mother, father and sister doubled over with cramps, Eddie took their places. He cried out from the bed, sweat pouring from him. The pain became a writhing snake in his stomach. "Help me. Please help me. Water! Give me water!" He cried out for a doctor. Black foam ran from his mouth. Although in real terms the time was no more than five minutes, in Eddie's dream, he writhed for hours in agony before dying.

The doctor looked up at the judge, waiting.

"No. Not yet. What else is there?"

Once again dials were fine-tuned. This time the image was of a young man in a police uniform. Eddie was offering him a bribe. The officer grabbed Eddie. They struggled. The policeman struck his head on a table and was momentarily dazed. Eddie took the officer's gun and began beating him. Eddie became the officer. When he was tired of hitting him, he shot him in the spine leaving him unable to speak or walk.

Judge Benton said, "That's it. I think he gets the idea of what his victims have suffered. Wake him up." Eddie came to, all pale and shaky. "How do you feel?" she asked. Eddie was unable to answer. When told to get down from the table, his legs wouldn't carry him. "Get him a wheelchair and release him." She looked down at Eddie. "Your life of crime just ended, Mr. Smalie. I hope you've enjoyed your virtual tour of the pain and suffering you've caused. Since your only living victim is the police officer you crippled, I felt it only fitting that you should share his fate."

Eddie left the court less than two hours after he had entered. As he wheeled himself down the hall on his way to freedom, one of his fellow prisoners shouted,

"Hey, you were right! No jail time. Lucky you. Bet you're glad you got the Dream Judge."

Josh shook his head. Took a few sips of whisky and looked at Steve and George. "Now you may think this fantasy judge stuff is nonsense. Let me tell you there's not a cop out there who wouldn't give a month's pay to make it real. Besides, this is a good way to blow off some steam. Everyone who tells the story adds their own favorite fantasy to it. If not out loud, then in their dreams.

"Here's another south of the border story, When you work out of San Diego, a lot of these come your way. This one kept us busy running from this side of the fence to the Tijuana side . . ."

Chapter 21
THE SPA TREATMENT

Advertisements for Chiquita's Health Spa across the border in Tijuana touted a week of dream fulfilling relaxation. For $5,500 you could expect a custom-tailored fitness program, wonderful personal services such as herbal wraps, facials, in-room massage, scrumptious spa cuisine, and your choice of challenging self-discovery classes and programs. Private accommodations boasted bubbling waterfalls and fish filled pools outside each room. The grounds were designed for quiet walks. Meticulously landscaped gardens with well-tended koi ponds, camellia bushes, and benches placed under trees promised to sooth frayed nerves. Motivational speakers presented sessions on personal fulfillment and offered private counseling. The gift shop was a shopper's delight of various products featured at the spa. The number of guests was limited to no more than forty at a time, assuring that each person felt pampered and important.

Away from the main building was another structure designed for maximum privacy. In this part of the spa only five guests resided; it was built to take as many as eight. The halls were softly lit, the floors covered with carpet to dull any outside sounds. Dr. Carlos made his rounds, checking on his special guests. In each room he monitored blood pressure, noted vital signs and marked charts with his findings. These guests went by code names according to the color of their doors, Ms. Blue, Ms. Pink and so on. Occasionally there were men, not often.

Young and handsome, Dr. Carlos, was eyed by every woman at the spa, if not for herself, then for an eligible daughter at home. The women in the special guesthouse blissfully slept through any thoughts along those lines. They were all tethered to lines feeding them a special blend of nutrients. They each had paid $20,000 to be put to sleep and starved until their excess weight came off. They were awakened every three days, walked around, bathed and given a check-up before being put back to sleep. The procedure usually took two weeks; if they still weighted too much, they could come back after a month and go through the process again for an additional $5,000.

On this particular night, the doctor left the Blue room, locking the door. He walked slowly down the hall to his office and sat with his head in his hands. Finally he straightened, picked up the phone and dialed. When he heard the click on the other end he said, "It's done."

Jim Duncan walked into the San Diego police station and approached the desk. The sergeant looked up. "My wife is missing."

"Missing persons. Down the hall." Sergeant Fillmore pointed to his right.

"When was the last time you saw your wife, Mr. Duncan?" asked Lieutenant Cummings.

"Two weeks ago. And actually, it's Doctor Duncan."

"Two weeks? And you're just now reporting it? I have to ask why."

"My wife went to The Golden Door Health Spa in Escondido to lose weight. She's always trying without much success, so this time she asked me not to contact her. She said she just wanted to concentrate on getting the weight off. She planned to exercise, eat right and in her words, 'do whatever it took.' She was determined."

"So what makes you think she's missing? Maybe she's just toughing it out and plans to come home a new, thinner woman."

"There was a family emergency. I tried to call her at the spa, but they said they didn't know anything about her. That was three days ago. She should be home by now, and I haven't heard from her. Naturally, I'm worried."

"What was the emergency?"

"Her mother's in the hospital. Iris would never stay away if she knew her mother was ill. Something's happened. I know it. I can feel it." He looked away.

"What do you do for a living, Dr. Duncan?"

"I'm a forensic anthropologist. I teach at the university."

Cummings snapped his fingers. "That's it. I've been trying to place you. You take classes out to the boneyard and train them to tell how long ago a person died and from what cause. Isn't that right?"

"Yes. That's correct. Most of the bodies in the yard have been donated by the state. Homeless people. Bodies no one claims."

"I remember going out there when I was a rookie. It gave me the shivers."

"It's definitely not for everyone. We have three full time professors training the next generation of forensic specialists. It's very important work."

"Tell me about your wife, Doctor. Who are her friends? What does she do? Is she employed?"

"She mostly does volunteer work for the library. She used to teach; now she claims her weight makes her too tired to work a full day. That's why she was so keen on this spa trip. I can give you a list of her friends. I'll have to wait until I get home, though. I didn't think to bring her address book with me."

"That's fine. Call me later. Meanwhile I'll start checking spas. Maybe she went to a different one."

Dr. Duncan drove to the university campus and went to the office he shared with Dr. Connie Tabor.

"Jim. You look terrible. Are you all right?"

"No, Connie. I'm not. It's Iris. She's missing."

"Missing! Oh my God, Jim! When?"

"I'm not sure. I mean she went to a fat farm two weeks ago and I haven't heard from her since. She asked me not to contact her. Said she wanted to concentrate on getting the pounds off, so I respected her wishes. Now I can't find her."

"Fat Farm? You mean a weight loss clinic?"

"Yes. She said the Golden Door, only when I called, they had no record of her. Honestly, I'm about out of my mind."

"You've been to the police?"

"Just now. They're looking into it. They're talking to her friends, people at the library, everyone."

"Are you sure you want to work today? You look pretty rough. I can take over the field trip." She placed her hand on his arm. "You know I'm here for you, Jim. Anything you need."

"No, no. Thanks, I'm better if I keep busy." He patted her hand and then removed it. "Besides, this is the first trip for most of these students. Sometimes the first one is hard on people. They don't know what to expect."

The van rumbled to the border inspection station, "Chiquita's Health Spa" lettered on the side in bright blue. "Dr. Carlos, we haven't seen you in a while. Where's Estaban?" The border guard knew all the Spa personnel.

"He had family business in Mexico City and we needed supplies, so I decided to drive. Besides, a day in San Diego seemed like a good way to duck my responsibilities at the spa." He smiled and handed the guard a twenty-dollar bill.

The border guard laughed. "You said it, Doc. We're all the same, looking for a change of pace." He waved the van through.

The night was cool, a pleasant change from the 80 degree day. Dr. Carlos sat in the van, waiting. A little after ten, a black

Ford truck pulled along side of him. "Have you been waiting long? I got here as soon as I could."

"Long enough that now we must hurry. I need to be back at the clinic in time for morning rounds."

"Yes, yes. Everything is ready. Give me a hand." They pulled the gurney from the truck and took it to the newly dug grave. The body was dumped into the open ground, dirt shoveled over it and tamped down. Clumps of grass and a few rocks completed the scene. "There. In a few weeks the students will be allowed to 'find' the body and start their investigations. Just another anonymous street person."

"Lieutenant . . ." Detective Able stood at the door.

"Come in. What do you have?"

"Not much. The Golden Door was a dead end. All of her friends thought she was going there. Mrs. Duncan obviously had other plans; no one knew about them. We believe we've tracked her as far as the Mexican border. She was seen taking the bus. One of the drivers remembers her. Then someone at the American Plaza said they thought a lady fitting her description bought a soda. But that's the end of the trail."

"American Plaza, that's the trolley station, right?"

"Right. So she probably was headed for Tijuana."

"Probably. But she could have gotten off at any one of the stops between the plaza and TJ. Ask at each station. Take some extra help."

"Lieutenant, that's about sixteen stops."

"Then you'd better get started." He looked at the detective. "Right?"

Dr. Connie Tabor led her students between neatly cordoned off gravesites. "These bodies have all been processed. You can pull the results from the lab library. That will give you ideas of what to look for. Your job will be to test the new bodies coming in to get as much information as possible. You will note probable time of death, information provided by the ME. And work on finding new clues as to the cause of death. Also you will note anything that might lead to further investigation."

"Anything like what?" asked one student.

"That's what you'll be learning. It's the 'anything' that often solves the crime."

She smiled. "I know this is all new and a little mysterious; just trust me. It's important work and invaluable to you as a forensic scientist."

"Lieutenant, we're pretty sure Mrs. Duncan went as far as San Ysidro," said Detective Able.

"From what we've learned, the lady was obsessed with losing weight. So check out the fat farms across the border."

"Wonder why she would lie about going to the Golden Door and then head for Tijuana?"

"I'm not sure. I want to re-interview some of her friends and her husband. Someone must have a clue."

During the next few days, the lieutenant spoke once again, to several friends of Iris Duncan as well as her co-workers at the library. One woman, Nancy Bellis, said Iris had confided that she was not happy in her marriage and wanted to lose weight to get a new start in life. When asked if that included leaving her husband, she said, "I had the feeling it might; she never said that exactly. Iris had the money. She inherited a rather sizable fortune from her parents. Jim makes a fair salary as a teacher, but their lifestyle is dependent on her money. Also . . ."

"What is it?"

"Well, this is strictly gossip and I hate to spread gossip."

Lieutenant Cummings cut in sharply, "Ms. Bellis, we're investigating a missing person here. Anything you say might be important,"

"Yes of course." Nancy Bellis looked down. "Well, the rumor is that Jim was having an affair."

Lieutenant Cummings sat in front of the desk. "Dr. Tabor,

we've been checking on health spas where Iris Duncan might have gone. We traced her to Tijuana and asked about her at the Rosarito Beach Hotel and Casa Playa Spa. We also checked LazerX in Tijuana. When we looked into Chiquita's Health Spa in TJ, we found that you own a rather large percentage of that spa."

"Yes. That's true. It's one of my investments."

"You knew that Mrs. Duncan had gone to a health spa to lose weight. Didn't you think it might be important to mention your interest in the Spa?"

"No. The last I heard, she went to the Golden Door. This has nothing to do with Chiquita's or me."

After the Lieutenant left, Dr. Tabor called Dr. Carlos on his private cell phone. "Is there anything I should know?"

"About what? The American police were here; there was nothing to tell them."

"You're sure? Everything is okay down there? I don't want any nasty surprises."

"I'm sure. Don't worry," Dr. Carlos assured her.

The students were eager to start their first "hands on" training. Dr. Tabor handed out slips of paper marked with the gravesite each team of two was assigned. "Here you go." She slid the paper with 666 across her desk.

Susan Foster read it quickly, put it in her pocket and turned to her partner, Michael Kane. "We've got 999. Let's go."

Michael manned the shovel while Susan took charge of the checklist given to them by Dr. Tabor. He uncovered the body and pulled back the blanket. "Susan. Look at this!"

Susan peered at the body. "It looks new. I mean this person hasn't been dead very long. Look at her hands. She has a professional manicure and her hair is styled."

"This isn't some homeless person. Maybe she willed her body to the college for scientific research."

"Maybe, but why is she dressed in a silk nightgown? And why is she wrapped in a blanket? Something about this doesn't seem right. Let's talk to Dr. Tabor before we go any further." Susan pulled the slip with the gravesite number on it from her pocket. She stared at it for a moment and then handed it to Michael.

"Oh boy! This is 999. We're supposed to be at 666."

"Lieutenant, line one. It's Dr. Tabor from the college."

"Dr. Tabor, Cummings here."

"We found Iris Duncan."

"Dr. Tabor, we won't know for sure until the medical examiner completes the autopsy, but all indications point to a drug overdose. The blanket she was wrapped in had the Chiquita Spa logo stamped on one corner." Lieutenant Cummings sat across the table from Connie Tabor in one of the interrogation rooms of the San Diego police station.

"I understand that; however, I have no idea how Iris or the blanket got there. As far as I know, Iris wasn't even aware of Chiquita Spa."

"Did you know Iris Duncan?"

"Of course. I occasionally talked to her at faculty gatherings. A rather dull person. Frankly, I was surprised that Jim stayed with her. He's so bright."

"The Tijuana police are assisting in the investigation," continued Cummings. When they went to the spa they found four sleeping women hooked up to IV's in a separate building. What can you tell me about that?"

"IV's? What are you talking about? Have you spoken to Dr. Carlos?" Dr. Tabor asked. "He's my partner. He runs the day-to-day operation. What does he say?"

"Unfortunately, we haven't been able to find Dr. Carlos. We were hoping you could shed some light on what's going on."

"This is crazy!" Dr. Tabor said. "I don't know anything about any of this. I think I'd better call my attorney."

"That's probably wise."

"Jim, how are you doing? This whole thing is so awful. I can't even begin to guess how Iris got wrapped in a blanket from my health spa, much less how she got left at the training farm. But now the police think I had something to do with it, and to top it off, Carlos has disappeared."

Jim Duncan looked out of bloodshot eyes. His clothes were the same ones he had worn the day before, when the police had called to tell him about his wife. "You, Connie? Why would they think you're involved?"

"The clues all point to Chiquita Spa and I'm the owner."

"But that's crazy!"

"That's what I said; they don't see it that way. Jim, you don't think they know about us, do you?"

"No. Besides, that has nothing to do with this mess."

The cell phone rang. "It's me. I'm in a safe place I need money to disappear for good."

"How could you have been so stupid? The spa blanket!"

"Hey, get off my case, Doc! Remember you were there, too. How come you didn't think of the stupid blanket?"

"How much? I can't risk taking too much out of the bank. It'll raise questions."

"Bull! You set this up. There's plenty of money. Let's see, twenty grand a pop, times an average of five women every two weeks for two years, that's *mucho dinero*."

"Back off! You got paid. Where's your money?"

"No way can I go near my bank. That's the first place they'll look."

"Okay, okay. This is not the time to get into it. I can put my hands on about ten thousand cash. That's all."

"Bring the money to the McDonald's just inside the Tijuana border Wednesday at noon. I'll be there waiting."

"How am I supposed to get away? Wednesday I'm scheduled to lecture at the college."

"Your problem, Doc. Just be there."

Wednesday at noon the doctor arrived with the cash, watching anxiously for signs of Carlos. "Hey, Doc." A voice behind dark sunglasses came from out of nowhere. "Sorry I'm late, I had to be sure no one was with you. You have the money?"

"Yes. It's all here in this plastic bag under the McDonald's food."

"Clever. Now I can have lunch on the road." He smiled. "I'll be back when things cool down to get the rest of my money."

"Don't call again." The doctor turned to leave. Two pedestrians and a man making a purchase at the McDonald's window stepped up. "You're both under arrest. Come quietly."

Back at the San Diego police department, Detective Able asked, "What made you suspect the husband? All clues pointed to Dr. Tabor."

The lieutenant smiled, "Motive. Susan Tabor had no reason to kill Iris Duncan. Her husband had plenty."

The night chilled, so the men moved into the house and lit the fire. They had about a fourth of a bottle of Jack Daniels and one cigar left. *A bag full of money. That's a Big Mac I could have used*, he thought.

"Now this story may or may not fit in that book you're writing because it isn't exactly a crime. It's a slice of life that shows the twists and turns fate can take . . ."

Chapter 22
BE CAREFUL WHAT YOU WISH FOR

"Be sure. You must be absolutely sure. We can never go back. From this day on we will never, ever speak of this again, agreed?"

"Agreed."

Belita handed a tiny blue-wrapped newborn over to her sister. Alicia accepted the baby boy and handed her sister a tiny pink-wrapped bundle in return.

The girls then called the new fathers to come and meet their children.

Two years earlier:

Everyone in the church quieted down as the strains of music reached them. They turned to watch as identical twin brides with light olive skin, dark flashing eyes and jet-black hair escorted by their father, Juan Casas, came down the aisle. The swish of satin bridal gowns relieved the hush in the church. Tiny girls sprinkling rose petals from pink baskets preceded the trio. The flower girls parted allowing Juan to escort his daughters to the altar." Who gives these women to be wed?" intoned the minister.

"I do," said their father.

Juan kissed each girl's cheek then turned to sit by his sister.

When Juan Casas was seated, James Jordan and his twin Chris each stepped to the side of his bride-to-be. After the ceremony the minister turned the couples around and announced, "May I be the first to introduce you to Mr. and Mrs. James Jordan and Mr. and Mrs. Chris Jordan."

"So where are the four of you going on your honeymoon?" asked Bill Daley at the reception.

James, better known as JJ, answered for all of them. "CJ and Belita are going to Hawaii. Alicia and I are going to Paris."

"What, no togetherness? I thought the four of you were welded at the hips."

JJ laughed. "Listen, there comes a time when a man wants to be alone with his woman. I mean alone. *Comprende?*"

"Yeah. I get it. You must get tired of the twin thing."

"What twin thing?" said CJ, stepping up, drink in hand. "We're so used to thinking alike and looking alike that sometimes just for fun we trade places. No one ever knows the difference. We did it a lot when we were kids."

"Not this time," said JJ. "This is one time I want Alicia to know for sure it's me." They all smiled at his words.

"We're leaving," JJ announced. "Our plane takes off in three hours. We have to get going."

"Us too. Let me see if I can drag Belita away from her cousins. Aloha!" He waved at everyone and went to collect his bride.

Over the next year the young couples settled into their routines. JJ and Alicia bought a house a mile away from CJ and Belita. They socialized frequently and enjoyed their own sets of friends. CJ worked for Morgan Stanley as a stockbroker and made a very substantial living. Alicia stayed home enjoying painting and gardening. JJ was a computer genius called on to analyze and fix computer problems for companies all over the world. Belita taught kindergarten at Seventh Street School near their home. In February Alicia called her sister. "Let's have lunch. I have some exciting news."

"Great! I have something to tell you too." They laughed because each guessed what the other had to say.

In the restaurant they faced each other over glasses of iced tea. As if leading a band they raised their imaginary wands and chorused, "I'm pregnant!"

Amid giggles Alicia said, "JJ is so excited he can hardly sit still. He wants to rush out and buy baseball bats, mitts and balls. It's all I can do to restrain him. I keep telling him not to pin his hopes on a boy because sometimes girls come along too."

"That's funny because CJ is just as excited only he really wants a girl first. Talk about a buying spree. We have a closet filled with frilly dresses and pink ruffled panties. He says we can have a boy later. I think because the boys have an older sister he thinks that's the way it should be. Like you get to plan these things."

In the months that followed both JJ and CJ pressured their wives to get tested to see what their babies were going to be. They resisted on the grounds that they'd rather be surprised. Actually, in their eighth month, both had ultrasounds.

Monday, Alicia called Belita. "Come over. I have something to talk to you about."

The girls started a campaign to have their babies delivered by the family midwife who had delivered them in Cozumel, Mexico. "No way!" stormed CJ.

"Absolutely not!" yelled JJ.

"But it's a family tradition. It would make my father so happy," cried Alicia.

"Why are we just now hearing about this?" chorused their husbands.

"We didn't think. We didn't realize how much this would mean to our father," said Belita. The argument raged on for days, in the end the girls won.

A week before their due date, Alicia and Belita flew to Cozumel and were taken by car to the ancestral home of Juan Casas. There they were met with many hugs and kisses by the staff and Amata the *comadrona*, the midwife. The husbands stayed home asking to be called as soon as labor began. The following week at eleven a.m. both girls went into labor. They called CJ and JJ, assured them it would be hours, probably most of the day and into the night before they actually delivered. The boys made it to Cozumel by six that evening and, sure enough, there was plenty of time.

At two in the morning the men were excluded from the bedroom where twin beds had been set up for the girls. CJ, JJ and their father-in-law drank whisky and waited, listening to the moaning coming from the upstairs room. "If only their mother were still alive. She would be so happy," said Juan Casas. At three-thirty, with the help of the midwife and her assistant Alicia and Belita gave birth.

After the girls and the newborns were cleaned up and the babies wrapped in the traditional pink and blue blankets, the new fathers were called in. Alicia proudly presented JJ with the son he had longed for. "I knew it! I knew it was a boy!" JJ held his tiny son and looked in awe at the perfect child. "We'll name him James Juan after me and your father." He hastily added, "If that's okay with you."

Alicia smiled. "That's perfect. My father will be so proud."

CJ was equally thrilled. "Now my son will have an older sister to look after him."

"Whoa, cowboy, could we wait until this baby is older before we talk about the next one?" Belita gave her husband a tired smile. "I'd like to rest up before I do *this* again. One more thing. Are you still okay with naming her after your mother and mine?"

"Patricia Marie sounds perfect to me."

Five years passed, the families worked and played together until JJ was offered a job in Paris as head of the computer analysis division. "We can't afford not to take it," cried Alicia. "This is such a step up for JJ. Besides it's not like we don't have email and you can visit and . . ." Tears choked her making it impossible to keep talking.

"Don't cry, sis, it'll be okay." The sadness in Belita's voice belied her words.

True to their resolve, the sisters emailed daily, giving detailed accounts of the activities of their families and news of interest about others both knew. Oddly, each time the question of Alicia, JJ and young Juan visiting the States or the possibility of Belita and her family going to Europe came up, there was always a reason why it wouldn't work. Usually JJ's job would have him away from home.

"We're being transferred to Saudi Arabia for three years," Alicia emailed Belita and CJ. "I'm sick about it. JJ is pretty pumped. Juan doesn't want to leave his friends what can we do?"

Three years turned into five. By now it had been thirteen years since the two families had seen one other. In early March they received news that the girls' uncle, Manuel Casas, had passed away, leaving his vast fortune to the only boy in the family, James Juan. The money was to be administered by Alicia and JJ with approval from Uncle Manuel's attorney. The parents were to receive a generous administrative allowance. The will gave very strict guidelines as to how the money was to be spent. At thirty, he could take control of his fortune.

"This is so awesome," Belita emailed. "Who knew Uncle Manuel was so rich."

"Not me. This will insure a wonderful future for Juan. JJ is afraid he will be spoiled, I assured him that we'll be careful and train him to spend wisely."

"This is great, I do wonder why Uncle Manuel excluded Patricia Marie from his will."

"A male chauvinist thing. You know girls can't be trusted to handle money—yada, yada, yada. Unfair, I know."

Two more years passed before the money became an issue.

"Patricia is looking forward to college," Belita emailed her sister. "She wants to go to medical school. CJ and I want her to go, only the expense is mind- blowing."

"Maybe JJ and I can help. We do get a generous allowance, you know."

"Thanks. I'm not sure CJ would want to accept help. He's feeling a little fragile right now. The market tanked and there's a lot of talk about downsizing at his firm."

"I could have JJ talk to him. Would that help?"

"No. Don't do that, there is something. Call me on the phone. I don't want anyone to get wind of this."

Alicia had a sick feeling. She called her sister. "Belita, we agreed years ago *never, never* to breathe a word of this."

"I know, things have changed."

"Yes, more than you could guess." Alicia sounded sad.

"What are you talking about? What is it? Are you and JJ okay? I mean no problems between the two of you?"

"Nothing, really. Don't mind me. I'm just feeling the strain of all this."

"Strain! Strain! Alicia, what do you have to feel strained about? My husband's losing his job. He's worried sick and you and your family inherited a fortune. My family was completely left out. How do you think I feel?" She started to cry.

"Belita, what would you have me do? You want me to tell my husband that he's been raising his own nephew all these years? You want me to tell Juan he's not my son? You want to tell CJ and Patricia Marie the lie we've been living for all these years?" Alicia broke down into wracking sobs. "Just tell me, Belita, what do you want?"

Belita, too was sobbing. "I don't know. I don't know what I want." *Money, the cursed money. Why didn't Uncle Manuel leave it to charity?*

Over the next three years the two families became more and more distant. Alicia and JJ, with young Juan, seemed to grow increasingly prosperous. JJ continued to rise in his company, and with the additional funds from managing the trust, he was able to invest wisely. Belita and CJ, on the other hand, were in a downward spiral. CJ lost his job. They were relying on Belita's teaching salary to sustain them until he could get back on his feet. Meanwhile, medical school for Patricia Marie seemed an impossibility.

Belita emailed her sister. "I remember our promise, understand that we are in deep financial trouble. We need your help. You have to do something."

"JJ and I can help only to the extent of the stipend we receive for managing Juan's trust. I know JJ will want to help, but he must never know the truth."

"Alicia, I hate this more than you can know, I can't let Patricia Marie down. We promised her that she could go to any medical school she chose. She's been accepted at four top schools. We have to have money."

"Belita, don't do anything. Don't say anything. We're coming home."

Belita, CJ and Patricia Marie waited for Air France to land at LAX. JJ, Alicia and a lovely young woman came up the ramp to meet them. Alicia turned to her family and announced, "This is Juanita, our daughter." There was complete silence followed by bewilderment and then astonishment. "We wanted you to meet her before we explained."

CJ hugged his twin. "I don't understand. What's going on?"

"Let's go home and we'll explain."

Over drinks Alicia began. "We suspected from an early age that Juan was more girl than boy. JJ tried to entice him into 'boy' activities, but he always came back to dolls and dress-up clothes."

"It took us a long time to accept the truth. When we finally did, Juan begged for the operation that would change him into the girl he really was." JJ held out his hand to the girl by his side.

Juanita took up the story. "It's true. I always felt like a girl. I wanted to be a real one. Once Mom and Dad accepted me the way I am, they took me to doctors and had me tested. The tests proved that I was really a girl living in a boy's body. I started hormone therapy and last year I had the surgery to complete the transition."

"Now you know why we resisted coming home for all those years," Alicia added. "You can't imagine how the sex change has affected our lives. One major issue was Juan/Juanita's trust. The will clearly states the money is to go to a male heir. We've worked out an agreement with the attorney so that we can keep the money already paid. The money paid while Juan was still . . . Juan. We do have the will in court for a final ruling."

JJ broke in. "We've agreed that the four of us should share. It was unfair of Uncle Manuel to give the money to only one child. We have enough to send Patricia Marie to medical school and send Juanita to law school. She's hoping her uncle CJ will advise her since she wants to specialize in investment fraud."

CJ and Belita looked stunned. "I'm on overload," said CJ. "I don't really know what to say."

Patricia Marie was the first to recover. "Uncle JJ, Aunt Alicia, I think it's great to have a girl cousin. I'm just sorry it took so long to meet her." With that she turned to Juanita and hugged her.

"Thank heavens!" Juanita appeared to have been holding her breath. "You have no idea what this means to me."

Alicia, JJ and Juanita returned to their home in France. The sisters resumed their daily correspondence. The following year Alicia emailed, "News! The courts have upheld our request for Juan/Juanita's trust on the grounds that it was willed before the change therefore it belongs to her. Juanita is now of age to make some decisions and she has had the money divided. Half to her and half to Patricia Marie."

Juanita and Patricia became close friends through email. "Please tell me about the change," Patti begged. "How hard was it? What steps did you go through? How long did it take? Please tell me. I really need to know. I've never shared this with anyone before but . . . I've always felt more like a Patrick

~ 284~

than a Patricia."

"Actually it was the kid's grandfather who told me that story," Josh said. "Seems Patricia confided in him. She needed some one to talk to. Of course this was way after she was grown and had gone to med school. Don't know if she ever did anything about it.

"This next one is, unfortunately, far more common than people think I called it . . ."

Chapter 23
NEIGHBORS

The screaming and cursing died away. Sounds of a car door slamming, wheels on gravel spinning as a car sped down the driveway left an abrupt silence. Karen heard the back patio slider open and saw her neighbor walk out and sit on the steps leading to the backyard. She filled two cups with coffee and walked out her own back door, crossing the yard to sit on the cold step. She could see her neighbor's split lip and the beginning of a black eye as she approached.

"Here, maybe this will help." She held out a steaming cup of coffee and put her arm around her friend's frail, bony frame. "You know this can't go on. It's getting worse. If you don't do something to stop these beatings, they will only escalate."

"I don't know what to do. What about my kids? How will we survive?"

"This should be *for* the kids and yourself. If you let it go on you put them and yourself in increasing danger. Think about it. Marshal and I will help all we can. But, *you* have to take the first step."

"I know. It's just that in between everything is so good. Each time this happens it's like we clear the air and start over again. We're friends and lovers just like we were in the beginning of our marriage. Then…I don't know…something happens.

The eggs aren't cooked right, the baby cries, the dog barks, who knows what, anything, and the whole nightmare starts over." Tears streamed down puffed cheeks and were caught by a tissue now tinged with blood.

"Think about the future. How are you and the kids going to survive in this environment? The next step is hitting the children you know."

"Oh no! That's the one thing that would never happen. Whatever goes on is between us. The kids are never threatened. No, that's not a problem." The tears started to flow again.

"Okay, I'm telling you this whole situation is a time bomb. If you don't act soon the neighbors will act for you. Everyone hears the arguing and sees your face. You can have only so many 'ran into the door' accidents. The police are already aware of what's going on. It won't take much more before the kids are in foster homes, then what?"

Three weeks of peace and quiet passed before Karen heard the shouting next door and the sound of a car roaring off. She wasn't surprised to see her neighbor at her back patio door holding a wet washcloth over the right eye.

"You poor thing. Come in. Let me see to that eye." Karen rushed to the bathroom and retrieved an old blue ice bag, filled it with ice from the fridge and pressed it gently to the cut. "Oh, this is deeper than I thought. You need stitches. Grab the baby and I'll take you to the emergency room."

"I can't do that! He'll make me pay for it later. The hospital will have to report it.   That's all I need. If the police show up how will I explain it?"

"What's to explain? Take your kids and leave. Where are your parents? Why don't you go to them?"

"I can't do that. They were against this marriage from the first. Said there was something off about the way I was treated. I can't go to them now and say I was wrong and they were right. I just can't."

"Well, you can't let that eye go untreated either. You've gotten yourself in a mind trap. Somehow you think it's your fault. You think '*if only I hadn't done this or that. If only I hadn't said this or that if only...if only...* It's not your fault! Protecting the kids is your responsibility." She held up her hands. "I know. I know the kids are not in danger. What about the fact that they hear name-calling, cursing, and the sounds of you being beaten? What about the fact that they know those two fighting are their parents? Do you think for a moment this might be damaging to them?" Karen felt sorry for her neighbor. At the same time she was exasperated. "Come on. We have to get that eye looked after. Get the baby. You can tell them it was a car accident. Where's Toby?"

"He's playing with the Martin kids. I'll call and ask if they'll keep him until I get back."

The eye got stitched at the busy ER, antibiotic administered and the two were back home before five." I've got to hurry and get dinner on the table. I don't want a repeat of this morning."

Karen shook her head as she watched her neighbor pick up the baby and carry her into the house. As usual quiet reigned for days after the incident. Marshal looked up at Karen over his newspaper on Sunday. "The silence is making me a nervous wreck. I keep thinking it's the calm before the storm. Every time I hear a sound I jump." He smiled at his wife. "Crazy, I know. I'm on edge when they fight and on edge when they don't. I swear I'm almost relieved when the fight starts at least I can stop waiting. Why don't they just split up? Get divorced like everyone else. Staying together is un-American."

Karen patted her husband on the arm. "I guess it's hard to give up on a marriage, even a bad one when you have kids."

"Be doing those kids a favor if you ask me. That's no way to live."

Karen kissed him. "I agree, no amount of talking seems to get through. What else can anyone do?"

At five the next morning muffled shouts could be heard. Marshal half mumbled, "Well now I can sleep. I know when the next fight begins."

Karen retrieved the morning paper at six. She glanced at the neighbor's porch. She saw three-year old Toby holding his blanket and teddy bear. "Toby, honey, why are you sitting there?" Karen had a sick feeling in the pit of her stomach. "Come with me sweetie; are you hungry?"

Toby took his thumb out of his mouth long enough to say, "Toast un jab."

"Of course, I have just the thing for a boy like you. You can sit at the table with Marshal and have breakfast." Karen carried the little boy into the kitchen. "Marshal, look who came to visit. Can you fix him some toast and jam? I'm going next door to see if everything is okay." Karen gave her husband a worried look, which he understood.

"Hey Buddy. Sit right up here, let's see what we can rustle up." Marshal lifted Toby onto a chair sliding a phone book under him. "There that ought to do it. Here have some juice while I make toast."

Karen ran next door and rang the bell. When no one answered she turned the knob and stepped inside. "Hey, anybody home?" The baby crying was the only sound. No one called back. She started up the stairs to check on the child when she saw a bare foot protruding from under the dining room table. The coppery smell of blood filled her nostrils. "Oh no! Oh no!" She bent down, looked under the table and screamed. Marshal came on the run as soon as he heard her.

Police and paramedics were there in four minutes. Too late for medical intervention. By now the whole neighborhood mingled outside and had to be shooed back behind crime tapes. No one claimed to be surprised by what had happened, only that it hadn't happened sooner. Karen trembled as she gave the officer the information he asked for. The children's grandparents were on their way.

Josh turned to his assistant, "put out an APB. on..." He looked to Karen, "Do you know the full name?"

She squeezed her husband's hand trying not to cry. "It's Pat, Patricia Morris. I don't know her middle name. I kept telling him to leave. He wouldn't listen."

Josh looked thoughtful. "It's sad but true. People just get caught up in a vicious cycle and don't know how to stop. Of course, it's doubly true when the battered person is a man—the old macho thing." He blew a smoke ring, sipped his Jack, then continued.

"This next case straddled the border between Orange County, California and Las Vegas . . ."

Chapter 24
SLY GUY

Kathryn could make out shadowy figures standing in the dim light at the back of the parking garage. She could hear voices not words. The cold in the damp garage made her shiver. *Wonder why a big casino like the Flamingo won't put in some high watt bulbs. This is creepy.* She could see three men near where her car was parked. They seemed to be waiting for something. At the sound of her heels on concrete the men looked her way. Later, she remembered thinking they looked like actors in a play, waiting for their cue. Guns were in their hands. She began to back up. One man looked at her, then started shooting, not at her, at the man in front of him. The man fell and was shot twice more. Too shocked to cry out, Kathryn backed away and ran. *My God! I know that man!* She grabbed the first taxi she spotted. At home, shaking made it hard to dial the phone. "Jim, it's me Kathryn Castle," she said when attorney Jim St. John's secretary put him on the line. "I know this is going to sound crazy, I just saw Sylvester Guy shoot a man," her voice came out in a rush.

"Whoa, slow down, what on earth are you saying?"

"I'm telling you, I just saw Sylvester Guy kill a man. I was standing no more than fifteen feet from him. I'm telling you I saw it!"

"Calm down, take a deep breath. Now, are you all right? Are you safe? Come to my office. I'll send a car for you. You might feel better here."

"Yes, please. I'm scared."

Kathryn slumped down in the soft leather chair and began to recount the events of the evening. "I had just come from a meeting at the Flamingo. I was going toward my car when I saw four men. One of them seemed to be drunk, he was having a hard time standing up. Then I saw the guns. The odd thing was they seemed to be waiting for something. One of the guys, I call him Bowling Ball, was big and built like a linebacker. His head looked like a shiny, round ball. His voice was like gravel being tread on by heavy boots. At first I thought the second man was a teenager. He was slight of build and very pale, then I saw that he was nearly bald with only a fringe of hair around his head. Teenage Man and Bowling Ball were wearing jumpsuits with something printed on the back. Because of the angle all I could make out was P---S GA—. The third man was Sylvester Guy. I'd know him anywhere. He was wearing one of his signature tweed jackets. I tell you, Jim, it was *him*. The fourth man, the one who got shot, was short, fat and rumpled looking. He was either drunk or sick. Now that I think of it he looked kinda beat up. It's like they were waiting for me. As soon as they were sure I could see them, Bowling Ball growled, 'Shoot, shoot now or the next bullet will be yours.' Sylvester shot the man. I ran like the wind."

Sylvester Guy stood, holding the gun as he heard a group of gamers exit the elevator. Bowling Ball and Teenage Man bolted for the stairs. Guy looked numbly at the man he'd just killed. The gamers were suddenly standing a few feet away from him. For a moment there was stunned silence. Then, there was mass confusion. One woman started screaming, the men started forward, then stopped at the sight of the gun.

Guy's adrenalin kicked in, his message center started

working. His feet began to respond. He threw the gun in the general direction of the body with a pool of blood spreading around it. *Down the stairs, turn the corner, head south on The Strip.* Guy picked up speed as he fled past Ballys, Paris, Planet Hollywood and MGM Grand. He could hear MGM's lion roar at him as he fled in panic. By now he could feel cold handcuffs and the hot breath of some cop at his back. At last, he saw the Tropicana across the street from the castle-like Excalibur.

The mile distance from the Flamingo Hotel to the Tropicana, where he'd left his car, normally an easy sprint for him, became the longest run of his life. Every tourist lurched at him. Every siren, a call to run faster.

By the time he reached his car he was icy cold and perspiring. His thoughts raced, *keys, keys, I had them in my jacket. No, I put them in my pants, no jacket. I know they were in my jacket pocket.* His hands flew from pants to jacket and back again. When he finally closed on them, his hands were too numb to hold on. The keys clanged on the concrete floor. Down on all fours, he stretched his arm under the car. When they were at last in his shaking hand, the keyhole became a shimmering, hard to catch ghost.

Guy fled Las Vegas toward Los Angeles and Orange County. The landscape rolled past as light dimmed over the desert wasteland leaving it in total darkness. Some portion of his brain asked, *what idiot ever saw beauty in this, the cat box of the world? What the devil just happened? I've got to get home and figure this thing out before the cops find me. The people in the garage got a good look. If I'm stopped I'm dead meat.*

Out of the night, sirens whirled and whooped as they bore down on his Mercedes. Gripped in panic, he tried to think of a way out. They approached at frightening speed. Finally, he realized that the cars around him were pulling off to the right; he filed in behind a Fun Bus loaded with homebound partygoers. The police, followed by a fire engine, passed him without a glance. His overwhelming relief made him nauseous. He felt so sick he didn't think he could go on. It took all of his willpower to get back into the flow of traffic. Just before Barstow there was an overturned Bronco. There were already stretchers with bodies on them being loaded into the ambulance.

The desert landscape gave way to more buildings and evidence of population by the time he reached the 215 turnoff, south to Riverside or west to Ontario and south again to Orange County. The scenery was a blur, his only thought to get to a safe place and sort this mess out. He could hole up at the Red Lion Inn for a while and make some calls.

By Monday Sylvester Guy's picture stared back from the front page of the *Las Review Journal* and the *Orange County Register*. The victim was identified as Joseph Wainright, a businessman operating just on the edge of the law. He owned several small businesses including a pizza takeout place, a dry cleaners and an auto repair. Ex-cons on parole were his primary labor source. The police had watched him closely for years.

The papers identified Guy as an assistant district attorney from Orange County. His whereabouts were unknown at the time the papers went to press.

"Jim," Kathryn said, "you know Guy is poison. He's railroaded more innocent people than can be believed, including me. I'd love to see him go down for this. In all honesty it did look like those two thugs were holding him at gunpoint. I'm between a rock and a hard place. If I testify for him, the prosecution will claim I feared retaliation, or possibly that he had promised to go back and right some wrongs in my old case. If I don't say he was forced to shoot in fear for his own life, his side will cry revenge! What am I going to do?"

"First let's get you out of harm's way. Take a leave from your job. We'll stash you out of sight until we can figure this out. No one trusts Guy. He's done more harm to the legal system than anyone I can think of, yet even I can't believe he'd kill Wainright. How did the two of them end up in that garage? Something big time is going on. I think you'll be safer if you leave town until we know what it is."

After landing in Honolulu, Kathryn picked up a paper and started searching for a place to rent. She found a house on the leeward side of the island, away from the tourist traps. It sat on a small bluff overlooking the ocean. A rickety stairway led down to the beach. Sliding glass doors opened to a garden filled with flowers gone wild. The rooms were furnished with bamboo and rattan furniture. The only concession to modernizing was a fairly new fridge and microwave oven. *Perfect!*

Guy wanted to get his plan in place before the cops got to him. *First an attorney, he thought. I need someone licensed in both California and Nevada, someone I can manipulate. Someone too greedy for the money to care about his political future.*

After several calls to people who owed him, he realized, *I'm a pariah.* No one wanted to associate with him or his case. Finally, he hit the bottom of the barrel, *Manny Lopez.* The laziest, most inept, greedy attorney he could think of. Usually he would avoid Manny at all costs in case someone mistook them for friends. Just maybe this time, Manny was the man. *They don't call me Sly Guy for nothing,* he smiled to himself.

"Hey, Sly, my man. What's up?" chirped the voice from the receiver. Guy winced at the intended familiarity from a man he loathed as inferior, however, in all fairness, this was the very reason he called him.

"Well, Manny, I've got a little situation here and I thought you might help out." *Appeal to the little creep. Try to make him think he's one of the 'Boys'. Later I'll squash this bug; right now I need him.*

"Well, ol' buddy, what can I do for you?" laughed Manny. "I caught your picture on the morning news. Looks like you got a barrel of trouble for yourself. Unless this is some new kinda campaign strategy to get yourself elected D.A. next term." Contrary to what Guy believed, Manny knew what

Guy thought of him. It pleased him no end to have the high and mighty Sylvester Guy call him.

"I was set up, Manny and I can prove it. There was a witness."

"Where is this witness?" asked Manny.

"I don't know, probably hiding out scared; trust me, I'll find her."

"Well, well, isn't this pretty amazing? I was sure you thought I was too stupid to walk and chew gum at the same time, much less practice law. Now you call me to ask me to defend you. What happened, ol' buddy, did all your good *friends* turn you down? Were all of your chicken shit *friends* too busy to come to your rescue? Were all of them suddenly going out of town? Did they all have vacation plans they couldn't break, or were their schedules just so tight they couldn't possibly do your case justice? Soo sorry. Wish I could help, you know how it is," snickered Manny.

Manny's assessment, so close to the truth, made Guy's stomach turn. As much as he needed him, Guy couldn't suppress his anger. "Look Lopez," he growled, "I picked you for professional reasons only." *What a lie. When I get out of this mess, I'll choke this little jerk. Who does he think he is? I give him the chance at a high-profile case and he plays games. If there were anyone else, anyone at all, I'd tell him to kiss my ass.*

Manny's irritating voice came back on the line. He just couldn't resist a few low blows now that he had a chance. "It seems to me this may be payback time. You've done your share of sticking it to people; maybe one of them wants some revenge. Remember that Castle woman? You tried to intimidate her into signing a guilty plea and forfeiting her right of appeal. If Jim St. John hadn't caught you, she would have been sent up for a crime she not only didn't commit, she was one of the victims. Pretty fancy footwork, I'd say."

In a rage, Guy forced himself to calm down, then it hit him. "Castle, did you say Castle? That's her! That's the broad I saw in the garage. I thought there was something familiar about her. I know it's her! Manny, get her address. She's my ticket out of this mess."

"Whoa, pal. Let's discuss my fee first. I'll take your case. It'll cost you a million bucks up front, plus expenses."

"Lopez, are you nuts?"

"Look, Sly, I may be nuts, and or stupid or inept or any of the other names you and your tight ass friends call me, but I know that if there were anyone else in the world who would take this case, you'd never have called me, so cut the crap. It's your life. Take it or leave it."

He had no other choice. It had to be Manny Lopez. Manny could be manipulated and Guy had every intention of running this case. He did have some misgivings about the way he had perceived Manny. Maybe he wasn't so stupid after all.

A murder trial involving Sly Guy would spell instant fame for Manny. He had no illusions about his talent as a criminal defense attorney. He did know that once this case went to trial, his name would forever be in print as the man who defended the famous Mr. Guy. TV coverage would insure a lot of free publicity. He frankly did not give a hoot if Guy killed Wainright. Everyone knew Guy hated that man; still killing him seemed out of character, even for Guy. Manny and Sly were both bounty hunters, and this case would make Manny number-one big game hunter in this town. *The truth is, he thought, no matter how this case goes, I'll come out on top: I'll be famous, a million bucks richer and a hero to all the poor schmucks that Guy has coerced into confessions over the years.*

Once they agreed on terms, Manny hired a private detective to find Kathryn Castle. Next Guy called the Vegas police and told them he was coming in on Southwest Air, with his attorney the next morning.

When they arrived, Detective Josh Cummings led them back through the labyrinth of cubicles that passed for offices. The detective was a six-foot mass of muscle. His fixed scowl gave him the appearance of being permanently pissed off.

The effect chilled Guy. Manny sat back and enjoyed the show. "Okay, why don't you start at the beginning and tell me what happened?" Cummings growled.

"I know this sounds crazy," said Guy, "but, this is the truth."

"Crazy, I'm used to, B.S., I'm used to; truth would be a nice change." He smiled, the smile held no warmth. It never reached his eyes. The muscles in his face were totally unaccustomed to the activity.

"I was gambling, not doing too well, when a girl I know, Lila Green, invited me to her place."

"A hooker?"

"A hooker. I've known Lila for several years. I usually look her up when I come to Vegas; this time she found me. We were supposed to meet on the second floor of the garage at six. She wasn't there. I was waiting when two guys jumped me and stuck a gun in my back. Naturally, I thought, hold-up, then they dragged Wainright out from between two cars. He looked like he had been knocked around. The goons put a gun in my hand and threatened to kill me if I didn't shoot Wainright. *I had no choice.* After I unloaded the gun in him, the two guys made for the stairs. A woman standing there saw the whole thing. She can tell you how it happened. Anyway, the next thing I know, people are in front of me. A woman is screaming her lungs out. I panicked. I threw the gun and ran like a son of a bitch."

"Just a question. Why didn't you shoot the two guys?

"I wanted to, but there were two of them and one of me. They said if I tried anything one of them could kill me before I knew what was happening. I believed every word. Frankly, I was scared spitless."

For the next hour Cummings asked questions about the incident. He wanted to know more about the two men, their looks, build, dress, anything else they said. He asked about the witness. Guy told him all he could remember. He said he believed the witness was Kathryn Castle, a woman he prosecuted at one time, he wasn't positive.

Manny remained quiet during most of the interview, then said, "Now be assured, my client will cooperate in every way. He wants to clear this up."

In due course, Guy was released on $1,000,000 bail. The press couldn't stop pointing out that murder, even in Las Vegas demanded a higher amount. These things happen in Vegas, if you know the judge.

Odd, thought Cummings, Guy seemed real clear about the witness, then vague about the two men with guns in his ribs. All he really said about them was that one was black, the other white, both wore overalls. He would have dismissed them as figments of Guy's imagination if he hadn't remembered a statement given by Mr. Townsend, one of the gamers who found Guy standing over the body. Townsend remarked that he noticed a tow truck parked in the alley beside the garage. He said he remembered because of the license plate, TOW BIZ. Tow truck drivers might wear overalls.

Meanwhile, Cummings made a call. "Mr. Townsend, Mr. William Townsend?" he asked.

"Speaking," said Townsend. "What can I do for you?"

"Mr. Townsend, this is Detective Cummings from the Las Vegas Police Department. Do you remember being in the parking garage at the Flamingo Hotel on the twenty-fifth?"

"Of course I remember," replied Townsend testily. "How could I ever forget a thing like that?"

"Sorry, sir, I just wanted to be sure. I remember a remark you made about seeing a tow truck. Can you tell me any more about it?"

"I think I told you all I know. It was just an ordinary tow truck. I never would have thought of it if it hadn't been for the license plate."

"Please, would you tell me again? What color was it? Do you remember the name on the side? Was there anything else you can think of?"

"Okay. It was yellow, not new, kinda beat up. The only

really outstanding thing was the license. Oh, wait, I think I remember the name, started with P, Paul's Garage. Pete's Garage maybe. Pablo's Garage. I'm sorry I can't be sure, it was something like that."

"Thank you, Sir. You've been a great help. I really appreciate your time. I'll see you when the trial begins."

Josh turned to the phone book. Under auto repair he found four garages that began with the letter P. He started dialing. On the third call a girl's voice answered the phone. "No Biz like Tow Biz. Pete's Garage." BINGO!

He drove out Owens Avenue until he spotted Pete's Garage hidden between two dilapidated apartment buildings. Pete ambled to the front of the service bay, his paunch preceding him by two feet. What was left of his dyed black hair, fell in unwashed waves over one eye. "What's up?" he asked when Cummings identified himself.

"Looking for a coupla guys, might work here."

He described the two men, Pete said, "Yeah, I know 'em. But they don't work here anymore. Took the tow truck for a joy ride. Had to let 'em go."

Josh got all the information he could from Pete, including the real names of the two. Before he left he asked, "How long you been in business?"

"I'm the manager. Joe Wainright owns …owned the place. Don't know what'll happen now."

"Wainright? That's interesting." He handed Pete a card. "If you hear anything, give me a call."

"They have some money coming. I thought I'd hear before now."

"If they call, stall until you get a hold of me."

"Will do." Pete didn't need the law looking at this place too closely. With Wainright gone he could skim even more of the profits, at least until someone claimed the shop.

A few days later he received a call. "Detective, this is Pete from the garage. They're coming for their checks. I told them to be here at three."

"Thanks, I'll be there."

In Hawaii, Kathryn received a letter from Jim St. John. The trial was scheduled for July fourteenth. Bastille Day. Off with their heads! "A fitting day for a trial for a traitor," mused Kathryn. "A traitor to all of the oaths of office he had ever sworn to. A traitor to all the laws he had sworn to uphold and a traitor to all the people he had sworn to protect. My only regret is that I will be testifying on his behalf."

She made arrangements to fly back as Skipi Jensen, in case Guy's people were watching. During the flight she made friends with a young mother traveling with four small children, two sets of twins. Her offer of help to get off the plane was gratefully accepted. At the curb she handed her charges to their father and hailed a cab. No one takes much notice of two women herding small children. She checked into Fitzgerald's Casino and Hotel. It was convenient to the court house. Until the trial started she didn't want Guy getting his hooks into her. Talk about being in the middle. The defense was after her because they believed she would testify for the prosecution. The prosecution wanted her because they thought she would testify for the defense. *As my granddad used to say, "Shit and two is eight." I don't have a clue what that means, but it seemed to make him feel better for the saying.*

Guy called his team together in the hotel room he reserved at the Bellagio. Manny, Guy and two law clerks hired to assist him were going over their defense strategy. "What makes you think this woman will lie about what she saw in the garage? Does she know you?" asked one of the law clerks.

In a rare moment of candor, Guy told them. "Several years ago I convicted her of a crime she didn't commit. I told her if she didn't plead guilty the judge would send her away for ten years. Actually, we were focusing on her to protect her boss, a high roller who had made some heavy campaign contributions in return for keeping his name clear. Which is why she has to be found at all costs. Any word from our illustrious PI?"

Manny shrugged his shoulders.

Later that day, Manny received a letter from Jim St. John informing him that Kathryn Castle was prepared to testify. A number of phone calls to St. John went unanswered; his secretary informed Manny that Mr. St. John was unavailable.

Court: Day One

Spectators filled the room; a quiet hum of conversation filled the air. Sylvester Guy and Manny Lopez were in place, seated at a table facing the judge's bench. For the first day of court Guy chose a medium blue suit, light blue shirt and blue striped tie. Blue, the color of honesty. If the trial lasted too long he would have to buy more blue suits.

The bailiff stood. "All rise for the Honorable Judge Richards." The judge swept in. "Be seated," intoned the bailiff; the court settled back to listen.

Judge Richards asked if all parties were in attendance and ready to proceed.

"Yes, your Honor," came the reply from both Manny Lopez and prosecutor Carlton Bell.

The jurors filed into the jury box, each one either sneaking a quick peek at Guy or studiously ignoring him. Prosecutor Carlton Bell stood. Aristocratic confidence came to mind. Bell's build spoke of hours spent in the gym and time under a sun lamp. His suit spoke volumes about custom tailors, old money and a lifestyle not supported on a D.A's salary.

"Ladies and gentlemen of the jury. Thank you for being here," he began. "I don't anticipate a lengthy trial. The facts are clear. Mr. Sylvester Guy shot and killed Mr. Joseph Wainright. The prosecution will prove that Mr. Guy lured Mr. Wainright into the parking structure at the Flamingo for the purpose of killing him. You will hear things about the character of Mr. Joseph Wainright. It is no secret that Mr. Wainright lived on the edge of the law, but ladies and gentlemen, does this give Sylvester Guy the right to kill him? You know the answer to that as well as I do.

"The defense will present a fairy tale about two men who forced him to shoot the victim. The defense will compound this tale with a, yet to be found, hooker who supposedly will confirm his story of why he was in the garage. The defense will also present a witness of questionable honesty, a woman accused of fraud in California, a woman with past ties with the defendant. Sylvester Guy was the prosecuting attorney in her case. Does anyone else here smell a rat? Why do I have visions of money changing hands? Bell ducked his head into his chin and looked up at the jury with an *Oh come on!* expression.

The judge looked sharply at Bell. "Watch yourself, Counselor."

"Yes, your Honor." He turned back to the jury, "Ladies and gentlemen, do not be fooled by this witness. Do not believe anything she tells you. There is no polite way to put it. This woman is a liar, plain and simple.

"In the days to come I will prove everything I have told you this morning. You will come to believe, as I do, that this man deserves the heaviest penalty allowed by law. Thank you." Carlton Bell sat down, the complete picture of a man representing the truth, a champion of all victims no matter their background. The jury looked convinced.

Manny Lopez stood to deliver his opening remarks. The complete opposite of Carlton Bell, Manny had put on a newly pressed suit and fresh shirt that morning. He had his shoes shined on the way to court. He still looked as if he had spent the night in his clothes. He just naturally looked unkempt.

Once in front of the jury he wiggled, tugged at his tie, straightened his jacket, buttoned and unbuttoned until the judge was fed up. "Mr. Lopez, will you please get on with it?"

"Yes, your Honor, sorry," Manny cleared his throat, "Ladies and gentlemen of the jury, it is your great privilege to be allowed to be part of the judicial process of which our country is so very proud. This is not to discount the time each of you is taking out of your personal lives to be here. For this I thank you." The judge, jury and everyone present began to roll their eyes and sigh. This was not going to be fast.

What on earth is Manny doing? thought Guy. This is not the speech we worked out.

Manny droned on. "It is in the great tradition of our forefathers that we are gathered here to learn the circumstances surrounding this case. All is not as it seems."

The jury began to shift in their chairs as Manny went on and on about their privilege, their responsibility, their duty, their sacrifice, etc., etc., blah, blah, blah.

"Finally, ladies and gentlemen, we acknowledge that Mr. Sylvester Guy shot Mr. Joseph Wainright. However, he did not do it out of malice. He did it out of fear for his own life. He was forced at gunpoint to shoot Joe Wainright, and we have a witness to prove it."

Guy wanted to punch Manny in the face when he finally sat down. Through gritted teeth he said, "That was the sorriest opening I have ever heard. If they weren't trying to stay awake they were trying not to laugh. I may be convicted on the grounds that I'm too stupid to hire a credible attorney."

Court: Day Two

After dispensing with preliminaries, Carlton Bell called his first witness. "Mr. Townsend, can you tell the jury how you came to be in the parking garage of the Flamingo the night Mr. Wainright was killed?"

"We, that's my wife and me and our friends Bob and Jody Shultz, were on our way back to our hotel. We all wanted to change; we were going to see Wayne Newton."

"You weren't staying at the Flamingo?"

"No, we were at the MGM Grand, but we went to the Flamingo to play for a while. Well, we took the elevator to the second floor of the garage. We was all walkin' and talkin' when Jody starts to scream her head off. Like to scared the sh…" Bill Townsend turned beet red. "Sorry, I mean the dickens out of me. I thought she was havin'a stroke or somethin'. Then I seen this guy waving a gun and there's a body on the floor with blood all over the place. At first I think the man with the gun is after us then he just throws the gun on the floor and runs. Bob, Bob Shultz ran for security, the next thing I know there's suits and badges crawling all over." He seemed completely unaware that what he had just said was pure *NYPD Blue.*

Mr. TV man, thought Attorney Bell. "Did you see anyone else in the garage? Anyone at all?"

"I think there was a woman in a red outfit, I wasn't watching her. I was too busy with the rest of the stuff goin' on."

"Very understandable, sir. Did you notice anyone in overalls or jumpsuits?"

"No, I didn't. I think I did hear someone runnin' down the stairs when we first got there. I'd forgotten that until now."

"Thank you, Mr. Townsend. That's all I have. Your witness, Mr. Lopez."

Manny stood to approach the witness, as he did his sleeve caught a glass of water sitting on the table next to him, sending a spray over the table and onto some documents. A few minutes were taken to clean up the mess. Judge Richards waited patiently while the bailiff produced paper towels. "Sorry, your Honor, sorry," mumbled Manny.

Sorry! Oh yes you're sorry, thought Guy, trying to keep out of the way. *Sorry should be this moron's middle name.*

Finally, approaching the witness, Manny asked, "Mr. Townsend, will you tell the court what time of day it was when you and your friends went into the garage?"

"I'm not sure of the exact time, late afternoon, around four or five. I remember that because we wanted to go and get cleaned up for dinner before the show."

"And what was the light like in the garage?"

"Kinda dim. We joked about the casino makin' so much money and being too cheap to buy high watt bulbs."

"Mr. Townsend, if it was so dark, how can you be sure it was Mr. Guy you saw?"

"Objection! He said it was dim, not dark," called Bell.

"Objection noted, Mr. Bell," said the judge. "But since we

already know by Mr. Guy's own statement that in fact it was Mr. Guy, the question seems irrelevant. Where are you going with this, Mr. Lopez? The question is not whether Mr. Guy was in the garage. It is *not* whether he shot the victim. It's, *was he forced to shoot?* Please let's get on with it."

"Yes your Honor, sorry your Honor," stammered Manny. He turned again to the witness stand. "Mr. Townsend, you stated that you saw a lady standing in the garage. Given the poor light, isn't it true that you can't be positive there was no one else in the garage?"

"Well, I guess there could've been someone back in between the cars. I sure as he . . didn't go lookin'!" Again Townsend turned the color of pickled beets.

"Thank you, Mr. Townsend. Would you please describe the woman you did see for the jury?"

"I'm not sure. Kinda short, I think, wearin' somethin' red. Maybe a red pantsuit. I probably wouldn't have noticed her at all if she hadn't run."

"Mr. Lopez, again I ask, is this going anywhere?" Judge Richards inquired in a bored voice.

"I'm finished, your Honor."

"The court will recess until Monday at nine a.m." The judge left the room. The jurors left through their own door.

Court: Day Three

"The defense calls Kathryn Castle." Manny moved to the front of the courtroom. Kathryn had dressed carefully for this day in a pale pink skirt with matching sweater set. She finished the outfit with a string of pearls and pearl earrings. Her blond hair hung just above her shoulders in soft waves. She looked at the jury with steady blue eyes.

"Ms. Castle, is it true that you were in the garage of the Flamingo the night Joseph Wainright was murdered?"

"Yes, it is."

"Would you please describe the events of that night for the jury?" Kathryn described in detail what she had witnessed. She described the two men in overalls and how they held Sylvester Guy at gunpoint and forced him to shoot the victim. She also told of running from the parking structure in fear for her own life.

"Thank you. Your witness."

"Isn't it true that you had a prior relationship with Mr. Sylvester Guy?" Bell's voice took on a strident tone. "Isn't it true that Mr. Guy once prosecuted you for crimes in California?" He became louder and stood closer to Kathryn. "Isn't it true that you've been paid to make this *revelation* about two thugs holding Mr. Guy at gunpoint?"

"Objection! Badgering!" Manny practically jumped from his chair.

"Sustained," intoned Judge Richards. "Mr. Bell, you will refrain from any attempt to intimidate this witness. It has been established that Ms. Castle is here of her own free will. I will not have you bullying witnesses in my courtroom. Is that clear?" Turning to the court recorder, he said, "Strike the prosecution's last three questions from the record."

"But your Honor…"

"Move on!"

"No further questions for this witness."

Manny was so pumped by seeing Bell take a hit from the judge he could hardly contain himself. "Your Honor, I call as my next witness Detective Cummings of the Las Vegas Metro Police." He was sworn in and seated. "Detective Cummings, based on the description given by Mr. Sylvester Guy and the corroborating statements of Ms. Castle, were you able to identify and ultimately find the two men described as the men holding Mr. Guy at gunpoint?"

"Yes, currently both men are in custody."

"Have they given statements in regard to their part in this crime?"

"They have. Both men claim to have been at a party on the night in question. Neither claims to have any knowledge of the shooting."

The prosecution waived questions, reserving the right to recall Detective Cummings at a later time.

"The prosecution calls Mr. Harold Thebes to the stand." He dressed for the occasion in a purple velvet suit with gold piping and matching hat. He'd been here before. He was not worried. He had this covered. No one could touch him. He placed his hat on the table and ambled to the stand. The light of the courtroom glanced off his perfectly round, shiny head, giving him the somewhat incongruous look of having a halo.

"Mr. Thebes, are you aware of why you are in court today?"

Thebes nodded his head.

"Please answer for the court record," said Bell.

"Yeah," came the growl.

"Mr. Thebes, were you in the parking structure of the Flamingo on the night in question?"

"No."

"Mr. Thebes, were you anywhere near the hotel that night?"

"No."

"Please tell the court where you were that night."

"All of us was at a pizza and beer bash."

"By 'all of us' who do you mean?"

"Us guys that work for Wainright."

"Mr. Thebes, do you know Sylvester Guy?"

"No."

"Before today have you ever seen Mr. Guy in person?"

"No."

"Will you please tell the court if you had any reason to kill Joseph Wainright?"

"No."

"No, you won't tell us or no you didn't have a reason to kill him?" came the exasperated response of Carlton Bell.

"Counselor, you are badgering your own witness. Please conclude your questioning," put in Judge Richards.

"Nothing further, your Honor,"

"Your witness, Mr. Lopez."

Manny wasn't sure what to ask. He wanted to discredit the witness, he wasn't sure what would get the right response. "Good morning, Mr. Thebes." He would take a softer approach to put Bowling Ball off guard. "Please tell the jury how you came to work at Pete's Garage."

He shrugged, "I'm a good mechanic."

"There must be a lot of good mechanics around. How did he come to hire you?"

"Lucky, I guess."

"Mr. Thebes, isn't it true that you were picked out of a prison training program?"

"Yeah."

"Isn't it true that you were in prison for assault with a deadly weapon?"

Bell was on his feet in seconds. "Objection, your Honor, Mr. Thebes is not on trial here."

"Sustained! Mr. Lopez, confine your questions to the matter before us."

"Your Honor may I approach the bench?" asked Manny. Judge Richards waved both attorneys to come before him. "Your Honor, I'm just trying to establish that this witness has a prior, using a gun."

"Lopez, that doesn't have anything to do with this case," put in Bell.

"Are you nuts? It has everything to do with it. This cretin forced my client to shoot Wainright, and I need to prove it."

"Gentlemen, I'm in a good mood. Don't do anything to spoil it. I'm with Bell on this one. Proceed *understand?*"

Manny tried a new approach. "Mr. Thebes, do you know Mr. Wainright, the owner of Pete's Garage?"

"No."

"Have you ever met Mr. Wainright?"

"No."

"You are aware that he is the owner?"

"Yeah."

"Mr. Thebes, please tell the jury in your own words what you did on the day of the shooting."

"Went to work. Went to the party."

Worn out now, Manny asked one more question. "Mr. Thebes, where was the party?"

"Pizza place on the corner."

Swell, thought Manny, *almost a whole fucking sentence.* "No further questions."

Court: Day Four

"The prosecution calls Mr. George Grimes," intoned Carlton Bell. Grimes walked to the witness stand. Dressed in a pale tan suit that blended with his complexion, he had the appearance of a spirit without substance. His wispy hair was slicked down, either still wet from a shower or filled with gel. His knees felt weak, his mouth felt like cotton as he took his place.

"Good morning. Mr. Grimes, please, tell the court who you work for."

"Pete's Garage."

"I understand that, sir, but isn't it true that Pete's was owned by Joseph Wainright?"

"Yeah, I guess."

"Mr. Grimes, please tell us where you were on the night Mr. Wainright was killed."

"A party."

"A party? Could you please tell us who else was there?"

"Bubba, Steve, Joe, Pete, Harry an..."

"Excuse me, Mr. Grimes, can you tell us the last names of these men?"

"No, well Bubba, his last name's Thebes. And Pete, his name's Fuentes. I don't know the rest."

"Bubba. Would that be Harold Thebes?"

By now Grimes had a fine coat of perspiration covering his upper lip. "Yeah," came his wavering answer.

"Mr. Grimes, were you in or anywhere near the parking lot

of the Flamingo Hotel on the night in question?"

"No."

"No further questions."

Manny declined to question the witness. There didn't seem to be any point. He asked to recall Kathryn Castle to the stand. "Ms. Castle, I just have one question. Do you see the two men who were holding my client at gunpoint the night Joseph Wainright was shot?"

"Yes. They're sitting right there." She pointed directly at Thebes and Grimes.

Carlton Bell stood to make his summation. "Ladies and gentlemen, what can I say?" Bell looked puzzled. "The defense *has no* defense. The only one who positively places the two men in the garage that night is a less than credible witness with former ties to Sylvester Guy. The supposed gunmen have airtight alibis. The only possible conclusion is that Sylvester Guy shot and killed Joseph Wainright. We have no idea of his motive, there's no doubt that he killed him. Sylvester Guy confessed. The story of being forced to shoot is pure fabrication. You have no choice but to find him guilty. Thank you."

Manny got up to make his closing remarks. He buttoned and unbuttoned his jacket.

"First, let me point out that the witness was acquitted of the crime she was accused of when Sylvester Guy was Assistant District Attorney. Sylvester Guy put Kathryn Castle through a nightmare, and she has every reason to want him to suffer, however, because she *is* an honest person she came forward to clear him of this crime." He shifted from one foot to the other causing the judge to glare at him until he stopped. "The two men, Grimes and Thebes, are, in fact, petty criminals with histories of theft and assault with a deadly weapon. The evidence tells the story." Again he shifted his weight and buttoned and unbuttoned his Jacket. "Everything my client has told you is true. You have no choice but to find him not guilty!" Manny turned to sit down, tripped over his shoelace and caught himself before falling into his chair. Guy hid his face in his hands. Judge Richards glared and futilely pounded his gavel at the laughter coming from the audience seated in the courtroom.

Jury deliberations went on for three days. At last the call came, a verdict reached. Sylvester Guy, Manny and Carlton Bell waited while the judge asked if the jury had made a decision. "We have, your Honor," said the foreman. The clerk took a paper from the juror and passed it to the judge. He read it and gave it back. "We find the defendant Sylvester Guy not . . ."

"Yesss!" Guy pounded Manny on the back. "We did it!" he whispered.

"STOP!" The voice came from a woman entering the courtroom on crutches. Her head was bandaged a brace wound around her neck. The court looked up in stunned silence. "Stop, he did it!" The woman pointed to Guy. "He planned the whole thing. I can prove it!"

"What?" Manny looked puzzled. "Who is that?"

"Lila Green," whispered Guy. "I thought she split. I don't know what to think. She was supposed to be my witness." Manny gave Guy a thoughtful look.

Judge Richards motioned for the woman to come forward. "What's the meaning of this?" he asked, as bewildered as the rest of the courtroom.

"Your Honor, my name is Lila Green. I was supposed to meet Sylvester Guy in the garage at the Flamingo. I was supposed to be his witness."

"Your Honor!'" shouted Manny, "This is inappropriate!"

"I decide what's appropriate in my courtroom, Mr. Lopez. Now sit down."

Manny fairly crumpled into his chair. Guy looked stricken.

"Please, Ms. Green, be seated." While a stunned courtroom looked on, Lila Green made her way painfully to the stand. "Tell us what happened. Don't be nervous, just tell us in your own words."

"I've known Sylvester Guy for a long time. One night he

said he was playing an elaborate trick on a friend and wanted my help. He said all I had to do was be in the garage at four. He was going to pretend to shoot some man. He never said his name. I was to witness two other men holding him at gunpoint. He was going to give me five hundred dollars just to be there. I went home during the day and was on my way back to the casino when I had this horrible car accident. When I woke up, I had been in the hospital for weeks, it was then that I found out about Sly shooting Joseph Wainright. I knew then that Guy lied. Guy hated Wainright. Joe Wainright had been blackmailing him for years. Joe knew that Sly falsified evidence against a big time operator in Orange County causing the man to lose millions in a land deal. He knew that Guy had taken thousands of dollars from the man's competitor. I'm not sure how Joe found out, he had been milking Guy for a long time. If the truth ever came out it would have ruined Guy politically."

"How do you know these things? And why are you willing to tell this court?" asked Judge Richards.

"I know because Joe told me. I'm willing to tell the court because Joe was my husband. My real name is Lila Wainright. I didn't know the joke was to be on my husband."

Jim St. John met Kathryn at Morton's Steak House on Flamingo Road. Jim raised his glass to Kathryn. "To the victor. How does it feel?"

Kathryn smiled. "I'm still reeling. I was so relieved when Lila Green-Wainright showed up, poor thing, still in a cast and bandages." Kathryn took a sip of her drink. "I don't feel like *I did* anything. I just happened to be in the garage and they just happened to need a witness. I'll tell you this, it feels great to know Sly Guy wasn't so sly after all."

Jim took a sip of his drink. "Yeah, it'll be a long, long while before he gets out of prison. At least he'll be in good company. Maybe Thebes and Grimes can be his roomies. Manny Lopez is the real winner. He keeps an easy million bucks and still has his sleazy practice. Frankly, I think most of his clients deserve him."

Kathryn looked pensive. "No, the real winners are the people who won't be harmed by Sylvester Guy's brand of justice."

Kathryn and Jim spoke at the same time. "Hear, hear! Let's drink to that!"

"You've really been all up and down the map haven't you?" Steve said while George freshened Josh's drink.

"Yeah. I worked in San Diego early on, then migrated to Vegas. The last years of my career were spent around the Reno-Tahoe area. Linda and I liked the quieter life up north. Not that there wasn't crime, there was, plenty of it, still not the same kind of crime you find in the bigger cities. Or at least not as much.

This one happened up in the Reno area about thirty years ago not to long after we moved there. I call it . . ."

Chapter 25
BAD NEWS

The call came at the worst possible moment. Linda didn't hide her disappointment. "Could another five minutes make a difference? She's been missing for months. If she's at the bottom of the lake, then she's at the bottom! If we're going to have a baby we have to start it *right now*! If we miss the time frame we have to wait until next month. You know all that. Why am I talking to you?" She burst into tears. Josh Cummings put his arms around his wife and tried to comfort her. They moved to this small mountain community to get away from the stress and strain of city life. Doctors told Linda that she needed to be calm and stress-free if she wanted to get pregnant. When this job as sheriff came up, he jumped at the opportunity. They had been trying without success to have a baby for years. Linda kept saying her clock was ticking; her doctor said she still had a small chance of getting pregnant. Now, she said her clock sounded like Big Ben! He knew it would have to happen soon or it would be too late. They talked of adoption, in his heart he knew both of them wanted a child they had formed themselves. He tried once again to comfort her, she waved him away. "Go! Go, do your job."

He kissed her on her tear-stained cheek. "Honey, you know I have to. We'll talk later."

Grim faced men stood looking at the murky water. Bubbles rising to the top of the lake suggested where divers were searching. The sheriff looked skyward in time to see a tiny plane in the distance. A speck floated down from the plane. He shaded his eyes to better see. It looked like a parachute falling into the dense woods, he couldn't be sure. Probably an optical illusion caused by light bouncing off clouds. Or a bit of vapor trail created by the passing plane, he mused. A shout diverted his attention to the lake. Divers were coming out of the water, dripping in the cold morning light. One held something up, a woman's purse.

"This is all we found. No body. After we drag the car out maybe there'll be more."

"Okay, thanks, we'll wait." For a moment he thought about his wife. He knew how much she wanted a baby. He did too. Maybe it was time to reconsider adoption.

Hikers found the back end of Cindy's car sticking out of the water under the old bridge. Josh and his men searched all night. They found no sign of her. She had been missing for more than four months now; he figured the body would show up sooner or later, probably later. If the body were at the bottom of the lake caught on roots or wedged between rocks, it could be spring before rushing water dislodged it. After a spring thaw the swift-running water might push a body to the surface where it would float downstream.

Suddenly this small, sleepy mountain town had more than its share of crime. The theft of payroll money at Walton Construction was no mystery. Everything pointed to Luc Marten. He hadn't even bothered to wipe off fingerprints. So far, a statewide bulletin produced no results. The sinking feeling that Cindy played some role in all this bothered him. *Active participant or unwilling victim?* He hoped to be proven wrong. The fact that they disappeared within days of each other made it look bad for her.

Josh pulled himself back to the problem at hand. The

missing Cindy Arthur. With her car in the lake and most probably her body, he had work to do. Cindy clerked at the general store over on Pine Alps Avenue. A nice girl, he worried about her. Her boyfriend, Luc Marten, was bad news. The sheriff spoke to him when he first came to town. He kept track of parolees in his area. He knew that Luc spelled trouble. He asked Luc why he'd come to Pine Alps. Luc answered, "You know where you can go. I've got a right to be here. I have a job and I'm reporting to my parole officer. There's not a single thing you can do."

Josh remembered telling him, "You cause havoc wherever you go, Luc, always have, always will. Stay away from Cindy Arthur. She's a nice girl, don't mess up her life." Luc responded with an obscene gesture. Josh had even talked with Cindy, telling her that with her blond good looks and trim figure she could do so much better than team up with a guy just out of prison. He didn't realize that he was talking about three months too late.

Two weeks earlier Cindy called Luc. "Luc, honey, I don't want to bug you but you promised. If we wait much longer I'm going to start to show. Why can't we get married now?"

Luc hated it when Cindy whined. "I told you we'd get married as soon as I got some money. Look, I think we'll have enough by this time next week. Then we'll go someplace special and have a real honeymoon. You'd like that wouldn't you?"

"You know I would, Luc, honey, I can't wait much longer. I'm over three months along now. I can't get by with baggy sweaters much longer."

"I'll tell you what. I'll come by your place tonight and we'll plan our wedding."

"Really? You're not just saying that?" Cindy knew Luc's promises were not always reliable. He often broke dates or went days without calling. His jet-black hair and black eyes made Luc just about the best-looking guy in these parts. Cindy felt lucky to have him for a boyfriend, she did wish he'd pay a little more attention to her. Once he found out she was pregnant he'd become distant. Just lately, for some reason, he'd suddenly become more attentive. She remembered her conversation with the sheriff. He tried to talk her out of seeing Luc. He said that she could do so much better. Cindy remembered asking herself, how? The eligible guys in this town have no ambition, no brains, and all of them looked and acted like Neanderthals. At least Luc showed some ambition. She knew all about his prison record. He told her how he'd been framed for a crime he didn't commit. He said he wasn't bitter, he just wanted to make something of himself. He'd made big plans and he wanted her to be proud of him.

Luc did have plans. Walton Construction, where he worked, kept payroll cash locked up in the office safe. This month it would be close to a million and a half dollars. Business was good, Walton hired at least six new guys, making the number of carpenters, electricians, plumbers etc. about eighteen, if he'd figured right. Luc would come back at night and jimmy the door to the office. The safe was not a problem. He'd made use of his time in prison. He learned a trade. Safecracking. Luc's big plans included Cindy to help him.

"*Steal?* You're going to *steal!* Luc, are you out of your mind? Or what? That's all I need. Pregnant, not married and a nut for a boyfriend! What else can go wrong in my life?"

"Cindy, will you just listen for a minute? It's not like taking money from some poor schmuck. This is a big company with lots of insurance. They won't even miss it. Think what all that money can do for us. Think about our baby." Luc put his arms around Cindy and kissed her on the neck. "It's not like I haven't thought all this through. Nothing can go wrong. Trust me."

"I don't know, Luc. This doesn't seem right to me."

Luc could feel Cindy beginning to relax. He had a way about him that she found hard to resist. "Believe me, honey. I have everything worked out. Thursday, after the store closes, you be out front with your car. I'll drive by, put the money in the trunk and drive off. No one will even see us at that time of night. You keep the money for about a week, when I call, drive down to the lake. Go to the spot under the old bridge where we had the picnic last summer. You remember it, don't you?"

How could she forget? That's where her little bundle of joy got started. Her parent's death the year before left her orphaned at seventeen, Cindy yearned for someone to rely on. She did her best, still, she often felt lonely and insecure. Patting her stomach, she thought, *what's going to happen to us?* "I know where it is, Luc, but why do you want me there? Where will you be? Why aren't you coming with me?"

"Cindy! Cindy! Will you stop already? You drive me crazy with all the questions. Just do what I tell you and everything will be okay. Give me a few days and I'll call you on your cell. Be ready to move when I call."

"Okay, but I don't like it. It doesn't feel right. I'll pack a bag and keep it in my car so…"

"No! No! No bag, just your purse, like any other day. Don't bring anything else, and whatever you do, don't breathe a word to anyone. Promise?"

Thursday night, after everyone left, Luc quietly went to the construction office and broke the lock. He couldn't believe how trusting these guys were. All that payroll money in there and the lock could be busted with a few hammer blows. He could crack the old safe with ease. Fortunately one of the best, Jimmy Fingers, trained him. It took less than a half hour to open the safe and empty its contents into a burlap bag. He drove straight to the general store. Cindy looked ready to cry. "Don't start. Everything is okay. I'll call as soon as it's safe." He quickly put the bag in her trunk, kissed her and left in his old car.

He drove straight to Skyway Air and waited in his car through the night. When the first rays of the sun came over the mountain, he went into the office to find the owner, Mac, already drinking coffee and smoking a cigarette. "Hey, Mac.

How ya doin'?"

"Hey, Luc, ready to go?"

"You bet. I've been planning this trip for months. I can't wait."

Mac knew Luc as an ardent outdoorsman. He frequently took trips into the dense forest and lived off the land for weeks. This would be his biggest endeavor yet. Luc planned to parachute into the woods on the other side of the lake, use his skill at hunting to stay alive, and eventually make his way back to civilization. Luc called it his dream trip. He figured it would take him the better part of four months to finish the trip if snow didn't come early and hold him up.

Mac admired Luc's skill but couldn't understand giving up such pleasures as a soft bed and a softer woman. *Why, he wondered, would I want to sleep on the cold hard ground when I have a sweet wife and a hot dinner waiting for me at home? Oh well, to each his own.* "Okay, let's do it. The plane's all gassed and ready." They taxied down the runway with the sun in their eyes. Mac turned the plane to go around the lake, which put the sun at their backs. An hour later Luc pointed to the bare spot in the heavily forested area. He gave Mac a salute and jumped. Luc paid Mac to return a week later and drop a crate of goods. He told Mac it was prospecting gear. He said he thought there might be gold at the base of the mountain and he wanted to take a look.

Luc floated down, gently landing in the clearing. He had been here months earlier and knew the lay of the land. Base camp was set up farther into the trees by a stream that helped feed the lake. It would take him the better part of a week to make his way back around the lake. He quickly inflated the raft hidden when he'd first found this campsite. Adrenalin pumping, several miles could be made before nightfall, he wanted to get started. Even as a kid Luc prided himself on being self-sufficient. He and his half-brother trained to survive in the woods, killing and curing deer and rabbit. Books on edible plants and different methods of trapping game were his reading choices. He knew how to read the weather and could make a shelter from branches, deer hide or stones, anything available. The thought of taking the money and leaving Cindy crossed his mind. This idea was rejected on the grounds that she would provide added insurance in the event the sheriff and his men found him. The sheriff hated him, but Josh would never do anything to harm an innocent girl. She would be useful as a shield, if push came to shove. By the end of the fourth day he was making good time. Luc called Cindy on her cell and told her to be at the bridge in two days.

She grew cold, shivering as she waited in the ice-filled wind. The old bridge looked forbidding at night, not at all the way it looked when Luc first brought her here. *Then* she thought it looked romantic, *now* it seemed scary. She wished Luc would hurry. He said he'd be here. If it weren't for the baby I'd tell Luc to go by himself. *Without him I don't know how I could make it? The pay at the general store isn't enough to raise a child. And doctor bills! How would I manage? Doc says I'm not too strong. He says I need plenty of rest and special vitamins. How could I afford anything like that? Mrs. Olson knows. She told me she would help me and the baby, but I want my baby to have a father. She says Luc isn't reliable and I shouldn't believe his story about being convicted of a crime he didn't commit. They just don't understand him. I need Luc. As soon as we're married everything will be okay. I know Luc loves me.* Cindy hugged her coat to her shivering body trying to believe her own thoughts.

The raft soundlessly came up on the sandy shore. Luc pulled it onto the beach and was within feet of Cindy before softly calling her name. "Cindy, I'm here. Come on, hurry up, give me a hand." Luc opened the trunk of Cindy's old Buick taking out the bag of money. He quickly strapped the bag at one end of the raft. Together they started her car and gave it a push, letting it slide toward the lake. At the last minute Luc grabbed Cindy's purse and threw it into the open window. "Climb in the raft. We'll be gone before anyone knows we were here. They'll think you lost control and went to the bottom with the car."

"Luc, this isn't right. I can't do this. I don't want everyone worrying about me and thinking I'm dead."

"Yes, you *can* do it! Hey, don't back out on me now!" He softened his voice. "We have a whole life ahead of us. You, me, and the baby." He patted her slightly bulging stomach. The raft glided away as quietly as it had come, taking them farther and farther from civilization.

"Luc, I'm cold. You should have let me bring a heavier coat and a change of clothes."

"Cindy, will you quit! A heavy coat and more clothes, like a dead giveaway. What're you thinking? You can get warm as soon as we reach camp."

The trip back to base camp would take longer. They would be paddling upstream. Cindy really couldn't help and Luc tired of her constant moaning. A soft, cold snow started falling. As they rounded the last bend in the river, Luc hit a submerged rock that sent the two of them tumbling into the icy water. Cindy went down, then bobbed to the surface. Luc shouted, "Swim for the shore, it's not far!" He lunged after the raft, grabbing it before it floated away. He was able to pull it to shore, retrieving the money and his bow. A hole in the raft rendered it useless.

"Come on. We'll have to walk." Luc didn't seem to mind the wet and cold.

He set off at a pace that quickly tired Cindy. "Luc, please slow down. I can't go this fast. I'm tired and freezing. My stomach is cramping. Please." *My poor baby. What have I gotten us into?*

"Cindy, shut up, we have to keep going. If we stop you really will freeze. As soon as it's safe I'll build a fire. Don't think about the cold, just keep moving."

Cindy thought that Luc relished the challenge of making his way through the snow. She stumbled along silently on numb feet. The trees were scattered here, offering little shelter from the wind. *If only I could get warm. If only my teeth would stop chattering.* She kept hearing the words of the sheriff and Mrs. Olson. *Even Doc tried to warned me but, I'm too stupid to listen.* She tried not to cry. Tears only made Luc mad.

Finally, the woods became denser, darker. "Okay, we'll camp here." Luc picked a small bare spot within a ring of tall trees. A fire soon had Cindy feeling better. She was amazed when he started a fire with the flint from the backpack he'd managed to salvage along with the money. "I'll be right back," he said. "I'm going shopping."

"Shopping?" Cindy said to his back as he disappeared into the trees.

Gratefully Cindy huddled close to the fire holding some of the cold and dark at bay. She heard sounds in the woods. "Luc, is that you? Please, Luc, this isn't funny." She could hear rustling in the underbrush and twice she saw red gleaming eyes staring at her. Luc came into the clearing holding a rabbit by its hind legs.

"Sorry, this is all they had," he smiled. "I asked for a bottle of wine and some potatoes but…" he shrugged, "this is it for tonight." She smiled, relieved at having him back. She forgot for a moment the cramps brought on by hunger. Nothing had ever tasted as delicious as that roasted rabbit. Maybe everything would be okay after all. "We'll camp here tonight. Tomorrow we start early. I want to make base camp before the snow gets too heavy." They snuggled up next to the small fire. "Get some rest. We have a long day ahead of us." Cindy slept from exhaustion.

It took more than a week for them to make base camp. Luc could have traveled much faster. Cindy couldn't keep up. They took frequent rest stops and settled in for the night much earlier than Luc wanted. When at last they arrived, Cindy fell asleep wrapped in a blanket by the fire. It seemed to Luc that she was not breathing right. Luc was exhilarated. Mac had dropped the crate with supplies that included a small tent, warm clothes and snowshoes.

Over the next four months, they stayed close to base camp. Luc hunted and made arrows from hardwood from the forest. He practiced his skill with the bow and kept them supplied with meat. He dried much of it over the campfire and packed it in waterproof skins made from the hides of the deer he killed. Cindy tried to cook and keep the campsite clean. At least the crate Mac sent down had some warm clothes for her. Even though she didn't feel well, Luc insisted that she do her share. Her job consisted of gathering firewood, gutting and skinning the fish and the small game he brought back. He tried to teach her how to dry the meat over the fire, the smell made her nauseous. "Luc, I just can't do it any more. It's making me sick." Cindy held her hand over her mouth. A skinned rabbit lay on a rock at her feet. She ran for the woods. The sound of her retching disgusted him.

Snow fell, nights were freezing cold. Luc thought leaving base camp would be safe now. He planned to hike out of the woods and over the mountain range, eventually getting to Canada. He did not plan on taking Cindy. She would never make it. That night he packed his gear and left her sleeping a troubled sleep.

The day following Luc's departure, a hunter found a rubber raft caught in tree roots around a bend in the river. He brought a piece of silk scarf from the raft to show the police. The sheriff felt in his gut that it was Cindy's.

Josh took the piece of fabric to the general store and asked Mrs. Olson if she recognized it. "I can't be sure, it's so dirty and tangled, but it looks like the scarf Cindy often wore with her purple sweater. You know, sheriff, I told that girl to stay clear of Luc. I can tell trouble when I see it and he spelled trouble, big trouble with capital letters. I warned her. Yes I did." Mrs. Olson wanted to continue her tirade against Luc Marten, Josh thanked her and left.

Something had been nagging him for days. Now and then he caught a glimpse of it . . .then it disappeared. As he left the store and started toward his car, he looked up. The bright, clear day with sun on the snow made everything glitter. A small plane circled. A skydiver dropped from the plane and began his descent. He caught his breath. Now he remembered. The day they found Cindy's car he had seen a small plane overhead. He thought that something or someone fell or dropped from the plane. With his heart racing he headed to the outskirts of town and Skyway Diving School.

"Mac, did you take Luc Marten and Cindy Arthur somewhere about four months ago?"

"Nah, not Cindy but Luc, yeah. He likes to jump. And, he likes to rough it. He's always having me drop him into the woods on the other side of the lake so he can make his way back using just a bow and arrows to forage for food. Likes to live off the land, he says. Me, I like my creature comforts."

"When was the last time he jumped?"

"Let me check my books." Mac pulled out his appointment book. "Why? Didn't he make it back this time?"

"Did he have anything extra with him? You know, a big bundle, a duffle bag, something like that?"

"Nah, just his usual. He was dressed in those army camouflage clothes he likes, carried his bow and quiver of arrows. That's it. I warned him about the weather, he didn't seem to care."

Josh was disappointed. He walked toward his car. Maybe he was wrong about Cindy; maybe she *was* at the bottom of the lake. Mac ran out to the parking lot. "Hey Sheriff, I just remembered something." He turned to see Mac huffing after him. "I remember now, I dropped off a crate of stuff at Luc's base camp about a week after he left. He said it was prospecting gear. Said he'd heard there might be gold at the base of the mountain. You ever hear that?"

"Gold? Not in these parts. Sounds like somebody's pipe dream. Thanks, Mac." *What was really in that crate?*

He quickly organized a search party, other men trained in tracking and hunting in cold mountainous terrain. Doc Peters loaned his hunting dogs, said to have the best noses in these parts. "You after Luc for the construction robbery?"

"Yeah, I'm after Luc and I suspect Cindy Arthur may be with him."

"Cindy? Maybe I better come along. Cindy's pregnant. She'll be about eight months along by now. Last time I saw her she wasn't doing too well. I didn't figure she'd ever carry that baby past seven or eight months. Her vital signs weren't too stable. She really needed a lot of rest and good care. What happened? I thought she drowned."

"I'm not a hundred percent sure, this is a gut feeling. Yeah, come on. We can use the manpower." Doc collected his gear and followed.

The search party, twelve men in four rubber raft, left at daybreak. They started upstream from where Luc's raft was found stopping every few hundred feet to let the dogs sniff. The dogs were given a piece of Cindy's clothing and a shirt from Luc's cabin. Hours later they began to bark and run. They picked up the trail. The hunt was on.

Luc came down the mountain late in the afternoon, walking over rock polished smooth by ice, relishing, clear, freezing cold air. He went down a gorge filled with a dense growth of spruce, weaving a path through them, careful not to leave any signs of his passing. He slept that night in a huge hollow tree, protected from the cold wind. When morning came he chewed the last of the meat he carried in his backpack. He would have to hunt soon. He found a rock fall where several great slabs had fallen in such a way as to form a shelter. This would do for a day or two. Here, hidden from view, he could hunt and cure meat for the final push into Canada. He could build a small fire without danger of being seen. Luc stretched in the morning sun. It felt good to be battling the elements alone, without the aid of modern equipment, also without the encumbrance of Cindy. The decision to leave her was the right one. She would only slow him down. He felt powerful. He was congratulating himself on a smooth getaway when a faint sound came over the wind. Barking? Dogs? His good mood evaporated like smoke in a windstorm. Quickly, Luc climbed a high tree and scanned the area. Dense forest made it impossible to see anything; the sound of dogs barking became more distinct. Luc grabbed his pack and started off. He would have to skip hunting for now.

The dogs made their way through the forest, sniffing, barking, running. About a mile from Luc's base camp the trail split. One track went on to base camp, the other went north, through the woods. "He's headed for Canada. That's the only thing that makes sense!" shouted Tom Jenks. "We've got to catch him before he crosses over."

"What about this other trail?" asked Pete Marlow. "Looks like he went this way first."

"Yeah, I think he went that way and then came back through here later. Looks like that trail is older, this here looks fresh. Pete, you take one dog and follow the old trail. If you find anything, you have your walkie-talkie."

"Will do." Pete started off taking his own dog, Bitsy. The rest of the men went the other direction, following the hounds as fast as they could travel in the snow.

Luc could hear the dogs clearly now. He was hampered by lack of food and modern equipment, the very thing he sneered at earlier. He didn't know if it was better to stay put or keep moving. Now he could hear the distinctive chop, chop of helicopter blades. He could see men with rifles leaning out the door. Trapped! Dogs on the ground, rifles in the air. Luc tried to think, tried not to panic.

Sticking to as much cover as was possible he climbed to the top of the gorge and ran. He needed to find running water, a stream or runoff, where he could cross and possibly fool the dogs long enough to get away. "Stay where you are, Luc!" The voice boomed from the helicopter. "Stop! Don't do anything stupid. The sheriff's men are right behind you." Luc turned in alarm expecting to see men and dogs at his heels. As he turned, the soft gravel at the edge of the deep ravine shifted, throwing him off balance. He tottered on the edge, trying to regain his balance, arms windmilling in empty air. Men and hounds came into view; the lead dog ran barking and snarling toward him. Luc's last step was a ballet move, gracefully pirouetting him into empty space.

The sheriff, Doc, and three other men started at the other side of the lake where Mac said he dropped Luc and later his gear. He hoped to trap him somewhere in the middle. The search for Luc's base camp took little time. The men followed the stream until a clearing came into view. A small tent was at one side, the remains of a fire were a few steps outside the tent. Doc kicked the cold embers. "Looks like this is where he started."

A low moan startled both men. "What was that?" The sheriff ran to the tent. Cindy Arthur lay dazed and shivering. Her swollen belly looked obscene beneath one thin blanket. "Cindy! Cindy! Hold on. Can you hear me?"

Doc moved the sheriff aside. "Here, let me in there. Get some warm blankets and build a fire." Doc quickly took charge. "Cindy girl, can you talk?"

Cindy's eyes fluttered. "I'm so cold. Luc ran off. I'm gonna die."

"None of that talk, now. We'll get you to the hospital, you'll be fine."

The sheriff radioed for a helicopter. "Hurry, this girl is pregnant, she's been exposed to the cold for God only knows how long," he said to the dispatcher. That bastard! What kind of monster would leave a pregnant girl alone like this? This is a new loc even for Luc." He hurried back to the tent. Doc looked up at him, shook his head. "Help's on the way. Hang on, honey. It's going to be all right."

Cindy could barely whisper. "How could I have been so stupid? I thought Luc loved me. He said he loved me. We were gonna be married. I should have listened. Everyone tried to warn me, you, Mrs. Olson even Doc."

He bent over the distraught girl taking her small hand in

his big one. "Don't blame yourself, honey, Luc has always been trouble, big trouble. He's always been a smooth talker. Don't blame yourself for a minute. Even when he was a kid he could charm the socks off people."

"How do you know so much about Luc?" Cindy whispered. She grimaced as pain shot through her body. "My baby! My baby's coming!"

Doc moved the sheriff aside. "She's right. This baby isn't waiting for the chopper. "Get my bag. I need some things." He rummaged through his bag, found what he needed and gave Cindy a shot to ease her pain.

The baby came in a rush of fluid. He was small, wrinkled and squalling at the top of his lungs. Doc held the infant close to its mother. "Cindy honey, look here, meet your son."

Cindy's eyes clouded with tears. She reached out feebly for her baby. "My poor baby. What will happen to him? I know I'm not going to make it," she cried.

"Cindy, don't worry. Linda and I will take the baby. Don't worry about a thing. We'll take care of him until you get well. He'll be waiting for you when you get out of the hospital." The sheriff's voice was choked with emotion. "You asked how I knew so much about Luc. I know because he's my half-brother. We grew up together. Same mother, different fathers. This little fellow is my nephew."

The smile on Cindy's face was radiant. "Thanks. I know I'm not going to make it. Be a good father. Don't worry about giving him things; just give him all the love you can. Tell Linda I'm grateful. When he grows up tell him I wasn't a bad person." He had to lean down close to hear her. "Someday when he's old enough, tell him only the good stuff about me, will you?" Cindy stopped breathing before he could respond.

The whap, whap of the helicopter and a dog barking drew the sheriff from the tent. Cindy's body was strapped to a carrier attached to the outside of the runners. Doc sat inside holding the baby. Pete and his dog, Bitsy came into the clearing. Pete was holding a phone to his ear. "Yeah, yeah, I got it. Looks like

Luc took a high dive over the gorge. They're looking for the money and planning to retrieve his body; they'll probably have to wait 'til spring."

The small community turned out to say farewell to Cindy. *What a sad way to end a young life, he thought. Maybe we can do better by her baby. No! Not maybe, damnit we will do better.*
Later the sheriff and Linda stood at the nursery window. Baby Josh was out of danger. The doctor said that considering the lack of proper nourishment during his development he was making amazing progress. They could take him home. Linda was crying. Josh told her about his relationship to Luc. They agreed to tell Josh Jr. when he was old enough to understand. The doctor handed the baby to Linda, wrapped in hospital blankets. Her eyes clouded with tears, "I never thought I could be so happy."
Josh, holding back his own tears, squeezed her hand. "Me too."

"So, Josh Jr. is that baby. Wow, that's fantastic. I didn't know." Steve said.
"We never made a big deal of it. Junior grew up to be a wonderful man. He's married now with a family of his own, sent him to Harvard Law School." *Thanks to the money at the bottom of the gorge.* "He liked real estate law so that's his specialty. Just as well, criminal law pays better but I'm not sure the toll it takes is worth it." His eyes misted over and once again Steve and George thought he'd gone to sleep. His head fell forward causing him to start and then he reached for his glass. The cigar was burned down to a stub with a long ash attached.
"Can I light another one for you?"
"No, but thanks. I've smoked my quota for the night."
"Okay. Josh. How long were you in law enforcement?"
"Well, a long time. Let's see, beginning to end I guess over fifty years. I started out at eighteen, right out of high school

and retired at sixty-five and stayed on as a reserve officer and consultant for another five. During that time I worked in San Diego, Las Vegas and Reno, kind of moved up the states. A lotta memories, good and bad." The detective looked very old and tired at that moment. "You boys go along now. I gotta get my beauty sleep."

Steve said, "Thanks for having us. We appreciate hearing your stories. By the way, did they ever find the money?"

"No, never did. Probably still up there somewhere. Lots of people looked but they never found it."

"May we come back?"

"Sure, sure, come back and I'll share some of my pictures with you." The detective shook the empty bottle a little sadly.

"That was awesome. Let's come back Saturday and bring pizza and another bottle." George said. "Drop me off at the office so I can get my car."

"I can't wait to see his pictures." Steve added. "Hope he'll let us copy them for the book."

Josh Cumming passed away that night in his sleep. His son, Josh Jr. loaned the pictures to Steve and George. "This book will be my dad's final tribute. I know it would make him proud. It will be something for the whole family to remember him by. Please let me know when the book is published so I can buy the first copy."

"You'll get the first book off the press," Steve said. We both agreed to put aside ten percent of the royalties for your children. It's the least we can do."

CPSIA information can be obtained at www.ICGtesting.com
Printed in the USA
BVOW102136250313

316426BV00006B/55/P